"What the *kosst*?" said a man's voice from somewhere back the way she had come. Someone else was here. Someone Bajoran, apparently, for the curse was not one that a Cardassian would ever use. Ro Laren drew her phaser, more excited than afraid.

"Who are you?" she shouted.

"Who am I?" the voice answered. "Who are *you*? This heap is mine—we claimed it over a week ago."

A man emerged in the corridor then, a gray-haired Bajoran that Laren didn't recognize.

She lifted her phaser. "Don't make me ask again," she said coolly.

He slitted his eyes at her, his heavily lined face crinkling with the expression. He looked worried for an instant, but then smiled. "My name is Darrah Mace," he told her. "I've come here from Valo II. Now, how about you tell me who you are?"

"My cell found this ship two days ago," she told him, her phaser still trained on the stranger. "I was here first."

The man laughed. "Just how old are you? Twelve? You still haven't told me your name, by the way."

"I'm Ro," she said firmly, hearing the sound of the airlock starting to open. "And that will be Bram, the leader of my cell. It's two against one now, so you'd better shove off. This ship is ours." Laren stood her ground, her phaser still pointed directly at Mace's head.

"And just what do you propose to do with that?" The man smirked, folding his arms in a self-satisfied expression that infuriated her.

"Didn't you hear me? I said shove *off*." She indicated her phaser. "This thing's stun setting is broken, but the rest of it works just fine."

*Twelve!* She'd been fourteen for better than two months.

# STAR TREK®
# TEROK NOR

## NIGHT OF THE WOLVES

### 2345–2357

## S. D. Perry & Britta Dennison

Based upon STAR TREK
created by Gene Rodenberry,
and STAR TREK: DEEP SPACE NINE®
created by Rick Berman and Michael Piller

POCKET BOOKS

New York   London   Toronto   Sydney   Gallitep

Pocket Books
A Division of Simon & Schuster, Inc.
1230 Avenue of the Americas
New York, NY 10020

This book is a work of fiction. Names, characters, places, and incidents either are products of the authors' imaginations or are used fictitiously. Any resemblance to actual events or locales or persons, living or dead, is entirely coincidental.

This book is published by Pocket Books, a division of Simon & Schuster, Inc., under exclusive license from CBS Studios Inc.

First Pocket Books paperback edition May 2008

POCKET and colophon are registered trademarks of Simon & Schuster, Inc.

For information about special discounts for bulk purchases, please contact Simon & Schuster Special Sales at 1-800-456-6798 or business@simonandschuster.com.

Cover art by John Picacio; cover design by Alan Dingman

Manufactured in the United States of America

10  9  8  7  6  5  4  3  2  1

ISBN-13: 978-0-7434-8251-6
ISBN-10:    0-7434-8251-4

For Thad

*Sorry I was such a jerk during rewrites*

—B. D.


For Myk and the boys

—S. D. P.

# Acknowledgments

Britta Dennison would like to thank the following people for valuable creative or technical input:

Thad Dennison, Ben Burdett, Lucy Dennison, and a nod to Hans Lindauer. Thanks to James Swallow for raising the bar so high. Also, a massive thanks to Paula Block and Marco Palmieri for laying the framework and for taking a chance on me. I hope the gamble pays off.

For their emotional support:

My husband, Thad; my parents, Ben Burdett and Barbara Burdett; my sibs, Brooke Minas, Barbi Buresh, and Brady Burdett; the in-laws and baby-sitters extraordinaire, Judy Dennison and Annete Levy; also: Mike and Frani Grover and the rest of the Grover clan, all the mooks who read my blog, and Lucy and Ruth Dennison, for keeping me on my toes.

Extra super special thanks goes out to my BFF S. D. Perry, who has been a valuable mentor and invaluable friend.

S. D. Perry also thanks Paula Block and Marco Palmieri, James Swallow, and all the Trek writers, past and present; her marvelous husband, two perfect kids, and the lovely ladies at the School of Autism who keep the faith. Oh, and Britta, who's way, way cooler than she thinks she is, and also came up with all the really interesting parts.

# OCCUPATION YEAR EIGHTEEN

✦ ✦ ✦

## 2345 (Terran Calendar)

# Prologue

The Bajoran vessel fled into the Denorios Belt, chasing salvation it would never find.

Malyn Ocett fought the involuntary curling of her lips as the tiny ship tried to evade her; there was opportunity here, but also peril. As a newly minted dalin assigned to captain the Cardassian scoutship *Kevalu* on her first patrol of the B'hava'el system, this was exactly the chance she needed to prove herself worthy of the command that had been only grudgingly entrusted to her. But failure to stop the errant Bajoran craft would validate those who had opposed her assignment—and Ocett knew she had no shortage of detractors in the military—effectively ending her career before it could even begin.

*And that I will not allow.*

"Close the distance, helm," she said aloud. "Communications, open a channel."

"Target is receiving us, Dalin."

"Bajoran vessel. This is the Union scoutship *Kevalu*. You are in breach of travel restrictions. I give you opportunity to turn back and surrender to Cardassian authority or I will be forced to take action."

Silence answered her.

"They're increasing speed," her pilot said.

"Stay with them." The *Kevalu* vibrated as it pierced the

Denorios Belt, a tempestuous ring of charged plasma that encircled Bajor's star between the orbits of the seventh and eighth planets. Normally avoided by spacecraft as a navigation hazard, the Belt had in recent years become the obvious first destination for Bajorans foolish enough to attempt illicit travel out of their home system.

"Bajoran vessel. This insolence will not be tolerated. Power down immediately or I will open fire."

The alarming rise in terrorism since the start of the annexation had forced the enactment of strict regulations over space travel, which in the B'hava'el system was generally limited to Cardassian vessels and occasional trade ships from other worlds. Bajorans, by contrast, were forbidden to leave their planet without express authorization, and only under the most controlled conditions. But they were a surprisingly crafty and devious people, Ocett had quickly learned, capable and even determined to find gaps in the Cardassian security web through which they could slip. Under different circumstances, a ship caught in such an act would be destroyed immediately, but patrols were under strict orders to take prisoners whenever feasible; it was believed by some in Central Command that the capture and interrogation of terrorists would allow the Cardassians to obtain intelligence they could use to break the insurgency.

Still no answer from the Bajoran ship. The gil manning sensors reported that the vessel was preparing to go to warp.

Ocett tended to believe the Bajorans were nowhere near as organized as Central Command seemed to think. The randomness and utter lack of sophistication exhibited by the insurgents spoke to scattered and unaffiliated groups, not a network. But orders were orders.

"Tactical, power up disruptors and target their stardrive," she said. "Send them a warning shot—I want them disabled, not destroyed."

"Target acquired. Firing disruptors."

Ocett watched in satisfaction as light blossomed on the engine case of the oblong vessel's aft hull. "Direct hit," the tac officer reported unnecessarily. "Bajoran's stardrive is off line. However—"

The *Kevalu* shook against the impact of a particle beam. At first, Ocett wasn't sure whether to be angry or amused, but the tac officer's next frantic report put any notions of laughter out of her mind.

"Forward shields down! Emitters have overloaded! They're recharging weapons!"

Ocett's eyes widened as she leapt to her feet. "Fire at will! Helm, hard about!"

Letting fly with another salvo from its disruptors, the *Kevalu* pivoted to port, turning its exposed bow away from its quarry. Explosions ripped open the Bajoran vessel's hull and the ship broke in half, sending debris luminescing through the plasma field.

Ocett let out a breath. She was a little rattled; the confrontation had not gone at all as she'd expected. The Bajoran ship had been underpowered and should have been no match for the *Kevalu*.

She whirled angrily upon the tac officer. "What happened, Glinn?"

The young man swallowed. "It was the Denorios Belt, Dalin. Our shields were already taxed protecting us from the plasma field. Taking a direct hit on top of that overloaded the forward emitters. Perhaps if we had not—"

"This is a Union vessel!" Ocett snapped, cutting off whatever impertinent suggestion the glinn was about to make. "More than that, it is a Union vessel under *my* command, and I will tolerate no incompetence from its crew. You and the chief of engineering will begin work immediately to upgrade our shield emitters so that this unacceptable system failure never happens again. Do you understand me, Glinn?"

"Y-yes, Dalin," the tac officer stammered. "Permission to leave the bridge?"

"Get out of my sight."

Ocett waited until the glinn had departed, then discreetly exhaled again. "Helm," she said as she retook her seat. "Take us out of the plasma field and resume original heading."

The *Kevalu* bucked gently as it maneuvered through the Denorios Belt, and Ocett considered how narrowly she had escaped humiliation. Her failure to capture the Bajorans was galling, but at least their vessel had been stopped, and damage to the *Kevalu* itself was minimal. Still, she was acutely cognizant of the fact that any misstep in her early years as a shipmaster was potentially one from which she would never recover.

It was an unusual choice for a woman to join the military; few ever did so, tending to pursue more traditional careers in the judiciary or the sciences. Most personnel in those professions could remain close to home, be with their families. But since Ocett was unable to have children, it was unlikely that she would ever find a permanent mate. Family was the highest ideal in Cardassian society, and a woman who could not bear children was considered undesirable. Ocett knew that many women in her position would have been bitter, considering themselves condemned to a life of solitude. But Ocett had perceived her situation as an opportunity for a career that would otherwise be closed to her. She had the freedom to travel as far away and as often as the military required, and she had no familial obligations to keep her from dangerous duty. But she was still a rarity. It spite of her recent promotion, none of her crew seemed able to forget it—a situation that required constant reminders, in no uncertain terms, of her absolute authority aboard the *Kevalu*.

It was with that thought that the gil at sensors, a male

named Veda, spoke up. "Dalin, I'm picking up something unusual on midrange scanners."

"Less preamble, Gil."

"Yes, Dalin. It's an object in the plasma fields, about the size of a cargo container. Refined metal, and a faint power signature."

"Something from the Bajoran ship?"

"Negative. It's too far from the debris field, and the metallurgy is inconsistent with anything produced by Bajorans or Cardassians."

Ocett rose and went to the sensor station to see the readings for herself. What she saw gave her pause. Veda had definitely understated the matter: the ship's database seemed not to know what to make of the object, as apparently nothing like it had ever been recorded by a Cardassian vessel. And there was something else.

"This reading here," she said, indicating a specific segment of the datastream, "what is it?"

The gil frowned, apparently seeing it for the first time. "I'm not sure."

Ocett sighed. "Enhance your scan and report," she ordered. *Men. No head for the sciences. It's a defect of the sex— not inquisitive enough.*

While she waited for Veda's report, she considered her options. All things being equal, she would prefer not to have to interrupt her patrol to investigate an anomalous object, particularly one within the proven hazards of the Denorios Belt. But of course all things were not equal. Since the ship's automated logs would show that something had tripped the midrange sensors during its patrol, it would be inadvisable to ignore the object. She could file a report of the discovery, but since she wholly expected her superiors to pay significantly more attention to her reports than to any of the men's, she knew that if she overlooked a single thing, it would invite questions regarding her prudence. Her last option would be to beam the object aboard and conduct a proper analysis. She would almost certainly be accused of being overly zealous if she were to do that, but she felt it was favorable to the alternative—carelessness earned rebuke, especially for a female.

Veda made a puzzled sound. "Well?" Ocett said expectantly.

"Perhaps you should look at this yourself, Dalin."

Ocett's eyes narrowed as she leaned in. She arched an eyeridge. "There's a small fluid mass suspended in the center of the object," she said aloud, failing to disguise the surprise in her voice.

That caught the pilot's attention. "Some kind of weapon, then," he volunteered. "A volatile compound, or a biogenic device."

"No, I don't think so," Ocett said. "It's not exhibiting the properties normally associated with such materials. It's almost as if . . ." She looked up at the pilot. "Helm, take us within transport range of the object, speed one-quarter impulse."

"Dalin—?" the pilot began, but then reconsidered whatever he was about to say against Ocett's withering glare. "Acknowledged. One-quarter impulse."

Ocett pressed her comcuff and alerted the engineer in transport. "Gil Kretech, this is Dalin Ocett. Sensors have registered a small object of unknown composition. As soon as we're within range, you're to beam this object directly to the decon chamber so that it can be scanned and logged into the ship's database."

Her request was met with a brief pause. *"Dalin, if I may say so, our mission is not one of exploration. We are not a science vessel. I recognize that curiosity is a uniquely feminine trait, but—"*

Ocett cut him off swiftly. Males never had to tolerate

such impudence. "I would advise you to forget my sex and carry out my orders, Gil," she snapped.

His answer held the appropriate measure of meekness. *"I will report back to you as soon as transport is complete, Dalin."*

"See that you do. Bridge out."

Twenty metrics later, Ocett and Veda stood before the decontamination lab's observation window while the gil deftly manipulated the remote instruments that were separating the object into its constituent parts: an unadorned, roughly cylindrical capsule that turned out to be a stasis apparatus of some kind, and a small spherical module. But while the alien technology was of considerable interest, it was the contents of the sphere to which Veda directed Ocett's attention.

"There's nothing like it in the database, just like the container," Veda said as he studied the results of his new scans, which were flashing before them on the window as he worked. "But there's no question that your suspicion about the reading was correct, Dalin. The liquid is organic."

"Organic," Ocett repeated. She looked to the transparent sphere and considered its contents—a small quantity of amber hued liquid with the consistency of dark *kanar,* shimmering subtly in the artificial lights. She could not tear her eyes away for a moment, trying to determine—did she just see a ripple? A slight movement? Or was it only the effect of the containment field? "Is it—?"

"It's inconclusive. But some of the scans suggest that this substance could be—or maybe could have once been—some kind of life-form."

Ocett was pleased, for it seemed that she'd chosen wisely. Evidently they'd come across something of interest, after all. No one would complain if it proved valuable.

"Continue your analysis," she said, her tone cool. "We'll turn the substance and your findings over to the science team stationed on Bajor after we return to base."

"Yes, Dalin."

Smiling to herself as she made her way back to the bridge, Ocett was gratified to finally hear a touch of genuine respect in the gil's quick reply.

# OCCUPATION YEAR NINETEEN

◆　◆　◆

## 2346 (Terran Calendar)

# 1

They stood at the apex of the Janitza mountain range in the northernmost sector of the continent, the humid, cold air heavy with the scents of pine and nyawood trees. Third-Tier Gil Corat Damar turned to take in the verdant abundance all around, then turned again, his expression a mix of hunger and awe. The new prefect of Bajor stood behind the junior officer, watching, remembering the first time he'd seen Bajor for himself. He'd been a much younger man then, blinking around himself in wonder.

From their vantage point, the valleys far below were patched over with ovals of colorful farmland, fading into wild tangles of jungle and jagged forests. The shadows of moving clouds cast a traveling pallor along the hilly meadows, disappearing where the densely woven carpet of trees appeared almost black.

Dukat could plainly see Damar's thoughts as he took in the scenery; in his most lavish dreams, Damar could not have imagined a world like this. It was so far a cry from the cracked and sandy plains of their homeworld, with its hot, erose mountains of obsidian jutting from the barren land. Cardassian soil was good for little more than harvesting rocks, or fashioning into clay for making brittle pots. To see this bold illustration of color, of green and blue and rich red dirt, was quite literally breathtaking.

"So—tell me what you think of Bajor," Dukat said.

Damar hesitated, unable to look away from the lush panorama. Dukat was pleased with the hesitation, a sign of careful consideration, perhaps a weighing of words to find those that would most impress the gil's commander. Dukat had taken a special interest in Damar, was grooming him to be his own personal assistant, and knew that Damar understood the honor of being so singled out. In truth, pickings had been lean; today's Cardassian soldier, while certainly still the best trained in the quadrant, left something to be desired in an intellectual capacity. Corat Damar, fresh from officer training, stood out because he thought further ahead than his next meal, his next *kanar,* his next sexual conquest. Dukat enjoyed seeing a sharp mind at work, and, in truth, there was no satisfaction in being admired by a fool. He wanted his personal aides smart enough to appreciate his maneuverings.

*And they* do *deserve appreciation,* Dukat thought, smiling. *I'm here, aren't I?*

"How can these people . . ." Damar began, then shook his head.

Dukat understood. "It seems hard to imagine that the Bajorans could have just squandered all this natural wealth for so long a time."

"I . . . suppose they were content with their lot in life as it was, and perhaps they—"

Dukat chuckled. "I believe the word you mean to use is *complacent,* Gil Damar." He gestured with an open hand. "The Bajorans have only the most rudimentary understanding of what you and I would call progress. The abundance of their world has made them lazy and superstitious. They can scarcely grasp scientific explanations for natural phenomena, preferring to give credit to their 'prophets' for anything they don't understand."

Damar was silent. He'd know nothing of Bajoran religion, of course, a low officer from the homeworld, but he'd learn. Most of the ground troops and station guards never bothered, but if he was as bright as Dukat believed, he'd pick it up.

"Of course, as prefect, I do not intend to disrespect their beliefs," Dukat said. "As backward as their religion may seem, I believe it is in the Union's best interests to allow the Bajorans to continue to worship as they did before the annexation. Some of my predecessors didn't share my view, but I feel that certain concessions must be made to the Bajorans if we are to successfully mold them into dutiful Cardassian subjects. As it is, they have no appreciation for us, because they fail to see all the good we've done for them. They choose to focus only on the inevitable episodes of petty discord that come with any cultural modification. They're like children, clinging to outmoded comforts, afraid to move forward. I intend to change that."

Damar's expression was appropriately deferential. "You're going to revolutionize relations with the Bajorans, sir."

Dukat smiled paternally and placed a hand on Damar's shoulder before a brief, high-pitched tone sounded. Comm from the bridge.

Dukat pressed his comcuff. "What is it?"

*"We're approaching the station, sir."*

"I'll be right there. Computer, end this program."

The panoramic views that surrounded them skittered and vanished, revealing a dark chamber outfitted on all sides with imaging diodes. Dukat enjoyed watching Damar struggle to maintain an expression of indifference to the abrupt change. Holodeck privileges were usually reserved for upper-echelon officers.

"Shall we?" Dukat asked, gesturing toward the door, and the young man fell in at his side. Together, they walked toward the central main corridor of the *Galor*-class vessel. Soldiers stopped to salute as the two men headed for the bridge, the gul nodding pleasantly in turn. Each and every one of them would be under his direct command.

*Returned, in triumph,* he thought, holding his head ever higher. This was a great day for him. He had been partly responsible for securing Bajor's allegiance to the Union, but politics had kept him from his rightful place as overseer to the annexation. His "punishment" for alleged missteps, a protracted stint as warden of the Letau prison facility, had turned out to be a prime opportunity; it had given him a chance to display his acumen as a leader, while removing him from the treacherous power struggles taking place in Central Command. He'd had time to cultivate alliances, to subtly discredit his detractors, to work his way to a position that would allow for this exultant return. Now he was prefect of Bajor; he was back to command the fortress station that rose in the Bajoran sky each night, to make his name synonymous with Cardassian superiority. He was where he belonged.

"Sir, I . . . Thank you, sir, for the opportunity," Damar said as they neared the bridge. "For the simulation."

Dukat smiled. "It's a small thing, to be sure, but I suppose when I was a third-tier gil—of course, we didn't have anything like current holosuite technology in those days."

Damar nodded. "Perhaps when I'm able to take some leave, I'll be able to go to the surface and see the real thing."

"You may be able to do that, Gil Damar, although I would advise you not to underestimate the responsibilities of military personnel on the station. And—if I'm not mistaken—your betrothed will be on the surface, will she not?"

Damar's face flushed. His affianced was with the Information Service, if Dukat recalled correctly. Vela, Veja, something like that.

"Yes, sir. She's at the Tozhat settlement."

"Well, then. I imagine your time on the surface will probably not be spent climbing mountains."

Damar grinned foolishly. They stopped outside the bridge, the gil obviously hesitant to assume an invitation, and Dukat gestured for him to step ahead, feeling generous.

"The ship is approaching our new home, Gil. Would you like to come to the bridge?"

Damar positively glowed. "Yes, sir."

"Very well. Let's go and have our first look at Terok Nor."

Lenaris Holem had given up trying to keep his right leg from cramping. It was the moisture in the weather today, the swollen clouds above him threatening to spill their contents. He couldn't remember how long he'd been in this line, and since he didn't have a timepiece, there wasn't any effective way to be sure without asking someone else. He knew better than to ask the woman sitting on the ground behind him—old Thera Tibb was a notorious jabberbox, and the last thing Lenaris needed was to be trapped listening to her endlessly embroidered anecdotes about her children. Anyway, Lenaris was fairly certain she was asleep, which gave testament to how slowly the line was moving.

Lenaris looked at the man in front of him. He was approximately the same age as himself, in his late twenties or early thirties, with very sharp ridges on his broad nose, and a wild tangle of uncut curly hair. His clothes were rough, even shabbier than Lenaris's own. He most likely didn't have a timepiece, either. Still, Lenaris was so bored and uncomfortable, he thought he might as well strike up a conversation.

"Do you have any idea how long we've been standing here?" he ventured. It was always a little ill-advised to speak to strangers when one was away from home. If the person you spoke to happened to belong to a higher *D'jarra,* he or she might take offense at your attempt to engage in conversation, depending on their caste. But many Bajorans—Lenaris among them—held those things in much lower esteem since the effects of the Cardassian occupation had become more widespread.

"I believe we've been here since first morning prayers." The man nodded at the glint of B'hava'el, piercing a thin ray through a break in the cloud cover overhead. "So, assuming my knowledge of the sun's position is correct, we've been here for at least six hours."

"Six hours!" Lenaris exclaimed. "I knew it had been a long time, but—"

"I could be overestimating," the stranger admitted, "but if I am, it's only by half an hour or so. I'm certain first morning prayers were going on when I got in line, and you didn't come along much later than that."

Lenaris folded his arms and sighed. These food ration lines were getting more intolerable by the day. His stomach was empty, aching from the days since he'd had a substantial meal. "I can't believe the spoonheads put us through this, day after day," he muttered, "and still have the gall to claim that they're trying to help us."

"The . . . what? Did you say . . . *spoonheads?*"

Lenaris cleared his throat. It was unwise to throw around such a blatant slur, when there were collaborators everywhere. "I mean, uh . . ."

The other man laughed. "I don't know if I've heard that before," he said. "Spoonheads. It does suit the Cardies, doesn't it?" The stranger stuck out his hand. "My name is Ornathia Lac, by the way. Or just Lac."

Lenaris took the man's hand and shook it. "Lenaris Holem. Where are you from, Lac? I don't believe I've heard of the Ornathias."

"Oh, I'm not from around here." He seemed not to

have any inclination to speak further, but Lenaris was bored. He eyed the other man's earring.

"A farmer?" Holem asked carefully.

The man nodded, but said nothing else.

Lenaris went on, trying to put Lac at ease. "My mother came from farmers. She married outside her *D'jarra*." He chuckled, and then clutched at his stomach at a mild twinge caused by the laughter. He was pretty sure he had been working on an ulcer for the better part of a year. "She always had a rebellious streak, which my father says I inherited. She was from the farmlands near the northern Relliketh province—is that where you come from?"

"No," Lac told him. "I come from inland of the Tilar peninsula, across the channel." He held out his hand, palm up, and looked toward the sky. "Did you feel a drop?"

Lenaris shook his head. "By the vineyards? What are you doing all the way over here?"

"The vineyards are part of my family's old estate," Lac answered, conspicuously ignoring the latter part of the question. "Though the Cardies took part of it over a decade ago, when they were still trying to colonize, my family still controls some of that land."

Lenaris nodded, curious as to how Lac had come to be at Relliketh. The only way to get across the channel was to go by Cardassian ferry or skimmer, and he wondered why the farmer would go to such trouble and expense. The man didn't offer any further explanation, however, so Lenaris thought he'd do best to let it lie.

"So," Lac said, after a moment of silence. His eyes flicked to Lenaris's earring, a rather plain one that did not include his family's caste designation. "What's your *D'jarra*?"

Lenaris was a bit taken aback; it had once been considered impolite to inquire about a person's *D'jarra,* if he didn't display it on his earring, or offer the information when introducing himself. But times had changed, and

Lenaris supposed there wasn't any reason not to tell the man. *"Va'telo,"* he said.

Lac's eyebrows did a little jump. "You're a pilot?" he asked, sounding hopeful. Most *Va'telo* were pilots, though some were boatmen, and in the old days, many had driven the groundcars.

"I *was* a pilot," Lenaris corrected him. "I used to do some transport work before the spoon—er—Cardassians shut down the textile mills along the channel. Times have been lean for a long while, though. I had to . . . sell my ship." It pained him to speak of it even now, two years later.

Lac nodded sympathetically. "The Cardies have disrupted nearly everyone's life, I suppose. My family still farms some of our land, but production is down to a tenth of what it was—and then the Cardies take most of it anyway, to meet quotas. It might seem backwards for a farmer to be standing in a food ration line, but—"

"Nothing makes sense anymore," Lenaris agreed.

Lac was quiet again, and Lenaris wondered if he hadn't said something wrong. The farmer was difficult to read. Lenaris shook his cramping right leg back awake again, not sure if he should continue the conversation.

"Have you ever flown a warp vessel?" Lac suddenly asked.

Lenaris laughed sharply. He'd been barely a boy when the Cardassians started to restrict warp travel. "How old do I look to you?" he said, then instantly regretted what might be perceived as unkindness in his tone. "No," he said. "I haven't. My father, of course—but he's long gone."

"Did your father ever tell you anything about flying a warp vessel?"

Lenaris swallowed. "A few things," he said. He looked down at his feet as he thought of his father, who had died from a simple untreated infection when Lenaris had still been in his teens. The Cardassians had placed a week-long block on travel between provinces after a terrorist strike, with no exceptions. Hemmed into a particularly remote area in Relliketh, Lenaris Pendan had died before a medic could get to him. Another indirect casualty of the occupation.

Lac nodded. "I didn't mean to make you uncomfortable," he offered.

"No—it's all right, it's just—I don't particularly care to think about my father."

"Oh," Lac said. "Was it . . . Cardies?"

Lenaris shrugged slightly. "More or less."

Lac looked apologetic. "I don't mean to sound so . . . forward. It's just that . . . well, I think I've heard your name before—and then when you said you're a pilot—"

"A pilot without a ship," Holem reminded him. This conversation seemed mired in depressing topics.

"You won't need a ship," Lac told him. "I have one."

Lenaris's eyebrows shot up, but Lac went on as if he hadn't just said the unlikeliest thing one could have expected from a farmer.

"I do recognize your name," Lac said, his voice taking on a confidential tone. "You know Tiven Cohr, don't you?"

Lenaris was no less surprised. "I . . ." He wasn't sure whether to confess to it or not. Tiven Cohr was involved with Lenaris's old resistance cell, a group he hadn't associated with for the better part of a year. This was not the sort of thing one was generally eager to discuss with a stranger.

"Look, Lenaris," Lac said, suddenly sounding a bit urgent. "I know we just met, but . . . you seem reasonably trustworthy. And if I'm right about that . . ." He lowered his voice. "I have something to show you that, as a pilot, you might find interesting." He glanced at the overcast sky. "That is, if we ever come to the end of this line."

As if on cue, it began to rain, at first the slightest suggestion of cold drops prickling the back of Lenaris's neck, and then an out-and-out downpour. He crossed his arms tightly across his chest, sniffling as the water soaked his hair and rolled down the tip of his nose.

"What kind of thing?" he asked Lac, who had assumed a similar posture.

Lac smiled mysteriously through the sheets of rain, and leaned closer, to speak to Lenaris over the plunking and splashing all around them. "It's a warp ship," he whispered. "A *Bajoran* warp ship."

Lenaris stared in disbelief. "Where?" he asked.

"I'll show it to you," Lac told him, wiping the water out of his eyes. "But first, I want you to do something for me."

"What's that?" Lenaris said uncertainly, shivering in the rain.

"Take me to Tiven Cohr."

"I can't," Lenaris said, feeling slightly relieved. He didn't want to get mixed up in whatever this fellow was proposing, especially if it involved Tiven Cohr. "I don't know where he is."

Lac looked disappointed. "But . . . could you find out?"

Lenaris frowned, poking his toes in the edges of the deep puddles that were suddenly emerging. "I don't know," he said.

The rain was beginning to let up, as quickly as it had started. Lac gave it another try. "You couldn't even maybe tell me where you last saw him? Anything like that?"

Lenaris grimaced. They were coming closer to the front of the line, where they would soon be within earshot of the collaborating Bajorans who ran the ration checkpoints. "I suppose . . . there are a few things I could tell you," he said.

Lac grinned. "Then it's settled," he said. "I can take you to my shuttle tomorrow."

"Your shuttle?" Holem said. He hadn't intended to sign on for whatever it was Lac was offering, but the farmer only nodded. Holem was bursting with questions, but as the line edged closer to the ration station, he could not ask them. He would have to be satisfied with finding out after he'd received his rations, and with the way his stomach was churning, he hoped the food would taste better than it smelled.

Professor Mendar cleared her throat loudly, and several of her students sat up a little straighter in their chairs. Miras Vara absentmindedly tapped a stylus against the surface of her padd, trying not to think about lunch. This class, a required postgrad overview of the Cardassian territories, was always difficult for Miras because of its unfortunate time slot. She was sure that many of the students, if not most, had the same problem. It didn't help that the content of the course was mostly irrelevant to Miras's primary concentration, homeworld agriculture. She'd spent six years studying ponics and soil components, and enjoying every minute of it; a quartile of politics and geography, treaties and borders, and she was bored stiff.

"Today, we begin our study of Bajor," the professor said, her hair a sleek black helmet on her rather mannish head. "I have prepared a brief presentation. I hope it will illustrate the importance of the development of new weapons for the future of our world, and open a discourse on ways in which we might better incorporate alien cultures."

Miras stifled a yawn and programmed her padd to download the images from the mainframe.

"I have to warn you that some of this material may be disturbing," the professor continued, and Miras sat up straighter, glancing over at Kalisi. Her classmate arched one delicate ridge, smiling slightly. The other students murmured to one another.

"Quiet, please. These are uncensored images, given to us by a correspondent for the Cardassian Information Service. She has risked her life many times to bring the truth about the Bajoran annexation to the Cardassian people. Normally, these images would not be displayed for the general public to view, as there are those who would manipulate this kind of material as ammunition for dissent. However, I am confident that my graduate students know better."

"There was a man in my sector who was a dissenter," Kalisi whispered across the aisle. Kalisi Reyar was one of Miras's closest friends. "I haven't seen him for a long time."

"He was foolish to make his opinions known," Miras whispered back.

Kalisi's gaze flicked to the front of the room before she replied. The professor was wrangling with her console. "He couldn't help himself. People with beliefs like that usually have a disorder that prevents them from understanding loyalty to anything but their own desires. A defect in their lateral cortex makes them abnormally egocentric, and the same disorder keeps them from having any impulse control. I learned about it in socio-deviance."

Miras turned forward as an image on the teacher's display lit up the darkened room. There was a long, slow pan of a massive pile of rubble, smoking composite materials spilling from the front of a large building. Soldiers in deflect suits were using displacers to shift through the wreckage.

"This ruined building is located at one of the older Cardassian settlements," Professor Mendar explained. "You can see that it has sustained considerable damage in an attack by rebel Bajorans. Of course, the vast majority of Cardassian structures remain unharmed. But for the soldiers who were garrisoned in this building, for the men and women who worked here . . ."

Miras leaned toward Kalisi. "My cousin was stationed on Bajor for a little while, before being sent to the border colonies."

"My father says the border colony skirmishes are a

waste of Cardassia's resources," Kalisi said promptly. "We should be putting more focus on Bajor."

Miras did not answer. Her own parents had often expressed the opposite belief. Many Cardassians had strong feelings about the conflict with the Federation over the border colonies, but Miras felt it wasn't appropriate for a woman to make her political opinions known. Anyway, it was not the function of a scientist to question military affairs, only to answer the call for improved technologies, to better the Cardassian quality of life. She had often thought to herself that Kalisi was too outspoken for a woman, but she adored her friend just the same. Miras had no illusions about her own future—she would work at the ministry, part of a team developing agrochemicals, or studying soil–plant microbe interaction; she would marry and bear children, as expected by her family and by the Union, and while it was all quite dull, she supposed, she was content with her prospects. Kalisi, though, beautiful and ambitious, an engineer and a programmer . . . Miras couldn't imagine such a plain, quiet life for someone like Kalisi.

"This is one of our most productive mining facilities on Bajor," Professor Mendar went on, images of tunnels and rocks flashing up, a number of the soft-faced Bajorans moving carts of rough-hewn stone across the screen. Without ridges, their faces seemed vulnerable and bland, their coloring quite sickly. Not an attractive people. "We have found a dizzying array of geological resources on the planet, and our latest estimation suggests that through their acquisition, we will extend Cardassian mineral productivity for decades, perhaps centuries."

The next image was of a crashed vehicle in a forest, a skimmer perhaps, its broken metal body half hidden by the deep green of the surrounding plants and trees. Miras felt a spark of real interest, looking at the tall woods, the lush undergrowth. She leaned back to her friend again. "This is giving me an idea for my thesis project."

"Me, too." Kalisi's whisper was no less excited.

"Beyond the usefulness of the topsoil analysis, just think of all the undiscovered flora and fauna . . ." Miras marveled at the possibilities. Xenoecology was her current favorite "tangent," a class that was also taught by Professor Mendar. "What would it be like to be part of a research team stationed on Bajor?"

"If I were to go, it would be to study how to make Cardassian weapons more effective there. I hear the climate is nearly intolerable."

Miras started to reply, but the latest image on the teacher's display caught her eye, and she gasped in horror.

Professor Mendar continued her narration. "I know that what you are seeing is very disturbing. But I think it's important that you understand who will be the true beneficiaries of better Cardassian technology."

Miras looked away. The picture was too much. Half-starved Cardassian children, their eyes hollow and black beneath their cranial ridges, stood miserably in a hut made of reeds. Their faces were smeared with reddish Bajoran soil, their black hair tangled, their clothing barely more than rags.

"These are the children of families who were once stationed on Bajor—families who were killed, or who simply disappeared. They have no place in Cardassian society now."

"But where will they . . . what will they do?" Miras was so flustered that she spoke out of turn.

"Please raise your hand, Miss Vara. When they're of age, they'll be offered placement in the military, perhaps trained for some menial labor. They'll be transported wherever the Union needs them most."

Miras studied the hopeless, unsmiling faces. "But isn't there something we can do for them now?"

There was a murmur of disapproval among some of the other students, and the instructor hesitated before speaking. "We can ensure that there are no more like them in the future."

Miras wanted to say more, to plead their case, but she knew better. The integrity of the family structure was the very core of Cardassian society. To take on a child of another's blood, to give them resources meant for one's own children . . . It simply wasn't done. In leaner times—and not so long ago—orphans had been cast into the streets to live like animals. Euthanasia, while not common, had neither been rare. It had only been in the past few generations that any subsidy had been made for them by the government. Orphans were better taken care of now than at any other point in Cardassian history, but it was still a sensitive topic. Seeing their small faces, though, she'd been unable to keep silent.

The film jumped to reveal another shot of the makeshift orphanage, and what Miras saw next disturbed her even more. This time, she remembered to raise her hand before asking. "Those alien children in the back of the room—are they also . . . ?"

"Yes. The Bajoran insurgents are truly so ruthless that they will even kill their own kind, if they suspect that they might be assisting the Union. Those children are probably the sons and daughters of Bajorans who cooperated with the Cardassian government and were subsequently killed by heartless terrorists. We must understand that we are dealing with an enemy whose ideals are very different from our own. We must not make the mistake of trying to sympathize with their position, for the Bajorans are not like us."

"Kalisi," Miras whispered. "We *have* to focus our thesis projects on Bajor."

Kalisi nodded vigorously. "I already know what mine

will be," she told her friend. "What do you think of 'Weapons for Peace' as a title?"

A look from Professor Mendar, and the two students fell silent, turning their attention back to the presentation.

As the class came to an end, Miras approached her professor eagerly, with Kalisi close behind her. "Professor Mendar, where can I find the latest datafiles from Bajor? Kalisi and I would like to research the annexation for our final thesis projects."

"That is an excellent idea, ladies, but I'm afraid there is currently very little data available to the public. Study of Bajor is a relatively new pursuit, considering the growing pains that are still under way in winning the loyalty of the Bajorans. Most of what you will find is related to the geology of the planet. If you've anything else in mind, you might not have much to go on."

Kalisi interrupted. "Is there anything comprehensive on Bajoran atmospheric peculiarities, as opposed to Cardassia Prime's?"

The teacher looked doubtful. "You're welcome to look at whatever the Ministry of Science has on file."

Miras felt a spark of excitement. "Do you think we might contact the information correspondent who captured those images? Perhaps she might help us. If you're at liberty to say her name, of course."

The teacher nodded. "That information is indeed open to the public. The correspondent's name is Natima Lang. Yes, I think you would be well-advised to speak to her. You'll find her to be a very knowledgeable, accommodating, and patriotic woman."

*Natima Lang.* Miras filed the name in her short-term memory, deciding she'd try to contact the woman right away. She'd been planning for some time to do her final project on aerobic soil processes in Cardassian sand clay, but the images of Bajor . . . She felt suddenly quite certain that her focus had to be on some aspect of Bajor. It was unlike her to make such impetuous decisions—that was more in Kalisi's line—but she was clear in her mind, as though the decision had been made long ago.

"My children." Kai Arin's distinctive voice was edged with kindness that was comfortable but firm. His words rang gently through the Kendra Shrine, settled over the congregation like an embrace.

"I know that many of the faithful have come to believe that the Prophets have abandoned them. But I urge you to hear my words. The Prophets have a plan for Bajor. It is when things become most difficult that our faith must sustain us. You must follow the prophecies as laid out by our forebears. You must adhere to your *D'jarras*. Leave politics to those in the designated political realm. Continue to concentrate on your roles in society as individuals. It is through the *D'jarras* that the machinery of Bajoran life will continue to run smoothly, each Bajoran a crucial component of the whole. Unless every last component works together, the machine will break down, and Bajor will become dysfunctional, its societal inner workings broken beyond repair."

The faithful murmured their approval, and Vedek Opaka Sulan, who stood at the door of the shrine with a ceremonial chime, murmured along with them, as she had through all the day's services. But, try as she might to stifle it, her heart ached with doubt. She could not ignore the Cardassian soldiers who stood just beyond the door of the religious shrine, listening to the kai's every word.

Arin was not the most popular kai in Bajor's long and storied religious history; in fact, many Bajorans had refused to accept him when he took the position a few years after the formal occupation by the Cardassians, believing him to have been elected falsely under the alien regime. The church had been affected by numerous schisms at that time, and many Bajorans had simply abandoned formal religious services altogether, though most still believed in the Prophets. Arin often chose to address these concerns in his sermons, but his thinning congregation seemed only to grow thinner as time went by.

Opaka wanted to believe that there was true conviction behind the kai's words; she had long felt that those who accused the kai of being a puppet for the Cardassians were simply weak of faith. Her personal thoughts on the matter had always been that the kai spoke from his own heart, that he genuinely believed in advocacy for the *D'jarras*. And yet, as time went by, Sulan could see more and more evidence that the *D'jarras* were hurting Bajor more than they were helping it. In the written words of the ancient ones, she found more and more references to the idea that the *D'jarras* were based solely on tradition rather than on actual prophecy. Yet she struggled, for she feared that she had simply fallen victim to the murmurings of the doubtful—although she considered herself a sensible person, not easily swayed by popular opinion. In many ways, she had never felt her faith tested so strongly as it was being tested now.

As the evening's final service concluded, Opaka bid good-bye to the Bajoran worshipers as they filed out of the sanctuary, and then gathered together the ceremonial items to be put away in the reliquary. She turned to acknowledge her fifteen-year-old son Fasil, who waited for her in the pews, amusing himself by whittling on a bit of kindling he had picked out of the firewood. Opaka was exhausted—she had stayed awake too late the night before, studying prophecy—and she looked forward to joining her son for dinner in their small cottage, but her persistent unease remained. She had considered speaking to the kai about her concerns, but something held her back. She did not want him to perceive her questions as an accusation in any way, and she knew she must think carefully about how to approach him.

Someone spoke behind her. "Vedek Opaka, you seem troubled."

She turned, still holding chimes and braziers. It was Gar Osen, an elder vedek who served as close counsel to the kai. She liked him well enough, though he had always seemed a bit reclusive to her. It was typical of him to ask after another's concerns, but rare for him to share his own feelings.

"Thank you, Vedek Gar. I suppose I was just considering . . ." She hesitated, but Gar's expression was so effectively compassionate that she decided to unburden herself of her thoughts. "In regard to the kai's sermon today, I . . . confess I often wonder at the efficacy of the *D'jarras* in today's world. I don't mean to say that they should be abandoned, of course, but—" She paused, but Gar's expression hadn't changed, and she felt encouraged to continue.

"Perhaps the Prophets don't always mean for us to passively wait for answers to fall to us," she said. "Perhaps the Prophets expect us to find conviction within ourselves when things become difficult, to call upon our own individual strengths and weaknesses, and . . . perhaps a redefinition of the *D'jarras* *is* in order, considering the circumstances. I say this only because it seems that so many of the castes have become irrelevant in this new climate, and they serve to divide us, at a time when unity is so . . . imperative . . ."

She trailed off, fearing that she had said too much. Gar's silence had finally unnerved her, and she waited for him to weigh in with an opinion of his own.

"Vedek Opaka, it seems you have given a lot of thought to this matter. Would you like it if I were to speak to the kai on your behalf?"

"Yes," she told him, flooded with hope and relief. "You understand—I only want to open a dialogue. Perhaps the kai has something to say that will help me to better understand his approach."

Vedek Gar nodded. "Perhaps he does, at that."

He took Opaka's left ear between his thumb and forefinger, and she closed her eyes as the energy of her *pagh* was revealed to him.

"Your *pagh* reflects deep sincerity, Vedek Opaka." He bowed slightly, and left her.

Opaka bowed in turn, and went to put away the ceremonial items, pleased that she'd spoken after all.

The man's name was Thill, Thill Revi, and he was as coarse and unappealing as most Bajorans. Natima could have interviewed him for the story over her office's secure line, but there was also going to be a minor "summit" at the base where Thill was in protective custody, a conference of all the base commanders in the Rakantha province; the Information Service needed a representative there. Her supervisor hadn't wanted to send her—the military base and the small Cardassian community it protected were near a heavily forested area in Rakantha, not a secure area in spite of the heavy concentration of soldiers there—but most of his male reporters were on assignment, and she was one of his best filters, fast and clean. He'd assigned her a recorder and a travel permit and told her not to linger.

*As though I'm on vacation,* she thought, looking into the narrow, damp face of Thill Revi as he studied her press badge. They sat in one of the base's small meeting rooms, thankfully heated but otherwise unpleasant, bare, and ill-lit. Her "escort," a base garresh, leaned against the far wall looking entirely bored. She was glad to be covering the conference; it would stream as a lead piece, worth the price of the last-minute travel, a cramped transport full of leering soldiers, a tight deadline . . . But another interview with one of *them* took some of the shine off.

Thill handed back her hardcopy pass, his expression too alien to understand. Suspicion? Anger? The Bajoran had graying hair and thin lines around his nose and mouth. When he spoke, his voice was sharp and nasal.

"You say you want to know about Mesto?" Thill asked. "Write a story about it?"

Natima nodded, and spoke with a patience she didn't feel. "Produce it, actually. As I said when I contacted you last week. I'm doing a piece about the Bajoran approval of Union annexation, focusing on men and women—like yourself—who've accepted our presence here, and have chosen to help us, in spite of the risks from Bajoran insurgents."

Thill's narrow face grew narrower. "Well, I don't know about that," he said. "All I did was tell our town liaison about Mesto Drade. He told the commander here, and they arrested him."

Natima checked the recorder, adjusted the angle slightly. "He's your neighbor, is that correct?"

"Farm next to my outfit," Thill said. His tone was sullen. "Don't know that that makes him a neighbor."

"Tell me how you found out what Mesto was doing," Natima said. Usually such an open-ended invitation started them talking. Most of the Bajorans she'd interviewed were only too eager to explain themselves, to convince anyone who might listen that they weren't really like the others, the *collaborators*.

Thill folded his arms. "You hear things. Drade, he thinks—he thought he was better than me. Farmer's no better than craftsman, though, no matter what anyone says. We're the same on the wheel."

*D'jarras*, she thought. The caste system. She stifled her distaste at the ignorance of his beliefs, reminding herself that he'd been raised into his cultural superstitions; it wasn't his fault. "Mesto was hiding the parts of a nearly complete warp reactor in his barn, along with stockpiles of chemical explosives. Your decision to turn him in probably saved lives."

Thill looked sour. "Ruined mine, though, didn't it? It's not just the rebels, you know. None of them—my 'neighbors'—none of them ever treated me real good. My family *D'jarra, Ke'lora,* is low on the wheel, see? I'm a tanner, come from a long line of tanners. It's a respectable position, you know, working the skins. 'And as the tradesman plies his wares, so the tanner scrapes the hides, so the ranjen studies the Word.' That's a direct quote from the Book of Seasons, isn't it? But all those high-caste types, they don't want to shake hands with someone like me. Same with my da, an' his da before him. Good men, treated poor."

His expression darkened. "Since I told about Mesto, though, no one will even *look* at me. I went to the market day after the soldiers came, and they wouldn't even sell me a drink of water. I should have expected as much. They say they believe the Word, but when Drade stopped farming, when he openly shunned his Fate, they all looked the other way. Someone had to stop him, that's all. "

His mouth pinched even tighter. "Never thought they'd do what they did to me, though."

Natima nodded along, trying to appear empathetic. It was a common story. Even after all this time, the Bajorans ostracized, harassed, even threatened "collaborators." Thill was at the military base because a week after he'd informed on Mesto, someone had tried to burn his house down, with him inside of it. He'd come to the base for protection. Usually informants weren't offered any kind of shelter, but the station commander had personally benefited from the seizure of the warp reactor and explosives; he'd granted Thill a temporary sanctuary.

*Not that he deserves it,* she thought. Thill hadn't been trying to help the Union, turning in a plotting terrorist; it was all some petty revenge, over hurt feelings and ridiculous cultural tenets. Still, she'd get nothing further from him by sharing her thoughts on the matter.

"It's . . . commendable, that you chose to see Mesto Drade brought to justice," Natima said, glancing down at her notes. "His name has been on a list of people with possible ties to the terrorists for some time, but his priority status was low. As I said, your decision undoubtedly saved lives . . ."

She waited for him to pick up, to detail his story, but he only stared at her, his lined, hard face as still as stone. She resisted looking at her chrono, aware that the first meeting of the Rakantha base commanders would soon begin, if it hadn't already. It was being held in the base's main building, behind the barracks. Her feature on "helpful" Bajorans wasn't due for another week, but she'd be up late tonight, filtering footage from the conference. There would be material for the civilian net on Cardassia, sound bites for the propaganda channels, other strings that would be sent to high-ranking members of Central Command; best she be there to record it.

*Wrap this up, then.* She'd get no help from Thill, but she had more than enough footage of Kubus Oak, droning on about brotherhood between the races. She'd cobble something together from the other interviews.

"Well. I appreciate your agreeing to meet with me, Mr. Thill . . ."

There was a sudden, heavy rumbling sound, stilling her words. Natima recognized the sound instantly; she'd spent long hours watching feeds of terrorist attacks. An instant later, they heard shouts, heard the keening whine of phaser fire. The garresh who'd taken her to meet Thill had snapped to attention, was talking low and fast into his comm. Natima and Thill both stood, the Bajoran's long face and darting gaze giving his fear away.

*The conference.* The base had been attacked, was perhaps still under attack. The explosion had come from behind the barracks, she was sure of it. Natima scooped up her recorder, turned to the door. She was too excited to be afraid, thinking of the footage she might be able to capture. The garresh stepped in front of her, physically blocking her way.

"We'll stay here until we get the all clear," he said sharply.

"I'm a reporter and qualified filter for the CIS," Natima said, meeting his tone. "And I'm aware of the risks. I could—"

"You could *die,* Miss," he said. "I'm assigned to keep you from harm, and my orders stand. You're not going anywhere."

"What if they come for me?" Thill said, his voice high, his eyes moving, moving.

The garresh sneered at him. "Then we'll let them have you, Bajoran."

Thill sat down again with a low moan of terror. Natima glared at the soldier, frustrated, aware that if she'd been a man, he would have let her go.

*If I were a man, I wouldn't have an escort in the first place.*

The garresh's face was set. Outside there were more shouts, but no further explosions, no more weapons fire. A hit-and-run, probably, like most of the terrorist attacks on Bajor. The rebels were cowards, they were fools with firepower, randomly attacking anyone and anything Cardassian. Natima hoped that no one in the settlement had been injured. There were families there, wives and children of soldiers, civilian scientists . . .

*They don't care who they hurt,* she thought, sitting back down, and finally felt a whisper of fear for herself. In another few moments, she, too, would have been at the conference.

Thill had his head in his hands, was mumbling to himself, repeating something over and over. She leaned in, caught his plaintive whisper.

"I don't want to die, please the Prophets, please don't let me die, I'm sorry I did it, I'm sorry about what I did, please don't let me die . . ."

Natima leaned away from him, unable to hide her own sneer. Praying to gods that didn't exist, to absolve him for turning in a terrorist . . . so that he might be saved from another terrorist, one of his own kind. And outside, soldiers had surely been injured, perhaps killed. She'd tried to keep an open mind since coming to Bajor, but what a miserable, self-serving people she found them to be, never content, reckless and violent and primitive.

She held her recorder tightly, waiting to be told it was safe.

## 2

Gil Damar watched Gul Dukat as the prefect surveyed the operations center from the upper ring that extended beyond the prefect's office, overlooking the soldiers at work. Damar thought the gul looked pleased, and he thought of the great responsibility that went into commanding such a large and impressive facility. Dukat caught Damar's eye then, and he ambled down the short staircase into the lower level, where Damar was filling out shift-end reports.

"What do you think? Is your new assignment to your liking, Gil?"

Damar nodded. "Yes, very much, sir. The station is . . . it's not what I expected."

Dukat smiled and gazed around appreciatively. "Yes, the Nor-class is really quite breathtaking when you first see it in person. Seldom have elegance and power been fused together so effectively."

Damar worked quickly to finish up his reports, with the Gul standing nearby. It seemed to Damar that Dukat wanted to continue his conversation, and he wondered if it would be better to abandon his duties to speak to him, or to continue at his task. He could feel Dukat's gaze on him as he worked.

"Most of the shops already have leases pending," he

offered, continuing to file. "I believe the Promenade businesses will be a striking success."

Dukat broke into a smile. "I'm pleased to hear you say
that. I admit, I had my doubts about the Bajoran merchants'
readiness to move their business to an orbital venue. But
most seem to understand what a truly great opportunity
this will be for Bajoran trade relations with other worlds.
For those Bajorans smart enough to open businesses here,
there is a lot of latinum to be made."

Dukat began to walk, and Damar hesitated at his station
before the gul beckoned for him to follow. "Let's have a
look around the Promenade, shall we?"

"I . . . Yes, sir."

The two left ops, heading for the station's center of
commerce. It was a number of levels below operations, part
of Terok Nor's upper core. As the lift began its descent, Gil
Damar marveled at the construction techniques that had
gone into assembling this station in such a short time. A
third of the materials had come light-years to be assembled
here, much of the components prefabricated elsewhere and
systematically fastened into place.

The Promenade was a tri-level ring of commercial
spaces and observation decks, which also housed security and the station's infirmary. Several shopkeepers were
already beginning to set up their wares to offer to the Cardassian soldiers and to the vast numbers of Bajorans who
would soon be coming to work at the ore processors.

"Just think, Damar. Soon this station will be full of happily working Bajorans."

Damar looked around, envisioning it. The Bajorans
would be quartered in community housing near ore processing, given a place of their own, although there would
be those who earned private quarters, in the station's inner
habitat ring. Dukat had spoken of plans to turn one of the
Promenade spaces into a Bajoran shrine, to make them feel

more welcome; it was a revolutionary idea, and a brilliant one. "It's a wonderful opportunity to show the Bajorans how they can profit by partnering with us."

He could see that his answer pleased the prefect. Dukat nodded firmly. "Yes, Damar, exactly! Someday we'll be providing work for all idle Bajorans, here and on the surface. We will eliminate the food ration centers, and help them to become self-sufficient instead of relying on Cardassian charity. I commend the efforts of those who have conspired to provide welfare to our hosts, but I fear that the newer generations are learning only helplessness and a sense of entitlement from our repeated handouts. They have no gratitude, as they have come to expect us to feed them."

An aide who had come up behind them quickly fell in step with the prefect.

"Gul Dukat," the garresh said. "Your Bajoran intermediary is here and is waiting to meet you."

Dukat turned to the aide, looking puzzled and a little annoyed. "My intermediary? Do you mean Kubus Oak? I've already spoken with that pest at least a dozen times today."

Damar barely succeeded in concealing his surprise at hearing Dukat's belittling of Secretary Kubus. The gil had met him earlier in the day, and Kubus had struck him as the sort of Bajoran who genuinely appreciated how his world could benefit from its association with Cardassia. That enthusiasm, coupled with his lifelong political acumen, made Kubus the ideal liaison between the prefect and the Bajoran government. Damar wondered what the man had done to earn Dukat's apparent disdain.

"Not Secretary Kubus, sir. It's Basso Tromac. He has been appointed to take care of any . . . personal errands you may need fulfilled here on the station or on the surface of Bajor . . . ? You requested—"

Dukat nodded. "Ah, yes. Thank you. Have him wait outside my office. I'll be there shortly."

The aide left them, and Dukat continued to walk, his hands locked behind his back. "I want to trust the Bajorans," he confided to Damar, "but they make it so difficult. It won't be easy for me to invest any confidence in a Bajoran assistant."

Damar nodded, thinking he understood. "But it is best to have someone of this world as a go-between, to help prevent cultural misunderstandings," he suggested.

"Exactly! You're quite perceptive, Damar. And yet, I think it would be wise to put this Basso Tromac up to a little test of loyalty, wouldn't you say?"

Damar supposed that sounded reasonable, and he nodded. They walked a few minutes more, Dukat pointing out salient features of the station, explaining the concepts that had birthed his vision—a central core encircled by two rings, connected by several well-spaced crossover bridges; as many as 7000 people would be able to live comfortably in the habitat ring. The outer docking ring supported the massive pylons that housed ore-processing. The station was comfortable as well as functional, with a design aesthetic that spoke to the unique sensibilities of the modern Union. Terok Nor was truly a feat of Cardassian engineering.

The two officers finally headed back for ops, Damar noting that Dukat was purposefully taking his time, making himself late for his meeting. The young gil lingered behind at his station when they reached the station's uppermost level. Standing outside the closed door of the prefect's office was a Bajoran man with a characteristically crinkled nose, the skin of his forehead so strangely pink and smooth, like the belly of a *marga* fish. A glinting adornment dangled from one of his ears. Damar attempted to keep his eyes on his work, but he could not help but regard the man with curiosity. He had seen only a very few Bajorans up close. He watched the exchange in the periphery of his vision.

"You must be Basso Tromac, my new personal aide," he

heard Dukat say. The man answered only with an inclination of his head. Dukat conspicuously did not invite him into the office, which Damar thought odd, but imagined it was part of the test Dukat had been talking about. "There's something I would like you to take care of right away."

"How may I be of service, Prefect?" The Bajoran sounded compliant enough.

"Many of my officers here are far away from the comforts of home. They are lonely—for the companionship of women. I would like for you to go to the surface and return with some attractive Bajoran females, to ease their loneliness."

Damar was stunned, but he noted that the Bajoran man had not even blinked.

"I will see to it immediately, Prefect." Basso bowed as he made to leave.

Damar stole a glance at Dukat, and found that the gul was looking right at him. Embarrassed, he trained his gaze back to his workstation where it belonged.

"Report to my office, Gil Damar."

Damar reluctantly ascended the steps, hoping that his expression did not reveal his discomfort.

Dukat ushered him into his office and gestured for Damar to sit. "You appear . . . unsettled, Damar. Was it the request I made of the Bajoran that upset you?"

"I apologize for eavesdropping, Gul, I did not mean to—"

"Think nothing of it, Gil. Only tell me what is troubling you."

Damar cleared his throat. "Well—sir, I know that it isn't unheard of for officers to sometimes . . . seek comfort when they are away from home. It isn't that, sir. It's just that . . . the Bajoran women . . . they are so different from us. It seems . . . unusual . . . *unnatural,* to think of . . ."

Dukat's smile slipped away. "Gil. If you are going to

serve on Terok Nor, you must come to terms with your own xenophobia. The Bajorans are different from us in many ways, of course. But those differences are primarily cultural. Biologically, we are actually more alike than we are different. As for what distinctions there are, we Cardassians must learn to bridge those differences if our two peoples are ever going to come together."

"Yes, of course, Gul Dukat." Damar was embarrassed. He knew that the gul had much to teach him, and he desperately hoped that he was wise enough to recognize the lessons as they came. He hoped he would never do anything foolish enough to cause him to fall from Dukat's favor.

After a single night spent in the settlement outside of Relliketh, Lac had persuaded Lenaris to accompany him several *kellipates* away, into the tangle of forest outside the town, not far from where Lenaris's old resistance cell had once hidden. First, they had scouted the area where Lenaris thought Tiven Cohr might still be living, but the area was long abandoned. Lenaris doubtfully suggested that Tiven might have gone farther into Relliketh, though he wasn't sure if Tiven even had family there. Still, Lac seemed undeterred, happy to pursue Lenaris's scanty leads.

Since meeting Lac, Lenaris had felt a stir he hadn't felt in some time. Something in the other man's demeanor reminded him of Lafe Darin, the man who had inspired him to join the resistance in the first place. Lenaris had been much younger, then—not much more than a kid—but he still clearly recalled that sense that he *had* to fight back against the Cardassians, no matter the cost. That he would rather die than settle into hungry and despondent defeat. It was a mindset he thought he'd lost after Darin had died.

It was getting dark as they approached the area where

Lac said his flyer would be. Nightfall was the best time to travel beyond the Cardassian-imposed boundaries; the alien soldiers did not take well to the chill brought on after sundown, and Bajorans could expect few encounters with them during the night.

After much inconsequential small talk on their careful journey, Lenaris decided to satisfy some of the more compelling questions he had for the farmer. "So, Lac," he said finally, taking a deep breath. "You never told me how you knew Tiven Cohr in the first place."

It was already too dark for Lenaris to see the other man's expression, but Lac paused before answering, as if deciding what to say.

"I didn't know him personally. A friend of mine met him a few times."

"In what capacity?" Lenaris pressed.

"The resistance."

Lenaris was a little surprised by the man's candor, but not his answer; he had assumed as much. He thought again of Lafe Darin. When Darin had died, Lenaris had sworn off further involvement with the resistance, but he was still far from having been beaten into a submissive subject of the Union . . . and he had often wondered what it would take to make him care again. Darin's death shouldn't have been a surprise. Anyone involved in the underground had to understand that the only guarantee in the movement was that people were going to die. Friends, brothers and sisters, husbands, wives, even children. Still, Holem had been unprepared for just how much his childhood friend's death had affected him.

"Tiven Cohr is in the Halpas cell," Lac said matter-of-factly. "At least, he was a year ago. I heard you were, as well."

Lenaris wasn't sure how to respond.

"It's all right, Holem. I'm fighting against them, too. At

least, trying to. Some friends and relatives of mine are trying to scrape together a resistance cell. But Tiven Cohr—I just wanted to contact him regarding another matter."

Lenaris thought he knew. Tiven Cohr was an engineer whose reputation far preceded him. "The warp ship?"

"I heard that he was the best. He worked on warp vessels before the occupation, didn't he?"

Lenaris nodded. "Yes, he did," he said. "But it's like I told you—I haven't seen him in some time."

"Well, you're the first lead on him I've found in months," Lac said. "You know more than I do, and that's got to be worth something."

They curved past the stand of dead and dying trees, thin shadows in the darkness. Lac led them into the woods, taking a trail that Lenaris could barely see by the glow of Bajor's distant moons.

"It's right up here." Lac gestured to something beyond a tangle of brittle tree limbs. Holem could not quite make out what it was as they approached the small clearing; he could only see a dark, angular heap of something that appeared to be covered with old leaves.

Lac began to tug at a corner of a tarpaulin that had been tossed over the ship, woven with strips of canvas and covered over with foliage.

"I don't believe it," Lenaris marveled, as the little ship was revealed underneath the covering. It was an old Militia raider, the kind that had been fairly common twenty years ago . . . when there had still *been* a Militia.

Lac stepped inside the ship, ignoring the question. "Do you want to fly her, Holem?"

"Really?" he said eagerly. "You'd trust me to—"

"Sure," Lac said. "I'm not much of a pilot, myself. You're the *Va'telo,* after all."

Lenaris stepped inside, looking at the name painted on the side of her hull. The *Lupus,* named after the crafty animals that roamed Bajoran forests, sometimes picking off farmers' livestock. "Where did you get this thing?" he asked.

A smile played around the corner of Lac's mouth, and Lenaris had already determined that Lac was the sort of person who did not smile without significant provocation. He was obviously pleased with his ship, as every pilot was. "This one belonged to my grandfather," he explained. "We have others, mostly built from the cannibalized parts of other ships, and even a few built from scratch. But this one is the template."

"But . . . you said you come from farmers. Was your grandfather . . . ?"

"It was a hobby for him. He wasn't allowed a master's license, of course. He never made it out of the atmosphere. But he loved to fly, when he could, and he was quite good at it, too." He tapped the ship affectionately. "He managed to hide it from the Cardassians when they started putting restrictions on possession and operation of flyers and spacecraft. It wasn't that difficult—it didn't occur to them that a farmer would have an old Militia raider stored in his barn."

Lenaris hesitated. "How do you keep the Cardassians from tracking your fuel emissions? For that matter, how are we going to stay under the security grids? Do you have some kind of . . . shielding device?"

Lac smiled again. "Nothing that sophisticated. I've studied some of the flight patterns of the delivery vessels that go back and forth across the channel, and I try to stick to their schedules. The Cardassians don't pay much attention to back-and-forth travel around here. Anyway, if it ever came down to a chase, their flyers have proven to be pretty wobbly in the atmosphere. I think there's a good chance I could give them a run for their money—and an even better chance that you could."

Lenaris supposed this was a satisfactory answer, and he

was flattered that Lac had already put so much faith in his abilities. He strapped into his seat, feeling a rush of real joy as he prepared to lift off. He adjusted the ship's thrusters to bring the craft straight upward, out of the trees, enjoying the familiar pull of gravity, the sensation of leaving it behind. He kept the vessel low, learning the console as he piloted them toward the peninsula. It wasn't until fifteen minutes later, when he was nearly to Tilar, that he remembered the other part of his question—the one that Lac hadn't answered.

"How *do* you keep the spoonheads from tracing your fuel signature?" he asked.

"Balon," Lac said, without missing a beat, and Lenaris's hands tightened on the flight yoke. He could feel the blood draining from his face.

"Balon!" he exclaimed. "You're joking!" Balon was a highly unstable fuel, out of use for over a century before the Cardassians had come, due to an unfortunate tendency toward spontaneous combustion.

Lac waved a reassuring hand. "Don't worry," he said. "Some friends of mine have figured out how to isolate the most unstable components of it, in its liquid form. We've been converting it to a safe fuel source for quite some time now. The Cardies don't bother to scan for it, since it's been out of use for such a long time."

Lenaris relaxed, but only slightly. He felt as though he'd just been told he was strapped to a "safe" bomb. And if Lac was overestimating his friends' expertise, then he could expect to walk with the Prophets somewhere around touchdown time—Lenaris hadn't landed a flyer of any sort in well over a year, and without knowing the terrain, he was likely to make a rough reunion with the ground.

Lac leaned forward to the ship's sensor display, an old-fashioned model with blinking, geometric glyphs showing the other craft in the region. A large, green triangle came into view, and Lac tapped it with his finger. "That's the landing point," he declared. "I programmed it in myself," he added proudly.

"I hope your friends know what they're doing . . . with the, uh . . ." Lenaris trailed off, not wanting to be insulting, but still—the balon mishaps of yesteryear were well remembered by anyone in the *Va'telo* caste.

"Don't worry, Holem. I've done this at least a hundred times, and I'm sure you're far better at it than I am."

Lenaris couldn't help but squeeze his eyes shut when the raider came into gentle contact with the ground, a perfect landing if he'd ever made one. He opened his eyes slowly and let out a hard breath. "All in a night's work," he said, his voice trembling ever so slightly. His hands still clenched the flight yoke.

Lac wasted no time in pushing back the raider's glacis plate. "Well, come on then. I'll take you to the settlement, and then tomorrow we can have a look at the warp ship, weather permitting."

On rubbery legs, Lenaris followed the farmer, wondering for the hundredth time what he was getting himself into.

In the dark, he could see the uneven outlines of the buildings up ahead. Lac led him toward the center of a ramshackle town, and Lenaris got a clearer picture of where the farmer lived. The buildings were mostly comprised of scrap, piled up on the foundations of crumbling houses from long ago. This was a town that had been destroyed by Cardassians, he deduced, at least a decade ago, and then rebuilt with whatever pieces of debris the surviving Bajorans could find.

"We haven't always lived like this," Lac explained. "My family's farm is some distance from here. I resettled in this area with my cousins just about eight years ago. We've had a few more stragglers join us since then, adding more dwellings as we were able to come by building materials."

Lac's definition of "building materials" was loose. Uneven bits of stone were plastered into place with dry mud on some of the more substantial houses, but many were thrown together from old sheets of metal and smart-plastic that were clearly salvaged from Cardassian refuse.

Lac came upon one such improvised structure, bigger than most of the others, and pulled back the door, made of several thin tree branches stripped of bark and twigs and crookedly lashed together. "Hello?" he spoke into the darkness, and after a moment, a half circle of light appeared underneath the crack of what must have been another door. The half circle widened as a door was thrown back, and out stepped the most beautiful woman Lenaris had ever seen, shaking sleep from her almond-shaped green eyes. She smoothed a thick, black curl behind her ear. "You're finally back," she said.

"Lenaris Holem, I'd like you to meet Ornathia Taryl," Lac said formally.

Lenaris extended his hand. "Your . . . wife?" he said.

Taryl laughed, a vibrant sound reminding Lenaris of a little bell his mother had once kept on a dais, back at his childhood home. "His sister," she corrected.

Lenaris hoped he didn't look as relieved as he felt as he clasped the woman's forearm. Her skin was smooth and warm.

"Taryl is the one who made the original breakthrough with the balon," Lac said, clearly proud of his sister.

"Really?" Lenaris said, incredulous. Research into stabilizing balon had eluded scientists for over a century. "I can't believe a farmer could just—"

Taryl's pretty face suddenly darkened. "Farming isn't just planting beans, Lenaris. It takes tremendous knowledge of soil chemistry, climatology, gene splicing and plant biology—"

"I'm . . . sorry," Lenaris said, mortified. "I meant it as a compliment."

Taryl did not look especially appeased, but she let it drop. "It wasn't just I who made the discovery," she said. "My fiancé worked on it with me. He—"

"It was you who made the discovery," Lac said. "Don't be so modest."

Taryl shrugged. "So," she said, gesturing to Lenaris. "Are you going to tell me why you've woken me up to introduce me to him?"

"He's a pilot," Lac said. "And he knows Tiven Cohr."

Taryl's mouth twisted as she appeared to process the news. "The warp ship," she said softly.

"Don't tell Seefa," Lac said. "I know he thinks it's a lost cause. But I still think—"

"He's my lover, not my keeper," Taryl said lightly. "I won't tell him." She looked Lenaris up and down. "You really know where Tiven Cohr is, Mister Lenaris?"

"Call me Holem," he said. "And . . . I might be able to find him."

Taryl nodded toward her brother. "Lac has been trying to locate Tiven Cohr for almost two years. Word of mouth, coded messages sent through the comnet—all have been dead ends."

"Well," Lenaris said, "I'll certainly do my best to help." He tried to sound earnest, though he had come here without any real certainty that he could—or even wanted to—find Tiven. She turned and left them, and Lac escorted Holem to a room with a rough pallet where he could lie down. He thanked his host, and as he lay awake, he considered. He had only just met Taryl, and apparently she was engaged . . . But she still seemed enough of a reason to follow through on his promise. He wanted to impress her . . . And he thought that perhaps there was some flicker of dissent that still burned inside him, not entirely snuffed out by the overwhelming defeat he had faced when the Halpas cell had broken apart.

✦  ✦  ✦

Natima Lang adjusted the volume on her communications screen, but it did little to correct for the subspace static invading her conversation. Transmissions between Bajor and Cardassia Prime were often full of interference during the early months of the year, when the disturbances in the Denorios Belt wreaked havoc on the subspace relays.

"I'm sorry, I'm going to have to ask you to repeat that last question," Natima told the young woman on the other end of the line.

*"I was asking if you wouldn't mind sending along some of your latest notes—I mean, anything that you don't mind parting with . . ."*

"Don't be silly, Miss Vara, of course I'll send you whatever I have. I admire you for having the astuteness to focus on Bajor. So many Cardassians are unaware of what an important venture this is for our future. They see it as just some distant, faraway place, without really comprehending how beneficial this annexation has been for the Union."

The girl nodded, her expression sincere and attentive. Natima was pleased. It galled her that so few people took much of an interest in what was happening on Bajor. The improved quality of life on Cardassia Prime was directly attributable to the Bajor mission. She wanted so much to impress upon her fellow Cardassians Bajor's importance to the homeworld, so they would not take for granted the efforts of their government.

*That will change,* she thought, studying the grainy face on the screen. Miras Vara seemed bright and enthusiastic; a few more like her, and Bajor's import would be fixed in Cardassia's consciousness.

*"Thank you so much, Miss Lang. Like I said, I haven't narrowed down to an exact topic, but I'm hoping that looking through your notes might help to inspire me. Oh, and please, call me Miras."*

"Well, I hope my notes will be helpful for you, Miras. And you may call me Natima. Now, I must warn you—the materials I will be sending you will include raw footage. These images must not be shared with anyone outside the Ministry of Science."

"I do understand. Although I'm curious—how did the Ministry of Science come to have the footage of those children in the Bajoran orphanage? Doesn't the Information Service consider images like that to be too provocative for public exposure?"

Natima's gaze flickered away from the viewscreen for a moment while she answered. "Yes, you're right—it is a very politically charged topic, that of the orphans. But because the images were being sent to an institution of learning—"

"But—if you don't mind my asking—why capture those images in the first place?"

Natima coughed. "I suppose I felt that . . . those children . . . that Cardassia might want to be made aware of some of the reasons we continue to send troops here. If you'll excuse me, Miras, I have an appointment I must be getting to. I hate to cut our transmission short, but . . ."

"I understand. Thank you so much for agreeing to help me with my project. I look forward to receiving your notes."

Natima tapped off the comm screen and sat back for a moment, closing her eyes. She did not hear her friend Veja Ketan enter her room, and was startled when Veja greeted her.

"Did I hear you say you had an appointment, Natima? I didn't know you'd scheduled anything for this weekend."

Natima stood from her chair. "I did say that, but I was really just trying to end the call. It hurts my eyes to look at the screen for so long."

"It wasn't a man, was it?" Veja's tone became playful, something that always annoyed Natima a little. Veja had romance on the brain since she'd learned that her fiancé, a third-tier gil in the military, was to be stationed on Terok

Nor. Natima had yet to meet Corat Damar, but Veja had taken a number of leave passes since he'd come to Bajoran space, the two of them meeting at the Cardassian settlement in Hedrikspool. She was always prattling on now that Natima should be looking for a mate.

"Hardly."

Veja toyed with the long, glossy black plait that curled around her left shoulder. "I was just on the comm myself."

"Talking to Gil Damar, I'd wager."

Veja smiled, playing at being embarrassed. "Yes, it was Corat. He invited me to go to Terok Nor, in just a few weeks! Can you imagine how exciting it will be to tour a brand-new state-of-the-art facility just as it begins to go into full operation?"

"Hm," Natima answered. "I suppose it would be interesting to have a look. I've been waiting for the service to send one of us up there to cover it, but I guess the military doesn't want any correspondents touring until it's better established."

Veja's face was dark with excitement. "Yes, well, now we have the chance!"

"What do you mean, *we*?"

"Well, perhaps Corat will have a friend for you. There are hundreds of eligible military personnel on that station—"

"Veja, I keep telling you and telling you—"

"Yes, I know. You're not here to find a husband. But that's exactly why you probably will find one. Don't you see? That's how it always works."

Natima sighed. She didn't really feel like tagging along on a date with Veja and her betrothed. But she wanted to see the station. She brushed at a dirty spot on her white tunic while she considered. The crumbly, ubiquitous Bajoran dirt had already ruined so many of her favorite things. It was enough to make her want to dress all in drab browns, like many of the Bajorans she'd seen. She regarded the smear of dirt for a moment before nodding.

"Okay, I'll go with you. But don't try to fix me up with anyone, please. And we should come up with some sort of signal, if you and Damar want to go off alone."

"Oh, we won't need a signal. If we want to go off alone, you'll know it. Trust me."

Natima rolled her eyes, hoping the station would be worth it.

Vedek Opaka bowed to her son, who stood at her left, and then she bowed to the woman on her right. She recited from Taluno's Seventeenth Prophecy with the rest of the congregation, and then she closed her eyes, to silently thank the Prophets for another day.

Once a month, the vedeks were free to join the gathering of faithful like any other worshipers, their spiritual duties adjourned. Although Opaka loved serving the Prophets, she also looked forward to these days, especially for the opportunity to be with her son. Fasil usually stood with another family until services were concluded, waiting for his mother to complete her tasks so that they could go home to their small cottage, a short distance beyond the sanctuary, and prepare their daily meal.

She smiled at Fasil. He was a good boy, responsible, with a strong sense of right. She had truly been blessed. But he was growing so quickly . . .

Vedek Gar had stepped to the front, and she turned her attention to him. She was looking forward to his sermon. It was during services that Gar's quiet, enigmatic qualities were temporarily suspended, giving way to reveal a fiery and inspirational spirit.

"My brothers and sisters," he began. "It inspires me to see such a strong turnout on a day like today, when many of us would prefer to be outside, to enjoy the sunshine. I know that when the weather has been so unpredictable, many of us feel as though it has been an eternity since we have been warmed by the sun. I commend you for choosing to come to services, for remembering to honor Those whose light replenishes our spirits." He smiled broadly, but then his expression gave way to one of deep regret.

"Of course, it brings to mind an allegory. One with which I know you are all familiar. For there are some among us who, in these times of despair, begin to wonder if the warmth and comfort brought to them by the Prophets will ever return. And as they lose their faith, they begin to lose their way as well. And even when the Prophets are felt again, like the sun on an uncertain spring day, it is not to Them that those wayward travelers attribute their good fortune. Instead, they believe that it is only by their own initiative that fate begins to smile upon them. They forget where proper thanks are due."

The congregation responded with a collective affirmation.

"The Prophets ask so little of us. They ask for our faith, and nothing more. And if we have faith, we know that we must continue to walk in the paths laid out by our fathers and mothers."

Sulan recognized the last bit as a fragment of familiar prophecy. *Let him who has tilled the soil till the soil, for the land and the people are one* . . .

It was a common theme, one that appeared numerous times in prophecy. *The land and the people are one,* the importance of the harvest, and the importance of those who facilitated it; each Bajoran assigned to his or her role, an elaborate, ancient system meant to promote peaceful cooperation among all strata of society—no one role less important than another. Though some may have held more prestige, it was understood that without even one element of the *D'jarras*, Bajor would cease to function. At least, before the Cardassians came, that had been the way.

Gar began to recite the rest of the verse as it appeared in her mind. "*. . . but the land will cry fallow without the efforts of the many. She who is a merchant, he who tends to the sick, she who guards the flocks, all must look to their own callings, and follow in the paths laid out by their fathers and mothers.*"

Opaka bowed her head and clasped her hands together, feeling humility swell in her breast. She knew that Gar had chosen this message deliberately. Though it was a favorite topic of Kai Arin's, Gar had never previously chosen to address the abandonment of the *D'jarras*, not directly.

"My brothers and sisters," Gar continued. "It may seem a small thing, *tradition,* in the face of hardship, in the fluctuations of a hard spring. But we all know that those Bajorans who choose to participate in acts of terrorism have begun to advocate for the dissolution of the *D'jarras*. I know there are those of you who have become impatient, waiting for the Cardassians to restore our full privileges, to want to shirk your natural-born identity and perhaps take up the mantle of some other profession in the meantime. But those lost privileges will never be restored if the Cardassians cannot trust us. And if these uprisings of violence do not cease, I fear that this essential trust may never come to be. Only patience, and faith in the Prophets, will bring about the better world we so desire. The message of the resistance is tempting to those whose faith has faltered—fight, destroy, let our anger rule us. But make no mistake—the men and women who turn from the path that fate has assigned them, who encourage others to do the same, will serve only to hurt us all. They build a wall between us and our Prophets, Who weave the Tapestry in which all our lives are threaded."

Opaka Sulan's humiliation was soundly complete. She pressed clasped hands against her face. Tears of shame threatened.

"What's wrong, Mother?" Fasil whispered, his hand—nearly an adult's hand—pressing against his mother's shoulder with still-childlike concern.

"Hush, Fasil. After the sermon concludes, I will speak to you."

"I'm sorry, Mother, I didn't—"

"Shh!"

Fasil turned his attention back to the service. Sulan watched as her son faithfully raised his hands and murmured the ancient chants in concert with the Bajorans around him. A heavy lump formed in Sulan's throat to see Fasil so nearly grown, and so like his father.

Fasil regarded her with curiosity as they left the shrine. "You seemed unusually affected by this morning's message," he said cautiously, as the two walked the distance to their old stone cottage. The air was warm but humid from days of rain, the weeds suddenly knee-high at the sides of the worn dirt path. The cottage was located halfway between the shrine, with its adjacent monastery, and the ancient ancestral castle that still stood at the edge of the woods to the south, the Naghai Keep. The fusionstone structure had withstood much of the destruction that marked the early years since the Cardassians declared Bajor an annexed world.

"Yes," she told her son. "Vedek Gar reminded me that I must never forsake the Prophets, no matter my personal misgivings about the occupation."

Fasil was quiet for a moment. "I believe Vedek Gar was trying to manipulate the congregation," he said.

Sulan was surprised. "Fasil!"

"I'm sorry, Mother."

Neither spoke again as they came upon their little house, nestled up against a wide thicket of trees that was just big enough to be called a forest. The cottage had served many purposes throughout the centuries: as a buttery, a tool shed, even a coop for livestock. Opaka Bekar had claimed it years ago, just before the birth of their son, when he and Sulan were both prylars at the second Kendra Shrine. It was generally accepted that married couples lived separately from the rest of the priory. At the time, Sulan was anything but happy to accept the squat little structure as her home. The cottage had never been much, and it still bore evidence of its past as a storage facility and a pen for animals. But Opaka had come to love it. She knew how very lucky she was to even have a roof over her head, let alone one as·sturdy and comfortable as this beloved little house.

As they entered, Fasil went immediately to the cupboard in the corner where the wooden dishes were kept. He removed two bowls and watched his mother as she lifted the lid from an iron kettle on the woodstove.

" 'For the land will cry fallow without the efforts of the many,' " he said, after a moment.

Opaka, tending to the *kava* root that had been stewing all afternoon, nodded as she watched her son lay two ceramic spoons down at the table. "Yes, that is the prophecy, Fasil. I'm pleased that you know your verse."

"Mother, the land is crying fallow now."

She began to say something but then stopped, realizing that she had no appropriate response. She moved to the far wall and used a long stick to prop open the window situated just below the peak of the high ceiling. She grunted with the exertion of the task; she had often wondered why whoever built this cottage would have put the only functionally opening window in such an inaccessible position. She supposed it was for security reasons, but that didn't explain why the glassed-in window was fashioned much more like a heavy door than a window.

"Much of Bajor goes unplanted these days, it's true," she told her son. "But it isn't as though the entire world is in famine. Most of us have enough."

"How can the efforts of the many serve to sustain Bajor, when so many of the *D'jarras* have become obsolete? Only a handful of pilots are allowed to fly, and most can't afford their own ships. Soldiers and police ceased to exist when the Militia was dissolved. Writers and artists have been all but outlawed. Scientists and engineers are deprived of the opportunity to work, unless it's directly in the service of our occupiers. Fishermen and farmers still thrive where the land and waterways have not been poisoned by mining, but even then, Bajor's bounty is forcibly given up to feed Cardassia Prime."

It was an argument he'd made before, one she'd sidestepped as best she could. It was not for a vedek to concern herself with politics, only to tend to the faithful and serve the Prophets. But Fasil, it seemed, was determined to discuss the matter.

Sulan turned and regarded her son with a glimmer of wonder. Had she thought him a boy, only a short time ago? He was no mere extension of his parents. He was his own individual, and was fast becoming an outspoken adult.

"Mother," Fasil went on, "I heard you speaking to Gar about your concerns the other day, and I know he agreed to speak to the kai for you. But either Gar missed your point entirely, or he just used your faith in order to placate you. You did not tell Gar that you wanted the kai to denounce the *D'jarras*; you told him only that you wished to speak upon the matter, to have a reasonable discussion. I believe that Gar is trying to distract you."

"To what purpose?"

Fasil shook his head, and Opaka stared at him. Her training and her faith labeled his words blasphemous, but she knew Fasil, too. Knew his heart. Knew that his mind was one of the keenest she'd ever encountered.

"Don't you remember what Kai Dava once said? He said, 'It is in the time of struggle that we must become as one.'"

Sulan was familiar with the verse, though it had been written long ago. It seemed to reference the ancient era before Bajor had become a united world, when its many nations had finally begun to lay down the arms they had raised against one another. She had not considered that those words could apply to their present circumstances. She nodded slowly, and sat down at the table. There was truth in what he said, but there were many truths. He did not yet understand the complexities of such things.

"Fasil, I know that you are no longer a child," she said softly. "And you are so like your father. He would be proud of you. But Kai Arin's beliefs are not without—"

"My father would still be alive if it weren't for the *D'jarras*."

"Cardassians killed your father when they attacked the city, Fasil. Not Bajorans."

"I blame them both," Fasil said stubbornly. "The doctor who refused to treat him because of his caste—"

"It was out of respect that a doctor of the laity refused to treat a prylar."

"And it cost my father his life."

Sulan did not want to continue this line of conversation. She rose from the table and went back to the *kava* at the woodstove, trying her best to chase memories from her mind. She could not block them out, not entirely. The recollection of when she had first learned of the attack on what was left of Korto, and the following realization that Opaka Bekar had gone into the city that morning . . . Her husband had decided to sell a small piece of heirloom jewelry, determined to make that year's Gratitude Festival a memorable one, with a proper feast. But he had chosen the wrong day to travel.

"Mother, you know that most Bajorans have abandoned their *D'jarras* anyway, out of practicality. What other choice have they had? If they are going to ignore the *D'jarras*, many of them feel that they might as well ignore the other teachings of the Prophets as well. Now that the Tears of the Prophets have all been destroyed, or lost, or stolen by the Cardassians—for we all know who have really taken them—many people are beginning to believe the Prophets have abandoned them. They need a religious authority to sanction what they've been forced to do, or else they will forget their faith entirely."

"The Prophets have not abandoned Bajor," Opaka said firmly. "We don't need the Tears of the Prophets to assure us that They are still there. We can hear the voices of the Prophets coming from our own hearts, if we take the time to listen."

"And what does your heart tell you of what is happening to Bajor?" Fasil asked. "What *will* happen, if we cannot come together?"

There was an answer, but she'd struggled so long to deny it, to adhere to what her own spiritual leaders had so strongly advocated. To embrace it as truth, she had to ignore a lifetime of teaching.

She'd had dreams. Since she was a girl, she'd had dreams about things. Fire and death. Struggle and rebirth. People she knew but didn't recognize. Her Orb experiences had been powerful, riddled with symbols and imagery that she barely understood, but the themes were clear and persistent.

*Always embrace the truth. Always speak your heart.*

"I don't need to be convinced that the Prophets speak to us," Fasil continued. "And perhaps the *D'Jarras* were once the best way for us to live together. But things are different now. You're right, the Cardassians were responsible for Father's death. They are a violent people. They've taken Bajor from us—and we've let them do it, clinging to a system that doesn't allow us to come together and stop them."

Sulan studied him, feeling slightly breathless. "Where did you learn to be so opinionated?" She wrapped a piece of coarse linen around the handle of the kettle and removed it from the fire. "Certainly not from me."

"From none other," Fasil replied, smiling. "I know that I come from stubborn stock, and for this I am grateful."

Opaka used a long-handled pestle to mash the *kava*, turning the clear broth into a thickened stew. "Fasil," she mused. "I see that you are becoming an adult . . . But the way you speak makes it seem as though it has already happened."

Fasil seemed to deflate slightly at her mild response, reminding her that he was still a child in some ways. "I don't mean to defy you, Mother."

"I know that. You have always been a good son." She sighed, smiled at him. "In truth, my heart tells me that you are right. The kai, what there is of the Vedek Assembly—they only wish to maintain the integrity of the faith, but this is no longer the Bajor of our forebears. Your assessment of the *D'jarra*s is what I believe."

It was a relief to speak it aloud, and she was suddenly hungry. A funny reaction to deciding that one's spiritual betters were wrong, but there it was. She brought the kettle to the table, dishing out small portions of the chalky soup.

Fasil hesitated before raising his arms in thanks to the Prophets for his meal. "If you believe it—then that is what you must teach."

## 3

Gil Damar busied himself triple-checking the conference room's comm feeds, to accommodate the individuals who would be "attending" the meeting via link. Among those would be Legate Danig Kell of Central Command, Dukat's immediate superior. Damar knew that this meeting represented a great deal to Dukat; it was his first chance, as Bajor's prefect, to actively demonstrate for these officials the direction he wished to take Bajoran relations. It was important that Damar and the other officers in charge of the preparations take care not to overlook anything.

As the visiting officials began to arrive, Damar stepped aside to let them pass, bowing or saluting each man as he took his seat around the heavy table. Four provincial overseers were attending in person from the surface, as well as six of the more influential base commanders; for most, this was their first visit to Terok Nor. Seven more officials would be present via link, and recordings of the meeting would be viewed by a score of other important men.

Damar lingered in the corner as Dukat had instructed him, waiting to be summoned by any of the attendees for a glass of *rokassa* juice or, for some of the coarser attendees, *kanar*. Damar himself couldn't stand the syrupy stuff, never having developed a taste for it, though he'd been known to take a glass in good company for diplomacy's sake.

As the attendees settled in, the comm links activated, Dukat stood up at the head of the oblong table and spread his hands. "My friends and colleagues," he pronounced, drawing out each word in his distinctive, slow dialect. "How pleased I am to be greeting you here today. I believe that this meeting, the first of many on this fine new station, will be noted for future generations as a historical event. For we will be discussing a new chapter in the history of Cardassian subject worlds. Specifically, a chapter describing the future of the richest and most successful annexation the Union has ever known."

Damar noted an undercurrent of mumbling skepticism, and he quickly made his way around the table to fill the dignitaries' empty glasses.

"*Thank you for that introduction, Gul Dukat.*" Legate Kell—whose countenance filled the largest viewscreen among several dominating the wall at the foot of the table—remained stoic as he assumed his place as the meeting's chair. "*We all know that the Bajoran annexation has not been without difficulty. The Bajorans have resisted our attempts to bring them to the level of Cardassian technological achievement. They have responded to our help with violence and destruction, frightening away civilian settlers and creating expensive setbacks for Cardassia. Yet, despite that, the Cardassian Union has enjoyed an era of prosperity and comfort due in no small part to the resources we have extracted from the Bajoran system.*"

Dukat, now seated, nodded sagely. "And with better management of the terrorist threat, our prosperity will only increase."

Kell smiled pleasantly. "*Indeed, Dukat, I am aware of your political platform.*"

Dukat smiled back, undaunted. "With your permission, Legate, I am eager to present to everyone the station's first productivity report."

"*By all means, Gul Dukat.*"

Dukat's long neck stretched very taut as he stood up straight, his bearing regal. "I am very pleased to report that according to preliminary estimates, the output from Terok Nor's ore processing units will translate to one hundred new ships in the fleet every three service quartiles."

Dukat waited as the room broke out in scattered applause. "I might add that those are very conservative estimates. But there's no use getting ahead of ourselves. I think it would be prudent to ask for a contingent of twenty legions to be sent to Bajor every two service quartiles, until the insurgency is entirely extinguished."

Kell made an indignant sound. *"Twenty?"*

"Indeed, Legate. As the output increases—which I believe it will in the space of a year—we'll want to be certain that the Bajoran perception of our commitment to them remains unshaken."

*"Gul Dukat, I must remind you that a very large contingent of fresh troops has been sent to Bajor within the last month, with more scheduled to arrive soon as part of your new strategy to impose defeat upon the resisting Bajorans. And what I haven't heard from you is the numbers regarding resistance casualties, which I'm told have not decreased in any significant measure."*

Dukat's smile tightened. "Perhaps you weren't aware, Legate, that the bulk of those troops sent to Bajor were redeployed to the colonies along our border with the Federation before it could even be determined that my strategy was effective . . ."

*"I am very aware of it. We are fighting a war on many fronts, Gul."*

"Of course. And yet none of those fronts holds as much importance for the future of the Cardassian Union as does Bajor. If we falter in any way, we send a message to the terrorists that they are winning."

*"If what you say is true, then your effective leadership becomes even more crucial,"* Kell said. *"I have the utmost faith that you*

*will successfully suppress the resistance with what you have been given."*

"Legate Kell, if I may say something," interjected Gul Darhe'el, at the table's corner. One of the regional administrators on the planet's surface, Darhe'el had for the last ten years overseen the mining operation at Gallitep, one of Bajor's richest minerological sites.

*"Certainly."* Kell nodded.

"It does us no good to downplay the Bajoran threat," Darhe'el said. "It may seem as though containment is a simple affair, but in fact the resistance has proven to be surprisingly resourceful, and their numbers are only increasing. This suggests to me, as it does to many, that all Bajorans have rebellion in their hearts, and to award them any freedom is an invitation to further attack." Darhe'el looked pointedly at Dukat when he spoke the last bit.

"I must respectfully disagree," Dukat replied, his jaw clenching only slightly. "My colleague has presented a very common misconception. In fact, the Bajorans are quite easily made compliant, as just a little leniency seems to go a very long way with them. While it is true that I plan to conduct most of my business from Terok Nor, I have been a student of this planet since first contact, and I will be forging personal relationships with individual Bajorans in order to foster an atmosphere of trust between our two peoples. I am certain that a gentle hand is necessary for maximum output."

Kotan Pa'Dar, the former scientist who now served as the civilian exarch at the Tozhat settlement, broke in. "I must agree with Gul Dukat, for a change," Pa'Dar said coolly, and Dukat acknowledged him with a curt nod.

*"Only time will tell which strategy is most effective,"* Legate Kell said. *"It makes no difference to me how the threat is contained, only that it is. Gul Dukat has been appointed prefect*

*of Bajor, and will manage the annexation as he sees fit—with the resources presently at his disposal."*

Damar saw the glint in the prefect's eyes as Kell spoke, though he didn't know what it meant. He knew that the two men had a history, and that Dukat did not hold Kell in high esteem, but the legate seemed to be supporting Dukat, and continued to do so throughout the surprisingly brief meeting. Dukat touched on a few other topics and wrapped everything up a short time later, announcing to those who were physically present that anyone who was interested was welcome to gather in the reception room for refreshments.

Damar deactivated the feed before he set about gathering the discarded glasses. Dukat had lingered behind to speak to one of the legates who had traveled from Cardassia VI, and as the legate retired to his quarters, Damar caught the gul's eye.

"I think the meeting went well," Damar said hopefully.

Dukat smiled, looking tired. "It went as well as could be expected, considering those fools from the civilian government were invited. So many of them have succumbed to weakness, and I know that at least a few have spread their biases around regarding the situation here. I have no doubt that Kell was unable to see them for the cowards that they are."

Damar was puzzled. The only "civilian" who'd spoken up had been Pa'Dar. "But . . . Pa'Dar . . . he agreed with you. It was Gul Darhe'el who said . . ."

"Yes, on the surface it would appear that Pa'Dar is aligned with me, and Darhe'el is not. But it is much more complicated than that, I'm afraid. It is always important to know who your friends are, who your enemies are, and what their ulterior motives may be for agreeing or disagreeing."

Damar felt awed in the presence of such a complicated man. "I am sure that Kell appreciates which men are sincere."

Dukat laughed. "Are you, Damar? I don't know where Kell stands at this point, although he at least pretends to have some faith in my abilities." The gul's expression narrowed. "As well he'd better. For although it's clear that very few can understand my strategies, I will be successful, whether Kell is willing to acknowledge it or not. You can make no mistake about that."

"I know you will be," Damar replied earnestly.

Dukat's expression grew more relaxed. "Will I see you in the reception room, Damar?"

"Oh." Damar was taken aback. "I thought it was reserved for attending officers."

"I don't see why we can't bend the rules a little, considering that I'm the one who makes them."

Damar was pleased, but in truth he preferred not to attend. Earlier today he had seen Basso Tromac with a group of scrawny and bedraggled Bajoran women, a group that he later saw being herded into the conference room after they had been cleaned up and dressed in tawdry gowns. He quickly deduced that they were meant to attend the reception, and the thought of mingling with the Bajoran females made him uncomfortable on several levels. "I am honored that you would extend the invitation to me, Gul, but I'm unusually exhausted this evening."

"Of course. No doubt you're eager to get to your quarters so you can place a communication to your beloved on the surface."

Damar smiled, thinking of Veja. "If you could see her, you would agree that I can't be blamed for my impatience."

"I don't doubt it, Damar. Still, it might do you well to come and socialize with the officers. You could learn a thing or two."

Damar spoke with unbridled honesty. "The only officer I wish to learn from is standing here with me right now."

It was not prudent to travel by foot for a few days after Lenaris's arrival at the settlement outside Tilar, for the spring rains had made it too wet to be practical. But when a dry day finally arrived, Lenaris joined Lac and Taryl as they picked their way through *tessipate*s upon *tessipate*s of unproductive land, some barren, some choked with noxious weeds. Without irrigation, these fields would doubtless wither into a dry tinderbox in the late summer, and Lac confirmed that wildfires were common.

Lenaris stopped along the way to pick wild *alva* fruits, which grew in abundance along the old hedgerows that had once marked the boundaries between farms. Lenaris had learned that dried *alva*s were a mainstay of the Ornathia diet, since they were plentiful and provided enough nutrition to ward off many serious infections. Lenaris popped the fruits in his mouth, savoring the burst of fresh flavor that was severely diminished once the fruits had been dried for preservation.

Lac had insisted that they walk. Though he was confident that the Cardassians could not trace the balon signature of his raider, he did not want to take any chances that the derelict warp vessel would be discovered, and so it was that the three had set out on foot to have a look at the craft.

"This was all productive farmland when I was a boy," Lac said, gesturing to the knee-high weeds that surrounded them. "We had the most reliable irrigation system on all of Bajor. It was built millennia ago, but it never needed to be restructured. The network of ditches, conduits, and underground canals was incredibly elaborate. I was always warned as a child not to go into the tunnels. They had never been mapped, so it was near-certain that you would get lost—if you didn't drown first."

"So, what happened to the waterways?" Lenaris asked him, though of course he already knew. It was the same story everywhere on Bajor.

"The Cardassians,"Taryl answered simply. Lenaris nodded.

Lac continued where Taryl had left off. "They dug up the main canals and diverted all the water to a point about thirty *kellipates* inland, for a mining operation that they abandoned less than five years later."

"What a waste," Lenaris said.

"Yes, it's their way. They're a very irresponsible people."

Lenaris laughed at the understatement.

Taryl broke in. "But really, we're fortunate that they stripped out the minerals they wanted so quickly. When they deserted that mine, they left us to go back to farming as we had before. But with the irrigation systems the way they are now, most of us have to rely on the elements for watering our crops. The Cardassians have their own system for delivering irrigation to the vineyards, but it's not sustainable. Some of us started trying to restore the canals, but most of us feel that fighting the Cardassians takes precedence over a convenient way to water the crops."

Lac grimaced. "The older generation, as I'm sure you can imagine, doesn't particularly agree with us. Which is why we don't spend a lot of time at our parents' farm anymore."

"The mining operation is near the village," Taryl explained, gesturing back to where they had come. "We followed the water, basically. Its most abundant flow is back where we built our houses."

"Does Seefa know where you are?" Lac asked his sister, and Taryl shook her head.

"He doesn't need to know where I am at every minute of the day," she said crisply. "So, Holem, do you know where this Tiven Cohr is, or not?"

Lenaris didn't care to discuss Tiven Cohr, but he wanted

Taryl to think him agreeable. "I think so," he ventured. "I know a few people who could possibly have spoken to him recently. People from my old cell."

"What happened to your cell, anyway?"

Lenaris frowned. Much as he wanted to engage Taryl in meaningful conversation, he did not want to explain how the cell had broken up. "Just went our separate ways," he said vaguely.

"Yeah, but—why? If the rumors are true, you had some very skilled people working together. Why would you throw all that away?"

"I don't think he wants to get into it," Taryl's brother said quietly, and Lenaris looked to his friend—for he had come to think of Lac as a friend—with gratitude.

"Is that it?" Lenaris said, pointing to some low foothills that were coming into view.

"Yeah," Lac confirmed. "She's right at the base of the smallest of those hills. They're riddled with kelbonite—the Cardassians' scanning equipment doesn't work well here. It's how she's avoided their attention all this time."

No one spoke as they came upon the massive ship, mostly buried in dirt and dense foliage. It was well camouflaged. Lenaris could see from the outline that it had been a mid-sized carrier. Someone, presumably Lac, had excavated part of one wing and a section of cockpit that permitted access to the interior. Ground birds had nested in the gentle fall of rock covering the ship, spiders had spun their webs across the dark, jagged entrance holes; the vessel had a desolate feel, dead and abandoned.

"You've gone inside?" Lenaris asked, his heart thumping.

Lac nodded. "A couple of times," he said. "It's a little spooky in there . . . but I didn't find any bodies—at least, not yet. I think whoever was inside must have bailed out before she came down—I couldn't find any escape pods."

Lenaris started to clamber up the incline that led to the exposed cockpit, Lac right at his heels, but Taryl hung behind.

"What is it?" Lenaris asked.

Taryl frowned and looked at her brother.

"You don't have to come in, Taryl," Lac said, sounding uncertain. "I mean—maybe you shouldn't have even come along, if—"

"No," Taryl said. "I want to come in. I just . . ."

"What?" Lenaris repeated, trying not to let his impatience show.

"It's just . . . I promised Seefa I wouldn't."

Lenaris looked to Lac for explanation, since Taryl didn't seem to want to elaborate.

"Seefa thinks—and some of our cousins as well— they think it's a bad idea to fool around with this ship. Besides thinking it's a lost cause, they're afraid the Cardies are going to find her. Once they've seen that she's been boarded recently, it's going to lead them straight back to the settlement."

Lenaris scratched his head. "Well, but . . . you're just farmers. You wouldn't pose any threat to them, just trying to find salvage out here to make your lives a little easier. They're not going to expect you to be trying to . . . to *fix* the thing, right?"

Taryl's mouth twisted. "Lac and I agree with you," she said. "But Seefa and some of the others are worried that the Cardies will find out that we've been using balon to power our impulse and sub-impulse vessels—ships that we aren't authorized to be flying in the first place."

"How would they—?"

"We've been shunting balon to the surface at a point near where the mining facility was abandoned—just a stone's throw from here, in a skimmer. If the Cardies were to find our laboratory, the place where we fuel our raiders—

they probably wouldn't continue to underestimate our abilities so much."

Holem frowned. He could see the logic well enough, but he couldn't bear to simply ignore the warp vessel here, just waiting to be fully excavated and repaired. With a warp ship, they could finally regain access to Prophet's Landing, or Valo II, or any of the other pre-occupation Bajoran settlements. They could conduct a serious assault on occupying forces if they could network with other Bajorans outside the system. Maybe they could even organize an offworld attack.

*That would surely make waves among the spoonheads,* Lenaris thought, with a helpless grin. He avoided the persistent voice that told him he just wanted to have a crack at flying a warp vessel. This was for the resistance. For his people, his world.

"She's been here this long without being detected," Lenaris said. "I say the benefits outweigh the risks. Let's just have a look inside. If the damage isn't too bad, maybe we won't even need Tiven Cohr. I know a couple of things about simple flyer repair—if we just put our heads together . . ."

Lac didn't need any persuading, but Taryl lingered behind for another minute before she finally succumbed to what she really wanted to do, anyway, and followed them inside the ship.

Vedek Opaka had set about on this day to tidy and sweep the dust from her stone cottage. Fasil had offered to help, but she sent him off to be with his friends, to enjoy the weather. Summer had finally come to the valley, which meant both good news and bad for the Bajorans who called it home. More and more people went without proper food and shelter with each passing year, and summer was a time for respite from the elements and the inevitably lean colder months. But the hot weather also meant more Cardassian activity on the surface. Opaka knew that many of the local resistance fighters chose to spend the summertime in hiding, plotting their next moves for the winter, when the Cardassian troops would again be at their weakest.

She'd learned as much from some of the people she'd been meeting. Opaka had taken the warming weather as her cue to begin meeting with the scattered groups of people in the valley who did not attend services: the elderly who could not travel far from their camps, the more cynical and despondent Bajorans who believed the Prophets had abandoned them, and of course the restless young people who had begun to live like nomads—many of whom fought in the resistance. These were the people, Opaka had decided, who most needed to hear the message. She'd begun to travel regularly to the camps on the outskirts of the village on days when her duties were light, speaking to whoever would listen. She didn't preach so much as try to make connections, to remind people that the Prophets were real and that Bajor had a future, and she had been pleased with the mostly positive reception.

She had changed the bedding, dusted and swept the result out the cottage's front door. She propped the door open and went to wrangle the wood-and-glass panel that covered the tall window near the roof, to air the cottage out. As she turned from the window, she started a bit when she saw the silhouette of a man standing in the doorway, backlit by the afternoon sun.

"Kai Arin," she said, bowing deeply. "You honor me with your presence. Welcome to my home."

"Thank you, Vedek Opaka."

"Please, sit." Sulan gestured to one of the turned-leg chairs at the wooden table in the center of the room.

Kai Arin sat and immediately began to make small talk,

something Opaka had come to expect from the kai when he wished to calm himself. Obviously, he had something to tell her.

"You know . . . did I ever tell you . . . this house, many centuries ago . . . Kai Dava used to live in it. Did you know that?"

Opaka shook her head. "No, I didn't, Your Eminence. I suppose I knew that someone lived here . . . I mean, someone besides the *porli* fowl."

"It's true, or at least, so I'm told. In fact, it is rumored that before the old shrine was built, he kept the relics here, in this very house."

"You mean, a Tear was kept here?"

The kai looked away. "It's only a rumor, of course."

Kai Arin's faraway look spoke volumes. Eighteen years ago, he had tried to save the Orb of Truth, when the Kendra Shrine was destroyed. He had tried to save it, but he had almost died doing so. He had never spoken of it, but Opaka knew he carried guilt, remorse for choosing to save his own life over making every attempt to save the Orb. The Orbs—the Tears of the Prophets—represented a fundamental aspect of Bajoran spiritual life, the ability to connect directly with the Prophets. No one judged Arin for what he had done—no one but Arin himself. He was a spiritual man, and felt keenly the responsibilities of his service.

She quickly changed the subject. "There was a fire here, I was told, long ago . . ."

Arin spoke quickly. "Yes, it burned the roof off, and the dwelling sat vacant for some time. It was later converted into a springhouse, or something of that nature. It was a toolshed when I first came here, and then, as you say, it was a coop for the fowl, with a *batos* pen on the other side. Funny, nobody seems to keep *batos* around here anymore."

"I suppose nobody can afford to feed them," Opaka said.

"Things are certainly different now."

Opaka nodded, recognizing that he was coming to his point.

"Vedek Opaka, I'm told you have begun to preach outside the sanctuary."

She breathed deeply, nodded.

"I commend you for wanting to bring your message to those who cannot or will not attend services, although that's usually left to monks in other orders besides yours."

"Yes, I understand, Your Eminence. I . . . was only following my heart. I believe this is what the Prophets wish of me."

"Perhaps you are meant to preach outside of the sanctuary, Opaka, but I don't believe that you are meant to spread dangerous ideas to people already impressionable in their unhappiness."

Opaka had nothing to say. She had known that it would eventually come to this, but not so quickly. She had not yet prepared a response.

"Vedek Opaka, it is our obligation to spread the words of the Prophets. And those words include the message of Bajoran tradition. It is not our place to reinterpret the Prophets' words to serve our own personal beliefs."

"But . . ." Opaka protested, "the *D'jarras* have been reinterpreted many times, Your Eminence. The drivers eventually became pilots. The ceremonial healers became modern doctors. The—"

"What you are speaking of has been a gradual evolution of the roles within the *D'jarras*, not a reassignment of responsibilities for people who were born to perform specific tasks. I understand that many people have been forced to become idle under the current circumstances, but what I see is that those who reject their birthrights reject other teachings of the Prophets as well. They eventually begin to take up arms against the Cardassians. The Prophets do not condone violence. They never will. And neither will I."

"Yes, Your Eminence," Opaka murmured.

"I'm glad you understand," the kai told her, and stood to leave. Opaka stood with him, gripping the back of a chair as they both stepped toward the door. But she could not let him go. She could not merely concede to him and pretend that she agreed, when she did not, and would not.

"Your Eminence, I do not condone the acts of the resistance, either," she blurted out. "But I believe that this is a time for Bajoran unity. Instead, what I see are angry and fearful people who have too much time on their hands and continue to mistrust each other because of age-old rules that no longer apply to the world we are living in. This has made us ripe for Cardassian exploitation. Can't you see? Before we are *D'jarra,* we are Bajoran, and we are all Their children. We must come together, must decide together what we wish for ourselves, for our *own* children."

Arin did not speak, only shook his head.

"Kai Arin, I confess I did not realize that you truly believed there was still wisdom in clinging to the *D'jarra*s. I thought that perhaps you were using this as a means to distract our people from the misery they see all around them, to try and hold fast to some remnant of our original way of life. But now I see that you and I will have to agree to disagree."

The kai's expression was unhappy. "No. If you will not renounce your message, then I am afraid I cannot let you remain at the sanctuary. If you continue to preach it, your status as a vedek will be revoked. If you spread these words, Opaka Sulan, I will have no choice but to issue an Attainder."

Opaka tightened her hands around the back of the chair. The thought of being sent away from the sanctuary stung her; the thought of leaving this house, this comfortable existence, and being forced to live like those in the camps frightened her terribly. Fasil had friends here, they both did. And to be Attainted, expelled from the community of faith . . .

" 'And by following *D'jarra,* the land shall know peace,' "
he quoted, and gave her an encouraging smile. "I sincerely
hope that you'll stay with us, Vedek. Your presence would
be sorely missed."

The kai left her. She sat down again, her heart heavy
with the fearful understanding that things were about to
change. The kai was not an evil man, but he was mistaken.
She could only be thankful that the cold weather was past,
at least for now. If they had to travel, it would be in the
summertime.

Natima followed a short distance behind Veja and her
betrothed, deeply regretting her decision to accompany her
friend to the new space station. Corat Damar was a typical
Cardassian male, arrogant and self-important, and could not
have made it more clear that he resented her presence here;
she silently cursed Veja for not having the foresight to tell
her beloved that she'd planned on bringing a friend along.
She looked dejectedly around the station as he gave them
their tour, finding it to be dark and rather imposing with
its broad and heavy classical architecture. It was impressive,
to be sure, but not really Natima's style.

Hundreds of Bajorans had already been brought in to
work in the ore processors, and Natima was curious to see
what went on inside the units, though Damar was reluctant
to bring the women anywhere near the Bajoran section of
the station. "It could be dangerous," he insisted.

"Veja and I are in dangerous situations all the time
when we report on what happens on the surface," Natima
informed him.

Gil Damar appeared disturbed. "The Information Service should know better than to send two young, unes-
corted women into places of danger."

"Oh, our superiors argue with me from time to time,
but Veja and I can take care of ourselves."

Veja nodded. "It's true, Corat. You don't need to worry about us."

Damar looked sideways at Natima. "I'm not worried about her," he replied.

Natima shot him a look of loathing, but he had already turned his back to her and was guiding Veja toward the operations center, apparently not interested in whether Natima was coming or not. Unsure where else she might go, she elected to follow them.

"So, why does Dukat allow these Bajoran merchants to sell their wares on the station?" Natima wanted to know. "Doesn't that interfere with Cardassian attempts at commerce?"

Damar did not look at her when he spoke. "The prefect wants to make the Bajorans more self-sufficient."

"Well," Natima snorted, "he isn't going to do it by allowing them to continue following their silly religion. I noticed there's a religious shrine on the Bajoran side of the promenade. I can't believe Dukat permits that sort of thing in a military installation."

"He has his reasons for everything he does," Damar told her.

"What do you know of his reasons?" Natima struggled to keep her tone even. Damar struck her as an ignorant toady, her very least favorite sort of person.

"I don't need to know them. Gul Dukat is a brilliant leader, and people like us can't be expected to understand the complexities of his plans."

Natima found his response laughable, but she kept her amusement to herself for Veja's sake. Her friend had already begun to look a little uncomfortable.

"So, what can we get to eat around here?" Natima asked brightly, changing the subject.

Damar shrugged. "There are replicators," he said.

"What this place needs is a restaurant of some kind."

Damar finally turned to face her, a look of distaste on his blandly handsome features.

"I'll be sure to pass your suggestion on to the prefect," he said, and turned away again, slipping his arm around Veja's waist. Natima decided that she might wait out the rest of the tour by herself, and fell behind to watch the two lovers as they continued down the Promenade. She approached a Bajoran merchant's shop to examine his strange wares, and wondered how badly the replicators here would foul up a cup of red leaf tea.

Miras had begun to wonder, in the last few weeks, if she shouldn't reconsider her final project. The images she had received from Natima Lang had provided her with only a few ideas. There were many, many captures of Bajoran farmland, some of it in active production, some barren and dry, and some entirely overgrown with weeds. Miras was fascinated by the obvious fertility of the world, but the lack of accessible hard data was making her quest for further information an exercise in frustration.

Kalisi had been more successful in her pursuits, having found a cache of declassified military files regarding weapon efficacy, and had decided to continue her original idea to study the weaponry used on Bajor. But Miras still wasn't sure if she should continue with her investigation into agriculture, for it had recently occurred to her that she would need at least one physical soil sample in order to make her project worthy of high mark. She wasn't sure if she could acquire such a sample at this late date, for the topic deadline was beginning to loom, and she didn't want to settle on a theme until she was certain she could gather all the necessary items.

Miras had been studying in her dormitory for most of an afternoon when she received a call from Professor Mendar. It surprised her not a little when she switched on the companel and discovered the image of her instructor staring back at her; it was unusual for a teacher to contact a student through a personal channel.

*"Miss Vara, I hope I'm not catching you at a bad time."*

"Not at all, Professor. I'm delighted to hear from you."

*"Miss Vara, I think you will be further delighted when you hear what I have to tell you. I know you've been hoping to acquire a soil sample from Bajor, and I've thought of a means by which you might be able to do that without having to wait for a transport to bring one back from the planet."*

"Really?" Miras was instantly hopeful.

*"Yes. I just remembered, the Ministry of Science came into possession of a Bajoran artifact some years back. The artifact itself may not interest you much, but what I remember most about it is that when we opened the shipping crate, we were appalled at how filthy the container was. The artifact was caked with dirt. Of course, we cleaned it up when we made the initial inventory report, but I'm confident there is enough left in that container for you to get a viable soil sample."*

"Oh, Professor, what a good idea! Thank you so much!"

*"Our window of time is quite short, however. I've arranged to have the artifact sent up to a laboratory for a few hours. Can you meet me on campus at the east facility within the hour?"*

"Yes, Professor Mendar, I'll be right there." Miras switched the comm over to contact Kalisi, who was slow to answer, her eyes bleary.

"Wake up!" she teased her friend. "Professor Mendar found a way for me to get a soil sample. She's sending a Bajoran artifact over to the lab right now, and I'm going to brush the soil off it for analysis."

*"What kind of artifact?"* Kalisi, who had undoubtedly been dozing over a textbook, rubbed her eyes.

"I don't know," Miras told her. "But if you want to see it, you should come along."

Kalisi shrugged. *"I guess I could use a break,"* she said. *"I'll meet you outside the transport in five minutes."*

Miras and Kalisi arrived at the east facility in time to see
Professor Mendar speaking with someone who apparently
worked in the ministry's storage facility. She was affixing
her thumbprint to an inventory padd when she saw the
girls approaching, and her usually saturnine features turned
to a pleasant smile. "Hello, Miss Vara, Miss Reyar. The container will be transported up to the main laboratory on
floor two." She offered the padd to Miras. "If you put your
thumbscan here, you will be able to open the shipping
container." Miras did as she was told.

Kalisi was excited. "Where did it come from? How did
the ministry come to have it?"

Professor Mendar bent forward as if she were telling
a secret, an uncharacteristically girlish expression suddenly coming over her face. "I was told that the ministry
acquired it at an auction of repossessed goods," she confided, "but there was a rumor—and of course, it's only a
rumor—that the item was on loan from none other than
the Obsidian Order." She stood back and waited for the
girls' reaction.

"The Obsidian Order!" Kalisi exclaimed. "That can't be.
They don't loan out their inventory." She said these things
with an authoritative air, and Miras wondered how her
friend even came to have an opinion on the matter. Miras
had an inkling that Kalisi's father was involved in some
confidential faction of the government, but so were a lot
of people.

"As I said," Professor Mendar replied, "it's only a rumor.
I had understood that the Order underwent some sort of
political upheaval over a decade ago, and certain . . . priorities changed. The ministry acquired the object not long
afterward."

Kalisi said nothing more until the professor had excused
herself, leaving them to find the laboratory on their own.
"She's talking about Enabran Tain," she finally told Miras

in confidential tones. "When he took over the Order, a lot of things changed."

Miras could only nod, wondering if her friend really knew what she was talking about. It was interesting in the context of the object they were about to look at, but Miras had never been one to concern herself with the potboiler gossip that often surrounded the Order.

Miras and Kalisi took the lift to the upper level and found the main lab. The cylindrical shipping container, sitting atop a stainless metal work surface, was quite a bit larger than what Miras had expected. It was as wide as the breadth of a man's shoulders, and half as tall as Miras herself. She put her thumbscan on the shipping container's security panel, and peered inside as the side of the container flipped open. It was indeed full of dirt—reddish Bajoran soil that was as fine as ash. Miras quickly set about capturing several samples in a vial, and calibrated a hand-held scanner to break down the soil's composition.

"Let's see the artifact," Kalisi suggested as Miras tapped out the results. Absently, Miras stepped back so her friend could look inside the container.

"I can't really see it," Kalisi complained. "Let's take it out and have a better look."

Miras balked. "It's enormous," she pointed out, though it wasn't so much big as cumbersome.

"Come on, aren't you interested in history?"

"What does a Bajoran artifact have to do with history?"

Kalisi laughed. "We aren't the only civilization in the universe, you know. Here, help me. I like looking at old things."

Miras helped her friend heft the artifact from the container, and the two managed to remove a four-sided object with exotic designs incised on each section. There were numerous polished stones set into the panels, hidden beneath the dirt.

Kalisi ran her fingers over the raised design on one panel, and then inspected the ruddy dust left behind on her pale fingertips. "The dirt isn't really embedded in it. This must not have been buried. Maybe it was windy when they put it in the container." She brushed her hands together. "Is there a database with ancient Bajoran characters in it?"

Miras shrugged. "I'm sure this thing has already been catalogued and examined," she said. "If you look in the university database, they're sure to have some information on it."

Kalisi was already tapping away at her padd, connecting to the university mainframe. "I don't see anything here," she said. "Maybe they just inventoried it and then never scanned it. How long ago did Professor Mendar say it had come in?"

"Over a decade, I thought she said."

Kalisi continued to run her fingers over the surfaces of the object. "Hmm. Look at this corner. It looks to me like it's meant to open up. Maybe this is really just a case for something." She knocked on it with a closed fist, and it answered with a dull clang. "I think it's hollow!"

Miras was doubtful. "I don't see how this thing could open," she muttered, and slipped her finger along the edge. She was a bit surprised to find something like a seam there. The object was not comprised of a single piece of . . . whatever it was made of—wood, apparently, though there was no indication of how it was held together. Miras tried to insert her fingers in the crack, and Kalisi joined in, prying at the edges, but it would not budge.

"Maybe you're right," Kalisi said, and glanced up at the clock. "I don't know about you, but I haven't eaten all day. I'm going to find a replicator."

"I'm not hungry," Miras told her. "I think I'm going to scan this thing and see if I can't find out anything about these characters."

"So! You're interested in history after all!" Kalisi walked away on a note of triumph.

Miras smiled after her. "Linguistics, actually," she called, as Kalisi left the room. Miras used her own padd to record the object's written characters. She flipped on a nearby viewscreen while she downloaded the scan to the computer's database. The machine made a barely audible whirring sound as the processors worked to recognize the writing, but nothing came up. Miras turned once again to the artifact, touched the corner where Kalisi had been so sure that she felt a seam. She ran her fingers down the side. This time there was a clicking noise, and the crack on the corner of the object widened noticeably.

Miras was overcome with an unexplained sense of dread, but as she put her hand on the object, it gave way to an even more unprecedented feeling of calm. She found that she did not want to take her hands away from the object, which felt warm where she was certain that it had been cool before. It did not occur to her to be curious about the change, which was curious in itself, but she felt so tranquil, she did not mind. She sighed out loud, and then gently pushed open the edges of the object with her hands.

The artifact was indeed a case, as Kalisi had imagined, and inside was a very unusually shaped piece of stone, an oblong rock with a slender middle that widened at the top and bottom. The color was nothing like the Bajoran soil, which had been a reddish brown. This rock was a blue-gray color, a little more like common Cardassian rocks, but still alien in texture.

Excited at this new development, she quickly changed the sensor setting and scanned the piece of stone to add to the soil sample database. She punched in a code on the computer to compare the readouts to the dirt she had already examined. What she saw bemused her profoundly, for there was nothing even remotely like it in any of the other recorded data regarding Bajoran soil and geologic formations. The database showed this rock to be a complete anomaly.

Miras stared at the piece of stone for a moment, full of questions that she knew could not be answered. She put out her hand to touch it, and for a moment she seemed to drift away from where she stood, forgetting herself . . . but she was jolted from her temporary daze when a comm voice piped into the room. It was Professor Mendar.

*"Miss Vara, are you there? We have to return the object to the storeroom now, or sign it out for an additional period. Is it ready for transport?"*

Miras reluctantly closed the case. "In a moment, Professor." She wished Kalisi were here to help her put it back in the container. She wondered if she was supposed to have removed the item at all. She couldn't remember what the professor had said about it, and she struggled for a moment to hoist the object back into the cylindrical container. She clicked it closed and brushed the leftover dirt from her hands. Dirt that should serve to make her project a success, she remembered. She gathered up the vial with her soil sample, the reason she had come.

"It's ready to go, Professor Mendar."

Miras watched as the container was transported back into the cavernous storage facility, and as it shimmered into nothingness, she recalled that mysterious sense of calm she had experienced when she had touched the artifact. She wondered what, exactly, she had just been looking at.

# OCCUPATION YEAR TWENTY

✦ ✦ ✦

## 2347 (Terran Calendar)

## 4

Opaka Sulan had just been asked the question that she did not know how to answer. It was not the first time she had been asked it, and she knew it would not be the last. But the question still distressed her, because it was such an important one.

Having left the comfort of the sanctuary, she and Fasil had begun to travel to the refugee camps, looking for charity wherever they could find it. Already she had found that a great many people were eager to hear what she had to tell them, and as she traveled from one camp to another, her audiences had begun to grow.

She was no longer calling herself a vedek, asking those who listened to her words to refer to her simply as Sulan, but she had encountered many who still continued to address her as Vedek Opaka. She did not dissuade them, only made it clear that the kai no longer approved of her viewpoints and therefore it was not right that she use the title herself. This seemed to satisfy the congregations—congregations made up of skeptics, travelers, elderly men and women, youthful rebels, and the pious faithful. They sat together on the hot, dry ground, the dust baked into a hard crust by the midsummer sun. And yet, still the occasional determined bunch of *salam* grass would grow in patches big enough and soft enough for some young mother to lay down her restless infant as she listened to what Opaka had to say. It humbled her to look beyond the insular life she'd led for so long as a vedek and to see how her brothers and sisters lived in these difficult times.

Though her congregations came from many walks of life, and had once belonged to all facets of Bajor's ruined society, they seemed to have one thing in common—they were hungry to hear Opaka's words. They were hungry to be told that Bajor could be whole again one day, if they would only forget their differences and unite against a common oppressor. Opaka had been revitalized by the eagerness and faith of the people who came to listen to her, so much so that she would occasionally be stricken with silently joyous bouts of tearfulness after her sermons had concluded.

*But . . . then there is this.*

"Do you condone the resistance? If you believe we must unite to be strong against the Cardassians, then you must also believe that it is right that we fight them. But the prophecies have always been clear on their advocacy for reason over conflict."

She had considered the question many times, and still had no clarity to pass along.

"We must look inside ourselves," she finally told the man, who was barely older than Fasil. He had long, sandy hair and wide-set, earnest eyes. "We must come to terms with our individual beliefs. It is not for us to judge one another, but rather to decide what each of us can do, ourselves, to make a difference. Above all, we must be unified—and in the Prophets, we can find that unity."

The crowd responded with exclamations of agreement, thankfully making any further comment unnecessary, and she moved to other topics.

Later, as the small crowd began to disperse, Fasil approached his mother. She could see his dark head as he made his way toward her through the cluster of people. He suddenly looked very tall to Sulan, with unusually broad shoulders for a teenager, and she realized that he must have shot up just in the span of their weeks traveling. His sixteenth birthday had come and gone, and Sulan could no longer deny that he was a man, his ideas and desires grown beyond her jurisdiction.

"Mother," he said. He sounded annoyed, and she instantly knew what he was going to say. "You skirted the issue. When that man asked you about the resistance—"

"My business is not to be an advocate for the resistance. I am here to address other matters."

"You're wrong. You must take a firm stance regarding the resistance if you want people to continue to listen to you."

Opaka shook her head. "I won't do it, Fasil. My message is not about fighting. My message is about setting aside our differences."

"So that we can fight."

She continued to shake her head, but she was disarmed, and her son knew it. It did gall her to avoid the topic, but she felt ill-equipped to deal with the matter. Her own feelings regarding the conflict were still complicated, but she refused to suppress the core of her message just because she hadn't yet sorted out how to approach every aspect of the concomitant issues.

"Mother, I may as well tell you. I've met some people here . . . and I've decided to join the resistance. I'm going to fight."

In an instant, Sulan felt her body rooted to the spot where she stood, paralyzed, though her hands seemed to move of their own volition. They crept to her chest and covered her heart. She could feel the same choking tightness inside that she remembered when she had finally accepted that Bekar was dead.

"You're doing what you feel you must do," he continued. "You left the sanctuary. You have begun to speak out
against the words of the kai. Almost nobody would dare to
do what you have done, but I believe that what you have
done is right. Now I ask that you support me in what I
believe is right."

She shook her head, her voice losing strength as she
spoke. "Let the others take up arms. Let someone else do
the fighting. I need you."

"Bajor needs me." His piercing dark eyes, framed by
thick eyebrows and the hollowness of a man-child who
had never eaten a full meal in his life, reflected a deep,
unwavering conviction.

She regarded the tall stranger before her with his unfamiliar build and impenetrable gaze, and she knew that she
could not talk him out of doing anything that he had set
his mind to do. "If the Prophets will it . . ."

"If the Prophets will it, then Bajor will be whole again
one day. But it takes more than the will of the Prophets. It
takes the will, and the strength, of the people."

Opaka clasped her hands together and then pulled them
apart, to raise them up in prayer. Fasil obediently closed his
eyes and prayed with his mother, and then he took one of
her hands in his own. "Don't be frightened, Mother. The
Prophets will be with me."

Opaka looked around the camp from where they stood,
taking in the flattened landscape and the limping figures
of exhausted people as they returned from ration lines, the
faraway clanking of Cardassian mining machinery and the
faint collective whimpering of hungry babies, too young to
understand why they had to go to sleep with empty bellies.
She knew she was doing right, could feel it in her medita-
tions each day, could see it in the faces of those who came
to listen. But with the sudden understanding that Fasil
would be gone from her soon, seeing the desolation that

had become their world, hearing the hungry cries of children—for the first time in her life she felt her faith flicker. She needed to believe that the Prophets still walked with them, needed it so badly ... But what if ...

She let the feeling go, refusing to follow it any further. She recognized it for despair, for the very thing she'd left the sanctuary to fight against. She turned instead to watch her grown son as he walked back to the place where he had made his camp, feeling her heart break a little.

Bajor would indeed be strong again one day, because of Fasil, because of all these children who had grown up under Cardassian rule, who didn't have a simpler time to reflect back upon. Who wanted better, and would fight to get it. It was in that instant that she knew she could not afford to forget her faith again. Not with what was now at stake.

Kira Meru stared at the Bajoran woman who appeared before her, facing her in the mirror above the severely designed Cardassian dressing table. She struggled to accept what she saw there. This woman's face lacked the scarred, rawboned quality she had come to know of her own reflection, and her hair—too shiny, too carefully arranged. If she stood, she'd see curves now, instead of bony lines. The heaviness in her eyes and in her expression, that wasn't entirely wrong, though it was more somber now than it had ever been. It would have eased Meru's mind considerably if she could have just made herself believe that the woman in the mirror was *not* her, but she knew that nothing was that simple anymore. She had to accept that this was her life now.

The place in her psyche that could definably be called her heart did a little dip as she thought of that contrast between *before* and *now*, but she eased out of it with remarkable facility. It surprised her, how quickly she had come to understand that there was nothing to do but accept it, that there was no sense whatever in allowing the horror of what had happened to her to reach out and pierce her very soul, that crying and curling up in a ball on the ridiculously massive and ornate bed in her quarters would do nothing to ease the agony of being torn away from her family. The only sensible choice was to forget these things, motherhood and love, and sweep herself into the mysterious cocoon of alien elegance, where her natural reactions had no appropriate place.

She touched her hair—the stranger's hair—and moved it away from her face, examining the new earrings that Gul Dukat had given her. They were not ceremonial in nature, only decorative. Though Dukat had not specifically told her that he did not want her to wear the traditional Bajoran ear adornment, when he had given her this pair as a gift this morning it seemed to suggest that she'd better forgo her customary jewelry for now. They were beautiful, the delicate spirals of metal reflecting a shimmering array of heliotrope and deep violet as they moved, with tiny blue stones at the curlicued base. They matched the pale purple of the tunic she now wore, a far cry from the body-hugging gown she had reluctantly donned when Basso Tromac had first brought her to Terok Nor with the other comfort women.

She started as someone entered the quarters, and then relaxed somewhat when she saw it was Dukat—although she never relaxed entirely when he was with her. Dukat had been very kind, it was true, but he was still a Cardassian, and he was still the reason that she was here, instead of down on the dingy, starving surface where life had been so difficult, and yet so much happier than it was here on this stark station. But Dukat was also the reason that her family was going to be looked after from now on, her children given extra food and medicine, never to cry out in hunger or sickness in the middle of the night, ever again. He had promised her.

"Hello, sweet Meru." The deep tone of his voice was like a heavy stone over fine gravel, but his languorous pronunciation still took the edge off some of Meru's discomfort. She had to appreciate that he had done his best to make her at ease. He had been refreshingly honest with her, confessing that when he "rescued" her from that overzealous officer at the reception, it had actually been a charade, something that Dukat had set up in advance in order to win her trust.

He had admitted to her how much it pained him to take this time away from his own family: his wife back on Cardassia Prime, his children of whom he was so movingly proud. Meru could see immediately that this man was lonely. He had brought her here because he was just as lonely as he had unwittingly made her, and she understood that it was now her job to do anything she could do to replace his emptiness with something warm, something that he could touch. Her own children's lives depended on it.

Meru knew that she should be revolted by him. She should have loathed him for separating her from her husband and her babies, and for making such a crude ploy to manipulate her. In truth, she was a little disgusted with herself for not hating Dukat, not recoiling from his every advance. But she didn't hate him. She had tried to make her friend Luma Rahl understand it, but maybe there was no understanding it. Meru was through trying to justify it. She wasn't happy, but ultimately she cared for Dukat, a little. They had been too intimate for her to do otherwise; she saw things in him that she believed no one else could have seen.

"Hello, Dukat."

"I've told you, Meru, I want you to call me by my first name."

"Yes, I know . . . Skrain." Her eyes flicked down as she said it. She was still so accustomed to a person's given name being second. Besides, she felt that his first name did not suit him. He was too polished a man to have a name that sounded so brusque, almost violent.

He sat down on the massive bed and patted the space next to him, indicating that he wanted her to come near. She stood up and moved to his side with a strange combination of reluctance and anticipation. While it pained her deeply to be unfaithful to her dear Taban, she had found in Dukat a generous and conscientious lover. In all her adult life, it had been rare for her to make love simply for its own sake, the uncertainty of home and the chaos of constant uprootings making those clandestine, stolen moments something less than thoroughly satisfying. Her couplings with Dukat were an entirely different animal from what she had come to know with her husband.

He placed his hands, such cool, bloodless gray hands, on the curve of her neck and stroked it with the back of his fingers. She shivered, not entirely from the coldness of his flesh. "I've just come from a meeting," he murmured.

"I'm sure you were wonderful," she said, meaning it.

His face broke into a smile. She had quickly come to appreciate his smile. "I wish you had been there," he said. "I could have used the support."

Meru only smiled back in return, knowing that it was all he needed from her until he was finished speaking.

"Legate Kell does not understand what I am trying to do. He thinks I'm a fool for abolishing child labor in the camps. He thinks my plan to bring in better medical facilities is costly and unnecessary. None of them understand that a drop of prevention is worth an ocean of cure."

"You're too compassionate for them to understand you." She brushed a strand of wiry black hair away from his face.

"It's the resistance," he told her. "Why must they continue to fight me? Can't they see that I have their best interests at heart? You experienced yourself what kinds of things they do—the recent attempt on my life, you would have been killed, too. They would kill a Bajoran woman in cold blood just to make a self-serving political statement."

Meru worked not to tense, as she always did when Dukat mentioned the resistance. While she did not agree with every action taken by the resistance fighters, she understood why they fought. She knew firsthand what it was like to go for days without any food, to watch your children suffer from cuts that wouldn't heal, their bodies too starved for what they needed to thrive. She could not honestly denounce those who chose to resist. And though Dukat was an unusual man among Cardassians, Meru knew it was no use trying to explain it to him. He was unusual, but he was still a Cardassian.

"What's on your mind, Meru?" Dukat tipped her chin up toward his face with his index finger. Meru smiled as brilliantly as she knew how.

"Only pleasing you after a difficult day," she told him. After all, she thought to herself, that's what she was here for. To provide comfort. She was a comfort woman, and it did her no good to think of herself in any other context.

Dukat smiled in turn, and pulled her close.

"Holem, didn't you hear me? I said, hand me that hyperspanner." Taryl's voice echoed through the corridor from where only her feet were visible in the light of Lenaris's palm beacon. She had been lying on her back for hours inside the cramped opening of the maintenance conduit of the old warp ship.

Lenaris's palmlight wobbled clumsily around the pile of equipment spread across the floor of the ship's engine room. He was no novice when it came to tools, but Taryl had things he'd never heard of before. "Is this it?" He handed her a cylindrical object.

She made an exasperated noise. "No, this is a magna-spanner. The hyperspanner is—oh, never mind, I'll get it." She hoisted herself from the tube with some difficulty, her movements casting oversized shadows across the convex shine of the inner hull. Lenaris, feeling useless, got out of her way.

The derelict vessel still rested in the same position as it had when Lenaris had first seen it, over a year ago, and it was likely no closer to being fixed now than it had been when he had initially inspected it with Taryl and Lac. Since he'd come to live with the Ornathia clan, the days had passed quickly, lost to the myriad small chores and errands needed to ensure survival. There wasn't much time to come out to where the vessel lay, and the only one of the three who had any inkling whatsoever of how the engines might be made to work again seemed to be Taryl, and she was also the one with the least opportunity to actually work on it. Seefa, her fiancé, still felt that the business with the ship could come to no good.

But Lenaris and Lac grew ever more determined to see the thing airborne—or at least, grew ever more determined to spend time in the foothills with the ship, tinkering with her instruments and comparing her schematics with the information they managed to gather from various contacts between Tilar and Relliketh. It was a minor obsession for Lenaris, one that he wasn't sure he ever expected to be ful-filled, but one that took up a great deal of his time none-theless, whether it was gathering information, looking for an engineer, or poking around in the ship itself.

Of course, time with the ship was limited to the inter-ims between the small operations that the Ornathia cell was beginning to plan and carry out. The cell was still in its infancy, and full-scale attacks were ill-advised at this point. The cell was comprised mainly of the Ornathia cousins and their spouses, none of whom had any real combat experience. But many of them were surprisingly resourceful when it came to refurbishing pieces of useful equipment. The latest venture was a plan to build a long-range communications tower, which would have to be erected on one of Bajor's moons, probably Derna. Missions planned outside the atmosphere had been very few and far between, however, and took months of careful planning. The tower would probably not be completed for another six months or so—and Seefa was once again vocally opposed to the whole thing, being of the general opinion that offworld travel was simply a bad idea.

Taryl continued to clang around inside the maintenance conduit while Lenaris held the palmlight, waiting for her next order and letting his mind wander. "Holem," she said, jerking him out of his daydream, "I need you to hold this guide wire while I solder."

Uncertainly, Lenaris stuck his head and shoulders inside the opening of the maintenance conduit. Taryl was forced to straddle his torso, the conduit much too small for the two of them. He took the wire from her fingers while she soldered the exposed portion in place, holding a small sylus-sized light in her teeth. He could feel his heart pounding as she worked, all too aware of her thighs encircling his waist, and he willed his pulse to quiet itself; he did not want her to know just how much it thrilled him to be in such close proximity to her . . .

"What the *kosst* is going on here?"

Lenaris dropped his palmlight and quickly ducked out of the conduit; the voice belonged to none other than Aro Seefa.

"Seefa!" Lenaris exclaimed. "I didn't even hear you."

Seefa ignored him. "I've told you and told you how dangerous this is. I knew your fool brother was still committed to wasting his time with this heap, but you?"

Taryl hopped smoothly out of the conduit. "Calm down, Seefa," she said. "I'm only having a look around." She lowered her voice. "I'm humoring my brother a little. This thing's a lost cause, of course."

"You shouldn't even be here," Seefa growled, but much of the anger had gone from his voice.

Taryl stroked his arm. "I know," she sighed. "But you know how persuasive Lac can be . . ."

Lenaris wished he were invisible, and to a degree, it seemed as though he was, to Taryl and Seefa. They often seemed to forget his presence—or that of anyone else—when they were together. He found it increasingly difficult not to resent it a little, especially since he secretly felt that his rapport with Taryl transcended her superficial relationship with her fiancé. But he couldn't let himself think like that. It would only cause trouble.

In very little time, Taryl seemed to have Seefa almost thoroughly appeased, though he still demanded that she come back to the settlement with him. "If you've got any sense," Seefa said to Lenaris, "you'll come along with us. And make sure you don't leave any tools behind. It's bad enough to leave evidence of our presence here, but I guess if the Cardies think we're stripping the ship for useful materials, that's one thing. It's another thing to let them get the idea that you might be trying to get it airborne."

"Right," Lenaris said tersely, picking up tools. Seefa and Taryl climbed the ladder from the engine room to the cockpit, and he was alone.

Feeling hopeless, Lenaris glanced at the schematic Taryl had been using. She was trying to put the auxiliary power core back online, a fairly simple affair for a trained, *D'jarra*-born engineer, but for a self-taught farmer from Tilar, perhaps somewhat beyond her abilities. And yet, Lenaris could see from what Taryl had been up to that she was at least on the right track. But fixing the auxiliary system and fixing the warp reactor were two very different things. If only Lenaris had really been able to find Tiven Cohr, or any experienced engineer—someone who had worked on warp ships before the Cardassians had come. That necessary expertise was in grave danger of being lost to Bajor forever. The Cardassians had put restrictions on such information, and it could be preserved only through word of mouth, the older generation to the younger. But constant violence, disease, and poor nutrition didn't make for the greatest life expectancy. Bajorans who had been adults before the occupation were becoming scarce.

Lenaris removed himself from the exposed cockpit of the half-buried vessel and clambered down the slope that had been created by the still-buried wing. He headed back toward the village, wondering if Lac had been having much luck with the latest attempts to reach another cell in Hartis province—to plan tandem attacks, and maybe even to get another lead on an experienced warp engineer.

Lenaris greeted a few of the Ornathia cousins and their spouses as he approached the settlement. They were fetching water to be brought back to the village; there still hadn't been any proper wells dug in this region, most of the Ornathias having traded their plows for coil spanners and phase inductors. There were over twenty small ships of various types in the Ornathia fleet now, most of them hidden beneath natural overhangs of kelbonite that occurred along the mountains just beyond the old mining site. The ships all required constant maintenance, but many of the Ornathias had proven very skilled in keeping up their craft.

Lenaris found Lac at a small corner work table that was set up in his little cottage. Lenaris had built his own dwelling, just a few paces from Lac and Taryl's house, but when in the village, he spent most of his waking hours here, with Lac.

Lac turned quickly when Lenaris drew back the rough door. "Holem!" he said excitedly. "I think these long-range transmitters are going to be ready sooner than we thought!"

"That's great, Lac," Lenaris said, "but that doesn't mean we should rush the Derna mission. We still need a legitimate Bajoran flight pattern to cover us. We don't want to underestimate the patrols coming out of Terok Nor."

He gestured at the roof of the cottage, referring to the orbital station that drifted far above them, visible as an ominous, winking star in the night sky. Every Bajoran was well aware of the heightened Cardassian security that had been falling into place since the station had gone online, a year before.

"Terok Nor is just another reason for us to push harder," Lac said firmly. "We have to raise our game, take bigger risks."

"Like the warp ship," Lenaris said.

Lac nodded, and the two friends smiled at each other, agreeing without words.

Joer Varc smoothed back his unruly shock of hair, the color of the sand dunes of Cardassia's nearby Cuellar region. It had once been a sensitive topic for him, the unusual color of his hair. In all his life, he had probably encountered only three other light-haired Cardassians, and the distinction had been considered a handicap for him when he had trained for the Obsidian Order. But he believed he had proven himself to be more than just a standout in a crowd, and though it had occasionally been suggested to him that he should darken it, so as to "blend in," he had resisted mightily. His hair was part of who he was, and to a degree, he liked the idea of being remembered for it.

He headed to his debriefing with near unwavering confidence, eager to begin his preliminary report. This had probably been the easiest and most successful mission he had ever accomplished. From now on, he was going to jockey for more assignments on Bajor.

This was the second debriefing he had attended this week; the first had occurred yesterday, with the Cardassian military. Varc's cover was as a military glinn, and he was obligated to perform duties just like any other military drone, though his promotion to glinn came through in a miraculously short time, and his ship assignments never lasted longer than a month or two. Nearly every ship in the fleet included an operative from the Order, and each one had to take meticulous care that his or her cover was never blown.

He quickly found the office of Limor Prang, and the door slid back so that he could enter. The older man sat behind a desk so large and so ancient, it seemed to be a permanent fixture in the room. But Varc knew it was actually a recent addition; this office changed location almost as frequently as Varc himself changed assignments.

The old man's expression revealed nothing as Varc entered the room. Prang addressed him by his code name, something he did not always do when the two were in private. "Ah, Mr. *Kieng*. You look confident," he remarked. Prang looked as though he was going to say something else, but Varc, excited, seated himself and spoke before Prang could continue.

"In fact, I am feeling confident, Limor. I obtained considerable intelligence from my latest target."

"Really?" The gaunt old man across the desk appeared distracted, glancing at something over Varc's shoulder for a moment before focusing back on Varc, who was fairly bursting with his good news.

"He confirmed that most Bajorans continue to abandon their castes. There is a religious leader who has begun to advocate for it, despite the pressings of the kai. He also confirmed that the resistance is gaining considerable headway in his region, and he gave me several names. He was very specific. Those will all be in my final report." He could not resist boasting. "I saw to it that his small daughter was in the room with us—he was quite preoccupied with her safety. It made him especially eager to answer my questions."

Prang did not smile, but he almost never smiled. "I'm pleased that you enjoyed yourself, Mr. Kieng. However—"

Varc anticipated his comment. "The man did not survive the interrogation. But it is of no consequence, for I still gleaned everything that was asked of me."

"*I* shall decide if the man's death is of consequence, Mr. Kieng. Meanwhile, your personal comm chip has the details of your new assignment. You will board a ship leaving for the border territories in approximately four hours."

"The border territories? Oh. Yes, sir."

Prang did something unprecedented then, continuing to glance over Varc's shoulder, probably at the timepiece on the wall. He smiled slightly, an expression that Varc was sure he had never seen before. Varc wanted to turn to look at what the old man could possibly be so amused by, but he felt it would be impudent.

"You sound disappointed," Prang remarked.

"Oh, no, sir—certainly not! It is only that I felt my expertise with the Bajoran people might be of further use there."

Suddenly, to Varc's great astonishment, he heard a voice somewhere behind him. He whirled around.

"I find it somewhat distasteful to interview Bajorans," the man behind him said. He was standing very near the wall, and he had been so eerily silent and motionless that Varc would never have imagined there was anyone there at all. Limor Prang had obviously known of the stranger's presence all along.

"And why might that be?" Prang inquired, as if it were completely ordinary for a confidential debriefing to be attended by a third party who had not even bothered to make his presence known. Varc was embarrassed and flustered that he had not seen the man.

The man's eyes were held open very wide as he spoke, conveying a sense of extraordinary eagerness. Varc found his expression disquieting, particularly the slight curl at the corners of his mouth that did not straighten when he spoke. "They appear to wither so easily, but in truth, I have found them to be very skilled at lying. Surprisingly so, really. They will often allow themselves to die before the truth is ever revealed. Torturing them is useless, and in the end, I'm actually left feeling a bit sad about the whole business."

Varc was dismayed at this admission, for it seemed to be an acknowledgment of weakness, but Prang's reaction was dispassionate.

"Now, a Cardassian interrogation—" the man went on, "there's a challenge I can appreciate."

It was Varc's turn to dispute. "I find the interrogation and torture of my own countrymen to be far more distasteful than that of aliens who conspire to destroy the Union."

The stranger continued to half smile. "Indeed. Except that if a Cardassian is a dissident—a traitor—then I can hardly regard him as a countryman. He is far worse, in my eyes, than any hostile alien, who likely retains loyalty to his own society's values."

Varc considered his reply, but to his great relief, Prang finally spoke up. "That's quite enough, Mr. Regnar. We can finish this report without you."

The slight smile still on his face, the man left the room as silently as he had been standing in it. Prang turned to Varc, clearly amused.

"I apologize for Agent Regnar's presence here. We were just finishing up his debriefing when you entered, you see. You began speaking before I could properly introduce the two of you."

"Did you hear the way he talked to me?" Varc said, outraged.

"I would advise you to avoid tangling with that one," Prang said. "They are already calling him one of the Sons of Tain."

Varc was more irritated than ever at this news, but knew he would do best to follow the old man's advice. Those agents who had fallen under the direct tutelage of Enabran Tain, the head of the Obsidian Order, were often referred to as his "sons." If this agent was indeed one of them, then it wouldn't matter what Varc, or any other agent, thought of him. It only mattered what Tain thought.

# OCCUPATION YEAR TWENTY-ONE

◆ ◆ ◆

## 2348 (Terran Calendar)

# 5

Lenaris was never so happy as he was when he was piloting a craft, whether it was within the atmosphere or out in open space. But right now, surrounded as he was by the seemingly endless vacuum of darkness, Bajor's nightside a vast black well beneath him, he felt his exhilaration heightened to almost dizzying effect. He felt . . . free. All the months of careful planning and preparation had been more than worth it.

A bubble of static surrounded an incoming transmission, and he remembered himself. He was not free. It was imperative that he stick to the boundaries of the flight plan until the crucial moment when Lac would take the plunge into Derna's atmosphere.

Lac's voice sounded light-years away, even though Lenaris actually had a visual on the fuel burn from his friend's tiny craft. *"I'm not detecting any interference in our communication channel,"* he said.

"Good," Lenaris said, at a loss for words. His exhilaration turned sharp, excitement changing to unease as the looming, skeletal figure of Terok Nor drifted closer into range. He'd had no idea what the station would look like, but of course this was it. The menacing curvature of the arms, arching possessively over the top of the structure like the bleached-out rib cage of a corpse—it could only be

Cardassian in design. Lenaris suppressed a shudder, and continued carefully on his course.

It was a simple enough exercise to fly their small ships around within the atmosphere—the Cardassians didn't seem to pay much attention to Bajoran comings and goings, and when they did, it had been established that their overpowered ships lacked the agility to chase a sub-impulse raider in atmosphere. But the raiders' capabilities in space were far less certain. The cell had only made a very few offworld excursions, and it had not yet been determined exactly how safe it was to be flying around in these tiny, vulnerable craft—they could withstand space travel, but they hadn't been built for prolonged voyages. The danger was made even greater by the fact that, without more sophisticated scanners than they currently possessed, the raiders had no means to detect each other except by comm.

And of course, there were the Cardassian patrols . . . *Mustn't forget those.*

"*Target is in sight,*" Lac reported.

Moments later, they began to approach Derna, an unassuming gray satellite partially bathed in glowing reflection from faraway B'hava'el.

"I detect no patrols in the immediate vicinity," Lenaris informed his friend.

"*I'm not finding any either,*" Lac relayed back. "*I'm taking the dive in ten . . . nine . . .*"

Lenaris, in closer formation now, watched as Lac's shuttle suddenly broke away from the safety of the flight path. If there were any patrol vessels that they had missed . . . if Terok Nor just happened to be doing a sensor sweep at the wrong moment . . . But there was no evidence of Cardassian presence, no nearby warp signatures, no Cardassian transmissions coming through on the comm, adjusted for enemy frequencies. Lenaris drew in a breath and followed Lac into Derna's atmosphere.

He broke through without issue, weathering the resultant turbulence, holding to the flight yoke as he experienced the temporary sensation of freefall. The raider caught itself, and there was Derna stretched out in front of him, a dreamscape, mostly barren but for a thin, dry algae that covered the plains of endless rock. He concentrated on setting down, trying not to think about patrols, about Terok Nor.

Lac had set his raider down a few *linnipates* from Lenaris, nearer to the wreckage of the Cardassians' ruined base, abandoned more than a decade earlier. He got out of his raider and began to unload the transmission equipment, while Lac assembled the components of a scrambler that would allow the high-bandwidth transmissions to escape the Cardassians' notice.

The two worked silently, leaving behind their equipment and a narrow-band homing signal so that others could find it, should it ever need repair. Then, with a breath of poorly masked excitement, Lac brought the transmitter online.

Finished with their work, they stood for a moment, both searching the cold sky, Lac scanning for Cardassian signals with an old tricorder. Satisfied that they were still alone, Lac gave Lenaris a definitive nod.

"Ready when you are," he said, and Lenaris walked back to his raider without another word.

He gave the engine a burst of fuel and prepared to lift off. He felt a vast relief—the hard part was over. Of course, breaking through Derna's atmosphere still posed some risk, but if they stuck to the same flight pattern they'd followed when they came through, the Cardassians would never know they'd taken to the skies.

Lenaris was the first to exit the atmosphere, and he wasted no time retracing their path back to Bajor. His ship safely back on course, he was practically home free. His confidence mounted as Terok Nor's imposing figure fell behind him, but then he realized that Lac had not reported back to him after breaking free from Derna's atmosphere. He put in a call—and simultaneously saw an unfamiliar power reading on his instrument panel. A patrol from Terok Nor? His mouth went dry.

"*Lupus 2,* do you read me? This is *Lupus 7. Lupus 2*—please respond."

Nothing but dead air.

Holem cranked his transmitter through seven different channels, repeating his request, until his panic finally convinced him to try an unsecure channel—one that the Cardassians could easily pick up. He was desperate. "*Lupus 2,* please respond." Bajor was coming closer, but he didn't dare try to turn back, or even slow down.

His comm crackled and he almost relaxed before he recognized the fragmentary transmission as Cardassian. "*Terok N . . . reporting . . . prisoner . . . ip . . . out."*

Holem could scarcely breathe. He spun the ship's dials frantically, trying to pick up any other transmission, but there was nothing else. Bajor loomed ever larger in front of him, and he had to prepare for the heat and violence of re-entry.

Swallowing his terror, he clutched the flight yoke and shot his raider through the turbulence. He struggled to orient the ship once it broke through, struggled with feelings of shock and disbelief as he pointed the little raider in the direction of Tilar. There was nothing he could do. Lac was gone.

It had been a full day of study and prayer. Final services had ended, the late meal had been taken; Kai Arin was exhausted when he finally retired to his chambers, hoping to read a bit and go to bed, and the last thing he wanted to do was discuss Opaka Sulan with one of the vedeks.

Especially Gar Osen. Vedek Gar had been very vocal in his opposition to Opaka's activities these past two years, ever since she had taken her son and left her stone cottage. Arin had publicly renounced Opaka's status as a vedek of the church, but he had not issued an Attainder, despite having threatened to do so. Vedek Gar had been trying to persuade Arin to make good on that threat ever since.

Of course, it was possible that Gar wished to speak of something else, he told himself when he answered the late-night rapping at his door, but the kai doubted it. And truly, it was just as well. He'd known for some time that he and Osen needed to speak; it could be put off no longer. Much as he did not wish it, the kai invited his old friend into the small library that served as his study chamber, trying to prepare himself for the conversation ahead.

Arin owed much to the vedek, owed his very life to him. When the old Kendra Shrine had been destroyed, Arin had tried in vain to save the Orb that had been housed there. He could still clearly remember stumbling through the smoke, the walls falling all around him, retaining the divine object his only thought. He would have died, but that Gar Osen had pulled him to safety.

Gar began before he'd even taken his seat, his tone pleading, his words coming rapidly. "Your Eminence, surely you are aware of the dwindling numbers of faithful who come to attend our services. Opaka's message is becoming widespread, not just in this province, but on all of Bajor. Others are spreading her teachings. Other vedeks, Your Eminence! You must denounce her words by formally Attainting her. You must stop this . . . this *wildfire* before it spreads any further."

Arin chose his words carefully. "The fire of which you speak has already consumed most of our world, Vedek Gar."

Gar was taken aback, as the kai knew he would be. "Your Eminence, what am I to conclude from such a statement? Surely you are not trying to tell me that *you* now reject the *D'jarras*? That you've . . . given up?"

Arin shook his head. "No, Vedek Gar. I have not given up. I have . . . reconsidered. In the two years since Opaka left, I have studied and prayed and thought upon her words. And I have come to see the power behind them. Bajorans are finally becoming free of the despondency that has plagued us for twenty years. They no longer see themselves as victims. They are fighting back."

"But of course you do not condone the fighting, Your Eminence. You *must* not condone it."

Arin was troubled. "I have begun to question many of my own beliefs, Vedek Gar. What you say is true . . . but our world has never known such a struggle, and I fear that if we cannot unite, we will be broken. A successful leader must be able to admit that he was mistaken."

"Yes, of course, Your Eminence, but you must tread lightly around this delicate matter—"

"Vedek, I should inform you that I mean to write a series of new sermons, with a very different message from what I have taught in the past. I will call for an assembly tomorrow, to announce the change."

"Your Eminence, I must—"

"I thank you for being such a valuable adviser to me over these many years, Osen," Arin said. "I will forever be grateful to you, for your counsel and your friendship. But I believe that for now, my closest adviser must be my own heart."

Gar's eyes flashed with anger. "Kai Arin, I believe you pay too much mind to false counsel, and not enough to the prophecies."

Arin felt a flash of annoyance. Had Osen just accused him of having a false heart? He gestured to an ancient book spread open on a kneehole desk behind him, an original printing of the Oracle of Spires, a collection of prophecies from long ago.

"Vedek Gar, I have studied the prophecies all my life. There are many verses that contradict what is said regarding the *D'jarras*. You know as well as I do that it is possible to twist the meaning of these verses to suit one's own agenda. I will not be accused of picking and choosing among the prophecies in order to bolster a particular argument." Arin was aware that his hand had tightened into a fist. He consciously relaxed it, and continued. "The Prophets have fallen silent to me, but I know They watch over us still, and make Their voices known to those who would listen. When I see how Opaka Sulan's efforts have been rewarded, I see—I *hear*—what Bajor is telling me to do. And I believe it is time to listen."

Gar was speechless as Arin dismissed him. The kai was ambivalent as the other man left the small chamber, sorry for his old friend—Gar had been unwavering in his faith, in his reliability as an assistant and counselor. They had worked closely together for many years. But Arin had come to acknowledge that the old caste system was not serving them well, and as Opaka and others like her had spread their message, he'd felt the change in the air, a feeling of *possibility* among the people that seemed like a kind of rebirth. Contrary to what he'd believed all these years, it had been far from injurious to morale for the people to leave their *D'jarras* behind. He realized that what he felt was mostly relief, to finally admit to Gar what had vexed him so in recent times. Gar had always been the greatest supporter of the *D'jarra* way.

He turned back to the book of prophecies he had been immersed in before Gar came to call. He found the verse he had been reading, and traced a finger along the line of text. *The time of accord shall bring an Emissary, and the Emissary shall bring a new age to Bajor.*

"The Emissary," Arin murmured, just before he felt cold fingers slip around his throat.

"I'm sorry," said a familiar voice, and the kai, clutching at those icy fingers, turned to stare into a pair of eyes that seemed strikingly reptilian, though Arin had never noticed it before. "I'm afraid I can't let you call that assembly, Your Eminence."

The kai didn't understand. He struggled, but the pressure only increased, and images of joy and sorrow and regret ran through his mind; it was as though it was all coming together, becoming a coherent story. His last thought was of the Orb he had lost, the great tragedy of his life in service to Them. . . . If Gar had not dragged him out of the shrine when he had, could he have saved the Orb of Truth? Could it be, as the people often murmured, that the Orb had not been destroyed at all, but . . . *taken* . . . ?

Black flowers bloomed in his eyes, and the struggle was too great, blotting out his thoughts, and then there was nothing, nothing at all.

Miras Vara sat up abruptly in her bed, sweating and cold. She swept her damp hair from the nape of her neck, breathing deeply as reality began to piece itself together again. She was in her bedchamber, in the small apartment where she lived alone, across the way from the Ministry of Science, where she worked. It had been a dream, only a dream . . . never frightening, exactly, but it was the same dream she'd had with increasing frequency in past weeks. This time, it had been different.

As always, she had been walking alone in the night, outside the periphery of Cardassia City where she lived and worked. Her feet had been bare, and the stony road had pierced her soles, but there was no blood, no pain. The ground beneath her, invisible in the dark, gave way to softness, coolness like nothing that occurred in nature, at least not on her world . . . And it occurred to her that she was going somewhere, some specific destination that she had never visited before, and that it was vital she continue on.

This was the part of the dream that she had experienced many times before—walking alone at night, a sudden understanding that she had a purpose, even though she didn't know what it was. But before tonight, she'd always woken shortly thereafter. This time, she had continued to walk for a much greater distance than ever before, traveling blind until the darkness gave way to the fragile light of dawn.

The ascending sun cast a yellow pall across the ground, which, to Miras's astonishment, was coated in something spongy with an undercurrent of subtle prickliness—something *green*. She knew what it was, but only from books, from her brief school rotation through the agri program.

In the distance, not far from a deep stand of wood—real, living trees—she could hear noises, not mechanical, not humanoid, but soft gruntings and cluckings that she recognized as being from animals, from livestock. She was drawing close to a farm. But Cardassians were not farmers, and Miras began to suspect that she was no longer on Cardassia Prime at all. It was then that she recognized she must be dreaming, the most realistic dream she could ever remember having.

She walked through the misty, early light. It was cool, but not uncomfortably so. She marveled at the scene unfolding before her. A farmhouse stood near the copse of dark trees—she'd never seen so many trees together. There were animal pens, a broad stable, a vegetable garden, variations of things she'd seen in captures but never in life—and yet everything was astonishingly detailed, the dirt floor of the yard, the strange, rich smell of growing things. Insects fluttered up from the ground cover, which was everywhere.

She approached a farmhouse, a sturdily built cottage

made of clay bricks, black clay like that which could be dug from Cardassian mountains. But she had already decided that she was on another world, and became more certain when she saw the figures moving beyond the windows of the small house. Though she couldn't make out their features, they were not Cardassian—they were leaner and more graceful than any Cardassian she had ever seen. And yet there was something familiar about them, too . . .

One of them emerged from the house then, and Miras felt her breath catch. The woman *was* a Cardassian—or, at least, she had the same Cardassian cranial ridges, with dark hair and pale gray skin.

*She's Hebitian.* The awareness dawned on her like the early light that played across the fertile land. An ancient ancestor, from the first great civilization to arise on Cardassia Prime. Miras had been to see the Hebitian ruins, and she realized suddenly that she was not on another world, after all. She was in another time.

The woman was carrying a jug, fashioned from the same ebony clay as the bricks that made up the farmhouse. Her long, obsidian-black hair was loose about her shoulders, and she was dressed in a white linen garment, cut on the bias to grace the curves of her body. She teased a strand of hair around one of her slender, tapered ears, and then she turned. She saw Miras, and smiled at her. Raised her hand.

Miras was startled, having somehow assumed that she was only observing. This attempt to interact . . . Her dream was realistic to the point of uncanniness. *Could* this be real? Could she have been drugged, somehow, and brought here without her knowledge? It was absurd to even think such things, but she was helpless not to, it was all so realistic.

The woman began to speak, and Miras could not at first understand her. The Hebitian seemed to realize it, spoke slower, more minimally—and Miras suddenly found that she could understand her perfectly well, as though she'd just remembered that she already knew the language.

*I do.* The words the woman used were presumably Hebitian, a language that all schoolchildren learned the fundamentals of, as their modern language was built upon it. She'd studied linguistics at university, as well. The third time the woman repeated her simple statement, Miras understood it perfectly.

"I have been waiting," the woman said.

"Do you mean—you have been waiting for *me*?"

"I have been waiting."

Miras looked around for any evidence that the woman could be referring to another—and was struck anew at the strange, rich beauty of this long-ago world, understanding now where she was. The landscape was hilly, but the hills were gentle and rolling, not the usual needle-sharp crags of obsidian that made up her Cardassia. The grunts and screeches of animals were clearer now, more pronounced, mingling with the sounds of a trickling brook somewhere in the trees and the *chir-chir-chir* of what she imagined were wood-crakes, birds that most experts believed had been extinct for centuries.

"I have something to show you. It is something precious."

"What . . . what is it?"

"It is for your eyes only, Miras."

Miras followed her into the farmhouse, not surprised somehow that the woman had called her by name. The room they entered was clean and filled with light, aesthetically pleasing in a utilitarian way.

The woman went to a wood table that sat against one wall. She opened a flat obsidian box that lay atop it, reached inside—and as she started to lift out whatever was within, the edges of Miras's perception began to blur. The colors of the room became indistinct, began to meld into

the cacophony of unfamiliar sounds and smells. She closed
her eyes, and then opened them again—

—and found herself sitting in her own room, kicking
at the bedclothes and pulling her sweat-soaked hair away
from the back of her neck.

She closed her eyes again, took another deep breath.
Tried to hang on to the indistinct image from the dream's
very end, wanting to know what the woman had been
about to show her. Something larger than the palm of her
hand, something flat with a slight curve, made from dark
polished wood and adorned with bright pigments. The
object was heavily carved with an ornate design, a design
that resembled . . . a face. It was a mask. The Hebitian
woman had been trying to show her a mask.

*What does it mean?* Miras lay back in bed, closing her
eyes again, but she slept no more that night.


Opaka Sulan settled for the winter at a large camp near
the northernmost edge of the Sahving Valley. There had
been a city here once, Genmyr, that had extended almost
to the edge of the forest, more than twenty *kellipates* away.
Genmyr had been a major textile exporter, in Bajor's simpler industrial times. The majority of the residents—those
who had stayed behind, who either couldn't afford to leave
when the occupation had turned ugly or had still believed
the Cardassians meant to treat them fairly—had chosen to
resettle after an "accidental" fire had swept through the city
many years before. The fire had destroyed the livelihoods
of hundreds of families, made the greater community even
more reliant on their oppressors. There were people who
said they'd actually seen a group of Cardassian soldiers set
the fire, but of course word was not proof and even if it
was, there was no recourse.

Many of the broken city's natives had made camp here
for more than a decade, year round. There were tempo-

rary shelters here, like Opaka's fabric tent, and there were a few more substantial dwellings, though nearly all the buildings had a transient quality, lending a kind of anxiety to the camp, as if all its inhabitants expected the day to come when they would have to pack up their families and move on.

The land itself was still mostly barren, but the valley was sheltered from the worst of the cold and there was a river only a few minutes away. It was a good place to winter, and many families came each year, seeking community in the hard months. The camp had already swelled to twice its size since the leaves had begun to fall, since the last of the meager crops had been harvested, and the former vedek knew that more would come—many more, to hear her message of unity. She hoped she was up to the task. The people here had embraced her as their guide in matters of spirit. Many were already coming to her for direction, alone and in groups, and while she did the best she could, offered advice from the heart and spoke what she believed, she was often afraid of faltering.

She sat on the floor of her shelter, alone. A few of the camp residents had taken it upon themselves to build her a wood pallet, which made sleeping on the ground much more comfortable. They'd wanted to do more, but she wouldn't have it; they had few enough resources, and she tried to see that all was shared.

She folded her arms around her legs, listening to the movements of life outside—children playing, people working together. Good sounds. It was often difficult for her to find a moment to herself, and usually she was thankful for it; the company of her spiritual family helped to stave off the loneliness that sometimes overwhelmed her, since Fasil had gone his own way. She'd been without him almost two full turns of the season, and still missed him terribly. But today she wanted to have a moment of peace, needed a moment to herself to reflect on the man who had been one of the greatest living inspirations to her—because he lived no more. She had received word that Kai Arin had been found dead in his sanctuary, apparently of natural causes.

Looking back, Opaka could see how her spirituality had grown under his tutelage, could recall many of his services that had touched her faith so profoundly, and she indulged in a moment of tearful regret as she recalled their last conversation. She wished she could have parted ways with him on more amiable terms. But of course, were it not for the disagreement, she would never have left. It was more reason to be grateful to him, for forcing her to be stronger, to be brave enough to do as she had.

Someone whipped back the flap of her makeshift tent, and she hastily wiped her eyes. "Yes? I . . . I wish to be alone for a moment, if it can wait."

"Mother."

She turned, and saw her son standing in the entryway of her rough home. It had been over a year since he had left to fight in the resistance, and many months had passed since he had visited her last—months during which she had not known if he was alive or dead.

His face was more gaunt than it had been when he first left, the soft edges of his childhood replaced with the craggy features of an adult. He sported a new scar that crept diagonally across his left cheek, but his eyes were still the same, warm and wise. She stood and hurried to embrace him, her tears joyful now.

After a long, lovely moment they parted, Opaka smiling up at her boy. She'd never been a tall woman; Fasil had gotten his father's height.

"It is good to see you, Mother. You are looking well."

"You also look well, my son. Of course, just to have you here . . ." Her eyes welled again.

"I can't stay long. I came because I heard about Kai Arin."

She nodded. "Yes. He was a good man, and he will be missed. Surely, you can stay a few days?"

He smiled at her, but did not answer. "I came to ask you what you have considered, regarding who his successor will be."

"I suppose there will be an election," she said. The Vedek Assembly was no longer a powerful force in her world, nor was it in the realities of the people she spoke with each day. Perhaps that was why the Cardassians still allowed it to exist.

"I imagine Gar Osen will be a candidate," she added, then shook her head. "It doesn't matter who the kai is now."

"It does matter," Fasil said. "I believe the next kai should be you."

Opaka laughed briefly before realizing that her son was serious. "Fasil, I have no interest in holding that office."

"Do you know how many people know about you?" Fasil asked. "And what better way to spread your message than under the authority of the kai?"

"I do not wish to be kai," she repeated. "Let the people choose who they want, it will not affect my work."

"The people will want you, Mother."

"The kai is chosen from the Vedek Assembly," she said. "I'm not even—"

"—a vedek anymore, I remember," Fasil said, a touch of young male exasperation in his voice, and she smiled, loving him so much that it hurt her heart.

"But think, Mother. This new prefect cares not about our religious beliefs. You would have access to travel permits, to political functions, to so many more people."

Opaka considered him seriously for the briefest of moments. If she were the kai, she could spread her message *everywhere,* she would not be dependent on word-of-mouth among small fringe groups. She might even have access to media—Kai Arin's Festival sermon on the *D'jarras* had been recorded and broadcast, had even reached Bajorans who had settled offworld . . .

But it was only a moment before the absurdity of it made her laugh again—Kai Opaka!—and she took her son's hand. "You must be tired," she said. "Let us eat something. Help me prepare food, and we'll talk of this later."

He grinned. "I admit, the offer of food is enough to make me agree to anything. It is very good to see you again, Mother. I have . . . missed you." He squeezed her hand, looking away, his face working to avoid tears.

Opaka was nearly overcome to see her son so affected. It seemed she wasn't destined to have dry eyes today. She embraced him again.

"I have missed you, too, Fasil. So very much."

The days had turned into weeks since the Derna incident. Lenaris had not entirely given up hope that Lac would return to them—his disappearance had been so abrupt, Lenaris still couldn't quite believe it—but he knew better than to mistake hope for possibility. Lac was not coming back.

Seefa, who had always leaned toward the anxious, had become convinced that the Cardassians would be coming for them any day now.

"The Cardassians have Lac's raider," he'd said, on more than one occasion since Derna. "They know he was using balon to power it, and they know there is a massive balon deposit right here. Mark my words, they will come. After that, it's only a matter of time before they find the rest of our ships and take us all to work camps—or worse. Most likely, they'll execute a few of us to make examples, and then—"

"Let's not get hysterical, Seefa. There are plenty of other balon deposits on Bajor." It was always Taryl who pulled him back. She refused to be rattled by what anyone had to say regarding Lac, choosing instead to approach the situation with her customary calm rationality. It worried Lenaris not a little that Taryl seemed so placid in the face of her brother's disappearance; he feared that one day the reality of it was going to hit her, and then—he didn't know what would happen then, for he had never seen Taryl succumb to the kind of upsets that he himself was prone to. Taryl had a fiery temper, but sadness and worry were not usually in her repertoire. Lenaris envied her for it. If he could have drawn on that kind of strength when Darin had died . . . Lac's disappearance held certain parallels to that particular tragedy, but Lenaris was determined to keep himself together this time.

Still, he was overwhelmed with guilt that it had been Lac who had been caught, and not himself. It was just dumb luck, of course. But then—Lenaris had forgotten to put in a transmission to Lac after exiting the atmosphere himself. What if he could have helped his friend somehow? He didn't know how, but still . . . He could not help but agonize over every detail of that ill-fated mission.

Meanwhile, Taryl had taken it upon herself to plan a rescue effort with some of the Ornathia cousins, much to Seefa's vehement disapproval. Taryl was certain that Lac must have been taken to Terok Nor, and to her way of thinking, they would have to stage an effort to smuggle him off the station. While the three were calibrating the sensor arrays on some of their ships, Lenaris had been present for one of many arguments that Taryl and Seefa had been having in regard to the matter.

"You have no idea what something like that would entail," Seefa admonished her.

"That's why we will have to gather information first," Taryl told him calmly. "The comm equipment on Derna will be helpful with that."

"It's ridiculous, Taryl. We don't even know if Lac is there! I absolutely forbid anyone from going to Terok Nor."

"You don't have the authority to forbid anyone from doing anything."

Lenaris cleared his throat loudly, and the two lowered their voices.

But, as she had been with her efforts to repair the freighter, Taryl was undaunted. In secret, she met with Lenaris and a handful of others from the cell who thought they could put together a rescue party.

It had been more than a month since Lac's disappearance when Taryl approached Lenaris, who was washing out some old metal cans with Ornathia Sten, someone Lenaris liked almost as much as he liked Lac. The salvaged cans would be reused for food, or else beaten flat to repair damaged hull plating.

"You've got a call on the long-range comm . . . it's from Halpas Palin."

*Palin.* Feeling a surge of real hope, Lenaris chucked the can to Sten, who caught it neatly, and followed Taryl back to Lac's empty shack, where the Ornathias' best communication equipment was set up. Work on the warp ship had been all but forgotten in the wake of the Derna incident, but Halpas had been a pilot since long before the occupation—he could certainly fly the thing, if he hadn't any ideas regarding how to fix it—and even if he didn't, he might be able to help locate Tiven Cohr. Lenaris had sent out word months before, trying to get in touch with his old contacts.

"Halpas Palin! It's Lenaris Holem!" he shouted into the comm.

*"No need to scream, Lenaris, I hear you loud and clear. Whoever posted the long-range comm towers did fine work. I got word from someone in Jalanda that you were looking for me."*

"For you—and Tiven, as well," Lenaris said. "It seems we

might have access to a warp vessel that could use a little . . . adjusting."

*"So, you're finally ready to apologize, are you?"*

Lenaris scowled to himself. "Did you hear what I said?" he asked. "A warp vessel, Halpas! Maybe we could forget the past for a minute and consider what that might mean for the resistance."

*"It was my understanding, Lenaris, that you were through with the resistance."*

Lenaris tried to swallow his anger, but it was not easy. The older man had always been an absolutist in every sense, never forgetting a single slight—Bajoran to his very core. Lenaris tried to forget the many times that Halpas had treated him like a child, the sneering and insistent reminding of every mistake Lenaris had ever made. And then the final, furious rift that had torn the cell—or what was left of the cell—apart for good. Lenaris had foolishly underestimated the old man's tendency to hold a grudge.

"Listen, Halpas," Lenaris said tightly. "Let's just let bygones be bygones. I've got a warp ship. One that I think has a good chance of being salvaged. And if anyone could pilot it out of the atmosphere, it's you. Now, if you know where Tiven Cohr is, then there's nothing stopping us from using this ship for a full-scale attack. Are you with me?"

*"I know where Tiven is,"* Halpas said. *"He lives near me, at the edge of the Berain Valley."*

"In the city?" Lenaris asked. He'd been to Berain City a few times.

*"I also know,"* Halpas went on, as though Lenaris hadn't spoken, *"that he wants nothing to do with you—unless you're willing to apologize, of course."*

Lenaris was incensed. He didn't have time to pander to the foolish politics of a couple of stubborn old men. "Forget it," he said sourly. "I'll find someone else who can fix it."

Halpas laughed, a faraway sound on the comm. *"Still as prideful as a batos,"* he said.

"Look who's talking," Lenaris muttered, and he ended the call. The warp ship wasn't a priority right now anyway; he had a rescue effort to help organize.

## 6

"Hello, my old friend." Kalisi greeted Miras warmly as the two met near the turbolift at the Ministry of Science. Miras was pleased to see her. Although they both worked in the same building, they rarely saw each other; they had been hired by different departments, worked in different wings of the facility. Kalisi's position in defense technology, sanctioned and funded by the military, held a great deal more prestige than the field Miras had chosen. Miras found her agricultural studies fascinating, especially from a historical perspective—for it was generally believed that Cardassia Prime had once been green and abundant, before a dramatic shift in the climate had turned it to desert—but she seemed to be one of the few who cared. Miras believed she had seen ancient Cardassia herself, in the unfinished dream that continued to plague her; while she had no illusions that their homeworld would ever again be so fecund, she held hope that it could again be made fertile.

*Not that it matters at the moment,* she thought. The dream came almost every night now. She felt as though her life had been put on hold, that she could not pursue any matter, personal or otherwise, until she could decipher its meaning.

"What was it that you wished to see me about, Miras?" In spite of her eagerness, Miras approached the subject hesitantly. "Do you remember that object that we examined just before we completed our final project? The thing from Bajor—"

"Yes, the dirty old box with the strange writing on the sides." Kalisi smiled. "It hasn't been *that* long, Miras. Two, three years? Of course I remember it."

"I've learned a few things about it. I learned—some time ago, actually—that it was probably one of the Orbs of the Prophets. Have you heard of them?"

Kalisi frowned. "Orbs of the Prophets? It *does* sound familiar—the Bajorans call their deities 'prophets,' don't they? So the item is ceremonial, then."

"Yes, in a way. The Bajorans believe an individual may have . . . experiences from exposure to these Orbs." Miras smiled, making an effort not to seem crazy. "Anyway, I've been thinking about it a lot lately, and I thought I might like to have another look at it."

Kalisi nodded slowly. "And you don't have high enough security clearance to access it."

"That's right." Miras felt a tinge of shame, for she didn't want her old friend to think that asking this favor was the only reason she'd contacted her. "I thought of you instantly, because I haven't seen you in such a long time, and wanted to catch up anyway—"

Kalisi laughed. "It's all right, Miras. I'll clear you to have a look at the object. I can arrange for it to be sent to one of the laboratories here at the ministry—would that be all right?"

Miras nodded enthusiastically. "Yes, that would be perfect. Thank you so much, Kalisi. In the meantime—would you like to have lunch with me?"

It was Kalisi's turn to look uncomfortable. "Actually, I can't. I wish I could, but my responsibilities right now . . . I usually eat lunch in my laboratory, while waiting for my downloads to complete."

Miras decided that she didn't envy her friend's position. There was no one pressuring her for results. "Another time then, perhaps?"

"Yes. Let's not make it quite such a long time between calls, shall we?"

Miras quickly agreed, and Kalisi ran her thumbscan on a security padd to allow Miras access to a vacant laboratory in the main building's lower level. "Room 109-green," Kalisi told her before they parted company. "Wait there while I arrange the artifact's retrieval."

Miras wasted little time, feeling a strange kind of giddy anticipation as she walked to the lab. She didn't know what she expected to find, looking at the object again, but she'd realized only recently that her strange dreams had begun shortly after her exposure to it. They'd been intermittent at first, but as the months had passed, as she'd settled into her new career, the dream had grown in frequency and clarity, almost becoming a part of her. She'd done more extensive research on the artifact and its possible origins in what spare time she had, and when she'd learned that the objects were said to inspire visions, she had made up her mind that she needed to see it again.

*And it's not as though I have anything better to do . . .* She'd had a brief, unhappy romance with one of her co-workers soon after coming to the ministry, a man who had since transferred to the private sector; she was not ready to engage in another relationship anytime soon, much to the displeasure of her rather traditional family. Pursuing this minor mystery had become something of a fixation for her, one she was eager to solve. The sooner she could put this behind her, the better.

The lab was small but brightly lit. Within an hour of her arrival, the artifact was once again transported in its shipping container. She thumbed the lock and lifted the heavy object onto the work table, thinking that perhaps she had lost her mind, after all. If she'd told Kalisi that she'd started to believe she was having visions of ancient Cardassia . . .

Just thinking it made her feel incredibly foolish, but she'd come this far; she was determined to see her folly through. She looked at the thing, the case—the "ark," in Bajoran vernacular. It did not appear that the object had been disturbed since she had seen it last. Traces of red Bajoran dirt still smeared the outside of the container and rested in the crevices of the characters and stones that stood in relief from the object's flat paneled sides.

Miras ran her fingertips down the side of the object, as she had before, wondering if she would be able to open it again. Perhaps there had never been an opening, she thought to herself; perhaps she had been slowly losing her mind ever since her first encounter with this thing. Why not? Maybe the Bajorans had visions because of some mind-altering chemical in the materials of the box, or in the Orb itself, one that gave Cardassian women frustrating dreams and irrational notions. But the seam was indeed there.

Miras gently pried at the corner . . . and stepped back in amazement as a brilliant light spilled from the vertical opening in the case. She knew she should be closing the case, calling for help, but the sense of tranquillity that she recalled from her prior experience had returned, compelling her to further open the case. The Orb inside was illuminated so brightly that she could not even make out its size or shape, and after a moment, she could see nothing at all, nothing but a white, piercing light that flooded her vision, her reality, her thoughts.

Blind and confused, she struggled to maintain her senses. From a pinpoint of distinction within the harsh flood of brilliant light, the shimmering figure of a woman began to appear.

"Miras." The Hebitian woman's voice was as gently rolling as the hills of the surrounding farmland, melting into place all around Miras as the impossible whiteness began to recede. "I have been waiting."

It was the dream . . . But this was no dream, this was happening. The woman led Miras inside the sparsely furnished little house of black brick, and walked to the heavy wood table. She reached into the obsidian box—

—and brought out the mask, turning to Miras. Miras half expected everything to dissolve as it always did as soon as the mask appeared, but she knew better, too. This, this whatever it was, *vision,* was real.

"The mask of Oralius," the woman said, and handed it to her.

"Oralius," Miras repeated, taking the delicate carving. She frowned. The Oralians had been a cult of some kind that had been extinct in the Cardassian Union since Miras was barely more than an infant. It was something that was rarely discussed, a topic that seemed distasteful to most, a superstitious holdover from an unfortunate time.

"Go ahead," the graceful Hebitian woman coaxed, and Miras slipped the mask over her face.

She turned to find herself alone in the house—but it wasn't the same house anymore. This new place was made of cool stones, coated thinly with delicate mats of velvety green foliage. Miras could smell the pungent odor of food cooking, foreign and overpowering. The ceiling was very tall, accommodating a rickety wooden ladder that stretched to a sleeping loft against the far wall. The loft was equipped with a door, situated very near the peak of the ceiling. Miras watched as an old man, an alien man with smooth, ruddy skin and an oddly slender neck, climbed up to the loft and exited through the door. After a beat, Miras followed him. He'd walked out onto a large wooden porch that overlooked part of a lush forest, with trees so giant and bizarre that Miras knew with certainty that she was not on Cardassia Prime.

*Bajor?* She believed so.

The man seemed unaware of her presence, and Miras continued to follow him as he walked down a set of stairs that had been built against the side of the porch, toward the back of the small home. When he reached the ground, he lifted a wooden hatch that revealed yet another staircase, this one curving down into an underground passage that had been dug next to the foundation. Miras seemed to float after him down the darkened steps and into a small chamber. The man did not sense her presence as he knelt down before a little hollow in the wall, a hollow that accommodated a four-sided object, tiled, bejeweled, with an oval lens on each face. Miras knew what he would do before he even did it; he opened the ark, and brilliant light spilled into the room.

She shielded her eyes from the glare of the Orb, washed over again with light before the room suddenly went dim. As her eyes adjusted, she found that she had been transported to yet another place—a room lined with books, and there were two other men in the room with her, Bajoran men. The cold, heavy air smelled of incense. From what Miras had read on the subject, the Bajorans' clothes indicated that they were religious officials of some kind. In fact, she knew who they were, she knew what their raiment denoted without quite knowing how she knew it. These men were Kai Arin and Vedek Gar Osen. The names and titles were unfamiliar, but she knew them anyway.

The men were engaged in an argument, a debate, perhaps, but Miras could not be sure what they were saying. One man, the younger, departed the room—dismissed, she thought. The older man sat down at a desk and began to read from a book, a very old one.

Miras tried to call to the older man, for she was convinced that he was in danger, and when she saw the first man reenter the room, she became sure of it. The younger man crept up behind the elder and slid his hands around his narrow throat.

Miras tried to scream, to move, but she could only watch, silent and still and horrified as the old man thrashed in futile resistance, as his attempts to break free grew weaker. She tried to pull at the mask she wore, hoping that if it were removed she would be transported away from here, this nightmarish experience concluded, but her limbs were like fog and she had no control over her hands, her fingers. She was not even sure if she was inhabiting her own body anymore.

The younger man closed the book that the dead man had been reading, and removed the ceremonial headpiece from his lifeless body. The vision became more dreamlike, blurry and indistinct, things occurring in a jerky, clicking fashion. The murderer looked up, and Miras wanted to shield herself and could not. He seemed to be looking for someone, looking for her—and she realized suddenly that he, too, was wearing a mask, one that bore a strong resemblance to her own. He hadn't been wearing one before, she was sure of it. He seemed to be looking right at her, and he reached up and pulled his mask away—

—and Miras was finally taken away from the unfortunate scene, just as she registered that the face beneath the mask was no longer Bajoran.

It had been Cardassian.

There was almost no time to consider what it meant, for Miras was suddenly home again, at the very center of Cardassia City, the environment grainy and one-dimensional, like a very old image capture. She recognized it, but at the same time she did not—for the capital of Cardassia Prime lay in ruins, great heaps of smoking rubble and debris blocking the streets, the aftermath of a devastating attack. Bodies were everywhere, Cardassian men, women, and children. The stench of death and burning composite was terrible, cloying.

In horror and panic, Miras squeezed her eyes tightly shut and tried once again to tear the mask from her face. At last, she was successful. When she opened her eyes again, she was in the laboratory, the Orb case was closed, and someone was pounding on the door. Before Miras had time to think, Kalisi burst into the room, her face reading fearful bewilderment.

"Miras! What happened in here? The inventory staff was trying to contact you, and the ministry computer indicated that you weren't in the room—that you weren't even in the *building!* They tried to transport the object out but they couldn't get a lock on it. They called me because the artifact was under my clearance, but then my thumbscan wouldn't open the door!"

Miras tried to slow her own frightened breathing back to normal, but she was still continuing to receive images and thoughts that were not her own, like faded pictures in a dream, like connections made in deepest slumber.

"Kalisi . . . I have seen the devastation of Cardassia Prime. I have seen . . . there is a man on Bajor . . . his name is Gar Osen . . . but . . . but it isn't his real name. He—he isn't really a Bajoran, he's there to—oh, he must not find the final Orb! Cardassia will be destroyed!"

Kalisi's eyes widened in concern and confusion, and Miras realized how utterly insane her ramblings must sound. Whatever had happened to her, she felt she must not embarrass herself or her friend.

"Forgive me," she said. "I . . . believe I need to eat something. How long have I been in here?"

"All afternoon," Kalisi told her, placing her hand on Miras's arm. "I think food is a very good idea." She glanced at the object as it was transported back to storage, her expression even more anxious than before, and Miras stumbled along after her friend, trying to straighten out her thoughts.

"There must have been a malfunction with the linkup to this lab," Miras suggested. "That must be why you couldn't contact me, why the object wouldn't transport to the storage facility."

"Of course," Kalisi said. "It might also explain why my thumbscan didn't work at first." She did not sound especially convinced. "Miras, I think I will take you up on your earlier offer of a meal. It would do us both good, I think, to catch up a bit. It has been a long time."

"Yes," Miras agreed. "Too long." Her head was finally beginning to clear, and she felt foolish for the nonsense that she had just sputtered, and unnerved by the things she had seen. There had to be a scientific explanation for what had happened, some technology—obviously, it had produced a dampening effect on the ministry's computer system. Considering the chaos she had caused, she knew that she would not get another chance to look at the Orb. And considering what she'd seen, she thought that that was just as well.

Lenaris Holem was dozing in his makeshift home when someone rapped heavily on his door. He stumbled to answer, blinking in the orange light of the setting sun. The visitor proved to be Ornathia Delle, a round-faced woman of about thirty, one of the people who was conspiring to help Taryl get her brother off Terok Nor.

"Holem," she whispered, looking around nervously. "Taryl says she's found something that could help us rescue Lac." She hunched down slightly, as if it would make the pitch of her voice even lower. "Someone contacted her— someone who says they've been on the station."

Lenaris stepped out into the dying sunlight. "I'll go talk to her," he said.

Delle shook her head. "She says not to. She said Seefa is getting suspicious."

Lenaris was getting tired of sneaking around behind Seefa's back. Since he'd come to stay with the Ornathias, he'd finally begun to understand why Taryl cared for Seefa; for all his pessimism and neurotic habits, the quirky young man was very bright and entirely devoted to Taryl. Still, if Seefa didn't like what they were up to, perhaps he should go elsewhere. Ignoring Delle's warnings, Lenaris headed for Taryl's house.

A few steps from her door, Lenaris was intercepted by Seefa, who looked troubled. Lenaris attempted to walk right past him, but Seefa addressed him directly. It seemed he'd just left Taryl, as he kept glancing back at her door.

"Seefa." Lenaris nodded in turn, trying to sound casual. "I've just come to check on the progress of those new sensors that Taryl said she was working on."

Seefa didn't seem suspicious, only worried, and maybe even sad. "She's very upset about Lac," he said, almost to himself. "I'm foolish to be putting pressure on her right now."

Lenaris was puzzled. It was not unusual for Seefa to suddenly blurt out strange pieces of personal information, but that didn't make this any easier to understand. "I suppose that's wise, considering her brother's disappearance."

"It's just . . . we've been engaged our entire lives. I don't understand why we can't just make it official. Taryl says that the middle of the Cardassian occupation is no time for a wedding. But I think she's wrong. We have to be able to go on with certain aspects of our lives; we have to be able to occasionally indulge ourselves with small measures of happiness where we can take it. Don't you think I'm right, Holem?"

Lenaris knew better than to get in a disagreement with Seefa, or even a discussion about how to live one's life. Taryl's betrothed was not the sort of person that one wanted to engage in argument; he was perpetually answering questions with more questions, or changing the subject so that any specific aspect of a discussion would never be fully addressed. Brilliant, perhaps, but tiresome.

"Sure," Lenaris said. "Yes." His heart dipped as he said it. He continued to work to put his own feelings for Taryl aside, all too aware that they were wasted. Although it wasn't what he truly wanted, he'd resigned himself to being her friend a long time before.

He looked out to the west, where the old road had once been. He thought he had seen a moving object in the sideline of his vision. In fact, there *was* something moving. It was a person, that much was clear, but whether it was male or female, Bajoran or Cardassian, it was much harder to tell in the fading light.

Lenaris walked a little closer to have a better look, Seefa following. After a moment, Lenaris could be fairly certain that the person was a Bajoran, probably a woman, and . . . she wore the raiment of a monk.

"It's Winn Adami," Seefa said.

"Who?"

"She's well known around here. She has long been advocating for a full-scale effort to repair the irrigation systems. Her order does not approve of the departure from the *D'jarras*—she's in favor of fighting the Cardassians, but she thinks the fighting should be left to others. She believes our responsibility is to feed Bajor, not to fight for it."

"Does she come to preach the castes, then?"

Seefa shrugged. "I imagine she has more reason than that. She disagrees with us, but she's still very well respected. Several years ago, she bribed a Cardassian official who was sending a large group of Bajorans from a nearby village to be executed. Because of her intervention, the shuttle was diverted to a work camp. She saved their lives."

"Really?" Lenaris squinted.

"Yes, really." Seefa sounded annoyed. He tended to take

offense at any perceived slight. "I had more than one relative on that shuttle. She must be coming to see someone here."

Lenaris decided the business about Terok Nor could wait until later. "Let's go out and meet her, then. Bring her some water. She must have come a long way."

Seefa appeared to agree without actually speaking, and together the two men fetched a gourd full of clean water before they began to walk along the dusty road to meet with the approaching traveler.

"Ranjen Winn!" Seefa called as they drew near her. "What brings you all the way out here?"

The monk appeared to be slightly younger than Lenaris himself. She was fair of complexion, probably originally from the north, with ruddy spots flaming high upon her cheeks—the day had been hot. Her pale hair was twisted into complicated designs at the back of her head, her eyes glassy in their colorlessness.

"Aro Seefa. Hello." She accepted the gourd that he offered her, and after taking a small sip she reached out and took his ear to read his *pagh*. She closed her eyes, and then opened them again as she released his ear. "You are troubled," she said.

"Not any more than usual, Ranjen."

She smiled tightly. "I have come to speak to someone in your village."

"Oh? May I ask who?"

"Ornathia Taryl. Can you take me to her?"

"Taryl? Of course." Seefa offered her the gourd again, and she took another sip, eyeing Lenaris with what seemed to be mild suspicion.

The three started to walk toward the village together, Winn continuing to look Lenaris up and down as if she did not trust him. "You are not one of the Ornathias," she observed.

"My name is Lenaris Holem. I'm from Relliketh."

"I've never seen you here before."

"I've been here about two years now."

"Two years." Winn turned to Seefa. "Can it really have been that long?"

"It was almost four years ago that you were here last, Ranjen," Seefa said.

"Four years," she said, her expression unreadable. "And I am still but a lowly ranjen."

Lenaris was not sure how to respond to her. The revelation was spoken without emotion, yet it seemed to upset the woman. They reached the village without further conversation, and the two men escorted her to Taryl's hut, though she already seemed to know where to go.

"Ornathia Taryl," Winn said formally as she entered Taryl's hut. Lenaris and Seefa stepped inside behind her.

Taryl was, as usual, working on something. She stood up from her bench and bowed before the monk.

"Now, my child, there's no need for that. I am hardly the kai—or even a vedek."

"You honor us with your presence, Ranjen."

Winn looked pleased at being addressed with such respect. "I have come with news of your brother Lac."

"Lac?" Taryl's hand floated to her chest, and Lenaris saw, for a beat, the emotion that she was denying herself. It was gone just as quickly, that veil of restraint back in place.

"One of the prylars in my order just returned from the Pullock system," Winn said. "It seems the Cardassians have a prison camp there, on Pullock V. As you may know, the Cardassians permit some religious officials to give counsel to their prisoners, if it is requested. One of the prisoners on Pullock V specifically requested that an official from my order be sent. That prisoner was Lac."

"Lac!" Taryl exclaimed. "He *is* alive!"

"He's not at Terok Nor!" This was Seefa. "I knew it, Taryl. I told you it would have been foolish to go there!"

"To Terok Nor!" Winn looked appalled at the very suggestion. "What kind of foolishness is this?"

"Nothing, Ranjen," Taryl said, shooting her fiancé a look of urgent fury. "Please, tell us what you know of my brother."

The ranjen was clearly unsettled, but she continued. "Lac wanted to be sure to send back word to you that he is alive. . . . He doesn't believe the Cardassians took possession of his ship—"

"He's letting us know that we're still safe!" Lenaris exclaimed. Winn glared at him, and he apologized quickly. "Forgive me, Ranjen." He turned to Taryl. "I've seen star charts of the Pullock system—it's not far from our own."

Taryl turned to Lenaris. "Are you saying what I think you're saying?"

"What is the meaning of this?" Winn demanded.

Lenaris continued to talk as if Winn weren't there. "Tiven Cohr," he said.

"No," Seefa argued. "Enough with the warp ship, already. Even if your friend *could* fix it, you're guaranteed a death sentence if you leave the atmosphere in that ship."

"You're underestimating what kind of a pilot Halpas Palin is," Lenaris informed him. "He fought the Cardassians in the early stages of the occupation. If anyone can do it, Halpas can. If I leave now, I can get to where he and Tiven live by tomorrow morning."

He smiled at Taryl, ever so slightly. "I'll even apologize, if that's what it takes."

Ranjen Winn was visibly agitated by this talk, looking back and forth between Taryl and Lenaris. "Any foolhardy attempts to travel offworld will only result in lives lost, more Bajoran prisoners in Cardassian camps!" she admonished.

Taryl turned to the holy woman. "He's my brother," she said simply, and went right back speaking to Lenaris. "You would do it, then? You would contact Tiven Cohr—even after what he said?"

"Of course I would!" Lenaris said. "It's like you said, Taryl—he's your brother. And my friend. We can do this."

Winn interrupted. "Your birthright is to till the soil, *not* to leave this world in a ship! Just look at what has happened as a result of farmers trying to be something they are not—your brother has been captured, and according to the monk who attended to him, the conditions in that camp will not sustain him much longer."

"My birthright is that of a pilot," Lenaris told Winn. "And if you say Lac doesn't have much more time, then we had better get moving quickly."

Seefa broke in. "No," he said. "Lac can't know for sure whether the Cardassians took his raider, and I believe they would have done so. I suggest we all leave immediately, without our ships. We should go back to the peninsula."

"Seefa," Taryl said. "Lac obviously sent us this message with the hope that we would come looking for him."

Seefa looked unmoved, shaking his head.

"Please," Taryl pleaded. "He would do the same for you."

"Lac would be the first to point out that it would be foolish to risk several lives to save one. I know how upset you must be, but, Taryl . . ." He reached for her, but she stepped away, her eyes flashing.

"How can you say that?" she snapped. "If there's any chance that we can save him, we should take it. Holem is going to find Tiven Cohr—and I'm going with him."

"By the Prophets," Winn said angrily. "The misguided words of a renounced vedek have penetrated the consciousness of this world so thoroughly that farmers leave their fields unplanted, choosing to fly off on suicide missions instead of providing food for their world. You were never meant to take to the skies, Taryl, and neither was your brother. Perhaps this result is the Prophets' way of telling us that Lac should have kept his feet planted on the ground—as should you. "

"Ranjen," Taryl said, her tone softer, "we have long disagreed on this matter. We mean no disrespect to you, but we must do this. *I* must do this. My mind is made up." She turned to Lenaris. "How soon can we get there?"

Seefa tried to interrupt again, speaking over Taryl in continued protest, but she paid no attention to him. Neither did Lenaris. He was already formulating what he would say to Tiven. An apology seemed a small price to pay for Lac's life.

Natima was exhausted and not in a mood to talk when she received the transmission from Cardassia Prime. She and Veja had been on their feet all day long, attending a press conference that addressed some tortuous rearrangement of the civilian government's leadership role in the Bajoran provinces. It was all she could do to filter a decent report out of her notes. It hadn't helped that she had been standing right in front of a man with a rattling cough, masking out half of the dialogue. Not that any of it was especially compelling.

To make matters worse, she and Veja were being sent to Terok Nor tomorrow for yet another long and boring press conference. Every time Natima went to Terok Nor with Veja—there had been four trips since their first—she was made to feel like a superfluous rudder on a ship. Veja would go off with Gil Damar, to whom she still had not been formally enjoined—they were waiting for Damar's promotion to come through—and Natima was left by herself while she waited for the transport to take her back to the surface.

She rose from her bed and answered the transmission with reluctance, but then brightened a bit when she saw that it was her young friend, the scientist Miras Vara. Miras had consulted with Natima a number of times in the past two years regarding various issues related to the agricultural situation on Bajor, since Natima had originally helped her with her student thesis project—one that had earned her the very highest marks, in the end.

"Hello, Miras," Natima said cheerfully. "It's good to see a friendly face from home."

*"Thank you, Natima. It's good to see you, too. I was wondering if you have a moment . . ."*

"Of course."

Miras seemed unusually hesitant. *"I have some questions for you that I fear you might find . . . odd."*

"Odd? You know nothing surprises me anymore, Miras. Not after some of the things I've witnessed here."

*"I know. It's just that . . . I learned some things recently. Regarding Bajor. And . . . I didn't know who else I could ask."*

"Learned them . . . how?"

*"I . . . Natima, I can't say. Can you understand that? You've had to protect sources before, haven't you?"*

Natima nodded wordlessly, puzzled and intrigued.

*"Do you know anything of . . . the death of a Bajoran religious official? I believe he is called the kai."*

Natima was taken aback. Matters of Bajoran religion were certainly not typical fodder for Cardassian discussion. It was possible that Miras could have learned the term "kai" from some source within the science ministry, but Natima was sure that nobody in the Cardassian Union would have reported the death of the current one. Dukat saw to it that Cardassians generally remained ignorant of his lenience regarding Bajoran religious practices. "How did you come upon this information?"

*"I told you, I can't say. I'm so sorry, Natima, but I just can't."*

Natima could not be sure if she should confirm or deny the story. It seemed irrelevant in the greater scheme of things, but it was so strange that Miras should even know about it. "What more have you heard about this?" Natima asked her carefully.

Miras again appeared reluctant to speak. *"There is someone named Gar Osen. He . . . I believe he may have been present when the kai died. He may have been the one who found the body, or perhaps he is someone close to the kai. I only wish to confirm that this information is true. Or simply that such a person exists. That is all I need to know, Natima. Have you heard of him?"*

In fact, Natima did know who Gar Osen was, only because she had learned that he was campaigning to become the new kai. Again, she was puzzled that Miras would know anything about it at all. Natima herself did much of the final edits on what information the service passed along to Cardassian civilians, and she was positive that such specific details about Bajoran religious officials would never have been reported. The very fact that Miras knew about something so obscure set off alarms. What else was being leaked to Cardassia Prime?

"Miras, I will see what I can find out for you," Natima said, hoping that her friend would not recognize that she was stalling. "If you don't mind waiting for a day or two . . ."

*"No, not at all, Natima. Take as much time as you need. You have my deepest appreciation for agreeing to help me with this."*

"Think nothing of it," Natima assured her. "In the meantime, I think it's best if you keep this information to yourself."

*"I've told no one of consequence."*

Natima wondered what Miras's estimation of consequence was, and she ended the transmission. Her thoughts raced as she sat back in her chair. How should she approach this situation? Miras was her friend, and she didn't want to get her in trouble. Natima was certain that the younger woman perhaps didn't understand how dire an offense it could be for her to be spreading around classified information. For although the specific information that Miras had referred to was not classified, the greater connotations of that information certainly were. If citizens on Cardassia Prime realized how much religious freedom Dukat permitted the Bajorans, there would be a great deal of public dissent, and Dukat surely knew it.

Personally, she disagreed with the prefect's policies—as new citizens of the Union, the Bajorans should be putting aside their antiquated superstitions, should be searching for ways to adjust to a more Cardassian mindset. Instead, they spent their time fighting against the inevitable, making life miserable for the good people who'd traveled to this inhospitable world to help the natives—thanks in no small part to Dukat's leniencies. But it was her job to see that the news from Bajor supported the Union's image of infallibility, not a task she took lightly. Her job was her life.

She told herself she'd think about it, but knew already that she'd warn Miras away from the information again and then leave it alone. She could not afford to jeopardize her own career, even for a friend. Whatever Miras decided to do, that was her business.

# 7

Lenaris made preparations to land the raider along a wooded plateau just beneath the highest peak of the Berain mountains. He was relieved to set down after their long, silent night—the light was strong enough in the sky now to make them an obvious target. He and Taryl had headed out without taking significant precautions that their journey was along a routine flight path—there simply hadn't been time.

"I don't think we should take the raider down into the valley," Lenaris said. "We've taken enough of a risk, crossing territory that's mostly deserted—but I used to fly in this area regularly, and the security grids are pretty tight just over Berain City. I had the pleasure of being stopped more than once in this region."

"Okay," Taryl said. She wasn't familiar with the areas around Relliketh, and wouldn't have been in a mood to argue, anyway.

"It's about half a day's walk from here," he told her. "We'd better take all the water we brought. I can't be sure that we'll come to any other sources along the way." Taryl nodded, tying several gourds of water around one shoulder. He tossed some dried *alva* fruits into his pack, and the two began their journey down the narrow ledges and pathways that wound through the trees and along the side of the mountain.

Taryl walked closely behind him, occasionally touching his shoulder to steady herself on the uneven terrain. Lenaris pushed branches aside, pointed out exposed roots. It had rained recently, and the air was clean and sweet. The smell brought back many memories.

"So," she said casually, after a while. "Are you ever going to tell me about why Tiven and Halpas are so mad at you?"

Lenaris sighed. "It's a long story," he said.

"Seems to me we've got nothing but time." She touched his shoulder again, and this time he stopped walking and turned to face her.

"Yes, I'll tell you," he said, deciding that it might do him good to speak of it to someone at last.

Taryl nodded, and they resumed their hike.

"I joined the resistance with my best friend," he began. "Our families had been close since before we were born. His mother took it especially hard when we decided to go off and fight. He was an only child, you see, his father killed when he was a babe.

"His name was Darin. Lafe Darin. He was very enthusiastic about fighting. He was . . ." Holem paused, tried to think of the easiest way to sum up their friendship. "We were like brothers. I suppose I knew that it was possible that one of us could be killed . . ." Lenaris did not look at her.

"But it's still very abstract, isn't it? To think of a loved one dying. Or disappearing. Before it actually happens, that is."

"Yes," he agreed, relieved that she understood. He ducked beneath a low-slung vine as they carefully made their way down an especially steep path. The terrain evened out again, and he resumed speaking. "As time passed, so many years of fighting together, maybe we had begun to feel a little invincible. I know he must have, considering what he did." He fell silent, lost for a moment to memory.

"What happened?" Taryl prodded gently.

"Our cell was one of the first to find out that the Valerians were supplying the Cardassians with weapons-grade dolamide," Lenaris said. The words were familiar, he'd thought them a million times, but had never spoken them aloud. "We had the idea that if we terrorized the Valerians, they would stop trading with Cardassia."

"Cut them off at the source."

"Yes. We found out where the Valerian freighters were docking, where they were unloading their product—at their processing camp, in the Karnoth mountains. It was heavily guarded, very difficult to get past the security there, but we believed we could do it. Well, some of us did. I admit, I was one of the skeptics. Darin, though—he was fearless.

"So, someone came up with the idea to put a bomb on one of the freighters. The trouble was, the security was set up so that you could get on one of those ships easily enough, but you couldn't get back off. That was where they would detect you. We found that out the hard way—one of the people in our cell tried to get aboard to learn the schematics. We never saw him again.

"I thought the plan should be scrapped until we figured out exactly how and where our man had been captured, but Darin was impatient. He and several of the others conspired—without me—to place the bomb on the ship anyway, even though whoever carried it would have to accept that he was almost certainly sacrificing himself. Death or capture."

"How did you learn about the plan?"

"I knew Darin was hiding something from me." Lenaris sighed. "I could just tell—I knew him so well. I followed him to the camp, and I tried to stop him. Tried to talk him out of it, but of course he wouldn't listen."

Lenaris shook his head, recalling the scene. "We had ugly words. He accused me of being childish, said that I was just angry at being left out. I told him he was selfish to be depriving his mother of her only child, and he reminded me that he had been risking his life for Bajor since the day he joined the movement—that we both had. That taking that risk was part of joining the resistance. Of course I knew he was right, but a mission where capture— or more likely death—is a near certainty . . . I couldn't get behind it. I actually took a swing at him when I saw that he couldn't be persuaded, but he ducked, and I missed him. He didn't miss me, though. We parted ways on . . . unhappy terms." He laughed bitterly at his own understatement.

"I watched the freighter take off from a point a few *kellipates* beyond the landing site. It almost came to nothing. The captain of the ship ejected the cargo less than a minute after taking off. He must have noticed that something wasn't right in the cargo bay, where Darin had planned to place the bomb. But the captain was too late; the bomb exploded just as he ejected it, and he lost control of the ship. I saw it come down."

He slowed, remembered the feelings of horror and loss as he'd watched the ship fall from the sky. "It seemed to take an eternity. It was hard to tell at first where it landed. I ran through the forest, following the smoke trail, just hoping that by some miracle of the Prophets, Darin would be alive."

He didn't look at Taryl, who had fallen in step with him. "But of course, that was impossible."

Taryl's voice was quiet. "You found it?"

"A few hours later, I suppose. It's hard to remember for sure. Several others from the cell got there about the same time. It was dead in the middle of the forest, far away from anything. It had sustained a lot of damage, took out a massive swath of the forest where it landed—incinerated at once, with little fires still burning when we got there. The landing gear was completely obliterated, the entry hatch fused shut—I tried to get in anyway, but I burned both my hands . . ." He remembered the smell of his own flesh burning, and went on, pushing it away. "Halpas acknowledged that there weren't any survivors aboard. He scanned the area twice—not that he needed to. Nobody could have walked away from that mess . . . and then everyone in the cell immediately started squabbling over the ship, before we'd even discussed what to do with the . . . bodies.

"I was outraged that they didn't even bother to acknowledge Darin's death, and I told them so. They said I was a coward, told me I'd been living in a delusion if I hadn't expected to lose a friend someday. They said that if I was so reluctant to sacrifice anything for Bajor, the cell was better off without me."

"Was that when you left?"

"No. It was after—after the . . ." He trailed off, began again. "They set up a guard, though I told them the Cardassians would come for the ship, if the Valerians didn't. They told me to stop being an old woman, and they put three men in charge of watching her for the night— including one of Tiven's brothers. It wasn't three hours later the Cardassians found the wreckage, and they didn't hesitate. They just dropped a bomb on her and didn't look back, making sure there was nothing we could salvage from her.

"Everyone was devastated. They could see I had been right, but of course they weren't about to admit it . . . especially Tiven, who was crazy with grief after the loss of his brother. I think they expected to hear 'I told you so' from me—which they wouldn't have—but they continued to shout at me just as they had done before. They . . . wouldn't let up on me, and . . . I lost my senses, a little bit."

He felt shamed, remembering the words he had spoken. "I . . . told them it was their fault, for not listening to me. . . . Tiven didn't take that very well, he called me a coward again, and I told him . . . I said that he shouldn't be so reluctant to sacrifice a mere brother for the greater good . . ."

He took a shaky breath.

Taryl spoke carefully. "It sounds like the incident produced bitter memories for a lot of people."

Lenaris nodded, silent for a moment before he spoke again. "You know what the worst part of it is?"

Taryl stopped walking, and Lenaris stopped with her. She turned to face him. "Tell me." Her voice was very soft.

"Taking down that ship interrupted the flow of dolamide to Bajor for exactly one month. One month, and then traffic went right back to the way it had been before."

Taryl met his gaze, and he saw a great sadness in her own. After a few beats, they started walking again.

The two hiked for several hours, moved down the deep forests of the foothills, still mostly untouched by the Cardassians. The Union had a mining operation north and east of these woods, partway up a ridge that bordered the Berain mountain range, but it was barely maintained, now that almost everything of value had been stripped from the soil and stone.

The threshold to Berain City seemed to be eluding them, but every time Lenaris started to worry that they were going in the wrong direction, he would see a familiar landmark, an assurance that he had not lost his way. Berain City held less than a third of its pre-occupation populace, but at least a few thousand people still called it home; there were signs of civilization among the trees this close to it, even coming from the mountains. Finally, he found the creek he'd been looking for, and the bridge—several old logs that had been lashed together to form a crude but functional crossing. Taryl looked down at the rain-swollen stream, hampered along the sides by bright green leaves that had fallen from the dense trees overhead.

She shook the string of gourds. "Not much left. Should we refill here?"

"No. The water looks clean, but it isn't. We're a ways downstream of a Cardassian tailings pond. I would drink it if I had to, but given the choice—"

Taryl nodded as she worked to keep her footing on the slippery old bridge. Lenaris took her hand, and she squeezed his briefly before they came to the other side.

It was just a short distance beyond the creek that they came to the edge of a clearing, one that had apparently been man-made, for there were several cleanly cut stumps dotting the yellow-green meadow. "This is the very out-skirt," Lenaris told her, "where timber used to be harvested. In the old days, we picked and chose among the trees to maintain the forest, but after the Cardassians came, people started getting more desperate."

The two passed through the rest of the forest, which bore evidence of the sustainable timber practices Lenaris had described. The first houses began to appear where the trees were still thick, and then the forest opened and they came to the lowest point of the valley, panning out with a spread of homes, businesses, shrines, and factories, a crooked river twisting through the center of town.

"How will we find him?" Taryl wondered, looking out at the city from the edge of the forest where they stood.

"Simple," Lenaris said. "We go to the nearest tavern, and we ask."

Miras was sick.

She had been struggling for some time now just to avoid falling asleep altogether, working until late into the night for days on end, reading in her bed instead of sleeping in it, fighting her exhaustion to the point of weakening her immune system. Now she had fallen victim to a viral infection of some kind, and was confined to her bedroom where she knew that the most sensible thing to do was succumb. Her aching joints screamed out for rest. She did not want to dream, but she also did not want to prolong her illness. She wanted to get better and get back to work as quickly as possible.

It was late before she finally fell asleep, and despite her exhaustion she still tossed and turned, agonizing over every detail of her past nocturnal experiences—and the one that had not happened in the night. The one that had happened in those lost hours when she had been in the laboratory with the Orb. She was sorry now that she'd ever pursued the artifact. It had affected her mind, somehow, and her only real hope was that time would make the instability fade, would return her peace of mind.

*Miras,* the serene voice of the Hebitian woman beckoned her into sleep. *Miras, I have something to show you.*

"Please, I don't want to put the mask on again," she said, and the blackness of sleep melted into the temperate little room in the black-bricked cottage. The Hebitian woman's face read tender amusement.

"No, Miras. You will not evoke the spirit of Oralius this time." She was holding the mask in her hands.

"Why do I keep seeing you? Why is this happening to me? Is it the Orb?"

The woman smiled. "This corporeal being to whom you now speak. Her name is Astraea."

Miras swallowed. "Do you mean . . . that *your* name is Astraea?"

The woman hesitated. "Astraea is a guide."

"A . . . guide?"

The woman went on. "Astraea is a lineage. My mother's name was Astraea, and my daughter's name will be Astraea."

"Astraea. Please, tell me why I am here. Is this a dream?" It was an absurd question, but she was desperate.

The woman put the mask on her own face for a moment. "All will be revealed. You must find the Book of the Hebitians—the Recitations, where it is all written."

"The book of . . . How am I supposed to find . . . Please, is this real? I don't know what I'm meant to do! Can't I just forget these dreams ever happened, wake up and go to the ministry tomorrow, as I'm supposed to? I don't want this!"

"The Book can be found just beyond the city. It rests within a vessel that is hidden in plain sight."

Miras tried to make sense of this puzzle. The city? What city? She must mean Lakarian City. The ruins. Where the Hebitian civilization had flourished, millennia ago.

The woman removed the mask, and Miras was startled to find that the woman's face had changed. "I am Astraea," she said, and her voice was different as well.

"But . . ."

She put the mask back on her face. "My mother's name was Astraea, and my daughter's name will be Astraea."

She removed the mask, and once again, her face had changed. Miras watched in fascination as the woman repeated the motion again, and then again. She continued to repeat the name Astraea, physically representing how the name was passed through many generations. As she cycled through each new persona, Miras could see that it was not only her face that was changing. Her shoulders were gradually broadening, her limbs becoming more compact, her skeletal ridges more defined. Finally, Miras understood.

"My name is Astraea," the woman said, removing the mask one last time, and Miras was stunned into absolute silence, for she recognized the face now.

Her own face.

Lenaris had started to wonder if it wouldn't be quite so easy to find Tiven Cohr after all. He and Taryl had been to three taverns; at each, the patronage knew exactly who Tiven was, but not exactly how to find him. But at the fourth place they walked into, Lenaris immediately spied Tiven himself, hunched over the edge of a wooden bar with a clay mug of *copal* between his hands, blustering his long-winded war stories and opinions to anyone who was listening—and that appeared to be nobody.

Tiven looked almost just as he had when Lenaris had last seen him, nearly three years before. His gray hair was twisted into several matted strands that were gathered at the nape of his neck with a piece of rawhide. His face was as heavily lined as a map, and his brown eyes seemed to look in opposite directions, belying a man with vision like a sinoraptor.

Tiven hadn't seen him walk into the bar. Lenaris approached quickly, Taryl following.

"This man's next drink is on me," Lenaris announced, though he had very little in the way of currency. He might have to do more than apologize just to get Tiven to stay in the room with him.

The old man's head turned abruptly. "Who the *kosst* . . ." He stopped and leaned back in his seat, looking at Lenaris as if seeing him for the first time—and not liking what he saw. He made as if to stand up.

"Please, hear me out," Lenaris said. He slid into the seat next to Tiven's. "Did Halpas tell you that I—"

Tiven's voice was as bitter as *makara* herb. "He told me that you're still as arrogant and full of yourself as ever."

"Please," Taryl interrupted, her voice almost shaking with pleading sincerity. "Mr. Tiven, my name is Ornathia Taryl. My brother's life is in danger, and I've heard that you're the best warp engineer on all of Bajor."

Tiven softened, but only by a fraction. "You brought a pretty girl with a sob story, eh?"

"She's telling the truth," Lenaris said. "When I was looking for you before—it was just because I thought a warp ship was an intriguing project—but now . . . my friend is in danger, and we need to leave the system if we're going to have any chance of rescuing him."

"Friends die," Tiven said.

"I know they do," Lenaris said. "I understand that."

Tiven turned to Taryl, his voice rough but not without sympathy. "Brothers die, too."

"My brother doesn't have to die," Taryl said. "We can save him, and you can help us."

"And what's in it for me?" Tiven finished the dregs of his cider.

"You could come with us," Lenaris said. "You always said how much you missed space travel—"

"Fine, I'll do it," Tiven said, slamming down his mug.

Lenaris was stunned. "What . . . what did you say?"

"I'll do it, Lenaris—if you just admit that you were wrong." He grinned.

"I was wrong," Lenaris said immediately. "I never should have questioned any of you about the mission, and I never should have said any of those things after it all went wrong, and I never should have left, and I never should have—"

"Whoa!" Tiven said, lifting his hands to his chest in mock defense. "I didn't think you were actually going to do it!" He laughed, gestured for the bartender to refill his mug. "This one's on you," he reminded Lenaris.

"Of course," Lenaris said quickly. "I'll buy you another one after that, if you want."

Tiven cleared his throat, looking away from them. "Truth is, Lenaris, you were right. Of course you were. We were all emotional after . . . what happened. I guess Halpas and I just resented you . . . for being young, and for knowing what you were talking about when you told us not to go through with it."

Lenaris said nothing, feeling nothing from Tiven's validation. It didn't matter who was right—he realized that now. Darin was still dead, Tiven's brother was dead, and Lac would be, too, if they couldn't get to him in time.

"I'll help you fix your ship, if she can be fixed," Tiven said, and pulled on his drink. "I've got nothing better to do these days, nothing but standing in ration lines and running up a tab at every tavern in town." He eyed the bartender. "Tabs that probably won't ever be paid," he said confidentially. "So maybe it's better if I get out of here for a little while. After all—you came all this way . . . and you even apologized!" He laughed, a drunken sound without much mirth. He was the same Tiven that Lenaris remembered, unstable, drunk, mostly well meaning.

Lenaris looked at Taryl, who was smiling with gratitude, the first time Lenaris had seen a genuine smile on her face since Lac's disappearance. "One more thing," Lenaris said, turning back to Tiven. "We need to find Halpas."

The old engineer nodded. "I know where he is," he said, "but whether he'll come is another story."

"He'll come," Lenaris said. "The chance to fly a warp ship? He'd never pass it up."

Tiven removed himself creakily from his stool. "You may be right," he said. "I confess, the chance to work on a warp engine is no small motive for me, either." He took one last draught of his cider. "After all," he added, "I'm an engineer by *D'jarra*—it's what I was born to do."

Kalisi had yet to make the breakthrough that would define her career, and though she knew she was still young, that she had years ahead of her, that didn't make her impatience any easier to tolerate. She was driven not only by ambition—she lived to make her family proud—but by a strong conviction that something needed to be done about the situation on Bajor.

Since coming to work for the science ministry, Kalisi

had been confronted with a lot of disturbing information about the annexation. Too many people had already died, soldiers, mostly, men of all ages, but primarily her own peers. Not even half her friends were betrothed; even a generation earlier, most, if not all of them, would have enjoined by now, been living with parents and grandparents, beginning families. The annexation was changing the heart of Cardassia, which had always been family, and she meant to do something about it.

She'd given it much thought, taken influences and variables into account, and had decided that what the Union most needed was a means to keep track of every single Bajoran on Bajor. The insurgents had managed for too long to slip beneath Cardassian sensors, hide in regions that were supposed to be off limits—where they were forming resistance cells and conspiring to kill soldiers. Kalisi felt certain that if she could successfully address this problem, she could alleviate much of the violence on Bajor. Unfortunately, all proposals for a full-scale identification system—twice, her own team's efforts—had been rejected. The officials in charge of Bajoran affairs had repeatedly insisted that, even if they could afford the exorbitant cost of such a system, they couldn't spare the personnel and equipment that implementing her ideas would require. She needed to approach the situation from a new angle.

Recently, she'd been developing an idea for an automated tagging and reading system, one that could function in the wintertime when the soldiers were hampered by the intolerable cold. She had been staying in her laboratory until late into the night, studying classified reports on past weapons failures and recent Bajoran attacks.

Kalisi's comm buzzed, and she jerked awake, unaware that she'd even been asleep. She rubbed her face, tapped at the panel. Who was even up this late? "Yes?"

*"Kalisi, it's me."* Miras Vara. Kalisi woke up a bit. She

hadn't expected to hear from Miras for a while, after that strange, stilted lunch they'd had, following the odd incident with the Bajoran artifact.

"Miras? Are you in your lab? What are you doing here so late?"

*"I could ask you the same thing, but I'm not going to."* Her friend smiled wryly. *"Kalisi, I know you'll think it's an odd request, but I need to look at the Orb again. It's . . . for a study I'm doing."*

Kalisi was instantly curious. Why would Miras ask to see the artifact this late at night? Not that it mattered anyway. "I'm afraid I can't help you, Miras. After the computer malfunction, it was pulled from general access. The director of engineering says she doesn't want anyone to take it out again until further analysis can be done, but it was put at the end of a very long queue. You've got a wait ahead of you if you want to see it."

Miras looked crestfallen. *"No, Kalisi, it's . . . I need to see it. I've got to convince the head of engineering to let me look at it, just for a few minutes. It wasn't the artifact that affected the computer system. It was . . . I don't know, but it wasn't the artifact."*

Kalisi kept her face impassive, studying Miras. They had agreed that the object must have had a dampening effect on the ministry's system. It was the only explanation. And now Miras denied it. Suspicious, to say the least.

"I'm sorry, but there's nothing you can do," Kalisi said. "You'll have to put whatever research you've got going on hold, unless you can convince engineering that it's something that can't wait."

*"Well, I guess . . . I'll have to come up with some reason to convince them to let me see it. I must. I must see that object."* Miras looked determined, and Kalisi felt more worried than suspicious now. They hadn't been in touch for a while, but Miras had never been like this. The Miras she knew was smart, sweet, slightly passive. Something about that artifact

was making her friend act very strangely. Kalisi knew that she had just recovered from an illness—she looked drawn and too thin—and wondered if the artifact might have had something to do with that, as well.

"Are you feeling all right?" Kalisi asked.

*"Fine, I'm well, thank you for asking."* Miras smiled, but her thoughts were elsewhere, Kalisi could see it in her face. They exchanged vague promises of future meetings. Miras gave her a distracted good-bye and faded from the screen. Kalisi sat back in her seat, thinking.

Maybe the artifact should be put under heavier security. Kalisi recalled some of what Miras had been raving about, after that strange incident—the destruction of Cardassia Prime. And shortly thereafter, she'd fallen ill, had been away from work for days . . .

Kalisi made a quick decision. There were people who could handle a thing like this, and her father knew them. It was late, but she decided it wasn't too late to bring up something that could be of importance to the Union, not if the artifact was truly dangerous. She reactivated her comm.

"Father? I'm sorry to call you so late—"

Yannik Reyar smiled gently at his daughter. *"It's no trouble, my dear girl. It's always a treat to hear from you. How is your research coming? Have I mentioned how proud I am, of you and your efforts?"*

"Thank you, Father, yes, you have mentioned, but it does me good to hear it again. Father, there is something I would like to discuss with you. This is a matter that I believe transcends the military."

His expression sharpened. *"Kalisi, I will contact you on another channel. End the call now."*

She did as she was told, and waited for another call to come through. This was standard protocol for any message relayed that might concern the Obsidian Order, though

Kalisi hadn't had much occasion to make reference to them before now.

Yannik Reyar was not actually a member of the Order. He acted as liaison between the Order and Central Command, and both organizations considered him an impartial entity. His position was unique, and important. Historically, there had been others like him, but none had been active in a time where there had been so much conflict between the two bodies. It made his job a dangerous one, especially since Central Command needed him more than the Order did—and the Order had the means to make him disappear at any time. They had the means to make anyone disappear, but Yannik's position put him at much higher risk. He knew it, and his family knew it, too. But he considered his work to be of value to Cardassia, and bore the risk with some measure of pride. As a result of her father's involvement, Kalisi had come to view the Order with a great deal of respect—in fact, she respected them more than the military, though the latter funded the science ministry's research.

The comm blinked as a scrambled message came through, and Kalisi entered a password to access her father's incoming transmission. "Is it safe to speak freely, Father?"

*"Yes, this channel is secure. What is it you wish to tell me?"*

"It will sound very strange, I'm sure. But . . . the Ministry of Science is in possession of an . . . object that may be of some significance. It came to my attention some time ago, but it's only been recently that I've learned of its apparent effects."

*"What kind of an object?"*

"It's a religious artifact from Bajor. But it seems to have technological capabilities that can't be explained—at least, not yet. The ministry's computer system was disabled for a short period when the object was being studied. The sensors gave false readings."

"Really?"

"The ministry plans to study it further, but . . . you know how inefficiently things are being done of late. It may be years before anyone gets to it. At any rate, after being exposed to it, my friend Miras was raving in a most disturbing manner, and then she became ill. Now she seems obsessed with the thing, wishing to see it again for some unknown purpose. Whatever it is, it has powers far beyond what meets the eye. I'm sure of it."

*"Now . . . just a moment. You say your friend was raving when she saw the object. And then she became ill?"*

Kalisi nodded. "She was speaking of the destruction of Cardassia. That there was a man on Bajor who was going to find something . . . I don't remember what it was . . ." Kalisi closed her eyes for a beat, trying to recall—the eidetic skill that so many Cardassians had perfected had never come easily for her. "Another of the artifacts, I believe. There are supposed to be a series of them. She was quite specific about a man called . . . G'ar, I think. G'ar Osen. But then she said it wasn't his real name, that he wasn't really a Bajoran. It sounded like nonsense, but she was obviously quite deeply affected. I admit, I've grown concerned about her."

*"G'ar Osen? And you believe it was this object that made her so hysterical? This Bajoran artifact?"*

"She's a very sensible person, normally. I'm telling you, Father, I have a bad feeling about this thing, as though it could be some kind of sophisticated weapon, sent under the guise of being a harmless religious object. I think the Order's scientists should see it. Central Command . . ."

She trailed off, knowing that her father felt as she did, about Command's disregard for the sciences, despite its funding of the ministry. But he still appeared uncertain.

"There's more, Father. A professor at the ministry told

me, long ago, that there was a rumor about the object. I did not take it seriously at the time, but she confided that she had heard the object may have had some connection to the Order. It's possible that during the transition when Enabran Tain took office, the item was somehow removed from the Order's storehouse. I couldn't imagine how such a thing could have happened, but . . ."

Her father frowned. *"When Tain became head of the Order, certain objects were alleged to have gone missing . . ."* His eyes went faraway as he seemed to make a decision. He refocused on her, nodding once. *"I will see to it that the proper channels are opened."*

"Thank you, Father. You are good to indulge me."

*"A father always indulges his children,"* he said, his broad face breaking into a kindly smile. *"Especially children who have always been obedient and who have always made him so proud."*

Gul Dukat delivered the news to Damar personally, coming down from his office landing to tell him. The two men faced each other, standing at Damar's station in ops. Damar was eager to return to his quarters so he could contact Veja and give her the good news, but he would not have dreamed of excusing himself from Dukat—especially considering that the gul was responsible for seeing to it that Damar's promotion had been approved so quickly. He was now a first-tier gil, up from second in under a year; he'd never imagined that he could have risen in rank so quickly. He knew that without Dukat's recommendation, he would not have.

"I can't think of a man better suited to climb so swiftly up the ladder of military responsibility," the prefect said warmly. "I wouldn't be surprised if you made glinn before the year was out, Damar."

"Thank you, sir. I am honored to be the recipient of such confidence."

"You've earned it."

Damar shifted a little. He wanted to excuse himself without seeming rude or ungrateful, but it seemed like an awkward moment to do so.

"Veja will be overcome when you tell her, I imagine."

"Yes. In fact I was hoping to——"

"I understand the two of you have planned a little retreat."

"That's right, sir. We're going to the old resort at Tilar."

"Ah, yes. The vineyards. I went there shortly after first arriving on Bajor. It's beautiful there, and usually very private. It used to get very crowded in its heyday, but after rumors started that Bajor wasn't such an ideal vacation spot—well, it's fair to assume that you and Veja won't have much company there."

Damar smiled. "I can't complain about that."

"No. Well, I'm sure you're eager to convey the good news to her. I will see you tomorrow morning, Gil Damar."

Damar grinned helplessly and made his way to his quarters. Veja was sure to be beside herself when she heard the news—for he would be a glinn even sooner than he could possibly have hoped, and when that happened, there would be no reason to delay the enjoinment ceremony any further. Veja would be able to conclude her work with the Information Service, and Damar could expect to have more flexibility in his assignments. He could even hope to be stationed in the Cardassian system, instead of out here on the frontier—for of course, Veja would want to go back to Cardassia Prime once they had been enjoined. He and Veja could expect to spend somewhat more extensive stretches of time together; even if he was called away now and again, it would be a distinct improvement over those sporadic lunches he had shared with her on the station, those too brief stolen hours on the surface. And, of course, they could begin extending their family. He could be a father. That was the part that Damar looked forward to the very most.

He hurried his stride, barely able to contain his excitement.

## 8

Lenaris had been right about Halpas. After rubbing
Holem's face in his unnecessary apology, the brusque old
pilot was all too happy to accompany them back to Tilar
to have a look at the warp ship, along with Tiven Cohr.
He was also happy to use his own little raider to fly them
back to where Lenaris had left the Ornathia shuttle, on the
plateau of the Berain mountains—Halpas knew the traffic
patterns like the back of his hand, and he had no fear of
being detected. "Stick to the legitimate paths, they don't
even look up from the scanners," he'd drawled. It was only
a few hours later that they met again in Tilar.

Before they'd even left the hidden hangar in the foothills, Ornathia Delle had shown up to inform Taryl of the
latest news—Seefa had gone.

"Where did he go?" Taryl asked, an edge of fear and
regret in her tone.

"I don't know," Delle said. "He wouldn't stop raving
about how the Cardassians are going to come here, soon.
He said we all need to take the shuttles and go—get as far
away from the balon as possible."

"I told him—Lac said they didn't get his ship!"

Delle shook her head. "He wouldn't listen," she said. "A
few others have gone as well. Tancha and Res and Vusan . . ."

Taryl looked lost for a moment before pulling herself together. "I can't go looking for Seefa now," she said. "We've got to get that carrier ready to go!"

Lenaris was prone to agree. Seefa could take care of himself. Lac, however—

Halpas and Tiven followed Lenaris and Taryl through the empty fields that lay between the village and the carrier's resting place. "What's all this about balon?" Tiven wanted to know.

"It's how we fuel our ships," Lenaris explained.

Halpas looked stunned, his heavy eyebrows moving back from his forehead. "You mean . . . like the ship you flew here? Are you joking?"

Taryl shook her head. "We distill the balon and isolate the nadion-affected components to stabilize it. We've been doing it for close to five years now, without a single incident."

Halpas and Tiven appeared impressed, and when Lenaris told them that Taryl had created the technology, they were even more so.

"Where did you train?" Tiven wanted to know.

Taryl flushed. "Self-taught," she explained. "My grandfather always said I had a knack for chemistry . . ."

"She's an excellent engineer as well," Lenaris told them.

"Not good enough to fix that carrier," Taryl said.

"Well, you don't have to be," Tiven said. "That's why I've come, isn't it?"

"Yes," Taryl said, "and I'm hoping to learn a thing or two as long as we have you."

Tiven frowned, and Lenaris wondered if he didn't like the idea of an overzealous would-be protégée getting in his way, but the old man said nothing.

They reached the ship in very little time, Halpas and Tiven both doing a terrible job of masking their excitement as they looked it over. "She looks structurally sound," Tiven announced. Lenaris and Lac had almost completely dug the ship out, and their diagnosis had been similar—these old carriers were built sturdy, and even some of the hardest impacts couldn't crack them.

Tiven practically scampered up the side of the wing, climbing down into the cockpit like a man twenty years younger, with Halpas close on his heels. Lenaris and Taryl came in afterward, when Tiven had tapped on a palmlight and was already halfway down to the engine room.

Lenaris followed Taryl and Tiven down into the engine room while Halpas looked over the navigation controls. The old engineer wasted no time in hoisting himself into the maintenance conduit, shifting about and making his inspection for only a few moments before calling out his diagnosis. "Anti-grav's completely shot, the aft piston coil array is fried, rear thrusters are in bad shape . . . and . . . it looks like the auxiliary power is . . . hm . . ."

"What?" Lenaris said.

Tiven bent his body so that his head emerged from the conduit. "Who's been working on the auxiliary systems?"

"That was me," Taryl said quickly. "A long time ago. I didn't make it worse, did I?"

"No, no," Tiven said, his head and shoulders again disappearing into the tube. "It looks like you would have almost had it, actually—you just need two self-sealing stem bolts on the transformer plate underneath the shock absorption circuit."

"Oh—I have some, back in my house!" Taryl exclaimed. "I can go get them right now!"

"That would be helpful," Tiven said. "And if you have a flange-type resistor wrench to torque down those bolts . . ."

"I do," she said.

"Maybe I'd better go with you," Lenaris suggested, feeling that his presence here was a bit superfluous. Taryl didn't discourage him, and they climbed out of the ship together, into the afternoon sunlight.

They walked through the fields in silence for a while, Lenaris simply enjoying her company, as he had been doing since they left Tilar. It was nice to spend time with her without Seefa along. He felt a stab of guilt at the thought, hoping that Seefa wasn't in any kind of danger, but he chased the thought away.

Similar thoughts must have occurred to Taryl. "I think I know where Seefa could have gone," she said glumly. "And I'm sure he wants me to come after him. He's testing me."

Lenaris didn't know what to say. He knew what he would have liked to say—that if Seefa was indeed testing her, then it was an unfair gauge of Taryl's loyalties. How could she be expected to choose between her brother and her fiancé? "Where do you think he is?" he finally asked.

"Back near his family's farm," Taryl said. "The Aro farm was adjacent to my parents' lands, when we were children."

"So . . . your marriage was arranged?" Lenaris already knew as much, but he hadn't heard it from Taryl, he'd heard it from Lac.

"Yes," she confirmed.

"How did you feel about that?"

She looked slightly put off. "I don't know," she said. "It's just how things were always done around here."

"But not anymore," Lenaris pointed out.

They did not speak for a few more minutes.

"Holem," she finally said. A subtle coloration in her tone had him very uncomfortable; he was sure now that she was upset with him.

"What is it?"

"You don't really like Seefa, do you?"

Lenaris bit his lips, cursing the notorious directness of the Ornathia family. "What makes you say that?" He wished with all his heart that something—anything— would distract her from this conversation. A house caught on fire, an underground tremor, the very voices of the Prophets calling out from above . . .

She looked away. "Never mind. You've just answered me."

"What is that supposed to mean?"

"You're chewing your lip like it was a piece of gristle. You always do that when you're uncomfortable."

"Well, maybe it's you making me uncomfortable." Lenaris instantly wished he hadn't said it.

Taryl looked annoyed for a split second before she laughed. "Oh, Holem. Be serious. What is it about him that you don't like?"

Lenaris was taken aback at her laughter. Why did she find it funny that he might be uncomfortable around her? In fact, sometimes he *was* uncomfortable around her, if only because his desire for a more meaningful relationship with her would periodically make his heart feel like it was going to break. But she probably had no idea that his affection for her was anything beyond platonic. She probably regarded him as she regarded her own brother. The consideration of that possibility brought back the unhappy sensation of heartache, and Lenaris blurted out his answer to her question without really considering what her reaction would be.

"He's not good enough for you, Taryl. That's all I have against him."

Taryl looked surprised, but there wasn't time to address the topic any further, for they had reached the village.

Lenaris followed her into the cottage, helping her to gather up the necessary items in a rough satchel. "Let me carry that," he insisted, making to sling the satchel over his own shoulder.

"I can do it," Taryl said, reaching for the satchel and sounding cross.

"Taryl . . ." Lenaris said, not wanting to finish, but

knowing that he had to. He couldn't have tension with her, not now. "Don't be upset with me about Seefa. It isn't that I have anything against him. It's just . . ."

"What?" she asked, and the anger had gone out of her voice. Lenaris thought that she wanted to hear him say it—he hoped she did—

"I can't help how I feel," he said stiffly.

She put her hand on his shoulder, as if to remove the satchel, but she didn't remove it. "And how do you feel?"

He couldn't say anything else, and he thought she looked disappointed for a moment before he realized that she was crying softly.

"Taryl!" he said, alarmed. "I . . . I'm sorry! Seefa will be all right . . . I should never have said anything . . . it wasn't my place . . ."

She came into his arms and he held her close, feeling as he did that it was wrong to enjoy it so much when she was so obviously hurting.

"It's not just that," she said, her voice muffled as she pressed her face against his chest. "I feel as though I was wrong to leave him. What if I never see him again, and the last words we had were angry? I'm . . . the only family he really has, since his aunt and uncle passed."

"You'll see him again. He loves you, and the two of you are going to be married." The words tasted less than sweet in his mouth, but he wanted, he needed, to console her.

"I don't *want* to marry him, Holem."

His body went rigid for a beat. He wondered if he'd heard her correctly.

"I care about Seefa, but I haven't wanted to marry him for a long time. Maybe I just got angry with you because . . . I felt so guilty."

"Guilty?"

"Yes. Because . . . I was . . . glad that he wasn't with me. With . . . us." Taryl began to cry again, her face pressed against Holem's shoulder, her body warm against his. He found that he could not resist holding her a little bit tighter. After a long beat, she turned her face closer to his, so that he could feel her breath on his skin. He brushed her forehead with his lips . . . and before he had quite realized what was happening, he was kissing the ridges of her nose, and then her mouth, softly at first, and then harder as she responded, and then his hands had begun to move across her back, underneath her tunic and around her waist, and her hands were finding their way across the front of his chest, and she had removed the satchel from his shoulder and it dropped to the floor.

Their clothes seemed to fall away as they tumbled to her bed in an eager meeting of mouths and limbs and fingers. They moved slowly, and then quickly, and then slowly again, becoming a single, breathing, living thing for a few stretching moments, their hearts and bodies perfectly in rhythm. Lenaris had been with a few women, had even loved two of them—but this was different, it was *Taryl,* and the depth of what he felt for her far surpassed any love he'd known before they had become friends.

Entangled in her arms, Lenaris felt like he could sleep for days, exhausted and happier than he had been since he was a boy. But there were things that must be done . . . things that he hardly felt like considering now that Taryl was here, pressed against his body. He wanted to just hold her a little longer . . .

But she stood up abruptly, retrieving her clothes from the rough floor where they had been discarded. She didn't look at him as she dressed. "Come on, Holem," she finally said. "We'd better get back."

"Sure," he said, quickly dressing and retrieving the fallen satchel to loop it across his chest. This time, she did not argue with him about carrying it. She seemed determined not to meet his gaze, and he sadly decided that if he hadn't wanted things between them to remain tense, he'd just done exactly the wrong thing.

Damar sat before the companel in his quarters with an unhappy knot in the pit of his stomach. He was not looking forward to this, but it could not be helped. He hoped she would understand; after all, his responsibilities were greater than they had been before his promotion. Veja had to realize that. She had to realize that his obligation to Dukat was immense. He entered Veja's communication code with a great deal of reluctance.

"You are looking beautiful, as always," he said, as Veja's face appeared on his screen. "It pains me to tell you that it will be longer than we might have hoped until I will be able to see you again in person."

*"What do you mean?"* Veja did not look like she was going to take this very well.

"My darling, you have my deepest apologies, but—"

*"Oh, no, Corat. Not the trip to the vineyards!"*

Damar hung his head. "Please, Veja. My duties to the station come first, no matter how much I wish it might be otherwise. You know that as well as anyone."

*"But, Corat, this trip was planned months in advance! How, at this late date, can your duties suddenly have become so pressing that you cannot even take a single two-day pass—only your third since you arrived, I might add?"*

"Veja, do not make this any worse. Dukat asked me if I would be willing to sacrifice this weekend for an important update to the security systems. What could I say? I owe my promotion to him."

*"You mean to say that he gave you a choice? And you chose to do a favor for Dukat, rather than to spend time with me?"*

Damar sighed, his patience waning. "Veja, that isn't how it works. Please, I need your support."

She was quiet for a moment, and Damar hoped she was

reconsidering her reaction, which he felt was tremendously unfair. If she was going to be the wife of an officer, she was going to have to learn to accept certain things. A soldier's duty was always to his superiors.

Her voice was cool when she spoke. *"Fine, Corat. It is regrettable that you cannot come along with me, but—"*

"What do you mean, come along with you? We will postpone the trip to a later date."

*"Oh, no, Corat. I requested this time from my superior, and he gave it to me. I'm not going to spend that time sulking around the settlement. I've always wanted to see Tilar."*

"Veja! Are you mad? You can't go away by yourself, it is far too dangerous to travel alone."

*"Of course, I'll bring Natima. She always has her weekends free."*

"Natima!" Damar scoffed. "She is hardly fit to ensure your safety! No, Veja, you've made your point that you are angry. I have apologized, but there is nothing more that I can do. Please, end this foolishness."

*"I accept your apology, Corat. But I am still going to Tilar. I'll be sure to contact you from the vineyards, to let you know what you are missing."*

Veja ended the transmission before Damar could argue further, and he smacked his palms in anger against the surface of his desk. He decided that she was probably only trying to bait him. He was not going to give her the satisfaction of contacting her again to argue about something so utterly preposterous. He turned off his companel and went to bed, anticipating a sleepless night.

Miras lasted another week before she made her decision, a week of deep consideration, of working up the nerve—a week of terrible, relentless dreams. She dreamed now, knew she'd fallen asleep because she had to watch it all again, relive the nightmare. The Hebitian woman was gone; now there was only the hidden object, the murder, the twisted, smoking ruins of her homeworld.

Someone touched her, and she woke.

It was a stranger, the man in the seat next to hers. "I'm sorry to wake you, but we've gone back down into the atmosphere, and we're approaching Lakarian City. The pilot says we'll be there in just a few moments."

"Oh, thank you, Mister . . . ?"

"Raaku."

"That's right, I remember now." They had briefly introduced themselves shortly after boarding the shuttle. Shortly after Miras had walked away from her old life, possibly forever.

The message of the recurring dreams had continued to unfold for her, although the images remained cryptic, violent, and strange. But she'd come to believe that the discovery of one of the Bajoran Orbs by a Cardassian would mean the end of their civilization—had come to believe it with all her heart, and that belief finally allowed her to embrace her insanity. She had no husband, no children. Her parents lived well outside the city, and she didn't see them often. Her job was interesting to her, but not especially fulfilling . . .

*And if I'm right about this—if this is a vision, a reality that will come to pass—then I have a responsibility.*

She had spent many hours reading through the texts she could find on Oralius, on the Oralian Way—and while many were simple propaganda smears, she'd seen glimmers of a strange but interesting philosophy here and there. From what she could tell, the Oralians were simply spiritual seekers, not the decadent cult she'd always believed them to be.

The brief recorded message from Natima Lang had provided the final push. It had been waiting in her transmissions only the day before, and had confirmed Miras's information about Gar Osen and the death of the kai—not directly, but clearly enough. Natima had been uncharacteristically grim, her expression solemn as she'd cautioned Miras not to continue concerning herself with affairs on Bajor. She'd added that going public with unapproved information was a punishable offense. When Miras had tried to return the call, she'd found that Natima was unavailable.

With clear evidence that there might actually be something to it all, Miras had acted. She'd packed a bag, made a few calls—and had then managed to scramble the Orb's access code in the ministry's database, making it impossible for anyone to retrieve the item without manually opening every single shipping container in the warehouse. All those years studying the ministry's filing system, preparing for her life's work, she'd learned a trick or two. There was a chance that nobody would learn of what she had done until someone actually attempted to find the Orb—but Miras wasn't about to take the chance that she'd be so lucky. She had stepped across a line, a step she couldn't take back.

The man seated beside her looked out the window of the transport shuttle, at the flat, endless desert stretching all around them, beautiful in the early morning light. "Have you seen the Hebitian ruins before, Astraea?"

"Not for many years," said Miras, remembering that she was no longer Miras. She had taken the name of the woman from her dreams, whose face had become her own. She was Astraea now, and after what she had done—traveling under a false name, deliberately misfiling the Orb—she could never go home. She hoped that she would find her confirmation, out here in the desert. She hoped she hadn't just thrown away her career, her *life,* for no reason at all. "I look forward to revisiting them."

In the fairly spacious control cabin of the Bajoran carrier, Lenaris and Halpas were having a look at some of the old ship's navigational systems. While Halpas confirmed that he had never flown this particular model, he was still familiar with most of her instruments. He pointed to a few components, explained their significance to Lenaris, who was feeling slightly overwhelmed with all the information he was quickly absorbing. This was different from studying old schematics—the knowledge Halpas carried included a great deal of information that never would have appeared in any manual.

"Those filter systems there are notoriously touchy," Halpas pointed out. "While these gauges over here can be sluggish at first, once you warp up they get a lot more loose." Lenaris nodded, taking it all in.

"The thing to remember is that a lot of the Cardassian ships have blind spots in their sensor grids, like their planet-based systems," Halpas said. He spoke this in confidential tones, almost as though he expected someone to be listening. "I can show you what I mean once we get out there—" Lenaris felt a thrill at this kind of talk, Halpas's confidence making it clear that this was really going to happen. "—and even more important than that, Cardassian ships have a tendency to require a power surge in order to arm their forward disruptors. As soon as they transfer power, everything else gets sapped—their navigational systems, their shields—and more importantly for us, their sensors."

Lenaris nodded vigorously. He tensed as a faint whirring sound went up on the bridge. The lights across the navigational array flickered once, and then settled into a constant glow. The auxiliary systems had already gone online half an hour before, but it was looking more and more like this mission was going to happen. He was actually going to travel at warp—he was going to leave the B'hava'el system. And he was going to rescue his friend.

Halpas walked him around some more of the ship's controls, quizzing him, pointing out subtle nuances he could remember from the sensor arrays. A few minutes later, Lenaris looked up as Taryl joined them in the cockpit, her expression bright and slightly anxious.

"The warp reactor is online!" she said. "Tiven said it was barely damaged at all—the biggest problems were the antigrav and the thrusters, but he thinks he's fixed those well enough for a decent takeoff."

"A takeoff!" Lenaris exclaimed. "I had no idea we'd be there already. We need to get a better idea of how we're going to mask this thing's signature before we can even think about it, or else—"

"Or else we just go for it," Halpas said.

Lenaris looked at the old man, expecting him to be either joking or ranting on one of his notoriously reckless plans—like the Valerian freighter, only this time, with him aboard instead of Darin. "If we do that, they'll target us before we're even out of the atmosphere," he said.

Halpas laughed. "You're thinking in terms of how a raider flies," he told the younger man. "A ship like this can break through the atmosphere in the time it takes a raider to power up its thrusters. We'll be halfway to Jeraddo before the spoonheads have even noticed us. And by then—"

"But once they have noticed us, we're as good as dead," Lenaris argued. "Their ships could outrun this thing even if it was operating at full capacity, brand-new. The trick is to stay *beneath* their notice."

Halpas shook his head. "We'll lose them," he told Lenaris. "You just leave that to me." He turned to Taryl. "So, just how many of these balon ships do you folks have?"

Taryl frowned. "Seefa took one, and then the other three who left must have taken at least two . . . we've got about twenty of them now."

"Twenty! We won't be needing quite that many. Let's get back to the village and bring a few of them here . . .

and while we're at it, I suggest we find some more volunteers. I'm not sure the four of us are up to storming a Cardassian prison camp on our own, no matter how remote the location."

Aro Seefa had successfully hidden the raider in one of the old drainage conduits, organized a modest food supply for himself, and made his bed. He'd slept, and woken with no idea of what to do next. The concept of leisure time was not one with which he was intimately familiar. In his experience, when there wasn't something to be fixed or retrieved or altered or built, you slept or ate. And neither of those options was feasible when his stomach was so twisted, knotted with a growing certainty that he'd done the wrong thing, leaving the Ornathias.

Seefa had explored these drainage tunnels and ditches many times when he was young, though his aunt and uncle, who had raised him after the death of his parents, had repeatedly warned him not to. The tunnels were ancient, whole sections caving each spring, and they still flooded in the rainy season. But they ran throughout the farms and vineyards of the Tilar peninsula, holding endless fascination for most of the children that had grown up here. Seefa's guardians had so many other children to look after—in all, they'd taken in fourteen occupation orphans who'd needed a home—Seefa had managed to explore the tunnels regularly, often using them to return to his family's lands, where he would hide in the shadows and daydream about being grown and in the resistance, dealing out harsh justice to the Cardassians.

Seefa's biological parents had been among the first Tilari casualties of the occupation. The Cardassians had announced that they would seize the Aro lands when Seefa was just a small boy. Like many of those farmers who couldn't conceive of leaving their land, his parents had refused to relocate, expecting the Cardassians to eventually give up and leave them alone. But of course, it had not worked like that.

Seefa's uncle and aunt, his mother's brother and his wife, lived on one of the farms that the Cardassians had ignored—an unremarkable *katterpod* field, adjacent to the Ornathias' portion of the vineyards, neither of which held much interest for the Cardassians. But the hilly, picturesque *tessipates* of the Aro family's famous coastal vineyards—which had been in Seefa's family for centuries—had been significantly more attractive to Bajor's occupiers. The climate, right on the water, was well suited to their physiology—the winters mild, the summers hot—and they had promptly claimed it for themselves, turning Seefa's childhood home into a Cardassian tourist attraction. Numerous resistance attacks over the years had made it less attractive, however, and the place was usually abandoned but for the handful of Bajoran collaborators the Cardassians had hired to keep it up.

His aunt and uncle had finally been relocated to one of the camps—for their own safety, according to the local Cardassian-kept magistrate—and the Ornathias had mostly managed to keep out of sight, moving to the far edge of their old lands. Many of the smaller farms had been allowed to continue—the Cardassians needed someone to refill their bread baskets—but they had refused to give up their stolen prize.

To be so near his family's rightful portion of the vineyards made Seefa's heart burn. He could smell the sea on the breezes that passed through the tunnels; a few moments' walk would take him to the ruins of the home where he'd once lived with his family. It was painful to be here. And yet, this was his home. This was the place he hoped to return to with his own family, where he and Taryl would raise their children, where they would someday die and be buried.

*Taryl.* She still had not come, though he was sure that she would know to look for him here. They had both played in the tunnels as children, had used them as adults to evade capture, more than once. He was left to assume that she was too busy trying to fix that useless carrier to be concerned with his whereabouts—assuming she even made it back from the trip with Lenaris . . .

Seefa felt his stomach knot tighter. He didn't like not knowing where she was, what she was doing. If anything happened to Taryl while he was just sitting here, he would never forgive himself.

It was the fear that finally drove him out of the culvert, thinking that it might be best to head back to the Ornathias, to wait for word. But as he emerged from the tunnel, he heard something that sent him toward the vineyards, instead, away from where his raider was hidden—the unmistakable sound of a ship landing close by. Not a Bajoran craft—it did not have the right kind of unhealthy growl. It was most assuredly Cardassian, a small shuttle, perhaps, or some similar flyer. They had finally come for him, and they had probably traced his balon signature, just as he'd feared. He'd led them straight to him, as easily as if he'd drawn them a map. *Foolish!*

He thought the ship had landed near the Cardassian "resort" in his family's vineyard. He crept toward it, moving slowly and silently, finally cresting a low hill covered in wild *jumja* trees to get a look. It was a transport shuttle, settled closer to the Ornathias' lands than his own—what he thought of as his own—and there were two Cardassians walking around. Technically, they were trespassing, walking on Ornathia ground, land still owned by Taryl's extended family; Seefa could see that they were on the wrong side of the hedgerow divider, although he supposed they didn't care. Why would they? Who would complain?

The Cardassians were women, dressed all in white. Not

soldiers, then? The dress of these two certainly suggested that they were civilians ...

Two women, alone and vulnerable at the vineyards? It had to be a trick. Perhaps he was being flanked right now, the women decoys.

Hide or attack? Run or fight? He didn't know, but seeing them just wandering around, touching the overgrown plants, acting as though they had some right to be there—it was infuriating. On top of his uncertainty and shame, his depressing memories—it was too much to tolerate. He quickly decided that he couldn't afford to be uncertain. He would act, for better or worse.

He pulled his battered old phaser, aimed directly at the two invaders, and sprinted down the hillside as fast as he could. The two Cardassians did not immediately notice him, but as he drew closer they heard him, and looked up. One of them screamed.

"Quiet!" Seefa snapped in a loud whisper. "How many are with you?"

"I—just us," said one of the women, the one who'd screamed. She looked terrified.

"But more are coming," the other said quickly. "Many more. Soldiers. If you leave now, you might get away."

Seefa squinted at the hot blue sky above him, saw nothing but a scattering of clouds. If she was telling the truth, he could run. Or it might already be too late.

"You'd better come along with me," he said, and gestured in the general direction of the nearest drainage tunnel with his weapon. They needed to get out of sight, fast.

One of the women started to speak to the other, in an urgent hiss. Seefa made an angry noise, and they fell silent.

They reached the culvert and entered the irrigation system, Seefa taking them in confused circles through the complicated labyrinth, wanting to be sure they couldn't be tracked. They walked for nearly a *kellipate*, quiet except for the sounds of one of them sniffling, the occasional drip of water. Seefa had to use his palmlight as the tunnels angled deeper, the chill of wet clay making him shiver. He had a vague intention of taking the women back to the Ornathia camp, but it would be a long walk.

"More will be coming," the bolder of the two women volunteered as he pointed them down another branch. Her low voice echoed. "They know that you're here."

"How did they track me? Was it the balon?"

"Yes," she said. "They've been tracking you for a long time."

Seefa clenched his jaw. He *knew* it. "How long before they get here?"

The other woman spoke in an urgent whisper. "Natima, is this wise?"

Natima seemed to think so. "Let me handle this."

"You had better tell me all you know," Seefa said darkly. He turned his palmlight to Natima's face. She squinted back at him, her lips tight.

"Have they tracked only me?"

The woman hesitated, her pallid face ghostly in the wobbling light. "They have tracked several of you," she said.

Seefa frowned. "Several? How many, exactly?"

"I don't know how many," she shot back. "I only know that it's more than one."

Seefa's heart hammered. If they were tracking shuttles, they might have followed Taryl, too; he needed to know before he risked taking them back to the cell, but it occurred to him that he had never really spoken to a Cardassian before, and he wasn't sure how best to manipulate them. What were they afraid of? What did they respond to? He had no idea.

"We know about all of you at the vineyards," the other woman said.

"Veja! Let me handle this," said Natima.

"What do you mean, *all of us?*"

"She's bluffing," Natima said. "We are only sentries. We don't know everything, we were only sent to confirm that you were in the area."

Seefa was confused . . . and finally, suspicious. "There aren't any more of us," he said sharply. "I'm the only one."

"You just indicated that there were more of you," Natima pointed out.

Seefa shined his light over the two women. Natima looked defiant, but something deep in her expression reflected fear. The other woman—Veja—appeared frightened out of her wits.

"You're civilians, aren't you?"

Neither woman spoke, confirming it.

Seefa sighed, kicking himself for panicking, not sure what to do. They were Cardies, but not fighters; he'd kill them if he had to, but he didn't like the idea. On the other hand, by taking a couple of tourists hostage, he'd made himself a target; someone would be missing a sister or a wife, a patrol would be sent to find their shuttle, and they'd surely find his makeshift camp. He couldn't take them to the Ornathias, not without endangering the entire cell . . .

*I'll have to kill them.* He didn't see that he had a choice.

"Just let us go," Natima said. "We won't tell anyone we saw you."

"You have our word," Veja added, her voice practically a whimper.

Seefa had to laugh at that. "The word of a Cardassian?" He gestured with the phaser, and the three began to walk again.

After a few moments, Natima spoke. "Listen, I . . . I need to relieve myself."

"That must be very uncomfortable for you," he said, without sympathy.

Natima arched an eyeridge. "You've no idea. I don't suppose there's a 'fresher available in these . . . facilities?"

"What do you think?"

Natima nodded. "If you wouldn't mind, then, couldn't I just have a little privacy for a moment? You could turn off your palmlight—no, I suppose you wouldn't do that. Or—I could go down that corridor there—" She gestured vaguely to a branch, just ahead of them, that intersected the main conduit they were walking.

Seefa regarded the woman and was struck for a moment by how . . . almost *Bajoran* she seemed. Something in her expression, the inflection of her voice, her simple desire to relieve herself without someone watching. The effect was unsettling, and certainly not something he would have expected from a Cardassian.

He flashed his light down the tunnel she had indicated, which was badly deteriorated. He knew that this one had no outlet, ending in a heap of sharp rubble—if she had any ideas of escaping, she'd be disappointed. "Fine," he said. "But your friend stays here with me."

"Thank you," Natima said to him, and turned to go down the conduit.

Veja stared at him like a *batos* in a slaughterhouse, her fear a palpable thing, and Seefa looked away. It wasn't his fault that they'd come to Bajor. They were victims of their own arrogance, their own erroneous sense of privilege, and he refused to feel bad serving as the hand of justice.

*I have no choice,* he told himself firmly.

## 9

Opaka accepted the offer of *deka* tea from Ketauna, smiling her thanks. She sipped, looked around his small cottage as Ketauna went to fetch his copy of Dava's Prophecies. Shev, Ketauna's neighbor, occupied himself lighting candles. It was late in the evening, the long summer light giving way to shadows in the little house. In her travels, she had encountered a few dwellings like this one, very nearly identical to the cottage she had once shared with Bekar, and later with Fasil, just outside the Naghai Keep. Most of them had a few minor differences, but they were built so similarly, of nearly identical materials and construction, that she had the unusual sensation of being back in her own beloved home. She missed it, sometimes very much.

"The eighteenth prophecy of Kai Dava," said Ketauna, reverently handing Opaka the open book. He was an artist, and had lived in the house his entire life. A kind man, he'd been a regular member of Opaka's informal sermons since the day she'd arrived in the small town of Yarlin, several weeks earlier. She'd stayed on when she'd realized how many travelers came through the village each summer; it was the biggest settlement along the pass through the northernmost range of the Perikian mountains, right next to a reasonably clean river tributary. She'd pitched her tent in Yarlin's spacious courtyard alongside a hundred others. A good many of them belonged to people who'd decided to walk with her, most from her winter camp, some who'd just shown up along the way—people who'd heard the message and were looking for someone to follow, it seemed, at least for a little while.

"Please, read it aloud," said Shev. Shev believed himself to be an expert on the life and prophecies of Kai Dava. He was a layman, but had several times told Opaka that if his *D'jarra* had permitted it, he would have gone into the clergy. "Ketauna showed it to me three days ago, and I was stunned at what it seemed to imply."

Sulan cleared her throat. " 'The dry ground shall be watered by a generation of sorrow,' " she said.

"That's *this* generation," Shev said knowingly.

Opaka nodded. "Perhaps," she said. She went on. " 'The tears of the people shall water the land, the Tears of the Prophets cast away.' "

"Because the spoonheads have taken them all," Ketauna broke in.

"We don't know that," Shev said. "They say the Orbs were all destroyed."

"The Prophets will look after them," Opaka said. And if They did not, that was also Their will.

"Go on," Ketauna said.

Opaka had studied this prophecy many years ago, but it had been such a long time, she would never have remembered this particular verse without having been prodded by these two, part of her ever-growing congregation. Sometimes, it seemed as if there were as many prophecies on Bajor as there were people, and they were often too cryptic to be deciphered. Ketauna and Shev had asked her here specifically to discuss this prophecy. It was not the first time she'd been asked to give her impressions of a prophecy since she'd begun traveling, and she was sure it would not be the last.

" 'But the Prophets have not shed the last of their Tears,' " she finished.

"You see?" Ketauna said, looking a little triumphant. "Now, what do you think that means, Vedek Opaka?"

Opaka had stopped correcting those who still addressed her as Vedek, although she felt a twinge of regret almost every time; for what, she was not sure. "I can't say, for certain," she told him. "Perhaps it means there are other Tears of the Prophets which have not yet been discovered."

"Well, this would be a good time for someone to find them, don't you think?"

Opaka nodded slowly. "It might seem that way to us, but only the Prophets know when the proper time will be."

"But you have read the prophecies of Trakor," Ketauna reminded Opaka. "He speaks often of the Orb of Prophecy and Change. Nobody has written of it since the time of Kai Dava—"

"Yes, there are many mysterious tales surrounding Kai Dava, it is true . . . but not all are fact. Many have theorized that the Orb of Prophecy and Change was simply another name for the Orb of Souls."

"Or the Orb of Contemplation," Shev added. "But the evidence seems to suggest otherwise. Did you know," he went on, "it was rumored that Kai Dava had an Orb fragment, a piece of one of the Prophet's Tears? They say he had it mounted onto a bracelet, which he wore until the day he died . . . and that it disappeared after his death."

Opaka had heard the story, along with many others about Kai Dava. The idea of someone using a broken Orb as their own personal token had always struck her as troubling, to say the least. Fortunately, there was no evidence to support the legend. . . . None that was known, at any rate.

Her expression must have reflected as much. Ketauna quickly changed the subject. "I suppose you have heard by now that Vedek Gar has been aggressively campaigning for the position of kai. He seeks to manipulate those of us who follow you, Vedek Opaka—he has declared your word to be the viewpoint of the church."

Shev broke in. "He has even moved into your old house. As though he is trying to be physically closer to you, as well as spiritually. I believe he means to deceive your followers."

Opaka nodded absently. She had heard such murmurings before today, and she was not sure what to make of them. She hoped they were at least partially true—that Vedek Gar really did believe the time of the *D'jarra*s was past, though the idea still surprised her. She had not yet had time to puzzle out what the greater impact might be. She looked out one of the windows. "It is growing late," she declared.

"Vedek Opaka, can I offer you a bed for the night? I would be glad to have you take my pallet, and I can sleep up in the loft." He gestured to a short ladder against the back wall of the cottage, and Sulan regarded it with some curiosity. There was a door at the top of it, in the same place as that inconvenient window of her own house—and it occurred to her that the window had probably once functioned as a door, just like in this house. It probably had been equipped with a loft as well, before the long-ago fire.

"It wouldn't be any trouble," Ketauna added. "I take in visitors all the time, especially in the winter. I would enjoy the company, really."

Opaka smiled. "It's quite all right, thank you. I'll return to the village before dark."

"But it will be dark quite soon," he protested.

Opaka turned to Shev, who lived in a similar abode just north of Ketauna's. "Does your house have a sleeping loft like this one? For I believe my old cottage was constructed in a similar manner . . . and it's a bit of a coincidence that I should think of it now, for it was often told that Kai Dava himself lived there once."

Shev answered with enthusiasm. "Ah, yes! The little house just outside the walls of the Naghai Keep—that *was* Kai Dava's house. Indeed, my house has a sleeping loft, just as Ketauna's does."

"Kai Arin told me that there had been a fire. . . . It must have destroyed the loft," Opaka mused. "The door was left behind, but I always thought it was a window."

Ketauna answered. "Yes, but if you had gone into your cellar, I suspect you would have found that the foundation of the house extended beyond the back, where the raised porch would have been, for in the old times, people used to sleep on those porches in the summertime, raised high above the ground so the tyrfoxes and cadge lupus wouldn't trouble them."

"My little house didn't have a cellar," Opaka said—

—and she saw something, then, in her mind's eye, a flash of dream like a memory, so strong and clear that for a moment, she could see nothing else. Ketauna's small home had disappeared. She saw a man in vedek's garb looking out over a vast and fiery pit. He wore a mask, and his body shook with some unknown emotion, one that made him tremble in its violence. She recognized the man, recognized Bajor's fire caves.

"Vedek Opaka, are you all right?"

*It's Gar Osen.* She didn't know how she knew, but she did. He stood behind an open door, his face hidden, the light of open fires dancing across his mask. And she knew things, then, things that she had no worldly way of knowing.

"Sulan?"

The worry in Ketauna's voice drew her back, back from what she knew had been a vision. A frightening one, but to hear the Prophets once more . . . to know that They had chosen her for this thing . . .

"I need to go back to my house," she said. *The cellar.*

"You mean . . . to your tent?" Ketauna asked her, taking her teacup. "At least let me accompany you—"

"No. I mean to my house . . . my house outside the keep, outside the Kendra Monastery. I need to speak to Vedek Gar. I'm going to go find my son . . . I will need him to help me." She spoke her thoughts, as certain of them as she'd ever been of anything.

"Vedek Opaka, can we help?" It was Shev.

Opaka looked up at him. "If you would like to come along, then you may. I believe it might be best to have some help. Yes."

"I'm coming too," Ketauna insisted.

"Yes," Opaka said again, her voice steady. "We'll all go. There is something in that house that . . . I must find. I must find it before Vedek Gar does."

The two men were silent, staring at her with something like awe, but Opaka had closed her eyes. She thanked Them for the burden They had placed upon her shoulders, praying that she would prove worthy.

Natima fumbled with the satchel that was tied around her waist beneath her skirt. Every little noise she made seemed to echo throughout the fetid hole she had been forced into, and she feared the Bajoran who waited for her outside the tunnel would immediately guess what she was up to. There were noises of dripping and sloshing that reverberated from everywhere; she hoped it would drown out her activity. From the satchel she managed to find what she wanted in the near total blackness—Veja's comm unit, with a direct line to Terok Nor. Veja had asked Natima to carry it for her in her waist-satchel, since she claimed it spoiled the neckline of her dress.

Natima activated the communicator, and waited for Damar's inevitable answer.

*"Veja, do you have any idea what the hour is here on the station?"* His voice over the communicator was louder than Natima had expected, and she moved farther down the clammy tunnel as she answered him, fumbling for the volume control.

"Damar! It's Natima! We're in trouble!"

*"What? Veja, I can't hear you. Did you say you're in trouble?"*

Still too loud. Natima pressed her fingers over the pinpoint of a speaker and moved even farther into the blackness. She could see nothing, hear nothing but the ever-present liquid sounds that rushed through the tunnels. She counted on the noise to cover her own, but it seemed that Damar couldn't hear her. She spoke louder.

"Damar! This is Natima Lang! A Bajoran has taken us hostage just outside of Tilar! There are more of them somewhere around here. He was speaking of something to do with balon, I got the impression it was important." There was no answer. "Can you hear me?"

*"I hear you now, Natima, but your signal is weak."* Damar's voice reflected something like fear. *"Is Veja all right?"*

"She's fine, Damar, I will look after her. But you must send someone. Did you hear all that I told you? There are more Bajorans around here, and this man is concealing something about balon."

*"I will send someone immediately."*

A crooked beam of light bounced into the offshoot. Natima whirled around, her fingers closed tightly around the communicator, as the Bajoran, dragging Veja by the arm, lunged at her, trying to get the device. Natima saw her chance and stepped to meet him, grabbing for his weapon, stuck in the waist of his tattered pants. She dropped the communicator but got her hands on the phaser. Veja ran when Seefa let her go to fight Natima for the weapon. The palm beacon fell to the floor, illuminating nothing.

They struggled in the cold dark, Natima's terror lending her strength—and somehow the thing discharged, a brilliant burst of light and sound that tore into the low ceiling of the tunnel. Debris rained down and Veja screamed—but only once, the sound cutting off abruptly.

Natima still had the weapon. Seefa scooped up the palmlight, moving its beam across the darkness, clouds of dust obscuring its meager light.

Natima trained the weapon on the Bajoran, searching the murky dark for her friend—and let out a cry when she saw the crumpled heap on the muddy ground, pinned beneath a massive mound of ceiling stones. She was not making a sound, but she was alive, her face pulled back in an expression of agony.

"Veja!"

The Bajoran was there even before Natima, scrabbling at the rubble. Only her head and one arm were visible beneath the pile of rocks.

"Help me!" he shouted.

Natima dropped to her knees, tried to keep the weapon trained on the Bajoran as she dug with her free hand.

"You might as well put that thing down," the man told her, without looking away from his work. "There was only one good blast left in the power cell."

Natima did not know whether to believe him, but considering Veja's condition it suddenly seemed unimportant. She put the weapon in the waistband of her skirt and began hauling the rubble away from Veja's body. Veja had started to pant, taking in short gulps of air, her eyes shining with fear and pain.

"Don't worry," Natima said, digging, babbling at her friend. "You'll be fine, we'll get you to a doctor soon, everything will be fine."

The Bajoran continued to pull at the rocks, but his expression was grim as he looked over Natima's shoulder, back toward the main conduit they'd left behind. He saw her looking and nodded in the direction of the tunnel.

Natima turned to look, felt her heart sink at what was illuminated by the dim glow of the light. Where the opening had been, now there was only a wall of crumbled rock and clay that continued to spill its gritty contents into the tunnel. They were trapped.

Gul Dukat finally looked up from his computer screen. "Balon? Are you certain she said balon, Damar?"

"I'm not certain of anything, Gul." Damar could feel each second tick by. "Except that they need help. We need to send someone to Tilar right away."

"Yes, certainly, but the part about balon . . . I received word, just about a week or two ago, that a Bajoran man was apprehended either on or near Derna. If I'm remembering correctly, traces of balon were found in the area after more extensive scans were performed. I didn't think much of it at the time, but . . ."

"He may have had something to do with the Bajoran who is holding the women captive," Damar said quickly. "But we must find them if we are ever to know for sure."

"Indeed, Damar, you have my authorization to take a shuttle to Tilar."

Damar was taken aback. He had expected Dukat to let him go, but not alone. "I will need backup, sir. There's no telling how many there are."

"I thought you said there was only one."

"Yes, sir, but . . . But perhaps more are involved. You know how the cells work."

Dukat nodded. "Very well, take Garresh Trach with you, I can't spare anyone else while we're installing the new security features. I'll inform the nearest ground division; they'll provide whatever else you need. Report back to me as soon as you find out anything more about the balon. Meanwhile, I'll try and see what I can glean from the Bajoran with the shuttle. I seem to recall that he was taken to Pullock V . . ."

"Thank you, sir." Damar promptly left Dukat's office and could scarcely keep himself from running to the lift, anxious to get to Veja, though he was still disappointed that Dukat would only appoint a single enlisted man to accompany him. He pressed his comcuff and raised it to his mouth.

"Garresh Trach, this is Gil Damar. Please meet me at shuttle pad 3. We're going to Bajor. I will brief you en route."

Natima and and the Bajoran had finally managed to clear the rocks and broken chunks of clay pipe from Veja's body, and now the man simply sat, speechless, watching Natima as she stroked Veja's hair and squeezed her hand. Veja had drifted in and out of consciousness, crying in pain during her moments of lucidity. A wet, seeping patch of darkness stained the front of her dress. Natima had found only superficial wounds to account for the blood, but had no doubt that there had been internal damage—how much, she did not know. Veja had finally swooned into a kind of sleep, for which Natima was grateful.

She sat back on her heels, trying to think. Damar would be looking for life signs in the vineyards, not wherever they'd ended up. By the time he widened his scan, Veja might be dead. She would have to find the little communication badge, tell Damar what had happened.

The Bajoran watched Veja, his expression strange. He seemed unhappy that she had been injured, as if he'd somehow forgotten that this was all his fault. Yet she didn't feel hatred for him, perhaps because she didn't feel it coming from him. His intentions, unclear before, were obscured even further. He'd been quick to help Veja—of course,

Natima had been holding his weapon by then, so it seemed likely that he was only trying to prove himself useful to avoid being killed.

"Should we try to dig ourselves out of here?" she finally asked.

"We disturb that pile of rubble, we're going to invite another cave-in," he said. He didn't seem angry or crazed, only tired.

Natima looked down the dark passageway in front of her, and pointed into the blackness. "What if we try to go that way?"

"I don't know. The tunnel ends in another pile of rocks. It's a dead end."

"We could at least check," Natima said. She stood up, looked around her feet for the communication device by the thin light of the palm beacon, lying on the floor by Veja. With the mounds of dirt and rock that had come down, she'd never find it, but unless there was some obvious way out, she'd have to look. It might be their only chance.

The Bajoran also stood, and Natima took a step back, hand on the weapon tucked in her skirt—and heard a synthetic crunch beneath her heel.

She forgot about the Bajoran, dropped to pick up the communicator. She tapped it, but it only squawked strangely in response.

"It's broken," she said, crestfallen.

"Give it to me," the Bajoran demanded, and Natima instinctively pulled it away.

"No."

"I might be able to fix it. I'm an engineer."

"You've never even seen anything like this before."

"I've fixed plenty of things that I had never seen before," he informed her drily. "I can do it. Just give it to me."

Natima hesitated. He might be able to alter the signal

somehow, to contact his cell. She knew full well that Bajorans could be frighteningly resourceful when they wanted to be. On the other hand, at least someone would dig them out. She handed it over.

Seefa popped the badge open with his fingernails, examined it closely with the palm beacon. "I think I might be able to fix it," he murmured. "But," he said, looking up at her, "if I do, your friends are just going to put me under arrest, send me to a work camp—or execute me."

"I won't let them," Natima said quickly, though she knew it was no use. Bajorans were suspicious by nature, and she had no doubt that Damar would not stand to see him live, after what had happened to Veja.

He put the badge in his pocket. "Let's have a look at the other exit," he said. "We'll have to consider all our options."

Natima looked down at Veja. She did not look well, her eyelids shiny and her breathing shallow. She did not like to leave her friend here alone, even if it was only for a little while, but she saw no other choice. She was not about to let the Bajoran out of her sight if she could help it.

Dalin Kruva of the *Hideki*-class Cardassian patrol vessel *Drakamair* was just returning to Pullock V from patroling the edge of the system when he received the systems-wide alert. Such transmissions from Terok Nor were not unusual, but they rarely concerned patrol ships that were this far from the Bajoran system. Open calls were usually for troops to go down to the surface of Bajor, with the very occasional bulletin in regard to a Tzenkethi or Federation vessel. The transmission was audio only, but Kruva recognized the prefect's unmistakable tone and cadence.

*"Patrol vessels, this is Gul Dukat. I have been alerted that there may be a handful of Bajoran insurgents who have begun*

*using balon-based fuel sources in order to avoid detection of their spacecraft. I am issuing an alert status in the following sectors . . ."*

Kruva was surprised at the Bajorans' resourcefulness, though he supposed he shouldn't have been. They weren't as primitive as they seemed. Not that he was concerned; the insurgents wouldn't come near him, not in balon-powered ships. It would take a balon vessel a week to get out of the Bajoran system, at best, and by then it would be out of fuel.

Yawning, Kruva turned away from the transmission as his ship's sensors read another vessel in the sector—a Cardassian ship, *Keldon*-class. He hailed the vessel.

"This is the patrol ship *Drakamair,* authorization code 1-1-4-7 *chavat.* Please state your code and your purpose in this sector."

*"This is the* Koeder, *outbound from Pullock V, authorization 8-9-5-5 po'tel. We are escorting Union officials back to Cardassia Prime."*

Kruva scanned the numbers and found them to be legitimate. The officials had been at the colony to witness an execution of Bajoran terrorists, political prisoners, and such; he allowed the ship to pass without further challenge, slightly bored by the repetitive nature of his work. He continued on his course, tuning the midrange sensors' sweep cycle to maximum. This area was often thick with Tzenkethi vessels, and some of the more adventurous Ferengi pirates operated in this region as well. It was a risk to divert power from the disruptor banks—it was not patrol procedure—but Kruva felt it was worth it. He rarely needed his weapons, and watching the traffic was his only diversion.

As he neared Pullock V, his sensors again alerted him to a vessel coming out of warp. He could not get an immediate read on the ship's type, but after a moment he discerned it to be an outdated Bajoran carrier, flying erratically as it slowed to impulse. It was obviously damaged, and posed no threat to him. Likely it was manned by Yridians or some other opportunistic people who had no qualms about using other species' technology, but the cryptic alert from Dukat had left him cautious.

"Bajoran ship, this is the Cardassian patrol vessel *Drakamair.* State your business in this sector, please."

The carrier did not respond, continuing to fly in a strange, lopsided manner. At least one of its thrusters was out. Dalin Kruva was becoming annoyed. "Bajoran ship, I repeat: state your business or I will open fire."

Suddenly, the carrier launched two objects the size of small shuttles. They began flying toward Pullock V, keeping in a tight formation.

Kruva ran a scan on the emissions of the two objects and detected nothing . . . But his scanners wouldn't pick up balon, not without recalibration. Kruva frowned. The lack of a detectable fuel signature seemed proof positive. But whether to pursue the small ships or the carrier was the larger question.

He decided to go the easier route, taking care of the tiny ships first. The carrier was practically crippled, he could finish it off anytime, but there was a slight chance that one of the other vessels could get away if he didn't act now. He quickly transferred power to the ship's forward disruptor banks, locking on to the nearest shuttle. He took it out easily, its blip on his transponder vanishing as the *Drakamair*'s weapons blasted it into twisted bits of floating scrap. Without a moment's hesitation, he targeted the second shuttle, which had managed to get just far enough to force him to power his ship a short distance before eliminating it as well. He turned his attention back to the carrier, but to his surprise, the ship seemed to be gone. Judging by the ion trail he detected, the ship had gone to warp. Powering up his sweep cycle, he followed the ship's warp signature, and he set a new course to give chase. He was not yawning now.

◆ ◆ ◆

Glinn Tedar's senses felt especially dull today. Although it was what passed for summertime on this continent, his fingers still felt stiff in the damp chill. The thin veneer of sunshine did little to stave off the bone-penetrating cold. How he hated this planet! He was counting the days until he would be sent home to his wife and family. The border fights would have been preferable to this backward, icy chunk of misery. He regarded the mud on his boots as he stepped out of the forest, wrinkled his nose in disgust. There was nothing so wretched on Cardassia Prime as this gloppy, sucking terrain that seemed to exist everywhere on Bajor, even when there hadn't been rainfall in weeks.

He had been careless in his rounds today, ignoring many signs that people had been in the woods. He'd spent countless patrols following such signs, and they never led anywhere. His outfit hadn't had much luck locating terrorists in this region. They either didn't exist, or they were just too savvy to leave evidence of their presence. At this point, Tedar didn't much care which scenario was true; he just wanted to get back to the barracks where it was warm.

He heard a rustling in the trees behind him and hesitated, hoping it would be another soldier from his squad, although they weren't supposed to meet back together for another *kellipate* or so. He raised his comm, ready to call for backup, but then relaxed. He saw a couple of Bajoran children picking their way through the forest. They looked awfully small, though Tedar couldn't begin to guess their ages. Bajoran children matured very differently from Cardassian, and they all looked like babies to him.

It disgusted him that the Bajorans allowed their children to roam so freely, running loose like animals. He would have had sympathy if he didn't already know them to be petulant monsters most of the time, probably from lack of decent supervision and tutelage. Cardassian children would never have been unaccompanied like this—in fact, Cardassian children would have been studying, honing their bodies and minds for the collective betterment of the State. There were games, but they were practiced rather than played, teaching skills necessary to become productive citizens of the Union.

Tedar wondered if he should acknowledge the children. Of course, they posed no threat to him, and they were not traveling outside the proscribed boundaries—there was no law against what they were doing—but Tedar thought there ought to be one, for their own safety. It annoyed him that these children would no doubt grow to be just as useless and defiant as the adult Bajorans were—that sort of attitude probably originated in the kind of lenient parenting that had allowed these two to roam about the forest by themselves. The children had come close enough now that he could see they were a girl and a boy, the girl being the elder of the two. She was scolding the smaller one, a brother, perhaps. Tedar wasn't sure—Bajorans all looked essentially the same to him: bland, fleshy features, crinkled nose. The girl child did have one distinguishing feature—her hair was a deep, fiery red.

Tedar decided to put a bit of fear into these two. "Halt!" he barked abruptly, and the children jumped. The girl dropped what she had been carrying, a rough drawstring bag, which fell and spilled its contents—several large, ripe *moba* fruit.

Tedar trained his disruptor on the frightened whelps, and bent over to pick up the fruit. "Where did you get these?" he asked the girl, whose expression wasn't as fearful as he'd expected.

"My papa," she said.

"Papa," the little one echoed, and began to snivel.

"Quiet," the girl whispered, but the boy began to

whimper even louder. The noise grated at Tedar's worn nerves.

"Stop that!" Tedar snapped, pointing his weapon directly at the pathetic little urchin.

"Don't you shout at my brother!" the girl screamed, and to his great consternation, she picked up one of the fallen *moba* fruit and tossed it directly in his face. Before he could quite gauge what had happened, the girl had grabbed her brother by the hand and begun to sprint through the forest, dragging the little boy behind her.

Wiping the sticky nectar from his eyes, Tedar was amazed at how quickly the child was moving, but he wasn't about to be bested by a couple of dirty-faced imps. He set off after them, catching up quickly, grabbing the little girl by her tangled, flame-colored hair.

"Ow!" she shrieked. "Let go of me!"

The boy cried out in baby-talk for his sister, and Tedar grabbed him by the arm with his free hand. The child fought to get away, but he weighed about as much as a bird, and Tedar lifted him off his feet with no trouble. The children thrashed in his hands.

Tedar suddenly felt very foolish, wasting his energy on a couple of squirming brats. "What are your names?" he demanded. "I don't mean to harm you, I just want to know where you belong."

"We belong in Dahkur," the girl replied, through gritted teeth. "This is our home, and you can't tell us we can't be here!"

He tightened his grip on the girl's hair, twisting until he felt a good many strands breaking away from her scalp. Tears were running down her face, but he could see that she was struggling not to cry. It made him all the more angry to see her fight against her natural response, and he gave her hair another firm yank before he threw her to the ground.

"I can tell you that I think you're a disgusting little churl whose parents are negligent to have let you in the forest by yourselves! You're lucky I have a soft spot for children, otherwise I might have shot you straightaway!"

"We aren't d–doing anything wrong," the girl insisted, her sobs finally having gotten the better of her. "You l-l-let my brother go right now!"

Tedar pulled the crying boy close to him. "Perhaps he would be better looked after in an orphanage," he suggested, "since your parents can't be bothered to keep track of him. He's practically a baby!"

The girl hiccuped through her sobs. "I look after him j-j-just fine!"

"Tell me your name, or I will take him to an orphanage—and you're welcome to accompany him, if you like."

"K-K-Kira Nerys, and R-Reon."

"Kira?" he repeated. He considered the name, knowing he had heard it before—knowing that it was supposed to mean something to him. And in a beat, he remembered. Dukat's Bajoran mistress—her name was Kira . . . something. He couldn't remember her other name, but he was certain that her family name was Kira—and that the Kira family was to be left alone. These children could be related to her, could even be her own. He released the boy's arm, and the child commenced to crying louder than ever, as if jostled awake from a state of shock.

"Go home," he ordered the girl. "Go and fetch your bag where you dropped it, and go home. I don't want to see you here again."

"But," the girl said, wiping the grimy tears from her face, "we were supposed to take that *moba* to Sorash Mabey. She's ill, and Papa said—"

"I don't care what your papa said," Tedar shouted, scarcely able to believe that this stubborn child would be arguing with him after he'd just done her such a tremendous kindness. "Just get out of here. If I see you again, I'll kill you."

It wasn't true, of course. Tedar could not have taken the risk of hurting any relation to the Kira family, but they probably didn't know that. Tedar shook his head, thinking of Dukat and his "cultural" exchanges—disgusting, and a lot of the men on the ground felt the same, but it was not wise to speak of such things.

He holstered his disruptor and watched the two children run back to retrieve their bag of fruit, balling his fists to ward the cold away from his fingers. This loathsome tradition of allowing children to . . . *play* . . . Tedar would never understand it. But then, it wasn't his job to understand things. He went where they sent him, did as he was told, and left the understanding to others.

Horrible planet. Tedar slogged on, wishing he was home.

## 10

Halpas was struggling with the controls on the old carrier, which had not behaved exactly the way he'd thought it would. It had been a long time since he'd flown a warp vessel, of course, and he'd never flown this particular model, but the ship was bucking and wobbling madly when it was not at warp, the inertial dampers damaged enough that they could actually feel some of it. Perhaps they'd taken it out a bit hastily, but he *had* managed to get it to the Pullock system, and that in itself should have warranted him significant congratulations.

Tiven Cohr, standing behind him, spoke up. "Do you think it worked?"

"I don't know," Halpas said. "We went to warp before I could see what happened." This was the second patrol vessel they had encountered since leaving Bajor's atmosphere; the first they were able to evade simply by exploiting the blind spots in their security grid; Halpas had been counting on them—and he turned out to be right. But they weren't so lucky with this ship—this spoonhead had already spotted them, and Halpas had been forced to launch a couple of their unmanned raiders in order to distract him.

"They're bound to find us eventually," Ornathia Taryl said.

"They might, but I'm staying in the wake of a Cardassian transport ship that passed through here. With luck, the patrol ship might actually pass by without noticing us."

"That would take a lot of luck."

"It took a lot of luck to get this scow spaceborne in the first place, let alone to warp." He grinned at Ornathia, whom he'd come to like despite himself. She was certainly a know-it-all, but then, she had been a surprising boon to the planning of this operation—for a farmer. Not to mention the business with the balon. It was hard not to be impressed by that.

"What'd I miss?" Lenaris entered the bridge from the shuttlebay, where he'd been supervising the launch of the autopilot vessels. Like the rest of them, he was dressed warm. The ship ran bare minimum life support; comfort wasn't a consideration.

"Nothing," Halpas said. "We went to warp before I could tell if the Cardassians took the bait. Now we've got to worry about whether or not they've picked up our trail."

Taryl was examining the sensor readouts. "I think they've picked us up," she said nervously.

"Looks that way," Halpas agreed.

Taryl looked around the room. "We'll have to launch another raider in their direction—give them something to stop and shoot at—then they'll have to power down their sweep cycle, just long enough for us to turn back around and sneak by them."

Lenaris shook his head. "We only have four shuttles left."

"I don't see that we have much choice," she told him.

Lenaris frowned. "If we need those ships to bail out later . . ."

"This isn't the time for cautious pragmatism, Lenaris," Halpas said. "We've got to do whatever works, or there might not *be* a later."

Lenaris looked as though he might argue, but then he glanced at Taryl and quickly backed down. "Okay," he said. He headed back to the shuttlebay to program another of the raiders for an autopilot launch.

Halpas was annoyed with the younger man's persistent pessimism, but he was not a man who spent too much time thinking too far beyond the most immediate step. Truthfully, he was a little surprised that they'd made it this far, but he'd always felt that way, in every mission he'd taken part in.

There were only nine of them aboard, the bare minimum needed to pop a prisoner free from one of the camps at home—and that was assuming they had schematics, practice time, probably some small intervention bought by bribe . . . They had none of that, here, their offworld venture entirely carried by Ornathia Taryl's wish to free her brother. Their plans were vague, their knowlege of the camp minimal; it would be a miracle if they managed to find Lac and get him back to Bajor.

Once the raider had been launched, Halpas watched the sensors closely, waiting to make the call. He couldn't afford imprecision, not now. The ship might have been damaged, but it was careful piloting that would make this kind of maneuver a success or a failure. A bad pilot couldn't save them from a Cardassian patrol even if the ship had been whole. His eyes glued to the transponder, he waited just another second, or less, and then—*now!* He reversed direction.

"I see their signature," Taryl said, pointing to an icon blinking on the sensors. "That's them. We've passed them."

Tiven peered over her shoulder, turned to Halpas. "Do you think they saw us?"

"They may have, but it looked like they dropped out of warp, probably checking out the raider."

"We can only hope," Lenaris said, returning to the bridge from the shuttlebay once again.

"We're coming up on Pullock V again," Taryl said. "Looks like the warp signature we're hiding in came straight from here."

"Are you sure that's Pullock V?" Halpas said. "How many planets are in this system?"

"Didn't you look at the charts, Halpas?" Taryl's tone was light. "I should have just committed to driving this heap myself."

Halpas patted the ship's flight control panel. "Who would keep her company while the rest of you beam to the surface?"

Taryl's finger was on the sensor array again. "Look, Halpas. Correct me if I'm wrong, but it looks like . . . the settlement's beam-shielded."

Halpas cursed. He hadn't expected this. A prison camp on a planet in an uninhabited system—why the extra security?

Taryl sounded worried. "We'll have to take the raiders down, time ourselves against their sensors."

"We can't take the raiders," Lenaris argued. "Two of them can barely hold two people apiece. We *might* be able to squeeze four into the third, but there's no telling how it'll behave with that much weight. And it won't leave any room for Lac."

"We can do it," Taryl said, though she sounded less than certain. "We have to. If we can get inside, we can shut down the shield. Then Halpas could use the transporters to get everyone else out."

Halpas nodded along, more certain by the moment that they weren't going to survive—and more exhilarated, at the very slight chance that they would. What they were attempting was unprecedented, which was why it might actually work. And they'd have help on the inside, once the prisoners realized they were being liberated.

*And it'll make those spoonheads think twice about who they're dealing with.*

"But—" Lenaris began, but he didn't finish, apparently realizing that it was the only way. "All right," he said. "Let's go below and tell the others. Tiven, you can ride with me."

"I'm riding with Taryl." Tiven grinned.

Lenaris rolled his eyes. "Halpas," he said, "set her in orbit, and stand by for our signal."

They nodded to him, and headed for the shuttlebay.

"I've located the transport," Garresh Trach announced. "Sensors show it to be docked at Tilar, just where it was reported to have landed."

"Well, take her down," Damar ordered irritably. He hadn't expected Veja's transport to be anywhere but at the vineyards.

Trach landed the shuttle clumsily, and Damar cursed himself for letting the younger man pilot. He had wanted to exercise his authority by being in command, but Trach lacked experience at everything.

"Do you see any Cardassian life signs?" Damar asked.

"No, only Bajoran. See for yourself." He pointed out the sensor results. A cluster of readings at the resort, undoubtedly groundskeepers and staff.

"We need better scanning equipment," Damar muttered.

"We might have more luck with handheld scanners," the garresh offered. "More precise, though we have to be in close range."

"Fine. Get me a tricorder, and bring one for yourself."

"Yes, sir."

The two men exited their shuttle and surveyed the land around them. The air was thick with humidity, and cool, but the sun was bright and warming. The vineyards were hilly, a wide expanse of land, green like Bajor's seas, with *tessipates* and *tessipates* of leafy vines, creeping up dark wooden stakes that had been driven into the dark ground.

The soil beneath his feet was rich and black, the long, spiky leaves that sprouted thickly from the vines rustling in the breeze, their deep green cutting sharply against the charged blue of the cloudless sky. Damar could see why the first Cardassians to Bajor had claimed this spot and why it remained a popular destination, even after the repeated terrorist attacks here in the early years of the annexation.

*Veja,* he thought, and felt his stomach knot.

Damar examined his tricorder readouts. Still no Cardassian biosigns anywhere nearby. Where were the soldiers? There was a base not a few hours away by skimmer.

· He contacted the base, spoke to the glinn in charge—his name was Ratav, and he had a short temper and was not afraid to use it. It seemed that a full half of their surface transports had suffered fuel-line sabotage by resistance hands, only the night before. Ratav's soldiers were pulling double shifts, and patrols had been rendered effectively useless for however long it took to repair the damage.

"But the situation here—" Damar started, aware that he was risking himself, arguing with a superior, but aware also that his position at Dukat's side meant that some allowances would be made.

Glinn Ratav obviously didn't think so. *"I'll be sure, once my working ships come back—after having run patrols for twenty-six hours straight—to send a squadron of my finest, to help you find your female."*

He said it with no trace of sarcasm, but the message couldn't have been clearer. Damar gave it up, promising revenge another day. It seemed they were on their own, at least for a while.

"We'll separate," he told the garresh. He called up a topo map on the tiny screen, traced out two paths that should allow them to cover the most ground. "Contact me at fifteen-minute intervals, unless you come across anything that could help us—anything at all, no matter how trivial."

"Yes, sir." Trach extended his scanner and headed off into the seemingly endless stretch of curly vines and wafting leaves.

Damar headed off at an angle, sweeping the scanning device, watching for signs that people had walked through recently. The smell of the air, of warm plant decay, the sounds of insects and small wildlife moving through the brush, all worked to distract him, but he could think only of Veja, of their last words together. He walked over a number of gullies and ditches, with muddy, standing water at the bottoms, swarms of insects hatching from the decaying muck. He came to wider trenches with steep sides, wide enough for a tall man to walk through, lined with flat, interlocking stones and outfitted with metal runners built along the vertical sides. Inserted into the runners were sheets of old metal, twisted and corroded with age. Damar stopped to examine one of them, and understood that it had once been used to dam the drainage ditch, probably during the dry months of summer. The ditch led to the base of a large hillside, where it disappeared into the ground. This irrigation system was extensive, to be sure, but it had run dry for some reason. Perhaps this leg of it had been cut off from the main water source.

He walked for a significant distance before he got anything—a weak biosign that appeared to be Cardassian. He moved the scanner about, watching the flickering numbers, followed its strength on a path that branched from his own. A second biosign had joined the first—they were definitely Cardassian, and there was a Bajoran with them.

*"A Bajoran has taken us hostage . . ."* Why had Natima called him, and not Veja? Damar moved faster, tearing through the virulent undergrowth.

He grew closer to the biosigns, drew his phaser—and watched, puzzled, as they started to fade. He reset the scanner and began again, but the readouts were the same, as though he were picking up signals through something, the density of that substance changing as he walked . . .

*Underground.* Those drainage ditches.

"Garresh Trach," he barked into his comcuff. "Lock on to my signal and report to me immediately."

Astraea was frustrated. She had been so sure that she would find something here in Lakarian City. She had been certain that she would find the original location of the ancient black stone cottage, either by landmark or . . .

*Admit it. You thought you'd* feel *it, sense something that would give you direction.* After a long day of searching, she was embarrassed by her previous certainty. She had scoured the area, the ruins, even the meager museums that displayed what was left of the Hebitian artifacts—anything that hadn't been sold off to help fund the military was exhibited here. But of what there was—broken urns, carvings, simple tools—there was nothing that spoke to her in any meaningful way.

She left the last preserved ruin, some sort of stable, to the few wandering sightseers and scientists that had shared her flight out, and started walking, lost in thought. The hot, dry day was soothing, though the dust was relentless . . . and she had gone back to struggling with truth and reality, afraid once more that she'd made a terrible mistake.

Her dreams were real—she had been so sure of that. The simple act of reviewing those images now, those fragments, affirmed their substance in her mind's eye. They *had* to be real. If they weren't real, she had jeopardized her future without just cause, had decided to leave her home, her career, her *family*—she could scarcely even acknowledge the profundity of what she'd given up.

She had not been gone long enough for anyone to really worry about her, she supposed. Perhaps she should go back home, confess what she had done, and accept the punishment? Certainly, she was guilty of no less than deliberate sabotage—a crime that was usually punished by execution—but the Orb had affected her somehow. Perhaps she would not be held fully responsible.

No. The effect it would have on her family, the disgrace of having a traitor for a daughter—it might be better if they never knew what had happened to her. It was already too late to go back.

She wandered toward the outskirts of the ruined city, checking her timepiece as she walked. She had booked transport on a shuttle to Cardassia II, scheduled to leave in the early evening. Her plan had been to find the book that the Hebitian had told her of—hidden in plain sight—and go into hiding for a while herself, plan her next move . . . dream whatever needed to be dreamed, to complete this insane quest.

She looked out at the flat horizon just to be absolutely sure that there was nothing here—no remnants of the last Oralians. Although, she corrected herself, they were not the *last* Oralians, they were probably the first. The last Oralians must have lived in Cardassia City, since they still existed when she was a baby.

Astraea stopped walking, the truth opening before her like a flower. Cardassia City! The last Oralians existed just decades ago, not centuries. If there were any remnants of the Oralian Way, it would be outside the last known enclave of planetside followers, which was in Cardassia City! In fact . . . Something so obvious occurred to her then, she was stunned that she had not considered it before. *Like something in plain sight, but hidden.* In her dream, the first of those significant dreams she had experienced, she had been walking toward the stone cottage from the city, from her home. It had been under her nose this entire time.

*I am looking in the wrong place.*

❖   ❖   ❖

Natima and her would-be captor had begun systematically moving rocks and heaps of dirt away from the dark branch of the tunnel they'd been trapped in. The Bajoran had climbed to the top of the pile to ensure that it was relatively stable, and now he worked at clearing the debris, lifting the heaviest rocks. Natima scooped dirt back into the tunnel with her hands and feet, ignoring the resultant scratches. As they worked, the palm beacon began to flicker.

"Will we be able to continue doing this in the dark?" Natima asked. Her voice sounded hollow against the cold, wet ground all around them.

"Let's just worry about what we're doing, all right?"

"But we should think about it before it happens, so we can formulate a plan."

"It's pointless to consider things that *might* happen. I think we'll come to the end of this before the palm beacon gives out."

"You think, but you don't know."

The Bajoran stopped working for a moment. "You certainly are preoccupied with foresight, for a Cardassian."

"What are you trying to imply?"

He went back to work. "Do I need to imply anything? Your people came here to steal our resources, and you burn the ground after you. I hate Cardassians, isn't that obvious?"

"Sure," Natima said. "And look where it's gotten you. Stuck in a tunnel with two civilian reporters. We'll probably suffocate in here."

"We won't suffocate," he said. "These tunnels are old, the rock has shifted. There's a wide rift not a minute's walk from where we are, on the other side of this heap."

Natima had nothing to say, she just continued to lift handfuls of rubble away from the blocked opening, and the Bajoran went back to work as well.

After a time, he spoke again. "This is where I hid when my parents were killed," he said. His voice was flat. "The soldiers came to force them off their land, and I ran away. I probably would be dead, too, if I had stayed behind."

"Ah," Natima said. "Your hatred of me has a point of origin."

"Of course it does!" he spat. "Every Bajoran you'll ever meet has a story like mine. Those who aren't orphans are widows, or they have lost children or siblings or friends. My story is so typical, there's hardly any reason to tell it."

Natima was quiet, struggling with an unexpected surge of guilt. She knew she had done nothing wrong. And the Bajorans had willingly accepted the annexation; they should have expected to have to make some adjustments . . . But she also knew how she might have felt if someone had come to her home and told her she had to leave. Forced her to leave, if she refused.

*If they had just cooperated . . .*

She wanted to maintain as friendly an atmosphere as possible. If she could show herself to be open-minded, compassionate, perhaps he would listen to her when Damar came, turn himself in without a struggle.

"Did you grow up in an orphanage?"

He shook his head. "No. We aren't like Cardassians, leaving their children behind. Bajorans keep their children out of those foul places, if it can be helped. I was taken in by relatives."

Natima bristled at what he had said, mostly because she knew it was true. She sat back from the pile of rock, clasped her scraped fingers tightly. "I'll have you know, I don't agree with the practice of leaving Cardassian children behind in orphanages. The trouble with people like you, you view Cardassians as if we were one person, with one opinion. We don't all agree on every aspect of our culture."

The Bajoran frowned, but said nothing. He continued working.

"I've seen plenty of Bajoran children in the orphanages," she added, "so don't try to pretend that the Bajorans are above leaving their children to fend for themselves. Usually, they are children of those who cooperate with the government—children who have done nothing wrong, and are left to pay the debt of their parents by people like you."

"People like *me!*" he exclaimed, but before he could finish, a stream of fine gravel spilled from the top of the heap. He leapt forward and grabbed Natima, shielding her body with his own. "Watch out!" he shouted.

A few of the larger rocks shifted, but nothing came down. She and the Bajoran pulled back from each other, both of them catching their breath from the scare. Natima stared at the man, confused. He had acted to protect her, after taking her hostage. What a complicated people these Bajorans were!

"Did I hurt you?"

"No," Natima told him, flustered. "I'm fine."

They heard a faint groan, echoing from the other end of the tunnel.

"Veja's awake," she said. The Bajoran nodded, stood, lighting the way with his flickering light.

Natima tried to hurry, but the light was failing fast. The muddy, rocky ground beneath their feet had to be navigated by feel, the dark a palpable thing around them, closing in, and she was afraid. She spoke again as they walked, working to keep herself focused. "The children in the orphanages—it's one of the few things that I have refused to censor about the annexation."

"Annexation?" He laughed, a bitter sound. "You Cardassians are so skilled in the art of the euphemism."

"What would you know about it?" Natima snapped.

"I have accessed your comnet before—I've read the reports you deliver back to your homeworld. Reports of happy Bajoran subjects, much-revered Cardassian leaders, Dukat's favorable reputation among the Bajorans. No mention of the resistance, except perhaps to report exaggerated victories against them—victories which have been few and far between, I might add."

Natima did not have time to answer, as they had reached Veja. She knelt beside her friend, the weak light showing them her mud-streaked face, tight with pain and fear.

Natima reached for her. "It's all right, Veja. We're trying to find a way out. I'm so sorry to have left you alone in the dark, but we have only one light."

Veja struggled to speak.

"Don't waste your energy. You need to rest." It was the Bajoran.

"Get . . . leave . . . I'm . . . okay. Go . . ."

"No, Veja. He's right—don't try to speak."

Veja shook her head and gasped weakly, gesturing back down the tunnel, the way Natima and Seefa had come.

"I think she's trying to tell us to get back to work," the Bajoran said, and Veja nodded before closing her eyes again, the tension in her face lessening as she drifted back into unconsciousness.

Natima looked up at the Bajoran, who would not return her gaze. "I'm sorry," he said quietly. "I never meant for anything like this to happen."

Natima stood up and tried to brush dirt off her dress before realizing how utterly futile it was—she was covered in grime and muck from head to toe, and she would be getting a lot dirtier before this day was done. She could not accept his apology, not with Veja so badly hurt, but she felt a need to at least acknowledge its sincerity.

"A lot of things happen that have unintended consequences," she said stiffly, and started back to the blocked entrance. The Bajoran followed, carefully lighting their way.

Lenaris and Taryl landed their respective ships less than a *kellipate* from the prison camp. It was as close as they could get, considering the complicated web of defense arrays surrounding the camp. The atmosphere was breathable, but thin, and Lenaris's head started to throb almost as soon as he left his raider. The air smelled strange—not bad, exactly, just a smell that Lenaris had never known. The very unfamiliarity of it made his stomach clench.

Lenaris and Delle met up with Taryl, who had ridden with Tiven, as the third raider thudded down. Sten and his cousin Crea leaped out first, followed by two brothers by the name of Legan, recent additions to the Ornathia cell. They were standing just beyond a patch of the strangest-looking vegetation Lenaris had ever seen—low trees with rounded leaves that appeared almost black in color, likely to compensate for the excessive distance of their sun. They provided good cover. If Pullock V had been a desert world, the operation would already be over.

"I read life signs," Taryl whispered, looking at her hand-held scanner. "But I can't tell if they're Bajoran. It's the shield—blocks out most of the signal."

Lenaris nodded. "Can you tell how many people are here?"

Taryl shook her head.

"Well, let's do it," Tiven said, and unslung his phaser rifle. Lenaris nodded, unslinging his own. The Legans both carried handheld phasers, while Taryl and her cousins were carrying pouches full of improvised explosive devices: slap packs and shrapnel grenades—unsophisticated, but they did the job.

Lenaris could see that the others were nervous, never having faced Cardassians in combat before. But he was too anxious and excited for his own sake to worry much about his companions' lack of experience. He felt that he was better at ground combat than just about anything else; he'd had a lot of practice when he had been in the Halpas cell with Darin. The two of them were so confident, they could have taken out an entire outfit of Cardassian soldiers from the ground. Once, they'd destroyed a massive bunker—just the two of them—and had done such a thorough job, the spoonheads hadn't even bothered to rebuild it. It was memories like this that Lenaris drew upon, scaffolding his courage, as the eight of them crept to the place where they expected the camp to be. They were always under-manned and outgunned—it was a fact of the occupation—but it was still possible to prevail.

As they edged closer to the Cardassian facility, a large, modern-looking operation surrounded by a low wall, they could see no guards, and they could hear no sounds of movement. It appeared completely deserted. Lenaris's tension went up a few notches.

"Are those life signs any clearer?" Tiven asked.

Taryl shook her head. "No," she said slowly. "There's no way to know what kind of opposition we're facing."

"Does it matter?" Sten asked.

Taryl shook her head. "No," she whispered. She edged a little closer, hesitant, looking at her scanner again.

"Maybe—" Tiven didn't have time to finish his thought, for a tight line of gray-armored soldiers had abruptly sprung up behind the wall, less than thirty paces from where they now stood, and each soldier carried a massive rifle. The volley of simultaneous fire erupted in a single, terrible, impenetrable barrier.

Lenaris's rifle was in his hands and he was spraying fire before he even had time to register what had just happened. His ears roared with his own heartbeat. He was only partially aware of the shots that originated somewhere at his side; presumably Tiven, but Lenaris only saw the ugly, reptilian faces in front of him, watched as they staggered and fell, one by one. He fired, fired again, and retreated, crouching back into the alien bushes.

The soldiers who had not fallen returned fire, though they did not advance beyond the low walls of the facility, only continuing to shoot like a single unwavering, mechanical entity, the same formation that Lenaris recalled they had often taken when on Bajor; if they were not advancing, it meant there were probably more of them, to replace those who fell. The shrieks from their phasers tore up the ground in blasts of cloudy, choking black dust, the blasts of fire erupting in perfectly timed staccato. It did not take long to confirm to Lenaris that there were indeed more soldiers coming; he heard their phasers before he saw them, marching forward from somewhere beyond the gates of the facility to fill in for their fallen comrades.

Lenaris took the briefest second to survey their own casualties. Delle was nowhere in sight. Sten's foot was visible a short distance away, poking out from beneath the brush ahead of him, but Lenaris could not gauge if he was alive or dead. Crea was dead, crumpled in the dirt. The Legan brothers were firing wildly in tandem. Tiven also continued to fire, and Taryl, ducking behind insufficient cover, clutched her bag anxiously, her expression wide-eyed with the fear of first combat.

"Go, do it!" Lenaris shouted to her, and she quickly snapped into action. She chucked the palm-sized slap packs with all her might, one after another as he continued to fire, covering her. More soldiers fell, but it was not enough.

"Tiven!" he shouted, risking a look in the old engineer's direction—and he saw that Tiven was on the ground, the upper part of his body a blackened mass, still smoking from the impact of Cardassian disruptor fire. Lenaris changed his position, continuing to fire. He still could not see Delle, and Sten appeared to be frozen behind the patch of bushes where he hid. One of the Legans had used up his power cell and was retreating, his brother continuing to fire methodically.

Lenaris made his way to Sten. "Go go go!" he screamed, firing over the other man's shoulder, and Sten jerked into action, dashing forward just far enough to pluck the phaser rifle from Tiven's corpse. With a cry, Sten discharged Tiven's phaser at the line of spoonheads, until there were no more standing. At least, none that they could see.

"Delle!" Lenaris cried out, but Taryl stopped him, her expression tortured as she shook her head. Sten had fallen to his knees next to his cousin's unmoving body. It had all happened too fast, was still happening. There was only a beat of ringing silence before they were made aware of more fire heading their way. Another line of identically dressed soldiers had just emerged from somewhere unseen, and there was no way of knowing how many more were waiting to replace these.

"Sten, your pack!" Lenaris shouted. The other man looked down at the satchel still slung around his shoulder as if he had forgotten it was there, and without wasting another second he pitched the explosive devices back at the camp—larger than those Taryl had used, meant to finish off the camp once they were done here—and it seemed to Lenaris that they were indeed done here.

The Legans had already retreated, both their phasers having run dry. "Let's get the *kosst* out of here," Lenaris ordered, and Taryl and Sten followed his lead, stumbling back through the squat trees, gasping, running for the shuttles. Lenaris sidestepped, firing back at the camp, hoping to the Prophets that they hadn't been flanked.

Powdery dirt and alien vegetation flew up beneath their boots. Taryl tripped and Lenaris snatched at her arm, yanked her after him, his head pounding as the first of the explosions tore through the thin air. Behind them, soldiers shouted, but they hadn't broken formation to give chase until it was too late. Sten and the Legans reached their raider first, and Lenaris pushed Taryl to hers before scrambling toward his own, blood thundering in his ears, expecting to feel the fatal blast to his back as he climbed into his vessel, his skin and muscles trembling in anticipation of it.

There were more explosions from the camp, one so big that it could only be the power station, a lucky hit. He fired up the raider, talking to himself, his voice a thready whisper as he frantically studied the sensors.

"Go, go, move . . ."

The instant he saw that Taryl was off the ground, he tapped himself into the air, imagining he could feel blasts of heat from the burning camp, pushing him toward the stars as he slammed on his comm.

"Halpas! We're running! Get ready to go to warp!"

If the Cardassians had flyers, they were too preoccupied with their camp to come after the Bajorans. The brief fly time seemed like an eternity, Lenaris trying to catch his breath, sure that each second would be his last. A bright-hot blast of light, a single pulse from a patrol ship's disruptors, and he'd be so much debris, blowing silently through icy space . . .

The carrier was waiting. Lenaris came in right behind Taryl, with Sten and the Legan brothers bringing up the rear. The bay's hatch clamped shut behind them, and Lenaris felt a quick jerk just before the inertial dampers kicked in and the old Bajoran ship went to warp. He clambered out of his raider, huddling against the cold, stumbling toward Taryl's craft. Taryl was still sitting in her cockpit, crammed in beside the Legans, who both looked to be in a state of shock. Taryl's head was down on the instrument panel.

Lenaris lifted the hatch, the fear finally hitting him.

"Taryl, are you all right? Are you hit?"

Taryl gasped once, twice—and started to cry, deep, rending cries of heartbreak that echoed through the dim, cavernous bay.

"Lac," she wailed, and Lenaris tried to hold her, but it was as though he wasn't even there.

## 11

Dukat was fuming as he tapped off the comm. The facility in the Pullock system had been badly damaged, and a good many Union troops were dead. He'd thought he'd been sufficiently cautious, sending soldiers to the work camp on Pullock V to oversee the execution of the prisoners there, which included the terrorist who had been apprehended at Derna—the man had given up plenty in the interrogation, confirmed that he'd tried to send word back to his friends. But even with that lead, Dukat had underestimated the Bajorans once again.

He sat back in his chair, his mood black. The average Bajoran's quality of life had improved dramatically since his rise to the office. He had promoted better health care, encouraged work-training programs, allowed them religious freedoms that they had no right to expect, and this is what they gave in return.

He started to call for Damar, but then remembered that the gil had gone to the surface; his betrothed had gotten herself into trouble, another hostile incident with a Bajoran terrorist.

Dukat templed his fingers, considering his next move. He did not particularly care to admit when he had made a mistake, but he knew that on very rare occasions, it was the best course to take. A change in tactics was required. He summoned Basso Tromac to operations, deciding how best to tighten the reins as he waited for the Bajoran to appear.

"You called for me, sir?" Basso stepped into his office not five minutes after being called. One thing to be said for Basso, he was punctual.

"I need you to deliver a message to Kubus Oak," Dukat said.

"Right away, sir." Basso slid a padd from his belt, fingers poised to record. "What message?"

"Inform Kubus that I am instituting new policies on Bajor, effective immediately. It will be up to him to be sure that the word is spread across his world. My men will be on hand to enforce these directives."

"Yes, sir," Basso said, suddenly sounding a little uneasy.

"Chief among them: no more religious counsel allowed in the work camps. In fact, we need to even the playing field for religious officials in general. I've allowed your priests a certain amount of leniency up to now, but I feel it is time for them to earn their keep, just like everyone else. All religious officials will receive work code numbers. And I believe we will be dismantling some of the monasteries. It is common knowledge that resistance members hide in them."

Basso was tapping away at his padd, his expression revealing nothing, but Dukat could see him swallow, hard. He was as superstitious as the rest of them, of course.

"Additionally, I am lowering per-month food allowances. And I am tightening restriction boundaries in Relliketh and Dahkur. I will post the specifics on the comnet."

"Yes, sir," Basso said. "Will that be all?"

Dukat nodded. "For now," he said.

Basso left him, and Dukat looked over transmission reports, trying to find the record from the patrol ship that had reported the balon shuttles in the Pullock system. He was having trouble locating it and became frustrated, considering that this was the type of thing for which he usually relied on Damar. Dukat muttered a curse at Damar's fiancée. Women could be so troublesome.

Dukat gave up on the transmissions and spent a few moments drafting his new directives, then uploading them to the Bajoran and Cardassian comnets. He then sent copies to the appropriate parties of interest—Legate Kell's office, the guls who oversaw surface operations. Dukat didn't bother himself overmuch with the details; what mattered were the bold, broad strokes. This would stir the rebels, make them reckless. His soldiers on the ground would make quick work of them, some small justice for the tragedy of Pullock V.

Hours later, he began to feel the intense solitude of command taking its toll. There was one other person who was adept at listening to his troubles, who might be able to ease his mind.

As he entered her quarters, he was immediately aware of Meru's posture. She sat on the bed with her back to the door, her head bent as she gazed down at her hands, her fingers twisting in her lap.

"Meru," Dukat said, wondering if she had already heard about the new directives. He looked to her companel. The screen was dark, but she had probably been at it, where she pored over the comnet reports on those days when she wasn't painting pictures or reading what passed for literature among Bajorans. The holosuites had never interested her, though Dukat had done his best to try and encourage her to use them.

"Hello, Skrain," she said, her voice hollow.

Dukat frowned. It was unusual for Meru to act this way. Even though Dukat knew she wasn't always entirely happy, she almost always managed to put on a convincing smile for her lover—it was one of the reasons Dukat had kept her around this long.

Dukat sat down on the bed behind his mistress, touching the back of her bare neck. He nudged away the few tendrils of hair that grazed her skin, having worked themselves loose from the arrangement on top of her head—similar to how a Cardassian would wear her hair, but especially striking on the delicate-featured Bajoran. "Is something troubling you, my dear?"

She shook her head, but she continued to avoid his gaze, and Dukat began to feel annoyed. She was acting a bit like a petulant child. He would find no solace from his worries here.

"I must go," he said irritably. "Gil Damar is not on the station. My duties will keep me busy for the next few days."

Meru finally looked up, and Dukat saw that her eyes were quite red, the edges of her nose laced with pink. A strange effect that Bajorans often experienced when upset, it did not flatter her.

Dukat turned away in disgust. "I won't be back tonight," he announced, and left the room.

Rain had come to the Kendra Valley, and a heavy downpour was soaking the muddy terrain that surrounded the old cottage once occupied by the Opaka family, the cottage where Gar Osen now resided. The same cottage that had been built in the time of Kai Dava.

Opaka Fasil pulled his oilcloth cloak over the top of his head to keep the fine spray of misty rain from his head and shoulders. Despite his best efforts, rivulets of water ran down the tip of his nose, and his fingers were cold and slippery where they clutched at the little shovel he was using to poke around the foundation of the little stone house.

"Quiet," whispered the older man who had come from his mother's camp—the artist, Ketauna. "The vedek will hear you!"

"He won't hear me," Fasil assured him. "I lived in this cottage for most of my childhood. It's very well insulated."

"But you're tapping the shovel right up against the house!"

"Let him work," the other man said, the younger one with the phaser pistol. His name was Shev. "If you're worried about it, go round to the front and watch the door. You can warn us if they come out."

The older man did as he was told without a word. In the half a day it had taken them all to reach the sanctuary, Fasil had learned that Ketauna was unexpectedly stodgy, for an artist. Fasil thought his sour mood might have something to do with the news they'd heard earlier, on their brief journey.

Gul Dukat had issued a list of new edicts. It was all that anyone could talk about. Among other restrictions, all religious personnel were to register with the work office for identification numbers within the next week, just like any other Bajoran citizen. Dukat was also planning to raze several of the sanctuaries and to discontinue the practice of allowing religious counsel in the work camps. The people of the villages and camps they'd walked through were horrified by the news, as was Fasil's mother, but it also gave her a legitimate reason to seek counsel with Vedek Gar, who apparently wouldn't see just anyone anymore. Fasil supposed they should be thankful for that.

Fasil found the ground near the foundation of the house to be quite soft underneath the superficial layer of rotten needles and leaves. It would have made excellent compost, he thought, for the little garden tended by the members of his cell. Beneath that was a layer of humus that gave way to rich, soft soil that lifted away easily, even with the unwieldy little tool he was using.

He dug quickly and quietly, Shev keeping watch. When the hole was deep and wide enough that he could stand in it, almost up to his knees, his shovel began to hit much more solid ground, a layer of soil that differed in composition, blackened, as if it had been burned.

A trap door. To the cellar. This *had* been wood, he could see by the splinters he was turning over with the sharp tip of the shovel. He was startled, though not terribly surprised, when the shovel *chunked* through the soft wood and hit air a moment later. Dirt and pebbles rolled down into the crack he had just made, rattling thinly as they hit the ground somewhere below. He scrambled up out of the hole, wary of falling through what he was sure was an old hatch. It was a wonder it hadn't caved in long ago, just from the weight of the soil.

Shev examined the hole from the edge, looking at the ovoid black spot in the center that seemed to open up into nothingness. "I have a palmlight," he offered, and produced a torch that he waved down into the hole. From the flash that crossed the small opening, Fasil could see uneven ground—a set of steps? Both men reacted to the sight, and Fasil felt his heart begin to pound in a fashion that was unrivaled by even the sketchiest missions he had been involved in with the resistance. He knew, now, that his mother had been correct. He was about to find something precious here.

*"There's a cellar behind our house. There's something there that belongs to us. Will you help me?"*

Fasil turned to the other man. "Hold the light while I finish digging. I don't want to fall through the hole."

Shev nodded wordlessly, and Fasil carefully set his feet back in the ditch he had dug. He scraped away the dirt that covered the old cellar door, checking his footing periodically, then started widening the hole with the shovel. The wood had rotted, swelled by seasons of rain, and it was only a matter of minutes before the ragged opening was wide enough to admit him.

Fasil put one foot through the inky black square, testing his weight on the rest of the old trap door. He put the other foot through, his feet dangling above the broken stairs beneath him. Shev handed over the palm beacon, and Fasil placed it into the waistband of his pants. He wedged his hands up against the sides of the hole. He looked up at Shev, who nodded without a word. Taking a tremendous breath, he lowered himself down into empty space and let his body fall.

Natima could not tell if the palmlight was flickering or if her eyes had simply grown too tired to see clearly. She had no idea how much time had passed since they had been taken belowground, but she was certain that it must be long past sundown by now. Her hands were covered with tiny cuts, her knees and elbows bruised and scraped. She was exhausted and hungry and scared for Veja, but oddly, it was the unpleasant sensation of the dried clay, jammed underneath her fingernails, that seemed to annoy her the most. She thought it might be the very thing to send her over the edge of tolerable misery.

"Hey," she said to the Bajoran. It occurred to her, not for the first time, that she didn't know his name. "Maybe we should take a rest. If we wear ourselves out, we'll never get out of here."

He shook his head and continued digging at the pile of dirt in front of him. "If we go to sleep, we may never wake up. I'd rather die trying to escape."

Now Natima was certain it was the palm beacon that was flickering, as it had been earlier. Seefa had adjusted something or other, made the beam softer, but now that was beginning to go, too.

"If you aren't going to sleep, you should make yourself useful with that communicator instead of just digging away in the dirt like a vole," she said. "The light is going to go out before we ever make a dent in that heap, and you know it."

The Bajoran finally stopped digging. "If we use it, I'm as good as dead," he said quietly.

"That isn't true! I promise I will tell them this was all an accident. I will tell them that you tried to save us. I know you have no reason to trust me, but I give you my word." She sighed, annoyed with his silence. "And anyway, what other choice do you have?"

He did not look at her, sitting back on his haunches to regard the tumble of rock, which looked very much the same as it had when they had begun digging. He heaved a sigh of his own. "I suppose I have to trust you. It's either my neck, or all of our necks. That's not much of a choice." He was quiet for a moment.

Natima spoke quietly. "Please," she said. "Please. For Veja . . . ?"

He turned. "Fine, I'll do it."

Natima picked up the light, crawled to her feet. "Let's go down to where Veja is. I want to keep an eye on her."

He nodded, and they walked the length of the conduit, picking through the rocks. When they reached Veja, the Bajoran held out his hand.

"Give me the phaser," he said.

Natima was taken aback. "What do you want with it?"

"I'll need some of the components in it to fix the communicator. Give it to me."

"But you said the power cell was dead."

"It is. That isn't the part that I need. There's a pin inside the trigger mechanism that I can use to reset the relay, to send out a general distress call."

Natima hesitated. She didn't want to give up the phaser.

The Bajoran looked annoyed. "Here you are, talking about trust. What am I going to do, shoot the two of you, so I can die in here without any company? Give me the phaser."

Natima knew it was no use, but she wanted to feel like she had a little leverage, at least. "What is your name?" she finally asked him.

He stared at her a moment, then shrugged. "Seefa," he said. "Aro Seefa."

Natima swallowed. "Fine, Aro Seefa," she said softly, and she handed over the weapon. Seefa crouched on the ground next to Veja, picking the weapon apart with his hands, and a thin piece of wire he had pulled from one of his boots. Natima set the palmlight down, focusing on Veja. Her breathing was a little less shallow now, her expression peaceful, but Natima knew she needed prompt medical attention.

She watched the Bajoran work as the light began to grow dimmer and dimmer, the gray shadows cutting across the orange light on his face. He was sorting through a handful of tiny pieces of metal and composite, carefully setting them aside. He removed the combadge from his pocket, cracked it open, and laid it next to the phaser's components.

"How do you know how to do that?" Natima asked. "I thought Bajorans weren't allowed to practice things like engineering, unless they work for the government."

"Bajorans do a lot of things they aren't allowed to do."

"But . . . who taught you to do that?"

Seefa shrugged. "People," he said. "Since nobody follows *D'jarra*s anymore, we had to learn by doing, not by being taught."

Natima was surprised, remembering some of her past interviews. "You mean, you don't approve of the caste system?"

Seefa snorted. "Hardly anyone does. It was never an efficient system, even in the old times."

"But your own government—"

"Right," he said. "Each and every politician appointed

by Cardassians, for being fastest to sell out their friends and family. Not *my* government."

Natima considered it. She had always believed the Bajorans' caste system to be remarkably foolish and backward, and it interested her to hear that this Bajoran actually agreed with her. And that others did, as well.

The light went out entirely for a split second before popping back on again, and Natima and Seefa both breathed in audible relief. "That's all I need," Seefa muttered. "To have to fix this thing in the dark."

Natima felt annoyed. "If you don't mind my saying so," she said, "if you had started work on it when I initially suggested it, we wouldn't have to worry about the light going out."

"You may find this to be madness, but I'd rather avoid calling on your friends for help," Seefa said. He carefully poked at the combadge with a curved metal rod he had removed from the weapon. An infinitesimal spark shot up, and Seefa dropped the device. He mumbled what she took to be some kind of Bajoran expletive and then picked it up again.

Veja groaned slightly, and Natima stroked her forehead ridges, quieting her.

"Of course, we wouldn't be here in the first place if you hadn't been so stupid as to attack a couple of unarmed civilian women."

"How was I supposed to know you were civilians?" Seefa said, looking up at her sharply.

"Two women wandering around a vineyard? Didn't you notice the way we were dressed?"

"Yes, but I didn't know if it was a trick . . . and women can be every bit as dangerous as men—if not more, in some cases."

"Our military does not usually employ women," Natima informed him.

Seefa snorted. "That's foolish," he said. "Half of your population wasted—twice as many people that could be fighting."

"Women are viewed very differently in our society than Bajoran women are in theirs."

"As less capable, because they carry young?"

Natima frowned. She had often thought the same thing herself, but she wasn't about to discuss it with a Bajoran.

Seefa reacted to her silence. "There are plenty of things about my own culture that I don't like. The *D'jarra*s, for example. There's nothing wrong with disagreement."

"My government doesn't look kindly on dissent," Natima said.

"That doesn't surprise me much," he said. "But if you can get enough people to listen to your viewpoint, then there's nothing the government can do about it, is there?"

"They can have those people arrested and executed."

Seefa laughed. "What a great society the Cardassian Union has created. Everyone must agree, or die. No matter how ridiculous or outdated the policies."

Natima said nothing. She felt that she should be furious with this man, this Bajoran man with the temerity to criticize her world, but she was too tired to argue with him. Too tired, and more than a little confused. She considered herself an upstanding member of the Union, but had sometimes questioned the wisdom of her superiors . . .

*You should not think on these things. Not here, not now.*

"I haven't been this hungry since I was a child," she said, determined to change the subject.

"Really?" Seefa had looked up again, his expression unknown to her, his eyebrows raised.

"We *do* eat, you know. Aren't you hungry?"

"No, I mean—why were you hungry as a child?"

"Oh," Natima said, realizing that the comment was somewhat more revealing than she might have intended it to be. "I suppose . . . you must know that our world suffered great hardships in years past. Before the annexation, many people on Cardassia Prime starved to death. We had to go elsewhere to find the resources to sustain our people."

"Ah," Seefa said. "Yes, I suppose I did know that, in a roundabout sort of way. So, your childhood was difficult."

He seemed to be mocking her, and Natima felt a spark of anger. "Yes, my childhood was difficult," she snapped. "My parents died during an epidemic, and they left me alone to fend entirely for myself. None of my relatives would have anything to do with me—lone children are seen as an unwanted burden, an extra mouth to feed on a world whose resources were already stretched thin. After nearly a year on my own, I was picked up by authorities and put in a terrible facility on Cardassia II, worse even than living on the streets had been. If it hadn't been for the Information Service . . ." she stopped, her breath coming fast. She couldn't imagine what had compelled her to share such details from her life with this . . . person.

Seefa had stopped working. "So," he said softly. "That's why you don't care for the orphanages."

Natima didn't trust herself to speak.

Seefa picked up the gutted phaser. "Before my parents died," he said, "I never went without anything. I didn't know the meaning of hunger."

"How cozy that must have been for you."

Seefa went on as if he hadn't heard her. "It's too bad, really."

"What's too bad?"

"It's too bad your people didn't simply ask for help. There was once enough here to sustain both worlds."

"My people tried to set up trade agreements with your world. We were turned away."

"So I understand it. But Bajor didn't need anything you

had to offer. We were self-sustaining, and it never occurred to us that a world would be any other way. If we had only known how dire your situation . . ."

"Cardassia could never be self-sustaining," Natima said. "Our world's conditions wouldn't permit it."

"But it must have been, at some point, before your people developed interstellar travel. Otherwise, how could your civilization have developed in the first place? Perhaps if you were to look back to the time when your world relied on its own resources, you might learn something. You wouldn't have to go about stealing from everyone else."

Natima shook her head. "That's absurd," she told him. "Cardassian civilization thrives on progress and technology. My people would never look backward toward a time when life was primitive, and . . . and . . ."

"And simple, and self-sustaining? Like the Bajorans'? We were happy here, before we were occupied and attacked and robbed. If Cardassia had followed our example instead of just . . ." Seefa stopped, and shook his head. "It's no use talking about it," he said.

"No, I suppose not," Natima replied. She enjoyed a good argument, but the thoughts their conversation had inspired were uneasy ones. And if Seefa didn't want to talk anymore, she wasn't about to try and make him. The communicator wasn't going to fix itself.

Damar could see what appeared to be footprints in the soft, ruddy-colored mud on the floor of the conduit. He nodded at Garresh Trach, who held his weapon ready. They moved into the dark, Damar switching on his palmlight to illuminate their way.

They didn't have the tracks for long; standing water on the passage's floor had filled in the murky impressions, prints that confirmed his earlier readings and Natima's message. Two women in sandals, a Bajoran's cracked boots.

They ventured deeper into the cold, dark passageway. The thought of Veja here, against her will . . . Damar moved them along quickly, watching his scanner.

A number of twists and they reached what appeared to be a main artery of the system. As soon as they stepped into the wider tunnel, the tricorder picked up a trio of life signs, faint but distinct. Two were Cardassian, the third Bajoran. Damar had to force himself not to run. The insurgents had shown themselves to be violent and ruthless and very, very careful. Recklessness on his part might put Veja further in harm's way.

They followed the signs down a smaller offshoot that was completely blocked by a recent collapse, recent enough that they could still smell the torn, sun-warmed soil in the air. Damar checked the tricorder again, recalibrating to medical. As close as they were, he could see that one of the Cardassian signals was quite weak.

He felt his fear give way to angry panic. One of them was injured, badly enough to alter a direct sensor reading. Could he attempt to find a back entrance to the tunnel? That would take too much time.

He wanted to shout, to call for her, but dared not. He could hear water rushing from somewhere, the sound echoing through the maze of collapsing tunnels, and reached up, touching the low ceiling. Flat rocks, lined with moist, crumbling clay. He crouched, touched the loose soil that had collapsed into the tunnel. It was soft.

*We'll have to go in from above. Leave one of the scanners so we can find this spot easily, dig somewhere past the blockage . . .*

He didn't want to leave, knowing that his beloved was just on the other side of the fallen rubble, perhaps hurt or even dying, but that was all the more reason to hurry.

"Garresh Trach," he said quietly. "We must briefly return to our ship for some equipment. Leave your tricorder here, we'll follow its signal back."

"Yes, sir."

Trach set down his tricorder and the two men hurried back through the tunnels, Damar refusing to second-guess himself. He had no time for doubt.

Opaka had made the *ratamba* stew she had been offered last as long as she could, savoring each bite. It was not only for want of diversion that she did so; it had been weeks since she had eaten such a substantial meal. Finally, she finished, smiling her thanks to the attendant prylar who promptly walked over and took her empty bowl.

"What do you have to say of my proposal, Vedek Gar?" she asked. In light of Gul Dukat's amended laws, she'd suggested that he consider officially disbanding the Vedek Assembly temporarily, so that its members might avoid further prosecution. She believed she already knew his answer, and knew also that he would take his time coming up with it, to show that he was giving it due consideration; it was why she'd asked.

The vedek smiled hesitantly. He glanced at the monk, gave a nod. The robed servant left the cottage, and Opaka prayed that her son had already finished his work, that the other two were keeping careful watch for him.

"I don't doubt, Sulan, that *Dukat* may very well elect to disband the Vedek Assembly," Gar said. "But I feel that it would be cowardly for me to run away from my people at a time like this, when the faithful will be seeking our leadership more than ever."

"There is logic in your answer," Opaka said. "But you cannot be of much good to the people if Dukat has you taken to a work camp."

"Now, Sulan." The vedek wore a pinched smile. "You cannot expect me to believe that you came all this way to discuss Dukat's new policies, for it would seem to me that you only learned of the announcement this morning. We only heard it last night. What was your true purpose for traveling all this way?"

Opaka had anticipated this possibility. "I . . . have come because I have been hearing rumors . . . that you are now beginning to support my position. You who were once so firmly opposed to the abandonment of the *D'jarras*—and I suppose I only wanted to find out if what I was hearing is true."

Vedek Gar nodded. "I see. It is true, I have begun to preach that the old ways are no longer effective for us, and that we would be wise to follow your advice. You see, I believe it is important for any official—religious or otherwise—to be flexible as conditions change."

"Certainly, Vedek Gar, I agree with you. But what I do not understand is, what exactly has changed that made you so abruptly shift your position? Other than the death of Kai Arin?"

Vedek Gar looked uncomfortable. "Sulan, I must inform you that I intend to reinstate you as a vedek of the faith, if I am elected kai. I am pleased, in fact, that you have come all this way, so that I can inform you of this decision in person. It would honor me greatly if you would rejoin us here at the monastery, though I'm afraid I can't offer you your old residence right away—" He spread his hands and gave an awkward laugh.

Opaka was not a political creature, but she understood now that he was. The awareness saddened her. The way she saw it, the Bajoran people needed hope and unity, they needed spiritual healing and a call to action, in support of their faith. She was only the messenger, a carrier of words, and sought no recognition for her acts. But she could see it through his eyes, too, listening to him speak. By endorsing "her" message, he would gain the support of "her" followers in the choosing of the new kai. It seemed inevitable that the ones who sought power were the ones most lacking the humility needed to truly lead.

*I will not judge,* she thought. She did not know his heart, no matter what her vision implied.

"Will you come back to us, Sulan?"

Even as he asked, she saw a hand appear in the window behind Gar, a simple shake of the fingers that represented success.

*They found it!* Was it as she'd seen? She did her best to keep her sudden excitement hidden, but she had no further reason to prolong their conversation.

"Vedek Gar—Osen—you have my apologies. I see now that my journey here was a mistake. I wish you luck in the outcome of the choosing." She stood.

Gar looked disarmed. "Sulan! You leave me so abruptly! Can I at least offer you accommodations for the night? You've come far, and we still have not discussed your status—"

Opaka smiled at him. "Your graciousness is appreciated, but my path lies elsewhere. The Prophets will look after me. I pray Their guidance will always be with you."

Gar's expression hardened slightly, but he stood also. "Of course," he said. He bowed to her politely as Opaka let herself out of the cottage.

Shev was waiting for her. He grabbed her arm and half-sprinted into the copse of trees behind the keep, practically carrying her. Her son waited there with Ketauna. Ketauna had his arms around a large object, too large to fit in his pack, wrapped in a piece of wool from his bedroll.

"It was just as you said, Mother!" Fasil told her. "A cellar, converted to a reliquary—"

"The Orb," Ketauna breathed, his face shining with the brilliance of new hope. "As you saw."

"We must go," Opaka said quickly. "We cannot stay here."

"As you say, Kai Opaka," Shev said reverently.

"Did you cover over the place where you— What?"

"You are the kai now," Ketauna said, nodding. "You were visited by the Prophets. The people will hear of this."

"After we find a place for you to hide," Fasil added.

"And a place to hide the Orb," Shev said. "The Cardassians will not find this Tear of the Prophets. We must all agree to keep this information to ourselves, until it is safe to reveal it. Do you agree, Your Eminence?"

Opaka nodded, too concerned for the Orb's safety—and their own—to laugh at her new title. She would refuse the position later, when she had time to consider her arguments, when she was sure the Orb was safe.

They started immediately, heading back toward the mountains, Opaka looking often at the bundle Ketauna carried. How precious, to find such a thing, at such a time! They could speak to the Prophets again, could seek Their wisdom upon the scourge of their world.

*You will be secret, but the faithful will know,* she thought, watching Ketauna shift the ratty blanket as he walked, carefully, reverently shifting the long-hidden Tear. The Cardassians would not take it—she had seen as much, in the knowledge granted her by her vision, her *pagh-tem-far*.

Things were unfolding as they should. She prayed again for strength, to do as They wished, to find in herself the potential that They had seen in her.

Basso Tromac walked in his usual quick manner as he returned from the shuttle pad. He carried a rather imposing bouquet of Bajoran lilacs, which embarrassed him somewhat. He knew what the flowers were for; Dukat always ordered them when he was trying to patch things up with his Bajoran mistress. Idle gossip saw to it that nearly everyone on the station knew, too. Basso supposed that he felt uncomfortable because he didn't like to advertise the prefect's business so blatantly; he considered that the ins and outs of people's relationships ought to be kept private.

He was relieved that he didn't see any other Bajorans on his way to the habitat ring, though he did encounter some snickering Cardassian soldiers. Basso wanted to believe that they were laughing because they found Dukat's personal life to be a source of amusement, but he knew that there was more to it than that. He knew that they had no respect for him, that they considered him nothing more than a simple errand boy, and consideration of this never failed to create a rise of fury in his throat. Well, at least the Bajorans were afraid of him. Though they sometimes acted bold, they knew that he could deliver a death sentence with a single transmission to Dukat. He supposed he should have pitied the idiots on the station for being so stupid as to have landed themselves in ore-processing. If they had only cooperated, as he had, their lives could have been perfectly comfortable. Although, he considered, there would always have to be *someone* left to do the dirty work. It was just the natural order of things, like the *D'jarras*.

Basso knocked softly on the door of Dukat's quarters. There was a door-chime, but Dukat had instructed him to always knock, and to always do it softly. The prefect answered the door with his usual stretchy smile. "Thank you, Basso." He accepted the flowers and turned away briskly.

Basso bowed. "Is there anything else?"

Dukat shook his head wordlessly and the door closed, but not before Basso caught a glimpse of Kira Meru, sitting on the bed with her head down. The back part of her dress was unfastened, which made Basso flush. The image of her bare back, the delicate knobs rising up from her spine, the golden color of her skin . . . Basso could not immediately erase it from his consciousness. He found it replaying back to him for a moment, and he was forced to swallow down a lump in his throat.

Something compelled him to linger for a moment in the hallway, straining to hear, but he couldn't make out much of anything. Just the low timbre of Dukat's rumbling voice. Basso didn't have to make out specific words to know what was probably going on. Not that it was anyone's business, but he was well aware of the nuances of Dukat's relationship with Meru. She would feign sadness for a little while, maybe about her children or something, and Dukat would be patient with her for much longer than Basso thought was reasonable. Basso had to admire Dukat's patience, for he himself had never been able to maintain much of it when it came to women. He supposed that was why Dukat was prefect—patience. An admirable quality, to be sure—one that simply did not come naturally to everyone.

He tried to listen at the door once more, until he caught himself and remembered the security feed in the hall. It reset itself after a few moments, and it wouldn't look right if he was still standing here when the sweep came back. He headed off to ops, trying to think of who would be most interested in hearing about Dukat and Meru's latest fight. Of course, it wasn't anyone's business, but having intimate information about the prefect had turned out to be a useful means of getting a captive audience from the Cardassians on the station, if only for a little while.

# 12

Natima had been sleeping, dreaming of a child in the orphanage on Cardassia II. He had been clawing at her arm, trying to get at a bit of bread she had been given, a piece she had intended to save for later, though she was as hungry as she had ever been. He was raking his fingernails down her arm, and she pushed him. He took a step back from her, and she was suddenly overcome with horror, for his breathing had become odd and shallow, squeaking grotesquely as he tried to take in heavy breaths.

"Here!" she cried out, throwing the bread at him. "Take it!" But he did not respond, his eyes bulging horribly in their sockets—and then she was awake, and she saw the flickering orange of the palm beacon, the Bajoran with his mud-matted hair, crouched in the corner over the broken communicator. And Veja. She was writhing, her fingers hooked into claws, and Natima realized that the horrible, thin squealing of her dream was coming from Veja.

"Seefa!" Natima cried, and the Bajoran's head snapped up—he had fallen asleep over his work. "Help me! I don't know what to do!"

Seefa moved quickly to Veja's side. He listened to her chest, and then he put his hand under her back. He lifted her up, slightly, and then moved her head from side to side.

Veja didn't seem conscious, but she continued to make that terrible hitching, gasping sound.

"From what I've seen, Cardassians have different physiology than Bajorans," he said. "Your bone structure, your internal organs—I'm not sure—"

"Is she going to be all right?" Natima knew he was no doctor, but the Bajoran had proven resourceful, and there was no one else.

Seefa listened for a second more, putting a finger to her lips. "Her breathing is very shallow. If one of her lungs was damaged . . ."

"What can we do?"

Seefa shook his head, started to answer—and then the high, whistling gasps ceased.

Natima was desperate with fear and horror. "Veja! Veja!"

Seefa leaned over her, pinched her nostrils closed and began blowing air directly into her mouth. Natima watched him helplessly, her panic building to levels she could not tolerate. She finally gave in, sobbing, too exhausted to resist anymore. She watched Seefa for a few minutes that seemed like an eternity, knowing that he was doing all that he could do, but that it probably wouldn't be enough.

They were so focused on Veja, neither of them turned at the rumble of falling rock, back by their dig. It wasn't until white light, strong, unwavering daylight, shafted into the tunnel that Natima realized what was happening.

*Oh, thank you, thank you!*

Seefa spared her a nod, went back to what he was doing, pushing air into Veja's struggling lungs. Natima stumbled to her feet, ran for the new opening, hearing a voice now, hearing a man—Damar?—shouting something—

—and then another section of the tunnel was falling, dirt and dust and rock raining down, and Natima realized she was too close. She stumbled back, tripped, fell badly—

and felt a sharp pain at the base of her skull as it connected with a rock.

She felt as though she were spinning, spinning away from herself. More of the ceiling had come away, but her vision was blurred and she could see only a ragged patch of whiteness that hurt her eyes. She tried to sit up, but a jarring, nauseating purple-tinged darkness washed over her. She felt sticky warmth seeping from where she'd hit her head.

*Stay awake, stay awake—Veja—*

Voices were coming from somewhere, men's voices. Shouting, Cardassian voices. More rubble falling down? Another shout. She flickered back to that boy, that boy who wanted her piece of bread. *You can't have it!* She clutched it as tightly as she could and a wash of brilliant red flared behind her closed eyes—a weapon's fire—and she remembered where she was, what had happened.

"Leave his body here," said the voice. "I'll carry Veja out, you take the other one."

*Damar.*

"He was trying to help us," she said, but only a struggling whimper emerged and it was too late, and the blackness that lurked around the edges finally closed in, bleeding her reality into dark. Natima slept.

After a silent and mostly uneventful journey back to Bajor, Halpas took the carrier back to the base of the protective kelbonite foothills. Taryl had rigged up a surface signal mask before they'd left to cover their takeoff and return, but they also got lucky; their flight was unchallenged, their set-down as quiet as the remnants of their crew. Nobody was speaking, least of all Taryl, who seemed to have been stricken into a state of crippling grief at the acceptance that her brother was beyond her reach.

They headed back for the village, and had just reached

the first dwelling when they were approached by Ornathia Harta. "Lenaris! Taryl!" she shouted. "We have to leave! I'm the only one left, and—"

"Calm down, Harta," Lenaris said. He looked around, saw no one else about. The ramshackle buildings seemed deserted. "What's going on?"

"We hacked into Cardassian comms this morning," she explained, her voice edged with anxiety. "We were able to confirm it—the spoonheads know about the balon! They're going to come looking for us. Our ships won't be safe for much longer."

"What about Lac?" Taryl said urgently. "Did you learn anything about him?"

"Taryl—" Lenaris began, but she ignored him.

Harta looked at her with haunted eyes. "There was a report we found . . . the prisoners on Pullock V were all executed yesterday. I'm so sorry, Taryl . . . but we can't think about it now, we all have to get out of here."

Taryl did not reply, she only buried her face in her hands and wept. Lenaris felt helpless as he placed a hand on her shoulder, knowing that it had no effect.

"Well, that's that," said Legan Duravit. "We'll take a ship and go, I suppose."

"The ships are all gone," Harta said, suddenly sounding defensive. "All but one, and that's mine. I only stayed behind to let you know what was going on."

Duravit looked incensed. "You've got a lot of nerve, Harta. We all worked on those ships, and they're as much ours as they are yours."

"It's everyone for themselves," Harta said stubbornly. "You have the raiders on the carrier, you can use those—unless you want to come with me. And I've told you what you needed to know, so I'm leaving—now." She looked genuinely sorry for a moment, and then she turned to go.

"How do you like that?" Legan Fin exclaimed, looking as though he wasn't sure whether he should stay or follow her.

"Let her go," Duravit told his brother.

"Well," Sten said, "I guess we'd better do as she says. I'm going to get a few things together, and then we'd better figure out where we're going, and how we're going to get there."

"There are still three raiders in the bay of the carrier," Lenaris said.

"My ship is still hidden in the rocks, if your cell hasn't taken it, too," Halpas added. "Though it doesn't run on balon, so I can't just park it anywhere."

"The balon ships might put us in more danger than your ship would at this point," Fin said.

"We'll have to find another fuel source," Taryl said, her voice dull.

"If anyone can do it, Taryl . . ." Lenaris said, trying to be helpful, but her expression suggested that she wasn't ready to accept anyone's optimism.

"We can go to Relliketh," Halpas said.

Lenaris looked at Taryl, hoping that she would agree to it, but she made no indication either way.

"Relliketh's as good as anywhere," Duravit said.

"I'd rather go home to my family's farm," Sten said. "I should tell Crea's mother that . . . what happened."

No one was making eye contact. It suddenly hit Lenaris, though it should have been obvious after what Harta had said, that the Ornathia cell was truly dissolving—just as the Halpas cell had done.

"Well," Lenaris said, his voice tight and disappointed, "maybe for now . . . before we all decide what to do . . . we could just make camp back by the carrier, away from the balon. The kelbonite should keep the spoonheads away from us, and from the shuttles, with or without balon."

"Fine," Fin said, and the others seemed to agree with him as well, though Taryl was still quiet.

Sten and the Legans went back to their cottages to retrieve a few things, but Taryl didn't move, her posture slumped and defeated. "Taryl," Lenaris tried, but she would not look at him. He finally gave up trying to reach her, and headed back to his own cottage to fetch a bedroll and a few other effects he might need to make camp for the night.

Natima rubbed the back of her head where the wound had healed. The dermal regenerator had made short work of the gash, but the hair on the back of her head was still stubble where the medic had shaved it to better access the wound. She had applied a special cellular treatment to stimulate the follicles and fill in the short patch, not sure why she cared at all, after what had happened . . . But she wanted to grasp on to some semblance of normality, even if it was only to look like her old self.

Veja had not been quite so fortunate. The medic felt reasonably certain she would make an almost-full recovery with no permanent neural damage, probably thanks to the breathing Seefa had done for her. But her internal injuries had been extensive, and the doctor had confirmed what every Cardassian woman feared more than death—Veja would never carry a child to term. She didn't even know yet; she had been heavily medicated since their return to Tozhat.

Damar had taken the news very hard, which Natima would have expected. According to Cardassian tradition, their enjoinment would be canceled. While it wasn't unheard of for a barren woman to take a lover, it was very unlikely that she could ever be an acceptable wife. Damar was not the kind of man to overlook such an old and widespread tradition. Natima supposed she had never

known a man who *would* have overlooked it. She dreaded
the time that Veja was lucid enough to be informed of her
condition. Many women chose to take their own lives
after sustaining such injuries. Natima didn't think that Veja
would do anything so drastic, but she feared for her friend
nonetheless. It was a terrible blow.

Still, Damar had not left Veja's side since she had been
taken to the infirmary. Gul Dukat had demanded that he
come back to Terok Nor to resume his duties and the gil
had flatly refused, a response that Natima could not help
but admire. It took someone of remarkable character to
refuse an order from the prefect. As she headed down the
hallway of the infirmary to pay her friend another visit, she
wondered if she might have misjudged Damar.

*Ask Seefa, see what he thinks.*

Natima shook off the thought before it took hold. Seefa,
their conversation, his death—it troubled her on so many
levels, she didn't know where to begin. As she had done
since waking up at Tozhat, she pushed the issue aside.

She stepped into the sterile, warm blankness of Veja's
room. Damar was, as Natima expected, asleep in a chair
next to Veja's bed. There were no attendants present. Veja
was still unconscious, or at least sleeping, and Natima
decided she'd do better to come back later. But as she was
backing out of the room, Damar opened his eyes.

"Miss Lang," he said formally. He had been noticeably
more polite to her since the incident, though Natima didn't
know if it was because his contempt of her had ebbed or
if he was simply too sad to be bothered with his former
opinion of her.

"Gil Damar. I apologize for disturbing you. I only came
to check on her status."

"It is kind of you," he said, his voice distant. "She is the
same."

"Has . . . has her family been notified?" Natima asked. "Because I was thinking that I could . . ."

"I spoke to her father. He has been . . . supportive, although he is understandably very . . . disappointed."

Natima remembered what Seefa had said about the Cardassian propensity toward euphemism, and she laughed, entirely unexpectedly. Damar gave her an odd look, one that contained a bit of the old contempt that she remembered so well from her encounters with him on Terok Nor.

"Forgive me," she begged.

"I see nothing funny here," Damar said icily.

"Of course not, Gil Damar. Except—"

She hesitated. She knew it wasn't her place to suggest such things, but he obviously loved her so. Perhaps there was a way, after all.

"Don't you find it somewhat queer that on our world, where children are valued so highly, we would cast away those children who have no parents? Children who could have found a home with women like Veja, who cannot now carry her own child, but longs to be a mother above all else? Hasn't it occurred to you, after all this, that—"

Damar looked positively horrified, and Natima knew she had crossed the line. "Gil Damar, I fear my female gift for curiosity and observation has gotten the better of me. It is only that I am so grieved for my friend that I forget myself. Please . . . I will leave you."

She turned and quickly left the room, practically running to get away. Her own apartment was quite close to the settlement hospital, and she broke into the cool outside air between the buildings feeling as though she'd forgotten how to breathe.

She felt embarrassed for herself, an unusual sensation, as she walked the short distance home. It had never been in her nature to avoid awkward topics just to preserve an air of comfortable formality. Still, she should have known better than to try and be philosophical with a man who was experiencing such suffering. And yet—

*And yet, their lives together need not be destroyed.*

It was not for her to say. She came to the gray building that housed her quarters and let herself inside, suddenly desperate for a long, dreamless nap. She couldn't remember ever feeling so tired.

Before she'd even closed her door behind her, her console lit up with an incoming transmission from Information Service headquarters on Cardassia Prime. Undoubtedly Dalak, and she'd have to speak with him eventually. She reluctantly took the call.

*"Miss Lang, I have been trying to reach you for some time. On behalf of all your colleagues here—and myself, of course—may I express sincerest regards for your health, after your unfortunate incident. I understand you're to make a full recovery?"*

His enthusiasm for her answer was markedly lacking, but she did her best to support the effort. He was her superior.

"Yes, Mister Dalak, although Miss Ketan was not so lucky. She has survived, but some of her injuries are permanent."

*"Indeed, Miss Lang. We've received the medical report. It is most regrettable. Still, I hear the two of you acted with outstanding bravery. It would make a good story, don't you think?"*

Natima was taken aback; this possibility had not occurred to her. "Oh! I suppose . . ."

*"This is just the sort of thing that the people love to hear. Military heroes, clever reporters, a depraved rebel killed. I would like you to deliver the story by tomorrow evening, Cardassia City time."*

"Uh . . . certainly. I will get on it right away."

*"Thank you, Miss Lang. Send Miss Ketan my goodwill."*

"Yes, sir. I will do that—as soon as she wakes up."

*"She isn't awake? Ah. Well then . . . anyway. Also, I under-*
*stand Gul Dukat put several Bajorans to death the other day,*
*going on a tip that you gave him—about balon? I think you*
*should run a follow-up story to that. The weekend crew ran it,*
*and the censor made a mess of it. I need you to handle it, if you're*
*feeling up to it, of course."*

Natima knew the story, and she knew that the cen-
sors had indeed made a mess of it—sometimes they were
so overzealous that the stories barely made sense when
they ran through. But she was feeling a bit harried right
now, having just recovered from a very stressful ordeal. It
wouldn't have troubled her a bit to have taken it easy for a
few days. "I . . . uh, actually . . ." she murmured.

Dalak interrupted smoothly. *"Good. I will expect that story*
*to run tomorrow morning, at the latest. I must go. Deadlines don't*
*rest for anyone, do they?"*

"No, they don't," Natima said. She had never particularly liked her boss, but she couldn't think of a time when
she had liked him less than right now. She rubbed the short
patch on her head again, tired, sick with worry, trying not
to think about Seefa or her new, conflicting thoughts about
the annexation, about Dukat, about her role in the Information Service.

That was when an idea occurred to her. The kind of
idea that demands a decision, that one cannot easily turn
away from once it enters the realm of possibility. It meant
risking her job, her all-important work . . . But not so all-
important in the way she'd always believed.

She felt her heart pounding as she began to type up her
report for the homeworld comnet, the image of Seefa's
face finally coming clear into her mind as she crafted her
words, polished her turns of phrase. The image of his face
the moment that it had dawned on her that he was nothing like what she expected him to be.

The comnet would get its story about the Pullock V prisoners tomorrow, but maybe it wouldn't be exactly the one that her boss had in mind.

Astraea kept her head down as she left the city. Her hair was loose, and she tried to use the long black tresses to shield her face. She'd debated using her shawl to cover her head, to guard her profile, but had finally decided that it might look suspicious. Even after she'd passed the last homes and buildings of the city's outskirts, she'd felt herself almost trembling with fear that someone she knew would see her, or worse, that her image had been uploaded to the military's facial-recognition system, and her brief ride on the city's shuttle had doomed her. Were her crimes serious enough that people would be actively looking for her? It seemed unlikely, although she'd surely been entered into the system by now, marked as a criminal. She had checked into a boardinghouse under her new assumed name, and nobody had come rushing to put her under arrest. Yet.

*I can always turn myself in, if I have to.* The thought was strangely reassuring; it allowed her to continue with her madness, knowing that there was sanity and reality, no matter how unpleasant, that she could return to.

She wandered beyond the edge of the city, where she finally found herself alone. She walked past the old manufacturing facilities, dating to hundreds of years before the annexation, sitting empty and ominous in the hot, dry, evening winds—a grim reminder to those who passed that Cardassia had once very nearly fallen into ruin. The thought of it gave Astraea a warped flash of the horror she had experienced when she saw those images of Cardassia destroyed, blackened, smoking, crushed perhaps beyond repair. A shudder ran through her entire body, and she pulled her shawl tightly around her.

Past the wide band of shadow-haunted industrial zone, she

reached the open desert, only a few thin vehicle ruts marking the expanse of cracked soil. Although she was looking at nothing, a field of blowing dust ringed with distant mountains so far away that she could easily block them with her hands, she thought she detected something here, something she had seen before. Was it wishful thinking that made it seem so? Or was this really the place where, centuries before, a small house had once stood? Meadows, a tiny stream, trees with birds in them? Was it simply the fantasy of a scientist who daydreamed about agriculture from things past?

She had walked a great distance, and her feet were sore. Though she had worn her walking shoes, she was not used to traveling as much as she had been doing in these past weeks; her movements were usually limited to the daily commute from her tiny apartment to her office in the science ministry. She had taken a public shuttle for part of her journey here, but, fearful of being seen, she had walked much farther than was probably wise. It pained her to think of the distance she was going to have to travel to return to the boardinghouse.

Examining the soles of her shoes, she thought she heard someone behind her and she stiffened, until she saw that a couple of stray hounds were fighting over something not far behind her, back near where the buildings began again. Her tension took on a different timbre, for she had always had a childish fear of the animals. Before the annexation, when Miras was a small child, her older brother used to scare her with tales of the giant wild dogs that fed solely on corpses, the remains of those who died of starvation, or during one of several poverty-borne disease epidemics. She had a vague idea that there were those who blamed the Oralians for many of the deaths from that time period; there had been great dissent, rioting, the overtures of civil war. She backed quietly away from where the animals were tussling, hoping they had not spotted or scented her.

A moment passed. The brief fight had reestablished whatever dominance existed between the two scruffy animals. One of the hounds turned its ugly, squarish head in her general direction, but did not seem interested in her. It padded away, followed by the other.

Astraea relaxed, turned to start walking again.

"Halt!" It was a man's voice, behind her, and Astraea froze. A Cardassian soldier stepped into view, a man with a broad forehead and a deeply scrutinizing expression. He had his weapon trained on her, though he lowered it upon reaching her. She imagined she looked quite harmless.

"I . . . I'm doing nothing wrong," she said faintly. "Only looking." She was not breaking any laws, but it was generally understood that people did not travel on foot outside the city. She knew that her very presence here was suspicious.

"Looking? For what? Trouble?" The soldier laughed haughtily at his own joke.

"No," Astraea said quietly. "I'm looking for . . . something that I lost." She instantly regretted saying it, for now she would have to follow it up with a legitimate story. "I mean to say . . . I'm just . . . looking at the view."

The soldier continued to regard her coldly. "What is your name, Miss?"

She thought fast. Now would be the time to turn herself in, and she supposed it would be wisest to just do so.

"My name is Astraea," she said, in spite of her best intentions. It seemed she wasn't ready to give up quite yet.

The soldier appeared taken aback. His mouth hung open for a moment before he spoke. "Astraea?" he repeated. It was his turn to sound faint.

She nodded, feeling certain that she had just guaranteed her own death sentence. She had now made a deliberate attempt to conceal her true identity to a soldier of Central Command. She might as well sign a confession.

"Astraea," the soldier said, blinking. "This name . . . is known to me."

What did he mean? She began to feel frantic. Was her alias already being associated with her true persona? In a panic, she corrected herself. "I mean to say, my name is Miras. Miras Vara. And . . . and I am from the Ministry of Science, and—"

"Where did you hear that name?" he said, his voice brittle and harsh again. "Astraea. Where did you hear it?"

"I . . . I . . ." Miras did not know how to answer, so she answered truthfully. "I heard it in a dream."

The soldier's expression changed, the hardness in his beady eyes quickly and fluidly transforming into earnest curiosity. There was a long pause before he spoke again, appearing to choose his words carefully. "I have another question for you," he said. "You said that you are looking for something. Are you looking for something . . . that is in plain sight, but . . . *hidden*?"

Miras felt her panic turn into something else. Was this a trick? How could this man—how could anyone—have known the very words spoken by the woman in her dream? She stared at the soldier for a moment before finally collecting her thoughts enough to speak. "Who are you?" she said.

His eyes seemed to bore straight into hers, scrutinizing, prying. "I am Glinn Sa'kat."

"Glinn Sa'kat—but I mean to say—"

Without breaking his gaze, he interrupted her. "You are . . . looking for the book," he said. It seemed to be a statement rather than a question. His voice was somewhat steadier now.

Miras answered without quite thinking about her answer, much in the same way as she had told him her assumed name. "Where everything is written."

The soldier stared at her for a long moment, his breathing seeming especially labored. "You had better come with me," he said, his voice possessing again a trace of the earlier gruffness with which he had ordered her to halt. But there was something else in it now. Something like disbelief, or possibly even fear.

Gar Osen woke at just past dawn and could not seem to get back to sleep. Beams of mild light, clouded through with a haze of ashy dust kicked up from the cold fireplace, were penetrating through the high window in the back of the cottage. One persistent finger of sunshine had landed directly on Gar's left eyelid. He pushed his face underneath the straw-filled bag that served as a pillow, but it was no use. He rose from his bed. He put his head down to stretch out his spine—the surgical alterations to his body had always made him feel so much more vulnerable, though in some ways, he could scarcely remember what it felt like to be in a Cardassian body. The stiffness in his current form might very well be a simple manifestation of his age.

As he lifted his head, he started and then gasped audibly. He was not alone in the room, though the other person was so utterly silent and still that he could have been there all night, as much as Gar would have noticed. "Who are you?"

The Cardassian rose noiselessly, an odd smile playing about his mouth. "Hello, Pasir," he said. "Did you get a good night's sleep?"

Gar was so taken aback at hearing his old name—it had been so many years since anyone had uttered it—that he could not immediately speak. He felt a combination of things, but mostly relief. Was he finally going to get some answers?

The man looked around the cottage. "How can you live like this, Pasir? It's so . . . primitive! Not to mention the cold." The man shivered to illustrate, and then laughed.

Gar was incensed. The other man acted very inappropriately for an agent of the Obsidian Order. "Why are you here?" He didn't really need to ask, for the use of his real name was enough to make it quite plain. "Where is Rhan Ico? She is supposed to be my contact—I've not heard from her in twenty years, at least!"

"I don't know where she is, I've never heard of her," the man answered, his voice reflecting disinterest. "Most likely, she is dead. Enabran Tain saw fit to clean house when he took over the Order."

*Enabran Tain?* The name was only vaguely familiar, and Pasir realized that things must have changed drastically since he'd lost contact with the Order. It was finally becoming plain to him now, why he'd been left to dangle alone in the dark all this time. "What do you want?"

"Well," the man said. "You probably haven't heard that the military sometimes tries to make use of the Order, since they've had so little luck with their own clumsy interrogations. They requested my assistance for what turned out to be a fool's errand, an absolute mockery of an interview in Dahkur." The man rolled his eyes for emphasis. "The military is frightened of its own shadow these days. But so long as I was here anyway, Enabran Tain had an idea of a means by which I might take care of a problem for him."

"A . . . problem?"

"Indeed, for it would appear that your purpose here has—shall we say—expired?"

"What do you mean? I still have a great deal of influence here! I—have a plan, you see. It was I who disposed of the old kai. And I have swung the general opinion of Bajor around to the abandonment of the castes. I will soon be the kai, and then—"

The other man sighed as he interrupted. "I must tell you that Tain was never entirely sure how he meant to use you, Pasir. You were simply a holdover from the days of his predecessor. And yet, he felt that having an operative in the field might prove useful to him in some small way. But if it's true what they are saying about Dukat's new edicts— and it is true—then what good could you possibly be to the Order when you are sent to a work camp with the rest of these Bajoran wretches? No, it is my understanding that although Tain had initially hoped for you to become the next religious leader here, this outcome is rather unlikely to occur, considering the current circumstances. And then there is the matter of the girl at the Ministry of Science . . ."

"What girl? What do you mean?"

"Your cover, Pasir. It has been blown, I'm afraid."

"Impossible!"

"It's true. Tain has considered the situation carefully, and decided that you have become more of a risk than an asset. Your mission is officially over."

"But . . . Dukat! He knows I am here, you must speak to him regarding these new policies of his. I know he does not mean to put me in harm's way—"

The agent laughed. "Dukat! Tain has no business with that fool they call the prefect. Oh, Pasir. You have been alone here for too long. It's a shame I don't have time to explain it all to you. It's rather a good story, actually."

Pasir began to feel desperate, taking a step toward the man. "Have you come to take me home, then?"

The man smiled. "I'm afraid not, my friend."

"Friend?" Pasir spat. "You are no friend of mine. If this isn't an extraction . . ."

It was quite before Pasir knew what was happening that the other man had moved so near to him, so near that a Cardassian phaser—those used by the Order, set to disinte-grate—could effectively do its job. He had time to register disbelief, but that was all.

✦   ✦   ✦

The agent stepped away and holstered his weapon. Pity, to destroy such a miracle of medicine. He'd heard that the process was considered something of an art. He let himself out of the cottage and headed back toward his skimmer without another thought, making so little noise as he moved that he might as well have been floating.

## 13

Lenaris woke up early the next morning, his body protesting against the effects of the night spent sleeping on the ground. Even after all the years spent in the resistance, he had never gottten especially used to sleeping out in the open.

He rolled up his things and observed the sky in the not-quite dawn, the stars still visible in the pale sky. Terok Nor winked as if it were chiding him, and he looked back down at the ground, feeling the impact of all that had happened.

He had been right about the Valerian freighter, but he had been wrong about this. The Pullock V raid had been a disaster, and now the cell had broken apart. Lenaris didn't know when he'd felt so thoroughly despondent; it had been bad after he'd left the Halpas cell, but this was different. This was worse.

The others were waking as well, but as he wandered the vicinity of the mostly empty field in front of him, he realized that Taryl was nowhere to be found. After circling the area in a panic and questioning the others, he ran back toward the village, calling her name the whole time.

The village was deserted. It had always been rough, but without any people in it—chattering, eating, working, or even sleeping—it looked positively eerie. "Taryl?" Lenaris called. "Are you here? Please, answer me!" He thought he saw a light on in her cottage, but maybe it was just wishful thinking. He headed for the little house, and drew back the door.

She was there, sitting at the corner worktable with a single light burning above her, her shoulders hunched. Lenaris thought she was crying, and took an uncertain step toward her. But when she turned, he saw with momentary shock that she was not crying at all—in fact, she was smiling.

"Holem!" she exclaimed, leaping to her feet. "I have to show you what I found!"

She gestured to the table, where a rudimentary comlink was set up on a tiny viewscreen. Taryl had been sifting through Cardassian comm traffic. Lenaris sat down and perused the small screen with the improvised keypad, using a clumsy translation program so that he could read the Cardassian characters. It was difficult to make out, but from what he could gather, the Cardassian comnet had run a story about Pullock V—but this was no ordinary Cardassian newsfeed, churning out propaganda about manufactured Cardassian victories. The casualties, the damage to the facility—it was all here, in plain language—at least as plain as could be interpreted by Taryl's translation software.

"Why . . . would they do this?" he wondered.

"I don't know!" Taryl said, delighted. "But I've already copied it and posted it on a buried channel of the Bajoran 'net where the Cardies can't delete it! Do you see, Holem? We'll be heroes!" She giggled, and then sniffed. Through her jubilance, she had still been crying intermittently, that much was plain by the pink blotches underneath her eyes.

"This is great!" Lenaris said. "If other Bajorans know that we staged an attack offworld—"

"A successful attack," Taryl added.

"It could help to fuel the resistance all over the planet!"

Taryl laughed again, wiping new tears away.

Lenaris kept reading past the point that Taryl had highlighted, and then he came to a part that he knew she was not going to react to quite so triumphantly. "Taryl," he said carefully. "Have you read this entire thing?"

She shook her head. "No, just the first part—it told me all I needed to know. I was looking for the article Harta was talking about, the one about Lac, and I found this."

"There's more to it," Lenaris said. "I think . . ." He pointed to the screen. She leaned over him to read it.

*A Bajoran man apprehended two Cardassian women in a drainage ditch outside the vineyards in Tilar province. The women, including this reporter, were safely recovered, but the Bajoran did not survive.*

"Oh," Taryl said, her smile disappearing. Lenaris quickly stood, helping her back into her seat. She sat down hard, her expression fixed, unseeing, as more tears coursed down her face.

"Taryl," he said softly. "It's okay . . . it will be all right . . . but—we have to go, Taryl. We can't stay here."

It took her a few moments before she seemed to hear him. "You're right," she said faintly, wiping her eyes and doing her best to pull herself together, though it was clearly an effort. "We have to go. Let's tell the others about this story. Maybe they won't feel quite so eager to just forget about the cell once they hear it."

Lenaris nodded, for he was hoping much the same thing. News that the Cardassians had actually taken significant losses from the attack did not make up for Lac's death, or that of the others—nothing would. But it was still a victory, and this article would make it a symbolic one. Hopefully, it could at least inspire what was left of the Ornathia cell into continuing to fight.

Lenaris watched her as she gathered a few things, and the two left the village behind them. He felt a combination of raw, palpable emotions as they left, not knowing where they would go, not knowing how they would get there. But as she turned to smile weakly at him, as if to convince him that she would eventually be all right, he knew it didn't matter, not now—for he would be going there with Taryl.

Dukat's back was to the door when Damar entered his office, and the sight of the turned chair made the gil's heart sink. He knew that Dukat was disappointed in him.

"You asked to see me, sir?" Damar finally spoke, beginning to wonder if the prefect even knew he had entered the room.

Dukat's chair turned around very slowly, and Damar winced internally at his expression. His head was tipped down, his mouth pulled tight. But he did not look angry, exactly. No, he looked . . . sad. And Damar realized that he had done more damage to the relationship than he had thought.

"Hello, Gil Damar," Dukat said. "How is your betrothed?"

Damar felt a tremendous crushing weight at the words, and he wondered if Dukat was deliberately trying to hurt him. "Our enjoinment . . . has been canceled," he said tightly. The burden of what he had just said was a miserable one, and he struggled to keep his composure.

"Ah," Dukat said. "So. You felt it necessary to work out the details of the transaction in person, on the planet."

"Yes," Damar said. "I wanted to be there when she woke up. I did not want her to learn the news from anyone else." As he said it, he felt a small surge of confidence, at least for his relationship with Dukat, for it had not been an unreasonable motive, and he felt sure that Dukat would recognize it as such.

"Indeed," Dukat said. "Personal matters can be so . . . complicated." He spread his hands. "It's a pity it had to occur when there was so much chaos going on here at the station. I suppose I hadn't realized just how much I'd come to rely on you."

Damar bowed his head and murmured an acknowledgment to the compliment.

"Unfortunately, it seems my superiors have other plans for you, Gil Damar. They are reassigning a number of my personnel to the border conflict. It seems there's been something of an outcry within the hierarchy, from a story posted by that woman you saved, the other one. I am afraid you have been selected."

"But—" Damar protested. "If it's all the same to you . . . I prefer to remain on Terok Nor. Even on the surface, if I'm needed there. Please understand, Gul Dukat, it was only the most desperate of circumstances that—"

"I assure you, Gil Damar, this was not my decision. I would prefer to have you remain here as well. But the changes are made. You will be leaving the station within the next three days."

"Yes, sir," Damar said miserably. He knew that Dukat had the power to override the transfer but had deliberately chosen not to, and he could not deny that it stung. Aside from the personal affront, he did not want to go to the border colonies. That he had ever been so foolish to think that diplomacy could solve the problems on Bajor! He wanted, he *needed* to stay here, to fight the insurgents. To kill them, if need be, for the expression that had been on Veja's face when he had told her what had been done to her. *To us.* He knew that the memory would haunt him, that he would never forget it. Not if he lived to be two hundred.

Cold and dead inside, he bowed again to the prefect and turned to leave.

"And . . . Damar?"

"Yes, sir?"

"Thank you for your service here. I shall . . . miss your companionship."

A sudden great sorrow blossomed in the emptiness, that he would likely never see Dukat again. "And I shall miss yours," he said, and meant it.

He turned and left the room as quickly as he could, struggling to hide his expression from anyone he might encounter in ops. He needed to go about gathering up his things. And there would be just a little time left to say good-bye to Veja, probably forever.

*"Miss Lang, you realize I could put out an immediate order for your arrest. Your actions translate to no less than treason!"*

Natima felt sure that Dalak was exaggerating, as he was wont to do. Though of course she was in trouble with Central Command, the offending report had been removed from the comnet before anyone on Cardassia Prime probably even saw it. The story had remained on the Bajoran net for significantly longer, but that didn't matter much—everyone here, Cardassian and Bajoran, already knew the truth anyway. For the most part.

*"What would possess you to even write such a thing, let alone fail to censor it? This is so unlike you, Miss Lang. I am practically speechless."*

How Natima wished the latter part was true! "You have my deepest apologies, Mister Dalak. I suppose I am just not myself after the ordeal I was put through over the weekend. I honestly can't tell you what came over me. I was feeling so much anguish over Veja's condition, and the stress of being in that tunnel—"

*"Of course, Miss Lang, I do sympathize."* Dalak softened his tone somewhat. *"Perhaps it was unreasonable of me to put you to your deadlines without giving you sufficient time to recover."*

"I would never suggest—"

*"No, no, Miss Lang, I insist. You must take an extra day for yourself."*

"An extra day. You are too kind, Mister Dalak. But what I really want to request from you is a new assignment. After all that I have seen and done on this world, I am eager to leave it."

Dalak's moon face managed to look impatient and surprised, at once. *"A new assignment! Miss Lang, you and Veja begged for the positions on Bajor. You may have forgotten, but I was very, very reluctant to assign females to such a dangerous place."*

"That's right, you were. And now I believe I have had my fill of what Bajor has to offer. It seems you may have been right, Mister Dalak." It galled her to say it, but she was really and truly through with Bajor. The temporary madness that had urged her to write that story, to imperil her career—worse, perhaps, to make herself known to those in power as some sort of dissident . . . She would cheerfully go back to reporting on petty crimes and the latest military promotions. She could live for a thousand years without ever seeing another speck of red Bajoran dirt and be perfectly content.

*"Fine, Miss Lang. I will see what I can do. But I have to warn you, I can't promise that you won't ever be sent back to Bajor after this. I need people with experience there. You were the best censor I ever had—before this slipup."*

"Thank you, Mister Dalak." Natima didn't believe his threat for a minute. She'd made him look bad; he would never send her back here. No, she had seen the last of this place—that much was certain. And she couldn't be happier about it.

"Glinn Sa'kat," Astraea said timidly, as she labored to keep up with the quick cadence of the man's footfalls, "where are we going?"

They were walking toward the periphery of the city, through the warehouse district, back toward the Paldar sector, where Miras had once lived.

"You will find out when we get there," the soldier told her.

"Am I in trouble? I told you, my name is Miras Vara. I . . . misfiled an object at the Ministry of Science. I am a criminal, a fugitive. Aren't you going to arrest me?"

Sa'kat turned to her. "No," he said. "I will not be arresting you—Astraea."

She was confused. "But—we can't go back to Paldar. I'll be— Why am I not under arrest? I don't understand any of this!"

"No," Sa'kat said, "I imagine you don't. You probably knew little or nothing about Oralius when you began having your dreams, am I correct?"

"That's right," she said, and the mention of the name Oralius confirmed to her what she had begun to understand—that this man was somehow connected to her dreams, to the Hebitian woman, the mask and the book.

"It is not an accident that we have met."

His proclamation did nothing to clarify her confusion. "Are you . . . are you taking me to the book?"

"You'll find out when we get there," he said again, and she was surprised to see that he was smiling.

"Glinn Sa'kat," she said carefully, "are you an Oralian? Is that what this is about?"

He walked a little slower, seeming to consider. "You know, I suppose I never considered myself to be an Oralian. There are no more Oralians, not really."

They came upon an old sidewalk, out of the city's edge and back to where she could set her feet on syncrete again. The hard surface, while somewhat punishing to the soles of her feet, was a relief to her ankles after walking in the unsturdy gravel and sand. They'd reached the dead industrial zone, haunted by shadows and hot, dry winds.

Sa'kat went on. "The last people to walk the Way disappeared many years ago. Central Command tried to round them up and exterminate them, ship them to Bajor and the surrounding colonies, where they were never heard from again. But they didn't get everyone. There were still a few left behind. They weren't killed, they simply . . . went underground. And then they stopped practicing altogether."

"And you—you were one of those?" It surprised her, since he appeared to be so young—not much older than she was, by her estimation, though it was not always easy to tell with soldiers. Something in their hardened expressions seemed to make them ageless.

Sa'kat shook his head. "No," he said. "I was not. But my parents were."

Ah. "The Way is not dead, only . . ."

"Only sleeping," he finished. "Waiting. Waiting for you." He began to walk quickly again, and she scrambled to keep up.

"But why me?" she protested. "As you say, I knew nothing of Oralius when I began to have those dreams, when I saw the woman by the creek. She showed me a mask! She said her name was Astraea—"

Sa'kat stopped walking. "You *saw* her?"

"Yes. Who . . . who is she?"

"She is—or was—a guide, for Oralius."

Miras shook her head, still not understanding. "Oralius, who was he? Why did people follow him?"

"Not him," Sa'kat corrected her. "Oralius, though She has no corporeal form, is usually referred to in the feminine, at least in the sect favored by my parents."

"No corporeal form? Like a . . . a ghost?"

Sa'kat laughed. "A ghost, a spirit, if you like. She follows no linear time, and She does not inhabit a body, like you or I. She is always with us, but She needs a guide, a spiritual vessel, to channel Her. We have been without a guide for nearly a century. After the death of the last guide, it was written that Her Way would collapse, until the emergence of the next guide."

"The next guide," Miras repeated. She was beginning to understand now. She was beginning to understand that Sa'kat believed *she* was that guide. Although she was not certain if she believed it herself.

"How can you be so sure that this is—"

"I can't be sure," he said, cutting her off. He resumed walking. "Nobody can be sure of anything, can they? But there are those things that we believe strongly enough, that we would be willing to take serious risk for them. That is the definition of faith, Astraea."

"Faith," she echoed, quite without realizing that she had spoken it aloud.

They had passed through the rusting dead zone and were beginning to come into the portion of the city that was inhabited. There were a few pedestrians milling around up ahead of them on the sidewalk, along with the occasional soldier, dressed identically to Sa'kat, patrolling the sector.

His voice dropped to a confidential tone. "I will tell you more of this when we arrive. You will be safe there. I have many contacts, in all facets of society, who will do whatever it takes to keep you from harm's reach."

Miras was overwhelmed. "And you will show me the book?"

"Yes," he said. "It is almost time to begin."

He smiled at her then, and she saw powerful feelings in his gaze: awe and fear, amusement, and a shining brightness that she could not name.

"It is time for us to be reborn," he said, and for the first time since she'd dreamed of the Hebitian woman, since her life had effectively been hijacked by the Orb, she felt as if things might work out, after all.

# OCCUPATION YEAR TWENTY-SIX

◆ ◆ ◆

2353 (Terran Calendar)

# 14

Nerys was crying as she made her way to the shrine nearest to her father's house, and she wiped her eyes with shame. She was no longer a child, she was ten years old, and there was no excuse for tears—not even after what had happened. Some people had to endure worse, much worse. And anyway, why should she cry when the Cardassians had let her go? She was safe, she could go back home to her father and her brothers—but that was just it, wasn't it? She was safe, but Petra Chan wasn't.

Nerys entered the shrine, looking hopefully for Prylar Istani. Her brothers and her uncle and cousins had all just dismissed her tears. They told her to stop behaving like this when really they should all just be grateful that they were together, while her father had been sympathetic but strangely distant. Nerys couldn't forget the look on Chan's face when the Cardassians had taken her away. How could she ever forget such a thing? It positively haunted her, and though she'd always lived with the aliens' presence, had even encountered a few very unpleasant soldiers in her short life, the day that they had come to Dahkur and taken away a dozen teenage girls in the village was perhaps the most stark and terrifying event Nerys had ever witnessed.

Nerys did not encounter Prylar Istani right away; instead, she found Vedek Porta tending the shrine. She tried not to let disappointment show in her voice when she greeted him, for though she respected the old man, she certainly could not speak to him about what had happened—and how she felt about it.

"Nerys, I'd take it you're looking for Istani Reyla," Vedek Porta said knowingly.

"Oh . . ." Nerys began, not wishing to be unkind, but the old priest merely inclined his head and went for the vestibule at the back of the shrine, where he soon emerged with Prylar Istani, dressed in her traditional orange robes. Vedek Porta left them alone, and Istani stretched out her arms.

"Nerys!" the kind-faced woman greeted her. "You've been crying. Come. Sit with me and tell me what troubles you."

Nerys sat gratefully on the bare floor facing the woman who had been a friend to the Kira family since before Nerys was born. Nerys felt as though she could confide almost anything to Istani, who always listened without judging—unlike her brothers—and with the feminine understanding that Nerys's father seemed unable to grasp.

"It's just . . . the other day, when the Cardassians came . . ."

Istani's face darkened, and she squeezed Nerys's hand. "Yes, Nerys. It was a terrible day."

"But . . . why? What did they want with those girls?"

The prylar's voice was soft with hesitation, and Nerys had the impression that she was concealing something from her. "Perhaps . . . they wanted younger girls, so that they can begin training them for a particular job that is easier learned in one's youth . . ."

"I told them," Nerys sniffled, "when they came to the center of town and began to select girls from the crowd, I shouted that they should choose me instead of Petra Chan . . ." Nerys began almost to sob now, for she missed her friend, the teenage girl who'd been like a mentor and older sister, and Nerys feared terribly for her safety. "But . . . but . . . ," she continued, "they said I was too young, and too scrawny . . . and Petra Chan isn't even that much older than me . . . and she's thinner than I am!"

"Nerys," Istani said, her voice soothing, "the Prophets will look after Petra Chan now, and you must thank Them for Their blessings. You and your family have always had plenty to eat, and you are together—"

"Not my mother," Kira pointed out, aware that she was being, as her brothers often accused her, a pessimist, only seeing the negative side of things. Of course she should be counting her blessings for having avoided whatever fate had befallen those teenage girls. She should be relieved that the Cardassians took Chan instead of her, but she didn't feel lucky or blessed—she felt guilty and angry.

"Nerys, my child," Istani crooned, reading the tortured agony in Nerys's face, "you will have to come to terms with your anger. We all suffer—it is part of the cycle of life. But it pleases the Prophets when Their children can transcend a life mired in misery, even in these . . . conditions."

Nerys said nothing for a moment, only finished having her cry, and then caught her breath, her head now resting on the prylar's shoulder. She thought, but did not say aloud, that if there were some way she could fight back, even a small way, if there were some way of surpassing these feelings of complete helplessness, maybe she could finally come to terms with how unhappy she felt. Maybe she could finally begin to achieve the peace she craved, the peace she knew the Prophets wanted her to have. But what could she do, as a ten-year-old girl?

Sitting there in the shrine, the last of her sobs calming themselves in her chest, she made a silent vow. She made it for her mother, and for Petra Chan, and for everyone else she knew who had been taken away or who had died. And mostly, she made it for herself; for the child who had never experienced childhood.

Dukat scowled when he received the call from ops; he didn't care for the way the new glinn in security delivered his messages. The manner in which the soldier bit off the ends of his words irritated Dukat, and he disliked that the man insisted on being referred to by his given name. The prefect had initially refused, but since nearly everyone else on the station had fallen into the habit, Dukat would maddeningly find himself referring to the soldier as just "Thrax."

*Too many eccentricities,* Dukat decided, *and he's too remote. Still, those are hardly actionable offenses.*

The comm signaled again. Dukat sighed. "What is it, Thrax?"

*"You asked to be informed when Gul Darhe'el's transport was on approach. It will dock in ten metrics."*

"Ah, yes," Dukat said, smirking as he considered the conversation that was about to take place. "At last he graces us with his presence. Have an honor guard meet him at the airlock. See that he is escorted directly to my office."

*"Acknowledged."*

It was not long before Dukat's office doors parted, and the dour-faced Darhe'el crossed the threshold, looking somewhat drawn. Dukat remained seated behind his great black desk, but pointedly did not invite the other man to take one of the guest chairs. "Gul Darhe'el. Welcome back."

"Prefect," Darhe'el said tightly. His voice was cold and hard, as always.

Dukat, by contrast, kept his tone gregarious. "And how was your stay on Cardassia?"

The other man was clearly fighting to rein in his contempt, which amused Dukat no end. Darhe'el always was too arrogant for his own good. "It was brief," he answered with exaggerated stiffness.

The prefect chuckled. "Yes, I expect it was. Congratulations, by the way, on receiving the Proficient Service Medallion. I must confess that I had wondered if you got the news about the accident at Gallitep while they were pinning the medal on your chest, or if they waited until the reception." Darhe'el's only answer was his cold stare, and Dukat finally rose from his chair, abandoning the game. "But we aren't here to discuss the honors that have recently been heaped upon you, are we?" He picked up one of several padds scattered across his desk, and slowly walked around to the other side, reading the report that was displayed on the device's tiny screen. "Dozens dead, with the number expected to rise in the coming days; even more permanently disabled; fully one third of the Bajorans and Cardassians in the camp believed to be afflicted with a malady we don't even have a name for yet . . . and all mining activity temporarily suspended." He tossed the padd back onto the desk. It clattered loudly as it landed. "I don't appreciate having to clean up your messes."

Darhe'el held Dukat's gaze. "We both understand what this amounts to, Prefect—the one issue behind which we have always stood together: insufficient resources to manage the annexation properly. Lack of adequate personnel, lack of proper equipment—"

Dukat snorted. "You're not going to escape responsibility for this by laying the blame at the feet of Central Command, that I can assure you. The fact of the matter is that *your* men mishandled a crisis that never should have arisen."

"I was informed that the AI failed to correctly identify a pocket of poisonous gas—a toxin of a type never before encountered . . ."

"This was hardly the fault of the artificial intelligence,"

Dukat snapped. "This was the fault of the men who were supposed to have been trained to operate the system, to correct for inevitable failures on the part of the machine— the men who serve under *you*. This is about your facility falling apart while you were enjoying the accolades of Central Command under the Cardassian sun."

For the first time, Darhe'el's face lost its scowl as his mouth spread into a thin smile. "Is the prefect asking me to resign from my post?"

Dukat's eyes narrowed. In fact, he wanted much more than to remove Darhe'el from Gallitep—he wanted him off Bajor. Darhe'el was a longtime favorite of Kell, and had been the legate's personal choice to become prefect of the annexation, before Dukat's secret maneuvering among the other members of Central Command had overridden Kell's decision and secured the posting for himself. Dukat ascended, while Darhe'el remained at Gallitep. But the fact that the two guls were on opposite poles when it came to Bajoran policy wasn't something that Kell had overlooked when he required Darhe'el to remain in charge of the mine. Of that Dukat was certain. Kell might be outwardly magnanimous, but he was unlikely ever to forgive Dukat, with whom he had long been at odds, for outmaneuvering him. Darhe'el was there to be Kell's thorn in Dukat's side . . . one the prefect was effectively powerless to remove.

"No," he finally said in answer to Darhe'el's question. Kell would never allow the other gul's removal, not while Gallitep was productive, and Darhe'el knew that. Even Dukat's political allies in Central Command would have none of it; they could hardly support the idea that the recently decorated Darhe'el bore responsibility for the mining accident. If anything, their public statements would emphasize the fact that, by taking place during Darhe'el's absence, the accident proved how vital he was to Cardassian interests on Bajor. Nor would they be persuaded that insufficient resources and manpower were to blame for what happened. In the end, Dukat knew, the fault would land squarely where it always did: at the feet of Bajor's prefect.

Dukat turned away from the other man and went back to his chair, speaking as he rounded his desk again. "Your file will be updated to contain an official reprimand. Gallitep is to be made fully operational again within five days. New troops will be provided to bring your personnel up to its previous level, and I'll speak to Secretary Kubus about replenishing your workforce. The laborers who were exposed will continue to work for the time being. When they show symptoms of the disease, we can assess whether it will be feasible to treat them—or if they would be better off at Dr. Moset's . . . hospital." The good doctor was always in need of new test subjects for his Fostossa vaccines. "For the next two service quartiles, you will operate as usual, but you will be required to deliver semi-quarterly reports and submit to inspections by officials of my choosing—"

"The AI will require an upgrade."

"You are hardly in a position to be making demands," Dukat snapped.

"And I didn't think I needed to remind you that Gallitep is by far Bajor's most productive—"

"*Was* Bajor's most productive facility. Terok Nor surpassed it some time ago, even before this . . . mishap."

"I meant to say on the *surface* of Bajor, of course," Darhe'el amended. "Though we both know that Terok Nor does not produce anything, only processes what Gallitep and facilities like it provide."

Dukat busied himself with one of the other padds on his desk, refusing to look up. "Perhaps you should get back to what's left of your facility now, Darhe'el."

"Are you officially denying me the upgrade I've requested?"

"Qualified personnel for such delicate work are at a premium, as you know perfectly well. But I'll see what I can do."

"And the executions?"

Dukat scoffed. "What executions?"

"The examples we need to make to discourage further acts of sabotage."

"This wasn't an act of sabotage."

"Does that matter?" Darhe'el asked. "News of the accident will spread, if it hasn't already. The insurgents will use it in their propaganda. The facts will be distorted to fit their ends. They may even claim responsibility for bringing Gallitep to a standstill, and that in turn will embolden their countrymen to contemplate more acts of terrorism. We have to stop it before it starts."

Dukat sighed. "I'll take your suggestion under advisement."

Darhe'el abruptly left the spot to which he'd rooted himself, and leaned toward Dukat with both hands on the gleaming black surface of the prefect's desk. His voice was surprisingly quiet. "You're throwing it away, Dukat. All of it. Bajor should have been brought under control long ago, but you insist on coddling these people. You want them to love you when you should be making them fear you. You've yet to learn that no one believes in benevolent despots."

"Are you finished?" Dukat asked.

Darhe'el straightened, his expression as he looked down at Dukat one of undisguised disgust. "Permission to disembark . . . *sir.*"

"Go home, Gul Darhe'el," Dukat drawled. "Go home to your hole in the ground."

Darhe'el turned and marched out without another word, leaving the prefect alone with his thoughts. Dukat sat back in his chair, steepling his fingers. The other gul's lack of proper deference was infuriating, but Dukat knew better than to succumb to it. Darhe'el might be Kell's favorite, but ultimately he was as powerless to harm Dukat as Dukat was to harm him. Let him bluster. In time Dukat would show them all he was right about Bajor.

Darhe'el was correct about one thing, however: Gallitep's AI software needed attention as quickly as possible to get the mining operation back up and running. But the Union manpower shortages on Bajor were ongoing, and he couldn't afford to wait for Central Command to process a request for a specialist to be sent from Prime—the accident had already put them dangerously off quota. The longer it took, the farther behind they'd fall.

It then occurred to Dukat that the answer to his problem might already be within easy reach. Perhaps there was someone at the Bajoran Institute of Science who was qualified to handle the job. . . .

Even as Dukat reached toward his companel to order Thrax to raise the institute, the console unexpectedly chimed on its own accord—in a specific pattern that Dukat knew denoted a personal call.

*From Bajor.*

He found himself glancing about his office guiltily before he answered, bringing up the image of a young Bajoran woman, sneezing uncontrollably.

*"Skrain,"* the woman said, between her violent nasal outbursts.

Dukat found himself backing away from the screen. "Naprem," he said, addressing the attractive woman, almost young enough to be called a girl. "My dear, whatever is the matter? Are you ill?"

She shook her head, unable to speak as another sneeze overtook her. *"No, Skrain,"* she said, taking an enormous, exhausted breath. She sneezed again and shook her head. *"Don't you know what this means?"*

Dukat slowly shook his head, trying to remember

what it meant when Bajorans started to sneeze like this. He found it more than a little revolting, actually. Cardassians did not generally have such noisy and appallingly *fluid* bodily functions.

"It mean—ah—it means that I'm going to—choo—I'm going to have a baby, Skrain."

Dukat was speechless, and watched her clear her breath for yet another sneeze.

"Did you hear what I said? I'm going to have our baby."

"How . . . wonderful," he said, his voice a little faint.

The room was sweltering. Laren could scarcely bring herself to take a breath; the air was searingly hot and smelled reptilian, the distinct odor of the filthy Cardassians who occupied it.

"Please," gasped Ro Gale, twisting his body in a futile attempt to relieve the pressure from his wrists. He was manacled to chains that hung from the ceiling. "Get my daughter out of here!"

The Cardassian interrogator ignored her father's pleas, his horrid skin as pale as fusionstone, his expression a mask of cruelty. His hair, the strange, distinct color of sunscorched grass, shone hideously beneath the hot lights of the room. "We're not finished here, Mister Ro."

Laren's hands tightened as she looked frantically for a way out. The cloying heat in the room was so intense, she feared she would lose consciousness if she remained much longer. She could not bear to watch her father be humiliated in this way. It shamed her; her father was supposed to be brave. He was supposed to fight the Cardassians, not cry and squeal like a child. She wanted to be out of this room. She wanted to be anywhere else but here, anywhere at all—

And then she was, bundled inside her sleeping bag, sweating between the layers of clothes and the coarse bedroll. She blinked. The light of dawn was just beginning to seep through the dense tree cover overhead.

*Dream, just a dream. Forget it.* It was what she told herself every time.

She wriggled out of the blankets and stood, began shaking off the dirt and leaves she had used to conceal the place where she slept, deep in the Jo'kala forest. The foliage here was so thick, the forest so wide, that the Cardassian ground tanks couldn't penetrate the hilly terrain beneath the dense, heavy-branched trees. Soldiers had to patrol it by foot— but no Cardassian knew the forests well enough to venture very deep inside them, not without heavy communications equipment that buzzed and chirped so loudly the dead could hear them.

She rolled up her "bed" and set about organizing her few things. Though it was not yet dawn, she knew it soon would be. She might as well get up and face the day; she didn't care to go back to sleep if it only meant having the same damned nightmare again and again.

She forced her thoughts ahead, going over what she had to do for the day. She stuffed her pack inside an old bag made from a sheet of Cardassian smartplastic, and slung it up around her shoulders, her phaser rifle fastened down around the bottom. She stretched her thin legs as she did this, and headed toward main "camp," where Bram Adir and the others were probably still asleep. The nightmare, the *memory* was still there, but it grew dim as she walked. She replaced the violence of her father's death with well-worn thoughts of what it would be like to put a phaser salvo right into the hideously grinning face of that oddly light-haired Cardassian. There were times when she could think of little else.

She had killed four Cardassians already. Four different Cardassian soldiers, on four separate occasions, with her resistance cell. She was one of the best fighters in this bunch, even though she wasn't quite fourteen yet. Some of the others in the cell still tried to get away with treating her like a child, but she knew better. She knew that her hide was tougher than that of many of the full-grown men she had met in her short time with the rebels. And there was nobody who could pick a pocket like she could, nobody who could steal a holstered phaser right from under a Cardassian soldier's bony nose. She had a talent for it; Bram had said so, many times.

Part of her ability came with her age, her deceptively girlish face. She knew this, and she took full advantage of it. It did the spoonheads no good to underestimate any Bajoran, but least of all Ro Laren.

It was with that thought that she spied Bram's bedroll in the ethereal light of the approaching dawn, and she picked up a pebble to chuck at his sleeping form. It pelted the heavy fabric of his dirty blanket, and he sat up like a spring-loaded toy. Bram rubbed his forehead, wisps of dark hair plastered across it.

"What the *kosst* . . . oh, Laren, it's you. I ought to have known. For Prophet's sake, girl, go back to bed! B'hava'el is just waking."

"Lazy, that's what you are," Laren chided him. She enjoyed pushing Bram's buttons. He was just so delightfully easy to rile.

Bram shook his head. "I don't know why I bother to keep carrying you along with us after all the grief you cause me, day after day . . ."

"Because you need me," Laren said.

"It's because you have nowhere else to go," Bram said, "and I have a foolishly kind heart." He removed himself from his improvised bed, stretching, and shook his bedroll clear of debris, much as Laren had done.

"I have plenty of places I could go," Laren said.

"Sure, of course," Bram said. "Go back to your uncle—"

"I'll *never* go back there!" Laren said. She turned abruptly from Bram and ran down to the creek to wash her face in the icy water. Bram knew he could infuriate her by mentioning her "parents," and he always had to play that card when he was annoyed with her, which was much of the time.

Laren had been on her own since she was twelve, when she ran away from her uncle's house for the last time. After Ro Gale was murdered, Laren's mother sank into such a state of despair that she had to be taken in by her family. She was no longer capable of looking after herself, let alone her daughter. Laren had been confused by her mother's reaction—she missed her father terribly, of course, and she understood being sad about it—but why would her mother turn away from her daughter, as well, the only person who might have been a source of comfort? And why subject her child to the random cruelties that had gone on in that overcrowded house, full of so many cousins and foster orphans collected from neighboring villages that her uncle didn't even know everyone's name? Laren wouldn't have dreamed of just . . . giving up, the way her mother had; a mother was supposed to protect her child. In this, both of Laren's parents had failed miserably.

After several attempts to strike out on her own, Laren was finally emancipated at twelve, when the adults from her extended family stopped coming after her. It was not the most unusual thing, on Bajor, for a child to be on the streets by herself. Common enough, in fact, as to be unworthy of remark. She was only lucky she'd never been picked up by one of the Cardassian orphan-catchers. Lucky, or smart.

Laren learned how to dodge the spoonheads quickly enough, and how to pick their pockets even quicker. From the older children on the streets she had learned how to break and enter, and how to manipulate simple security systems, even the computers that ran some of the rationing checkpoints. It was a skill that had come in plenty handy when she finally encountered Bram Adir, the man who had taken her under his wing and been a bit like a father to her. Like a father, only bossier, and without much affection. Laren had long ago decided that she preferred it that way. Anyway, who else was going to teach her how to fly raiders? She was hungry to learn everything, but flying off-world—it was worth the price of Bram's constant nagging and admonishments.

Laren rubbed her face with the creek water and shook the droplets from her fingertips.

Bram came up behind her just then, to fill his water-pack at the creek. "You know I was only having some fun, saying that about your uncle . . ." He trailed off.

"I know," Laren said sharply. "Are we ready to go?"

"Nearly," he answered. He capped off his pack, brimming over with cold water, and fastened the flat pouch around his back with a pair of straps. "Did you fill up your canteen? You're not sucking off my water like you always do."

"I only did that one time, and that was ages ago!" Bram had a long memory where Laren was concerned. She followed him as they returned to their base camp, near where the cell's four raiders were hidden. "Aren't we flying today, then?"

"Not today," Bram told her. "I got a tip about something on the surface, a few *kellipates* outside of town. We'll need you to override a security system—nothing fancy— just to let the rest of us in, and we'll take care of the heavy lifting."

She pouted. "Heavy lifting," she sniffed. "So I don't get to kill any spoonheads?"

"There won't even be anyone there," Bram told her.

"We're just pinching some supplies. When I said heavy lifting, I meant that literally."

Laren shrugged, supposing she could live with that. She withdrew her canteen from her improvised pack and shook it—nearly empty. She considered rushing back to the creek, but decided it wasn't worth it. Bram had plenty of water for the both of them.

Doctor Mora Pol's hands were trembling as he poured the bluish substance from one beaker into another. He held it up to the light, and then brought it back down to his work surface, where he could measure the changes with his tricorder.

"Pol!" The familiar, clipped voice piped up so suddenly from behind him that Mora nearly dropped the beaker.

"Mirosha, you startled me!" Mora was openly irritated in his reply. Doctor Daul Mirosha was the only other Bajoran in the facility. Although it retained its pre-occupation name, the Bajoran Institute of Science, the Cardassians had taken it over long ago, expunging nearly all of the Bajoran researchers who had once worked there. It had happened gradually, the scientists leaving the institute one at a time, a few finding their way to refugee camps with the rest of the idle Bajorans. But many of them had seemed to disappear—most likely sent to work camps, or possibly even executed. No one spoke of it, not even Mora and Daul.

The two Bajoran researchers knew that someday they, too, would most likely disappear. But for now, the two worked together in tight quarters, under tremendous pressure to yield results in the most unrealistic of time frames.

"How does it look?" Daul asked him, trying to peer around his shoulder at the beaker.

"Well, I suppose I'll tell you when I've run an active scan," Mora said coolly. "If you don't mind, that is."

"By all means," Daul replied, his tone equally cool. The

two men did not always relish each other's company. It should have been comforting to have another Bajoran face in the facility, but familiarity often bred contempt in these close quarters.

Mora initiated the scan. The test was chemical, a possible precursor to a treatment for Orkett's disease. He moved a step forward, to free himself of the sour breath of his lab partner, and then frowned at the readouts.

"Let me see," Daul insisted, reaching for the beaker, and Mora instinctively pulled it away.

"Just a minute," he snapped. "You're going to break it if you keep clutching and grasping like that."

"Are you two finished squabbling?" Doctor Yopal, the director of the institute, stood in the entry, her arms folded.

"We weren't squabbling," Daul said quickly, his arms falling to his sides.

Yopal wore the same expression as always, a face mostly bereft of any detectable emotion, aside from a very obviously manufactured upward curve to her lips; that curve was always there. Whether she was angry, thrilled, exhausted, or depressed, Mora could never be quite sure, for her expression never deviated, not even for a moment. He had come to expect no less from her, or from any other Cardassian.

Yopal was usually friendly, sometimes almost intimately so, chatting with Mora about various personal issues from her life just as his old Bajoran colleagues had. But it was all performed with that distinctive little half-turn of a smile, a subtle, consistent indication that her entire persona was a front, pasted over something else. Mora was slightly terrified of Yopal, in spite of her efforts.

"I must say, gentlemen, the state of your notes on this project has been less than satisfactory for quite some time."

"Doctor Yopal, I apologize," Mora said, his words tumbling out a little too fast.

"Yes," Daul spoke over him. "We have done our best to

master Cardassian syntax, but I fear that sometimes we focus too much on the work and too little on the vocabulary."

Yopal made an amused sound. "Men . . ." she began, the start of a familiar refrain. "You simply aren't capable of the same kind of attention to detail as women. I suppose you cannot realistically be faulted—you were born with the natural inclination toward immediate results, with less regard for the process of getting there. Sometimes, gentlemen, the journey is as important as the destination—often even more so. I find myself reminding you of this truth far more often than I would a female scientist."

Mora thought she might as well have been describing the difference between Bajoran and Cardassian, but he only nodded. "Of course, Doctor Yopal," he said with well-rehearsed sincerity. "Again, my deepest apologies. It won't happen again."

She moved on now, wasting no words. "Doctor Daul, I have news for you. You will no longer be working on this assignment."

There was a terrible moment directly after she spoke when Mora felt certain that he was about to see his friend for the very last time, and he immediately regretted all the moments of unkindness the two had shared. He tried to shoot his friend a look of appropriate apology, but Yopal was still talking.

"Because you have a background in artificial intelligence programming, Doctor Daul, I will be assigning you to begin work on an upgrade to a defective system that currently is in place at a nearby mining facility."

"A mining facility?" Daul replied. "You mean—at a work camp?"

Mora flinched inside, but Yopal was unmoved, as always, her smile intact. "Yes, Doctor Daul, at Gallitep."

Mora felt a shiver run through him at the mention of the facility. Every Bajoran knew about Gallitep. They knew it was a miserable, inescapable place, a place to be avoided at any cost.

Yopal went on. "The program is badly outdated, and . . . there was an incident, recently, that has warranted immediate attention."

"Certainly," Daul answered, his tone barely concealing the misery he must have been feeling.

Yopal nodded, tapped her chalky fingers against her upper arms. "Unfortunately, we no longer have many scientists on staff with this type of engineering in their repertoires. You'll be working mostly alone. As for you, Mora . . ." She turned, and hesitated.

An anvil of fear settled in on Mora's chest, his thoughts racing toward his deepest dread. He was about to disappear, like all the other Bajoran scientists who had once worked here, those whose expertise had become irrelevant in the sphere of what Cardassians considered to be useful research. He swallowed down a massive lump before he registered that Yopal had resumed speaking.

". . . an unknown sample of organic material, brought in several years ago, by a friend of mine in the military after it was discovered adrift in the Denorios Belt. It doesn't have any particular priority, but I just ran into her at a conference and I was quite embarrassed to have to confess that I'd not even taken a look at it yet. Just see what you can find out about it, and give me a report as soon as you're ready."

"Y-yes, Doctor Yopal."

She nodded to him, the half smile twitching a little before she took her leave of them.

"Thank you," he called after her. It seemed somewhat inappropriate to thank her, but he never missed an opportunity. Without Yopal's continued goodwill, he would have no job. A single misstep, and he'd likely have no life at all.

He watched Daul as he concluded his report on their current research, tidying his house for the latest project—

one that Mora knew amounted to collaboration with the Cardassians. But if it was collaboration that kept them alive, Mora was only too willing to comply, sick as it may have made him, and it was abundantly apparent that Daul felt very much the same way. What choice did they have?

Six months after the prefect had received the news about the outcome of his indiscretion with Tora Naprem, Basso Tromac was feeling hot with resentment. It was not a new sensation for him, nor was it one he liked much. He'd been Dukat's Bajoran adjutant on this station for seven years now, and he wondered if there would ever be a time that he would be treated with respect. He doubted it. Dukat was thoroughly unpleasant even to Kubus Oak at times, and Kubus was a man of great prestige.

Basso was fed up with having to deal with the Kira family. Taban was always surly to him, despite the fact that his visits meant extra food for his dirty-faced children, despite the fact that he brought medicine and goods that Taban was undoubtedly selling on the black market—despite it all, Kira Taban treated him like the enemy, and Basso was tired of it.

He was even more tired of being sent to deal with Meru, time and time again. Basso felt that Meru was a spoiled, inconsolable woman, and as she had gotten older, her demands and her tantrums had become increasingly unreasonable. She had far too much freedom on the station, which worried Basso from time to time. If she'd had the wherewithal, she could have made life very unpleasant for any number of people, especially Dukat. Basso had tried to delicately broach that topic with the prefect, but always met with dismissal; Dukat obviously thought Basso was merely put out at having to cater to his mistress, which did at least hold some measure of truth.

It disgusted Basso that Meru couldn't simply appreciate how lucky she was to have avoided the mines, for that was exactly where he felt she deserved to be. She had been pretty once, to be sure, but she was far from young now, and though Dukat saw to it that she was regularly afforded the latest in cosmetic treatments to keep her countenance youthful, the ever-present grief in her eyes aged her more than mere time ever could. It gave her a haunted presence, something that never failed to unsettle Basso. He despised being sent to look after her. He would have been happy never to have to speak to her again.

He entered her quarters, where she was seated behind an easel, working on one of her tiresome pieces of iconography. Although Basso had long ago rejected the meanings behind the *D'jarras*, he still held those from the artist sect in mild contempt, for he had been mistreated by a girl from the *Ih'valla D'jarra* in his youth.

"Hello, Meru," Basso said flatly. "I've been sent to see if you'll be needing anything for tonight. The prefect regrets to inform you that he has business on the surface."

The somber woman's mouth pulled down in a frown. "Again?" she said, in her mournful way. "He never used to go to the surface. Now he's down there all the time. I wonder what has changed recently?"

Basso knew exactly what had changed. He hesitated, considering the implications for only a fleeting moment before he said it. "Well, I suppose you weren't aware that Naprem recently gave birth to a baby girl."

"Naprem?" Meru leaned back very far in her seat as she regarded Basso with puzzlement. "Who . . . is Naprem?"

"Why, Meru, I suppose I thought you already knew about Tora Naprem. She is another of Dukat's . . . comfortgivers. She resides on the surface, however. I suppose Dukat felt it wouldn't be decent to have you both on the station."

Meru looked appropriately shocked, and Basso felt a cruel twist of amusement. Maybe now Meru would think twice about giving the prefect such a difficult time of it, if she understood how disposable she really was. "So, you'll not be needing anything, then?"

Meru shook her head from side to side, slowly, as if in a complete daze. Basso bowed to her and walked backwards out of the room, letting the doors close behind him. He chuckled unpleasantly as he left the room, but then he considered. He would have to handle the aftermath of this carefully. It would not bode well for him if Dukat were to learn who had leaked the secret to his station mistress. Basso began immediately to formulate his next move, for he would have to be clever to keep his own skin safe.

*It was worth it, though,* he thought. The look on her face ... Definitely worth it.

Dr. Mora ran through the security protocols for his computer, shutting down the laboratory for the night. It was late, and he was exhausted, but he considered himself lucky that he was even going home tonight—Doctor Daul had been spending many a night in the laboratory since he had been put on the artificial intelligence upgrade.

Mora considered the progress he had made with Yopal's anomalous organic material, which had turned out to be a gelatinous substance with the ability to mimic various forms about the laboratory—even a vaguely humanoid form. The Cardassians were quite impressed with what Mora had heretofore done with it, but beyond party tricks, Mora wasn't sure what further progress there was to be made with the *"odo'ital,"* as the Cardassians had begun to call it—the word for "unknown sample" in their native language.

Mora regarded the amber-hued liquid, the color of *copal* cider, stirring peacefully in a transparent container in the corner of the lab. He considered, with curious pride—as well as some measure of concern—that the liquid had increased in mass considerably since he began running his tests. He had enjoyed his work with the *odo'ital,* and would no doubt miss it once Doctor Yopal reassigned him to something else—for as soon as she discovered that his research was beginning to plateau, she would no doubt find a new project for Mora, possibly even something as unpleasant as Gallitep's mining operation.

He sighed heavily as he dimmed the lights and turned to go, but a strangely familiar sound stopped him in his tracks. He turned, looking around the lab, empty of life. "Hello?" he said, a little uneasily.

He was met with silence. He checked himself, chuckling a little at his own tired jumpiness, and turned again. And then again, there it was. A sound that was distinctly . . . well, it was very much like . . . it was a *sigh.*

Ever the scientist, Mora sighed again himself, louder this time. Sure enough, he was met with a response in kind, though he could not be sure where it was coming from. His face prickled as he considered the eeriness of it, but he had a strange hunch that he knew what was making the sound—for he had suspected for months now that the *odo'ital* was more than just a tank of glop. He'd been possessed of . . . a feeling, an idea. He believed the goo, unquestionably a new kind of life-form, was more than just some cellular broth. He begun to suspect it might actually be sentient.

Once more he sighed, and once more he heard a similar sound coming from the corner of the lab. He was sure of it now, it was coming from the tank, where the golden soup roiled and sloshed in its container, an approximation of Bajor's seas during a brilliant storm. The life-form was trying to communicate with him. Mora knew it. And this was the breakthrough he needed right now, to save his tenuous placement at the institute. He ordered the computer to put the lights back up. He would not be going home tonight after all.

Ro Laren's raider hung passively in space as she waited for a signal from Sadakita Rass, the pilot who was flying the scoutship. The Bram cell always stuck to the same formation when they left the Bajoran atmosphere, dodging the grids by staggering their signals in a particular fashion that confused the Cardassian patrol vessels. Laren tapped her sensor panel impatiently with her fingers before she got the chirp she was waiting for. She put on a burst of speed and quickly changed her direction.

It was not ten minutes later that she saw what her cell was after—the drifting wreckage of an alien freighter, first spied by Sadakita two days before. She had reported it back to Bram, who decided it was worth a second look. Laren had no means of confirming it, but Sadakita believed the vessel had belonged to the Ferengi, the alien merchants who sometimes dared venture into other star systems, even B'hava'el's, if it meant a big enough profit.

Laren could already see that the freighter had sustained extensive damage to its port side. Probably the inhabitants had bailed out of it, but she was surprised the Cardassians hadn't taken the ship yet. Maybe they had no use for it. Maybe they'd already stripped it. There was only one way to be sure.

Procedure was to wait for Sadakita to do another patrol sweep before they approached the ship, but Laren was tired of waiting. Though she had never docked on another ship before, she had a vague idea of how it was done, and she maneuvered her shuttle to the vessel's open bay, taking her stealthy little craft into the derelict's dark, gaping underbelly.

*"Laren,"* came a transmission; it was Bram, calling from his own raider. *"Is that you I see docking? Wait up on that. It could be booby-trapped."*

Laren considered, and decided Bram was being overly cautious. She didn't want to wait for him—he probably only wanted to be the first on the ship, anyway. She went ahead and docked, her tiny craft thumping crazily inside the bay of the hulking scow. It came to a rest inside a chamber flooded with blackness, and she put on her night visor. "My sensors say breathable atmosphere, and gravity," she reported back. "There must still be some kind of auxiliary power system intact, because the drop ramp came up behind me, so—"

"Laren, do not—I repeat—do not *exit your vessel! Stay inside it until I can get there. Sadakita's coming around, and I have to cover her before I can get to you.*"

Again, Laren scoffed at Bram's typical stodginess. He was always telling her what to do, and his advice was often wrong, anyway. She pushed back the glacis plate of her ship and took a deep breath. Her lungs did not collapse; she did not immediately begin choking on poison gases. Bram was afraid to take risks.

She hopped out of the raider, the night visor providing only a scant glow. She produced a palmlight and began to wave it about the bay. She could see nothing that interested her, only the most alien construction techniques she had ever seen.

Laren found an airlock and worked its thick double portals to gain access to the rest of the ship. Passing into the adjoining corridor, she spotted a bizarrely configured control console next to the airlock. It powered up when she touched it, and though it was mostly indecipherable to her, she managed to find the proper key that reopened the cargo bay for Bram. With that accomplished, she continued down the corridor; Bram was only going to scold her, and she wasn't in any hurry to listen to it.

She aimed her palmlight at a computer terminal she saw in one of the open rooms, and wondered if she might be able to hack into such an alien system. The challenge interested her, and she entered the room.

"What the *kosst*?" said a man's voice from somewhere back the way she had come. Laren stopped, confused. The accent, the timbre of the voice—it did not belong to Bram. Someone else was here. Someone Bajoran, apparently, for the curse was not one that a Cardassian would ever use. Laren considered her options. Should she go back to the bay and investigate? Did this person mean to harm her? She drew her phaser, more excited than afraid.

"Who are you?" she shouted.

"Who am I?" the voice answered. "Who are *you*? This heap is mine—we claimed it over a week ago."

A man emerged in the corridor then, a gray-haired Bajoran that Laren didn't recognize.

She lifted her phaser. "Don't make me ask again," she said coolly.

He slitted his eyes at her, his heavily lined face crinkling with the expression. He looked worried for an instant, but then smiled. "My name is Darrah Mace," he told her. "I've come here from Valo II. Now, how about you tell me who you are?"

"Valo II?" Laren repeated, shaking her head. "My cell found this ship two days ago," she told him, her phaser still trained on the stranger. "I was here first."

The man laughed. "Just how old are you? Twelve? You still haven't told me your name, by the way."

There was a low vibration beneath their feet, the sort Laren might expect from the closing of the cargo doors. Bram must have docked.

"I'm Ro," she said firmly. "And that will be Bram, the leader of my cell. It's two against one now, so you'd better shove off. This ship is ours." Laren stood her ground, her phaser still pointed directly at Mace's head.

"And just what do you propose to do with that?" The

man smirked, folding his arms in a self-satisfied expression that infuriated her.

"Didn't you hear me? I said shove *off.*" She indicated her phaser. "This thing's stun setting is broken, but the rest of it works just fine." Laren could hear Bram coming through the airlock. "Bram!" she shouted. "Draw your weapon! We've got company in here, and he's trying to steal our ship!"

Bram appeared behind Darrah Mace, hand phaser raised. The stranger turned a little, and finally seemed to accept the seriousness of the situation; he raised his hands above his shoulders.

*Twelve!* She'd been fourteen for better than two months.

"Who are you?" Bram demanded.

"Call me Mace," he said, his tone a bit more hesitant. "This ship is mine, and I'm going to take it. I've already been here three times, set up a signal scrambler so the Cardassians wouldn't find her. Why do you think the patrol ships haven't hauled her in yet?"

"Because the spoonheads don't do salvage," Bram said, but he sounded doubtful.

The other man scowled, though whether it was because of Bram's use of the racial slur or his defiance, Laren wasn't sure. "Look, you two. I'm taking this ship back to Valo II. I've already done some repairs on her—she's got air and AG, doesn't she? You think that's just luck? I'm willing to guess that neither one of you has ever set foot on a vessel like this before, let alone flown one."

Bram watched the man, his gaze scrutinizing. "We'll see about that," he muttered, and gestured Mace toward the bridge. Laren led the way with her palm beacon, looking back to Bram for an indication that she was going the right way. He nodded once, and made a point of loudly telling her that the "rest" of the cell members were standing by for his signal, still on their raiders outside. Laren nodded, pleased that Bram hadn't given their numbers away.

They came upon the cramped bridge. Whoever designed this ship could not have been much taller than Laren, for both Bram and Mace had to duck through the doorways, which were thankfully jammed open. Ro managed to squeeze to the front, interested in spite of herself.

"Let's see you get her online," Bram said gruffly.

Mace emitted a short sigh, clearly exasperated, and gestured for Laren to highlight a particular panel with her palm beacon. The wide circle of light fell on his hands, and he threw back a couple of switches, dancing his fingers over the keypad. There was a flicker of light, and then a ragged thrumming noise. The ship's power was back online, or at least, partially so—the lights behind Laren continued to flicker hypnotically, and the sound of the power core seemed an uneven chugging, like the throttle noise of a raider that was pushed into too low a gear for its speed.

"You can't possibly get this thing going . . . can you?" Bram seemed a bit awestruck.

"Of course I can," Mace said. "That's what I've been trying to tell you. If you'd like to come along to Valo II, you can stay aboard, but otherwise, you might want to get into your raiders and get off my ship, because we're going to have to go to warp."

Bram kept the phaser pointed at Mace, apparently trying to decide what to do. Laren knew that Bram was not about to kill another Bajoran, and neither was she. There were collaborators, of course, but this man clearly did not fall into that category. Still, Bram and Laren had an advantage with the phasers, and they weren't quite sure what to do with it. Order him to take it back to Bajor? Where would they dock such a thing, how would it behave in Bajor's atmosphere? She had no idea, and she knew Bram didn't, either. But warp ships were in notoriously short supply, and too badly needed to walk away from one—even a derelict.

"Oh, for fire's sake," Mace swore. "I knew this would happen."

"What?" Laren asked fearfully, for Mace seemed genuinely afraid.

"Look at this," he said, pointing to the alien ship's sensor screen. "That's a Cardassian patrol. The scrambler can't mask the energy emissions of an active warp reactor. It's time to go, now."

"Wait," Bram said, but then shook his head. "All right," he agreed. He finally lowered his phaser, probably realizing how ridiculous it was to be squabbling with another Bajoran when the real enemy loomed within striking distance. He put a call in to Sadakita, ordering the pilot to return to Bajor.

Mace didn't waste any time. He entered commands into the ship's internal computer system with startling efficiency, and the ship was trembling from its warp engines in almost no time at all. Laren expected to feel a discernible *whoosh,* something to indicate that she was traveling at warp, but there was nothing except the vibrations in the soles of her feet.

"Will they catch us?" Laren wanted to know. She was not often afraid, not since she was a child, but the thought of being captured alive was something that particularly frightened her. She was not usually concerned about it, so long as she was driving her own ship, for she had the utmost confidence in her abilities to dodge even the fastest Cardassian vessels at sublight. But this Mace fellow—well, she hoped that if the Cardassians came after them, they would just blow them up. Being taken prisoner was a possibility she could not even bring herself to consider.

"Not if I have anything to say about it," Mace assured her. "It's possible they haven't even spotted us yet. If they have, they won't necessarily take an interest if we're headed out of the system. It's no crime for a Ferengi vessel to be in Cardassian-controlled space, if they have legitimate business. If worse comes to worst, we talk to them—pretend to be a damaged Ferengi ship on our way home. "

Laren nodded, but her throat still felt tight.

Mace smiled at her. "Cheer up," he said. "I won't let anything happen to us."

Laren nodded again, thinking that maybe Mace wasn't such a bad person after all.

"You know, Ro," he added, "I think you're going to like Valo II."

## 15

Kubus Oak was in mid-sentence when the doors to Dukat's office abruptly slid open. ". . . which certainly makes the best economic sense. As always, your wisdom is—" Kubus stopped short, turning to see the highlighted silhouette of Kira Meru, flanked by a frantic Basso Tromac.

"I tried to stop her, Gul Dukat," Basso said. "But she wouldn't—"

"Thank you, Basso, that will be all. Kubus, we will continue this conversation at another time."

Kubus rose, barely acknowledging Meru as he swept from the room. Dukat gestured to his mistress. "Sit down, please."

She remained standing for a moment before finally sinking down into the seat that faced him. Now that she was here, she was not quite sure how to begin. She looked around, considering that she had never been inside his office before. So this was where he spent most of his time—or had, anyway, before meeting his new mistress . . . what was her name? Meru couldn't remember, but it wasn't important. She decided to get straight to the point.

"Skrain . . . you . . . you . . . have been spending a great deal of time away from the station of late, and I thought . . . perhaps . . . you had no more use for me." She took a breath, her gaze trained on the place where his heavy desk met the floor.

Dukat appeared shocked. "Meru! I can't imagine what could possibly give you such an idea. I love you, and you ought to know that by now. It isn't as though I think of you as a mere object, to be used and then discarded."

He went on, but Meru was not listening. She wanted desperately to convey to him that if he meant to be done with her, it would not hurt her feelings in the least, but she wanted to do it delicately, for she didn't want to give him the impression that she was eager to leave him. But in truth, she *was* eager. Since she had learned of his new mistress from Basso, she had finally begun to visit those forbidden thoughts that she had mostly learned to suppress many years ago—mostly. Sometimes she forgot herself, especially after a dream; dreams were a difficult matter, for she could not control them. Often, when she began to wake, she would feel as though she were desperately clawing her way back to her slumber, to go back to Taban and the children, even if it was not real.

But perhaps now she had a chance to do it in earnest. Much time had passed, and she wondered if her children would even recognize her, or she, them. Basso had stopped bringing isolinear recordings from the surface a very long time ago, and Meru's heart ached even to try and imagine what her children looked like now. Nerys, with her huge, expressive eyes and her bright, coppery hair—she would be ten years old now. Reon and Pohl, little men, not the babies she had left behind. And Taban . . . perhaps Taban had even remarried. The idea of it filled her with a nearly unendurable sensation of sorrow, worse even than the idea that he might be dead. It was selfish of her, hypocritical— but the thought of him having found love with another woman was nearly too much to bear.

Would any of them accept her back? Most likely they believed her to be dead, for Taban had originally sent word that he felt it would be better-if they didn't know what her true fate had been. Could she tell the truth, and would they be willing to forgive her? She didn't know, but she felt it was worth the risk, if only to see them again, if only to return to her homeworld.

Dukat had stopped speaking, and was waiting for her reply. She cleared her throat. "Skrain, I love you as well. I always will, and I will always appreciate all you have done for me. But if ever there comes a time when you feel you would prefer to . . . to move on from me . . . from our relationship . . ."

Dukat's puzzlement looked different now, and Meru hoped that he had at last begun to understand what she was trying to say. He gave her a terse nod, and stood from his desk, reaching out for one of her hands. "You've given me much to consider," he told her, his voice sounding oddly strained. "But perhaps this is not the most appropriate time for us to have this discussion. I will see you later this evening, if you will consent to have dinner with me."

"Of course," Meru answered. His question was a bit strange, as it had been many years since he had put on the pretense of "asking" her to dinner. Over time, he had dropped most of his formality when the two were together, speaking as plainly and honestly to her as Taban once had. Meru feared she had hurt him, and she squeezed his hand before she let it go. She would never deliberately hurt this man, but the idea of freedom—it was worth almost any price to her.

Doctor Yopal often insisted on observing Mora's research sessions with Odo—as he had taken to calling the "unknown sample"—but the frequency of her visits did almost nothing to ease the discomfort that resulted from her presence. Mora set a wide display screen in front of the tank, and then plugged an isolinear recording into his computer port. The display lit up with an illuminated diagram of a Bajoran vocal configuration.

"You see, Odo?" Mora said to the tank. "You understand this, don't you?"

Yopal snorted audibly, and Mora's face burned. He took up an electrostatic device from his work surface, a long-handled object with a probe at one end. He inserted the probe into the tank and set the cytoplasmic charge on a medium setting. The liquid in the tank immediately began to quiver, and in a steady motion the substance swept and twisted itself into a humanoid form, standing oddly erect in the center of the transparent tank. Odo opened his "mouth" and began making sounds, a rough, guttural sort of noise, akin to a clearing of the throat.

"Ah!" Yopal said, clearly impressed. "So, you have taught it to make noises, have you?"

"Yes, I have, Doctor Yopal," Mora said nervously. Odo had done better in the session last night, but increasing the charge actually had an adverse effect on his progress; he had to hold it steady at its current rate.

"*M-m-m*," Mora said, trying to get Odo to imitate him, as he had done the night before. "Mora."

"Uhmmmm," Odo replied. "Memmm. Memdoooo . . ."

Mora smiled. "There, you see?"

Yopal nodded vigorously. "Very impressive, Mora. I must say, I always assumed from the creature's . . . expression that it was indifferent to what we were trying to glean from it."

"I made that mistake as well," Mora admitted. "Though I knew his face was only an approximation of my own . . . it is hard to see past the impassivity written in his eyes."

Yopal kept her ever-present smile, but her tone was less than commending. "I must say, I am surprised you never before considered the possibility that this substance could have some level of awareness."

Mora was annoyed; in fact he *had* considered it, and had said as much. He imagined she was probably galled that he had inadvertently implied that she had made a "mistake."

"This is a perfect example of why women are better suited to the sciences," Yopal said. "Men simply don't explore all the possibilities. They tend to become stalled on a single facet of an equation, never knowing quite when to move on and branch out."

"Of course," Mora said, nodding deferentially.

"Well, Mora, I'll take my leave of you now. I look forward to reading your latest report on this matter."

"Indeed," he murmured, nodding to her as she left. He switched off the viewscreen. He reminded himself, as he put the electrostatic device away, that being condescended to by Yopal was still a welcome alternative to doing what Daul had been forced to do.

"Mmmm . . . memdo-mage," Odo said.

"Yes, Odo, that's quite enough," Mora said, and obediently, the pale "person" turned into a shimmering, twisting mass of fluid. Mora watched as he did so, for though he had seen it happen hundreds of times, it never failed to fascinate him.

Laren stayed close to Bram as they followed their guide from the freighter's resting place on an old landing field to the meager residences nearby. Mace explained that Valo II had once been a popular resort destination for many well-to-do Bajorans, but the colony quickly went into decline as more and more refugees fled here during the early years of the occupation. Now the primary continent—the only truly hospitable landmass on the planet—was dotted with slums, shantytowns, and nomadic encampments. They meandered through the outskirts of the village, strewn with a few tents and buildings constructed of transitory scrap, the dwellings becoming thicker and more numerous as they made their way into the heart of what passed for a city here. Laren was astonished; even Jo'kala proper was not so shabby as this. There were structures made of some kind of imported stone that looked to have come from Bajor, but the stone appeared too porous to bear up to the harsh winds of the current season; it was chipped and eroded on all the buildings that featured it. Most of the windows she saw were broken, with improvised covers of worn fabric or strips of old smartplastic, but some were simply left gaping open, the bits of jagged leftover glass coated with blowing dust. Everything smelled, like root broth and dirt and despair.

"My family lives here," Mace told them, gesturing to some kind of a heap of wood in front of him. "I'd offer you accommodations, but it's already a bit crowded. My son and his family live with us. His wife is pregnant, and her time is coming soon . . ." he trailed off.

"We're accustomed to sleeping outside," Bram told him. "You needn't worry about where to put us. We're a bit more concerned with getting back to Bajor, if we can."

Mace laughed sharply. "You're better off staying here, if you want my advice," he told them. "Anyway, I don't know if it can be arranged. The Cardassians mostly leave us alone here. Between trying to maintain their hold on Bajor and their ongoing border troubles with the Federation, they don't see us as being much of a threat to them. We're just eking out a living here; Valo II has nothing that they want."

"But you do go into Bajoran space, from time to time," Laren pointed out. "Like after the freighter—"

"Yes, and we still take in refugees," Mace admitted, "but we follow a strict procedure in doing so. There might be some way to get you back, but it will most likely be a few days, at least. We'll have to discuss it with Keeve and Akhere."

"Are they in your cell?" Laren asked him.

"Cell?" Mace repeated. "What do you mean?"

She wrinkled her nose. "The resistance," she said. "You are a resistance fighter, right?"

Bram held up a hand. "That's enough, Laren, don't interrogate the man." He turned to Mace. "She's just a kid," he said dismissively. "Smart for her age, but—you know."

"Just a kid, eh? Flying a raider, all by herself, out there in space just swarming with Cardassians . . ." Mace grinned at Laren, and she scowled ferociously back. She did not appreciate anyone's attempt at being overtly friendly; she found it suspicious. Still, a long-buried part of her visited the man's kindness with an infuriating sort of longing. She did her best to suppress it.

Mace looked up just then. "Ah," he exclaimed. "Here's the man I've been looking for."

"Darrah," greeted the other man, nodding at Mace. He was an older fellow, not much beyond Mace in years, but with a completely bald head and a rather ornate earring. It was one of the old D'jarra ones, denoting him as Te'nari. Not everyone wore the jewelry of their caste anymore, though of course everyone still wore some kind of adornment. It would have been as absurd as going without trousers to be seen without an earring.

Following at the man's heels was a tall boy, a teenager, with the greenest eyes Laren had ever seen. The two were clearly father and son, with a resemblance that went beyond their similar earrings: a kind of similarity about their noses and mouths, though the father's head shone with its hairlessness, and the son had a shock of very thick brown hair that hung nearly in his eyes.

Mace clapped his hand against the other man's forearm. "Juk," he said, "I brought back a couple of stowaways with me."

The bald man turned to regard Laren and Bram. "Where'd you find them?" he asked Mace, as if they could not hear him.

Bram answered. "Your friend here claimed a derelict vessel that we had our eye on." He extended his hand, which the other man looked at for a moment before taking it. "I'm Bram Adir, and this is Ro Laren. We're from Jo'kala."

"Jo'kala!" he exclaimed. "You mean—Bajor?"

"That's right," Laren answered him, unable to take her eyes off the boy who stood mutely behind his father. He did not appear to be much older than Laren herself. She hadn't had much interaction with people her own age since joining the resistance.

"I'm Akhere Juk," the man finally said. "I've been on Valo II almost my whole life, long before the Cardassians came, though my people were originally from Mylea."

"You're a *Te'nari*," Bram observed.

Juk shrugged. "We don't pay much attention to those designations anymore," he said, but Laren had a feeling that it might not be entirely true. She fingered her own earring, an old one of her father's that her mother had allowed her to take. *Sern'apa.* Caste was so unimportant that she paid it almost no mind—it was little more than a word. Its only significance for her lay in the fact that it was something of her father's.

"Neither do we," Bram said, "other than to find things to reminisce about. My mother's people were *Te'nari,* also."

"Ah," Juk said, and Laren detected a new light in the other man's eyes. It had always puzzled her, the old *D'jarra* system. The very idea that the adults would still pay any sort of homage to it was laughable. Just like most of the old ways. Foolish. Bram and Juk continued to jaw about their castes, and Laren shifted her weight from foot to foot, bored and impatient for something to happen. She looked over Juk's shoulder at his son, and their eyes met for a paralyzing moment. Laren quickly looked away, realizing that her face had been plastered with a sneer. She rearranged her features to look unreadable, benign, but still durable—a person to be reckoned with. It was the truth, after all.

The boy cleared his throat noisily. "My name's Bis," he said, the proclamation clearly directed at Laren. His voice was deep, but not quite like a grown man's; there was still a ragged softness to it. He took a step toward her. He extended his hand to her, and it was then that she flinched, as though she thought he meant to strike her. Ro wasn't much for shaking hands, and in fact, she supposed she had never really done it before that she could remember; she'd only seen adults do it from time to time. To her chagrin, Bis laughed at her. "What's the matter?"

She put her own hand out, her cheeks burning, and shook with him, without making eye contact. "This is all very friendly and everything," she said loudly and sharply, "but just where do you propose we sleep tonight? We haven't brought our bedrolls or anything like that—"

"Laren, you let me worry about that," Bram snapped, bossy as always.

"We've got plenty of room at my house," Juk suggested, but Bram quickly began shaking his head.

"No, no, we wouldn't dream of it. Just find us an empty building and we'll curl up in a corner. Even under a grove of trees—we don't need much."

Laren shot him an *are-you-crazy* look, for though it was true that she had often been reduced to sleeping in some very unaccommodating places, she couldn't imagine turning down an actual bed to do so.

"Let's take them to speak to Keeve," Mace suggested. "And then we can figure out where we'll put them for the night."

Juk and Mace went on talking, and Laren pulled Bram aside, speaking in hushed tones. "Why are you turning down his offer of a decent place to stay? Is it just that you like to be miserable?"

"I saw the way that boy was looking at you," Bram whispered. "We'll not be sleeping in their house."

Laren was indignant. "Now I *know* you're crazy," she said. "You would put a phaser in my hand, train me to fly a shuttle, encourage me to break and enter booby-trapped facilities . . . but you won't let me sleep in the same house with a boy?"

Bram snorted. "Let me tell you something, Laren. Bajoran teenage boys can be far scarier than even the most menacing Cardassian soldier."

It was Laren's turn to snort, but Bram kept talking.

"I ought to know about teenage boys. I used to be one." He laughed at his own joke, and Laren, though annoyed, couldn't help but smile a little—if only at the thought of Bram ever having been as young as she was.

Basso Tromac did his best to avoid making eye contact with any of the Cardassians as he headed to the Bajoran section of the Promenade. There were a handful of them who treated him with at least some facsimile of politeness, but the newcomers generally did not know that there was any distinction between him and the Bajorans in ore processing. They would often stop him and begin asking annoying questions if he looked at them the "wrong" way. Considering the sheer number of new personnel here, it was usually wise to just keep one's eyes pointed forward, at least until he came to the Bajoran sector, where he could again square up his shoulders, even add a bit of swagger to his gait.

He had almost made it to the heavy barricades that divided the station when Dukat's lazily authoritative tone spoke out behind him: "Ah, just the man I have been looking for."

Basso turned around quickly. "How can I be of service, Prefect?" He bowed a bit, as he always did when addressing Dukat.

"Basso, I have a question for you." Dukat spoke loudly over the din that was beginning to erupt beyond the gates—a fight breaking out, perhaps a lost child, some other trivial scuffle.

"Do you want me to go look into that?" Basso asked.

Dukat waved his hands. "No, no, I've got Thrax and a couple of the others patrolling back there, they'll get to it soon enough. Come. Let's walk this way." He pointed in the opposite direction, and Basso followed him. He didn't mind walking on the Cardassian side so long as Dukat was accompanying him; in fact, he rather enjoyed these rare opportunities to demonstrate for the others that he was no ordinary Bajoran.

"Basso, have you been seeing to Meru, as you have been asked?"

"Of course, sir." Basso took pains to keep his voice neutral, for he had anticipated this question. He did not have to guess at the tone of the meeting that had taken place between the prefect and his mistress in the office the other day.

"You haven't noticed her seeming . . . different, lately? Unsatisfied with her life here?"

Basso shrugged. "Certainly no more than before, sir."

Dukat's eyes narrowed and his smile wavered, and Basso quickly tacked on a follow-up: "I mean to say, she seems as happy as ever."

Dukat looked away, continuing to walk. The two passed several security officers, on their way to the Bajoran side, along with several miscellaneous soldiers and civilian personnel. Dukat nodded to each one, stilling their conversation until they were out of earshot. "Has she said anything to you about . . ." He trailed off as the chief engineer's assistant passed alongside them. ". . . Tora Naprem?"

Basso shook his head, but maintained a look of puzzlement on his face. "No, she hasn't said anything specifically about her—but now that you mention it, she did seem to indicate to me . . . well, I suppose I dismissed it as nothing, but it *does* seem a bit odd . . ."

"What?" Dukat demanded. "What did she say?"

"Well, she said that she worried that one day you would grow tired of her, if you ever found a younger mistress, someone prettier. She said she thought she knew how your wife must feel, having to tolerate dalliances by the man she loved . . ." Basso shrugged. "Nothing that any woman doesn't fear from time to time, but perhaps . . . perhaps she *did* learn something of Naprem . . . the new baby. It would seem to explain why she is suddenly—"

"She spoke of my wife?" Dukat asked sharply. He stepped into an empty pathway that led toward the habitat ring, and Basso followed him.

Basso nodded. "M-hm, m-hm, she did indeed, sir. She said, 'Poor Athra, it never occurred to me how difficult it must be for her—I almost feel in her a kindred spirit.' It was something along those lines."

Dukat looked furious, though he kept his voice low. "She spoke of my wife by name?"

"Yes, I remember it quite specifically."

Dukat looked troubled. "I have never told her my wife's name," he said. "You're sure she said those words?"

"I am quite certain, Gul, but you must know that she has the resources to find out just about anything she wants to know." Basso contrived an expression of sudden realization. "Oh, my. You don't think—you don't think Meru would ever try to contact your wife, do you? She is such an impetuous person, and so lonely for female companionship . . ." Basso stopped, and shook his head. "No, no, that's ridiculous, of course."

Dukat looked troubled for a moment. "Lonely?" he said, almost to himself. He turned to Basso, speaking louder now. "She has no means of contacting anyone."

"Well," Basso said, "that's not entirely true, Gul. She has been on the station such a long time now, she has learned how to bypass many of the security protocols that were originally installed to keep her safe. She doesn't necessarily choose to use them, but I've caught her leaving her quarters at unauthorized times, and fooling around with her library computer—"

"Why haven't you mentioned this to me before now?" Dukat snapped.

Basso did his best to look pained. "I have tried, Gul Dukat, I have really tried to discuss it with you, but you never seemed concerned when I pointed out that Meru had too much freedom . . ."

Dukat's eyes became faraway again. "Yes," he murmured. "You have tried to warn me. At any rate, we must tighten up the security that surrounds her."

"It's an excellent idea, though I'm not sure she'll tolerate it. She has always been so . . . ah, high-strung, we might want to ease her into the idea. Otherwise, she might try to resist you . . ."

"High-strung, yes. I suppose that does describe her, somewhat . . ."

"Although," Basso added. "If I may say—I sincerely doubt that she would really try to contact Athra, for revenge or any other reason—"

"Did you say *revenge*?" Dukat broke in.

"Well, it *does* make sense. Just as you were saying, she is a high-strung woman, and she does have a great deal of freedom to poke around, if she wanted to . . . and if it came into her head to try and make trouble for you . . ."

Dukat shook his head. "I am going to speak with her. You go on to ore processing. I will speak with you later." Dukat waved him in the direction of the turbolifts.

Basso headed for ore processing with a little more confidence than usual. It wasn't everyone who could successfully put a bug in the prefect's ear, so to speak. He hoped he could continue to steer the prefect in the proper direction, for if this went the way he wanted, he could finally rid himself of those duties that concerned Meru, and the effort of watching after her impossible family.

"My name is Mora." He had said it at least a hundred times today, and he was tired of the sound of his own voice. His mouth felt pasty, his throat sore from speaking, but he could not give up, not until Odo could repeat the words, and produce some indication that he actually understood them.

The shape-shifter gestured to himself, as Mora had been doing. "Mem," he said. "Mem-ma."

Mora sighed, exhausted. Did Odo understand what was going on here? Or was he merely mimicking the sound of Mora's voice? Could it be that he was not sentient after all—at least, no more than a tyrfox or a *batos*? He regarded the readouts on the electrostatic field that surrounded Odo's "head," and increased the frequency.

He continued to work with him for another seemingly endless round of call-and-response, with Odo's pronunciation gradually becoming more precise, and then less so, and then more so again. Mora believed that Odo was eager to please him, but then it may have only been an illusion brought on by Mora's own isolation. He occasionally feared he was spending too much time with the creature; he hadn't seen his parents in weeks, usually coming home to his family's residence long after they had retired for the night. And Prophets forbid he should ever meet an eligible woman! The idea of it seemed about as likely as the possibility that the Cardassians would turn tail and leave Bajor tomorrow. For better or worse, Mora was married to his work here, and he probably always would be.

"Mynameisssssmore . . . uh," said Odo.

"Very good, Odo!" Mora positively beamed, for this was probably the best pronunciation Odo had managed so far.

Odo's "eyes" occasionally rolled around, drifting lazily like those of a person touched in the head. It was an unsettling effect, though Mora had noticed lately that he seemed to understand the concept of "looking" at something. Right now, his gaze appeared to be trained on the door to the laboratory, and his expression was convincing enough to compel Mora to turn around and look. Sure enough, Doctor Yopal was standing in the doorway. Mora almost praised Odo for it, but Yopal spoke before he had the chance.

"Do you think he believes . . . that *his* name is Mora? Or do you think he even understands any of it at all?"

Mora felt immediately dejected, despite all the progress he'd been making this afternoon. "Well, only time will tell," he said stiffly.

Yopal went on speaking, her usual refrain about men and the sciences, and to Mora's grave embarrassment, Odo began to chatter behind her, a string of senseless syllables. "Mem. Dobake. Goobsine."

Yopal at first raised her voice to speak over him, but she abruptly stopped speaking after a moment, looking at the shape-shifter with curious surprise.

"Mem dobake good sine-tiss."

Yopal turned to Mora with openmouthed astonishment. "Do you hear what he just said?" She turned back to the shape-shifter. "Say it again, Odo'ital!"

"Mem dobe bake good sine-tist."

"That's right!" Yopal beamed. "That's right, Odo! Men don't make good scientists!" The Cardassian woman then did something Mora had never dreamed she was even capable of: she laughed.

"Odo," Mora began, not sure quite how to respond.

"He's making a joke, Mora!" She laughed again, and

Mora was stunned at how natural her laughter sounded. But even more alarming than the revelation that the Cardassian scientist was capable of genuine emotion was the change that had come over Odo's "face." The strange pulling at the corners of his mouth looked anything but natural, but it was certainly nothing that he had ever even attempted before today—at least, that Mora had ever seen.

"He's smiling," Mora said.

"Yes, he is," Yopal agreed.

This time, Mora laughed along with her.

Keeve Falor was a quiet-speaking man, dressed as shabbily as everyone else on Valo II, but with an even more elaborate earring than the one worn by Akhere Juk. Laren did not recognize the design; she only knew a few of the D'jarra symbols, and his was not one that she had ever seen before. Bram, however, seemed to know Keeve right away, though by his face or his D'jarra, Laren wasn't sure.

"Minister," Bram said reverently, as Juk and Mace began the introductions.

Keeve broke into a sheepish laugh. "Not Minister. Not for a long, long time." He extended his hand to Bram, who shook it warmly. "We're all more or less equals here on Valo II."

"But we do often defer to Keeve when a decision is to be made," Juk cut in.

Laren mentally nodded to herself; the D'jarras did still have some pull here, just as she had imagined. Keeve's D'jarra must have designated him to the class of politicians and civilian leaders.

The adults commenced to talking about what to do with this and that, where could Laren and Bram make their camp, how could they return to Bajor, the specifics of which did not particularly interest Laren—at least not while Bis was standing so near. She imagined that Bis had probably lived on this windy, dusty rock his entire life. He had never even seen a proper tree before. The foliage here was scraggly, with sparse leaves and dry, crackling branches, nothing at all like the grand forests in Jo'kala. She pitied him, a little.

Laren wondered many things about Bis. Had he ever seen a Cardassian, here on this world? Had he ever flown in a shuttle? Was he impressed that she had been in a raider all by herself?

"So, if you and your daughter would like, we could set up a tent for you, just outside of—"

"I'm *not* his daughter," Laren interrupted Keeve fiercely. She'd have expected Bram to have told him at least that much.

Keeve looked surprised, and a little amused. "Begging your pardon, my dear. So how is it that you came to be in a ship all alone, in Cardassian-controlled space?"

Bram answered for her. "I look after her," he said. "She's something of an orphan. My resistance cell has taken her in. We're teaching her how to fly—"

"I already *know* how to fly."

Keeve continued to look surprised, and Bram spoke quickly.

"Laren, please. My apologies—I've not done a very good job teaching her any manners. She lived on the streets, when I found her, running with a crowd of beggars . . ."

"I'm no beggar," Laren interrupted. "I stole things from the Cardassians. That's why Bram wanted me along, because I can break into their stockades better than any of the grown-ups in the resistance cell. He needs me to disable the security feeds before anyone approaches."

Keeve looked a bit unsettled as he turned to Bram. "She can't be more than twelve," he said.

"I'm fourteen!" Laren shouted.

"*Laren!* It's true, Keeve, the girl does have talent. She can hack into a security system like nobody's business, and I can't even begin to figure how she does it." He shot her a pointed look. "I'd never tolerate her impertinence if she wasn't good for something."

Keeve's expression reset itself to one of thoughtfulness. "Is that right?" he said, and he turned to look at Laren. "So, you fight in the resistance, do you?"

Laren decided she didn't like his tone. "Yes," she said sulkily. "And what do *you* do, here on Valo II, to try and drive out the spoonheads?"

Keeve's eyebrows shot up and he addressed Bram. "I see what you mean, about the manners," he said, one corner of his mouth twisted into a forced-seeming smile. He turned away for a moment to speak quietly with Juk and Mace, arguing good-naturedly in hushed tones. Laren could barely catch the gist of what they were discussing, but she was fairly certain it had something to do with her. Juk's voice rose above the others more than once, saying, "She's only a child!"

"You'll have to help me set up our tent, Laren," Bram said, apparently trying to draw her away from the conversation, but Laren did not answer, straining to hear what the other men were talking about. She caught Bis's eye as he shifted his attention from his father's conversation back to her, and she quickly looked away again, forgetting the men for the moment.

Keeve stepped away from the tight circle he'd made with the other two, and he turned back to Laren. "Well, Laren. If you can hack into Cardassian computer systems, then we might just have a little job for you. You ask what we are doing to fight against the Cardassians, and I'll tell you. We observe. We gather information. And we have a little reconnaissance mission that I think might benefit rather well from a little girl who knows how to bypass a Cardassian security system. A simple download at a hidden facility. Does this interest you at all?"

Laren lost her attitude in no time at all. "Yes!" she said. She stole a glance at Bis to see if he was watching, and sure enough, he was staring right at her. Her eyes met his for a moment, but she was too excited to be embarrassed. This was the perfect opportunity to impress him, and maybe she'd even get to kill a spoonhead or two.

# 16

Lenaris could not resist flicking out his hands to steady the flight yoke. His little brother turned to him, burning with annoyance, to judge from his expression. "I know how to do this, Holem."

"I know you do, Jau. But I keep thinking that you might want to wait until *after* we exit the atmosphere before you—"

"Leave him alone, Lenaris." Ornathia Sten spoke from where he crouched in the back of the raider. It was a tight fit with the three of them in the little ship, but since most of the cell's raiders had been taken to the Lunar V base, they generally had to commute in cramped quarters.

"I'm going to be flying on my own for this raid," Jau said firmly.

"Of course," Lenaris said, meaning to be reassuring, aware that he probably sounded condescending. As always, according to Jau.

Jau shook his head, and Lenaris decided it would be best to keep silent. Jau was sixteen, and though it was true he was as good a pilot as any of the grown men, Lenaris still couldn't help but regard him as a baby. The age gap was enough that Lenaris wasn't entirely sure how it was that Jau had come to be the gawky near-adult he was now; Lenaris had already left home to join the resistance before

Jau had even learned his first words. But this mission called for every available pilot, and he could not argue that Jau was capable. It was only . . . Lenaris wasn't sure what his mother would do if anything happened to Jau. He wasn't sure what *he* would do.

It was a long way to Jeraddo in a sub-impulse raider, the moon where the Ornathia cell had managed to store most of their raiders, since Pullock V. They couldn't keep all of their ships in Relliketh, where the cell was currently headquartered—as quickly as Taryl came up with new fuels, new ways to mask them, the Cardassians found ways to detect them, and the fleet was too large now to keep together.

The Ornathia fleet had regrown in recent years, as more people joined the cell. Some of Taryl's cousins who had originally fled back to their families' farms had returned to the cell after the Pullock V report had gained notoriety. Some of the raiders could still be stored in the Berain mountains, where the natural kelbonite in the rock shielded them from overhead scans, but the constant lifting off from the same location was risky, and Lenaris had suggested moving some of the shuttles to Derna, but Taryl had insisted that it would not be wise to keep the communications links and the shuttles in the same place. Halpas had been the first to suggest Jeraddo; the sparsely populated moon was of little interest to the Cardassians, their presence there minimal. It was the perfect place to hide their ships.

Lenaris tried to make conversation to pass the time. It never hurt to remind everyone of the basics, either. "So, we'll go in with a typical *kienda* fan formation, with me and Sten in the lead. Jau, you and Nerissa will flank, and—"

"I *know*," Jau said wearily. "And the Legans will be at the tail. We pull down until we're just about fifty *linnipates* above the base, and then we drop our ordnance in the center of four parked skimmers, and pull up. The blast should take out at least sixteen skimmers, if we position our explosives in the correct place, so make each hit count."

"Yeah," Lenaris said lamely. From the back, Sten chuckled.

Lenearis said little else until they reached the site, where they cruised over the forests of Jeraddo and quickly found the cave they had dubbed Lunar V. There were twelve raiders in all here, many of them engineered entirely from scrap, mostly by Taryl. These improvised ships lacked the comprehensive sensors that some of the older raiders were equipped with, though Taryl hoped to change that eventually.

It was one of these "newer" birds that Jau would be flying, since he was considered an apt enough pilot to compensate for the lack of equipment. The Legan brothers were barely competent fliers, and Lenaris would have been happy to have left them behind entirely, but they were short on pilots just now. Taryl was pregnant, and Lenaris wouldn't have dreamed of putting her in harm's way. She was safely back at Tilar, working on the communications upgrades. Halpas and a few of the others were on Derna right now, calibrating new relay towers to keep the cells on Bajor connected. And there had been an accident recently. The warp carrier had been taken out to try and make contact with some of the Bajorans outside the B'hava'el system, and it had never returned. Seven people were on that freighter, seven members of the extended cell, seven friends, brothers, sisters, parents, children—seven pilots. Lenaris had to make do with what was left.

The Legan brothers were coming in with Ornathia Nerissa, and Lenaris didn't trust them to take one of the scrap raiders. No, it was better to put them in the idiot-proof ships, though he didn't feel especially confident they wouldn't find some way of getting themselves lost—or, more likely, killed.

Lenaris quickly claimed his own shuttle, and they set to work. The little vessels had to be pushed manually from the cave, and the three men worked to move their vessels out into a more reasonable takeoff position, stomping through the heavy foliage and sidestepping the unusually large insects that patrolled the moon. The second of their transport shuttles docked while they were struggling, and Nerissa and the Legans emerged to help them. They managed to get each ship into position, each one loaded with appropriate ammunition, each double-checked according to Taryl's extensive list.

There were a few backslaps and encouraging words, and it was time. Each man or woman climbed into his or her vessel, all looking deferentially to Lenaris. It had never been said—at least, not within his earshot—but he knew they considered him the leader. It wasn't a job he'd lobbied for, but he couldn't deny the responsibility.

"Good fighting, everyone," Lenaris said, and pulled the glacis plate of his raider closed. He tapped in a few commands and lifted his shuttle into Jeraddo's mild sky, pushing through the sound barrier and out of the atmosphere in almost no time at all. There was little in the way of shock absorption. The inertial dampers did their best to keep up, but Lenaris was still rocked crazily about his cockpit before the shuttle broke into the openness of space.

He immediately tested the new sensor array that Taryl had come up with. He could see where the others were, and he tapped a command to each of them in code. Jau was the first to respond, and Lenaris felt a tightening pride in his chest, surpassed only by the residual traces of fear for his little brother's safety that still lingered.

*Prophets, keep him safe.*

Dukat's duties on this day had not permitted him to visit Meru as soon as he would have liked. For Dukat, there was no love that would ever transcend that which he shared with his wife, but between his few and far-between visits to Cardassia Prime, he grew lonely for female companionship. Most of his Bajoran dalliances had failed to hold his attention for long, but Meru was different. It could truthfully be said that he loved her. He may have been distracted lately by the birth of his new daughter, but his consideration of Meru had not faltered, only been put aside while he enjoyed the heady experience of having such close access to the newborn in his life. His children on Cardassia Prime had mostly been born while he was away on assignment, and he had been permitted to spend only brief stints of time with each of them while they were infants. His new half-Bajoran daughter represented a risky situation for him, but the cautious nature of the experience was easily displaced by the intense joy at her beautiful presence.

But today, he must not be thinking of Naprem and the little one; he must do what he could to make things right with Meru. For if what Basso was saying had any truth to it, she might have taken it into her head to do him harm. He was only too aware of the Bajoran propensity toward revenge—numerous attempts on his very life were ample proof. He considered a handful of Bajorans to be among the people closest to him, but he could not forget that they were a naturally mistrustful, jealous race. No matter how much he loved Meru, no matter what he did to placate her, he could never be entirely sure that she would not some-day turn on him. And he feared that the day might have come.

He entered her quarters without knocking, as he always did, for she knew to always be prepared for him, at every moment. It was one of the things he loved about her, that most often she was able to drop whatever she had been doing to come to him. Of course, there were those times when Dukat had been forced to exercise patience with her; she was only humanoid—only *Bajoran,* after all. She *was* remarkably cool-headed for a Bajoran, but she was still prone to occasional bouts of sulkiness. Dukat didn't always care for the effort of maintaining her, but she wasn't generally overly needy. He hoped that this latest rash of irritable behavior would pass, as the others had passed—usually easy enough to smooth over with a gift, or sometimes just a little extra time to herself—though lately, perhaps she'd had a bit too much of the latter. Dukat knew he'd better come up with a promise of a vacation of some sort, just the two of them, even if he couldn't immediately deliver it. He was a busy man.

"Hello, Skrain," she said, the same breathless way she always said it. Dukat had once found it to be interminably exciting, but it had lost much of its appeal these days. There was a part of him that now considered his relationship with Meru to be a bit superficial—even tawdry, compared to what he shared with Naprem. Naprem, so beautiful as she nursed their child, a nimbus of sunlight highlighting her hair, her cheeks . . . the backdrop of the elegant old estate he had chosen for her and the child, isolated, surrounded by carefully tended gardens and trickling fountains . . . The purity of the atmosphere did little to recommend those indistinguishable dalliances with Meru here on the station, in her artificially lit quarters, surrounded by the dozens of paintings she was always churning out—wooden-faced old priests from millennia ago. Dukat was sick of the sight of them.

He took her by the hands. "Meru. It has come to my attention that you've not been happy lately. I apologize that my business has taken me away so frequently. I propose that you and I plan a retreat for the near future—the two of us, for a week, perhaps. Anywhere you would like to go in the B'hava'el system—or farther, if you want. I can think of numerous places we've not seen yet."

Meru was quiet, appearing to be struggling with her response. "It's very kind of you, Skrain. You know how I've enjoyed the traveling we've done in the past. But I feel . . . that your mind, your heart, they lie elsewhere these days. I . . . I know about the child, Skrain, and I understand. And I was hoping that perhaps it would help you to understand my position, as well."

Dukat's breathing became tight. He did not want to lie to her, but he did not care to discuss Naprem, either. "Meru, whatever it is that has you so upset, I assure you it has no bearing on my feelings for you. Please, let's discuss happier topics. What can I provide you with that will ease you from this pall?"

Meru shook her head, appearing frustrated, and Dukat squeezed her hands. He began to speak again, but she cut him off in a rush of words. "Let me go," she said, her voice strangled. She began to cry. "I want to go home, Skrain, can't you understand that? I want to see my family again— my *husband!*" Her face crumpled and stretched unpleasantly, and Dukat let her hands slip away from his.

"I . . . see," he said faintly. He felt an unfamiliar writhing inside. He could not quite place the emotion he was experiencing. It was a combination of things, things he was not sure he could identify. Anger? Sadness? Embarrassment? Whatever it was, it was perhaps the most unpleasant sensation he could ever remember, and before he quite knew what he was doing, he had flung out his arm and knocked over Meru's easel, its contents of paint and canvas splattering and crashing to the floor. Meru let out a sharp cry.

"Skrain! Please—can't you see? I love you, but—"

"But it's not enough!" he roared. "It's not enough, all I've done for you, for your family—you would still choose your cowardly vole of a husband over a man like me, is that it?" He lunged for her, and he felt the back of his hand make contact with the hard surface of one of her well-sculpted cheekbones.

"No!"

Dukat abruptly stopped. Meru hid behind her hands, shoulders hunched in fear. A livid mark spread quickly across her face. Dukat turned slightly to see his reflection in the mirror above her dressing table, and he did not like what he saw—a panting man, his slick hair flung loose around his ears, an expression of dirty, dying rage still spread across his face. He straightened up, caught his breath, and smoothed his hair back, though Meru still crouched and sobbed.

Dukat did not care to think of himself as an abuser of women. He spoke coolly. "I have to go now, my dear," he said. "I will send Basso to see if you need anything, as always. Perhaps we will continue this conversation later, when we've both had time to clear our heads."

Meru continued to whimper and cry piteously as he left the room, and the sound of it made him sick to his very core. He was immensely bothered by the awareness that he could not erase the scene he had just created. He could pretend it had not transpired, but he knew that every time he laid eyes on Meru, it would return to him in all its shameful detail. Once out in the hallway, he quickly pressed his comcuff. "Dukat to Basso. Please meet me in my office immediately."

He did not like what he was going to have to do, but he could see no other reasonable alternative. As prefect, he was forced to make difficult decisions every day; some took their toll on his conscience, to be sure, but he never let that dissuade him from his duty.

Laren sat back on her haunches to regard the tent she and Bram had just finished assembling. It wasn't much, but it would do. Keeve had warned them that the nights this time of year could be quite windy, making it inadvisable to try and sleep out in the open—the lack of substantial tree canopy exacerbated the blowing dust, a condition that apparently caused respiratory problems for a number of the residents here.

"Why would they choose to stay on such a world if they have access to warp vessels?" Ro grumbled. "This place is worse than the worst parts of Jo'kala."

"Valo II wasn't always like this," Bram reminded her.

"But it's like this now," Laren pointed out.

Bram sighed. "They aren't welcome anywhere else," he said, tugging on a rope to test its strength. "Bajorans are outcasts on many other worlds, considered burdensome refugees. This place may not look like much to you or me, but at least they can call it their own."

He squinted toward the place where the "town" was located, and Laren thought he looked sad. She wondered, fleetingly, how old Bram was. What kinds of things had he seen as a young man, when he was her age, or younger, before the Cardassians came to Bajor? She had never really considered it before. She started to ask him, when a traveling speck caught her attention. Someone was headed toward their camp, and she thought it might be Bis. Laren started to tell Bram, who had ducked inside the tent, but then decided that she'd prefer to speak to Bis alone. She began to walk out toward him, to meet him before Bram would have a chance to notice that he was coming.

"Hi," she called out, as she came close enough to ensure that it was really him. "What're you doing?"

"I came to tell you something," Bis said, his green eyes immediately shifting away from her face. "My pa says to tell you that you can join us for breakfast in the morning."

Laren fell in step with Bis as she came closer to him, and began to deliberately walk in the opposite direction from Bram's camp. "How old are you?" she asked him.

"I'm sixteen just last month," he said, and cleared his throat.

"I'm fifteen," she said, before remembering that she'd already told Keeve she was really only fourteen. Bis didn't point out the discrepancy. "Do you ever fly those warp ships?" she asked him.

Bis looked ashamed. "I . . . have flown them with my father," he said. "Not by myself."

"Are you coming along, on this mission?"

Bis's mouth twisted. "I don't know," he said. "I want to, but . . ." His voice trailed off.

"What?"

"I don't know," he replied.

They continued walking in silence.

"I've never met anyone like you before," Bis suddenly blurted out. They stopped walking.

Laren felt a flush of excitement. "I've never met anyone like you, either," she told him. She took a step closer to him; perhaps now she would find out what all the fuss was about with kissing and the like, but just as she thought it might be about to happen, Bram's angry voice blared out from behind them.

"Laren! I don't appreciate your just walking off like that. Prophets' sake, I thought a wild animal had carried you off! If you're going to go wandering, you might want to give me a heads-up. Now, come back to camp, I need your help digging a latrine."

Laren wrinkled her nose with embarrassment and looked to Bis with apology. "I have to be getting back, anyway," he mumbled, and scurried off in the opposite direction while Bram herded Laren back to their miserable camp.

"What did I tell you about that boy?" he admonished, but Laren wasn't really listening. She dragged her feet on the way back, considering the possibility of sneaking out later on, but rejecting the idea on the basis of Bram's confounded twitchy sleeping habits. The man tended to wake up at the slightest sound; a useful trait in the resistance, but pretty infuriating for a pair of curious teenagers.

Mora's eyes grew heavy as he blundered through his notes; he knew Yopal would trouble him about the grammatical errors, but he couldn't be bothered with it now; he was tired, though excited. He'd managed a few conversations lately with Odo wherein the shape-shifter had demonstrated inarguable reciprocity; there was simply no longer any doubt that the being was self-aware.

"Doc-tor More-ah," Odo said from behind him, his newfound voice rough and guttural. Mora started. He'd been under the impression that Odo was "sleeping."

"What is it, Odo?"

"Doctor More-ah, Doctor Yopal. He is . . . not the same . . . as you are. He looks . . . not the same."

"She," Mora corrected Odo. "Doctor Yopal is a woman, Odo. There is a distinction between humanoid men and women, remember?"

"Yes," the shape-shifter said. "Woman. She. Doctor Yopal is a woman."

"That is correct."

"And men. Don't make good scientists."

Mora smiled reservedly. Odo had never stopped delivering this refrain from time to time. Perhaps it comforted him, as the first intelligible phrase he'd come up with on his own, but Mora failed to be quite as amused by it as he had been the first few times.

"So says Doctor Yopal, Odo."

The shape-shifter cocked his head, an affectation he had picked up somewhere. "Women look not the same as men."

"Well, it isn't only that she is a woman and I am a man, Odo. Doctor Yopal and I . . . we come from different worlds. Our features are dissimilar because we are of different races. There are many different varieties of humanoids in the galaxy, Odo, and they all have distinguishing features."

"Different. Doctor Yopal is different from Doctor Mora."

"Yes. That's correct. She is a Cardassian, and I am a Bajoran."

Odo said nothing for a moment, then he gestured to himself. "And Odo. Odo is not a Bajoran. Odo is not a Cardassian."

There was nothing in the creature's expression or inflection of voice to suggest it, but Mora had a distinct impression of sadness. "No," he answered. "Odo is a shape-shifter."

Odo said nothing, and Mora decided that he wanted to change the subject. "You have learned to speak so quickly, Odo. Did you understand what I was saying, before I began my attempts to coax you to speak on your own?"

Again, Odo's face did not change much; though the shape-shifter had been experimenting with expression, he was revealing nothing now. "Understand. Odo did not always . . . understand. But some sounds . . . some words, began learned."

"Why then, did you not try to speak?"

The shape-shifter tried a smile, an effect that never failed to unsettle Mora. "Odo did not know if Mora wanted it."

"You mean, you didn't think I wanted to hear you speak?"

The shape-shifter nodded jerkily.

"Well, there was plenty you could have said!" Mora exclaimed, but Odo only continued to stare, his strange, barren expression continuing to reflect absolutely nothing to suggest what might have been going on in his brain, as though "brain" even applied.

Mora cleared his throat. "I've got to finish my notes, Odo. Why don't you go back to your tank."

Odo said nothing, just obeyed. As always, Mora was left with the hunger to know more, though he had no choice but to follow a certain protocol. Had he been left to his own devices to study the shape-shifter, he would have carried out the process much differently, but it was imperative that he perform in the manner laid out by the Cardassians, for there was no telling what would happen to Odo if Mora were pulled off this project. Indeed, Mora had come to regard the shape-shifter as more than just a "project," for he saw Odo more often than he saw his own parents. With as much time as he spent with the shape-shifter, teaching him, testing him, he almost felt that Odo was part of his family, now.

Dukat had called Kubus Oak to his office to harangue the man about his failure to deliver more workers to Gallitep in a timely manner, for the mines were still operating at far below capacity since the accident, now six months gone. Kubus was full of excuses, as usual. He claimed that Dukat had warned him never to pull his workforce from Dahkur province, which was utter nonsense—Dukat had never said anything of the sort. He advised the so-called "secretary" to tell his men to pick up any stragglers found outside the proscribed boundaries and bring them to Gallitep at once, for Darhe'el had been contacting Dukat on the matter with annoying frequency.

Kubus was just leaving to go back to his quarters and do whatever it was he did in there, when a breathless Basso Tromac arrived in his office, unusually late to the briefing.

"My apologies, Gul," Basso said. "There was a mechanical problem at the docking ring that needed to be resolved. It could not be helped."

"Well, you've missed the conference," he told the Bajoran. "Kubus is just leaving, and I've no reason to repeat our conversation. Although . . . I do have a question or two for you, Basso, if Kubus will excuse us."

The Bajoran official took his leave, and Dukat immediately set to interrogating his aide. "Have you come from the hospital?"

"Yes, sir. I took the last shuttle back, but as I said, there was a problem at the docking ring and all passengers were briefly detained while the engineers—"

"I'm not interested," Dukat said tensely. "I want to know of Meru's condition. Is it—"

"Terminal, yes, sir. Doctor Moset confirmed that it is a particularly virile strain of the Fostossa virus. She is not expected to make it through the week."

Dukat's chin dropped on his chest. "Such a tragedy for one so young," he said softly. "I suppose I will have to go look in on her in the next few days . . ." He felt a genuine regret as he said it. A hard ache persisted in his chest, thinking of her, frail and nearly lifeless in the clinical isolation of the hospital—yes, he'd better go to her, soon. He owed it to her to make her final moments as comfortable as possible. Although perhaps she would prefer to see her Bajoran husband . . .

Dukat felt his face darken in resentment as he remembered the sob caught in her throat. *"My husband,"* she'd said. After all the years he'd spent with her, everything he'd done to make her happy . . . and at the back of her mind, always it was *him.*

Dukat looked up at Basso, who was waiting to be told what to do next, for like all Bajorans, he scarcely had a mind of his own. "I will see what I can do to visit her," Dukat said.

"It is understandable if you can't make it down to see her," Basso said. "You are a busy man, an important man. You can't be expected to keep constant vigil by her bedside while she wastes away—"

"That's enough," Dukat snapped. "You've done your job, now get out of here."

"Yes, sir," Basso said obediently, and left the office.

Dukat sat down heavily in his chair. He wanted to unburden himself from thoughts of Meru, but it was proving difficult.

*Difficult decisions have to be made every day,* he reminded himself. Being prefect of Bajor was not an easy job; it required great strength of character. It required a man who did not allow his personal feelings to distract him from those things that must be done, discomfiting as they might sometimes be.

Lenaris's raider entered Bajor's atmosphere like a dart. He clung to the yoke, the thrusters propelling him at dizzying half-impulse speed, too high a speed for even the best Cardassian pilots to keep their ships underneath the atmosphere without losing control. The little raider tore through the air, the proximity sensors clicking madly as he came closer to the target, and he reduced his speed, keeping his attention divided between his ship's course and the transponder signals that told him whether the rest of his team was still with him. They all were, though the Legans were predictably straggling a bit, but not so much as to compromise their formation. Lenaris prepared to descend.

The blood rushed to his face as his ship looped and fell, a straight plummeting nosedive toward the surface of the planet, the hills and glens of Musilla province rushing at him. There was a Cardassian naval base directly below, a "secret" installation that the Ornathias had learned of through contact with another cell operating in this region.

Lenaris kept his direction steady, correcting for sideslip and watching his altimeter fervently. He dropped closer and closer to the surface, trying to remind himself not to glance away from his instrument panel for even a second. The temptation to do so was nearly irresistible, as he had no guarantee that the base was really down there, aside from the testimony of another Bajoran he'd never actually met in person. But if the resistance was to work on a global scale, it was imperative that he trust his faceless contacts. The base was below him. It had to be.

He got his confirmation in the form of an automated missile, showing up first as a hot blip on his transponder and then streaking across his viewscreen. He expertly maneuvered around it, though he felt panic overtake him for an instant when he saw his brother's craft yawing dangerously on his proximity sensors. Jau corrected and the missile went straight for the Legans, who were flying too close together, as usual.

"Come on . . ." Lenaris held his breath. Duravit managed to pull up in time to avoid it, but the blinking light that represented Fin's ship did not come back on again.

*No!* He didn't even have time to cry out, another missile was coming. This time, Lenaris took it out with his phaser banks before it came close enough to be in dodging range.

The formation was broken now, with only Nerissa still pulling straight down in a determined line. "Good girl," Lenaris muttered, and hoped she'd have the wherewithal to take out any more missiles by herself.

He set his ship back into a nosedive, and another missile came after Sten's ship, which had veered far off to the side, swooping back almost into its original course. Sten managed to steer the missile away from the others, and Jau took it out before it got too close.

Nerissa dropped her explosives pack and a cloud of fiery orange debris came billowing up from the base below them, her raider riding the wake of it. Lenaris pulled up to avoid the blast front, trying to tap in a code to the other ships—*proceed with formation*. But only Sten seemed to have gotten the transmission, for the others were still flying in erratic confusion.

Lenaris decided he could pay them no mind, and continued on with the task at hand, plummeting toward the surface and ejecting the load of explosives just a few *kellipates* above the military ships that he could now see, lined up in neat rows. He pulled his flight yoke abruptly to his chest and felt the bottom drop out of his stomach as the force of the movement pinned him to his seat. The blast erupted behind him, and his ship twisted violently in the sky before he could straighten it out again. Another blast followed, and he knew that one of the others had dropped his load as well. Three out of six wasn't bad, though he hoped at least one more could manage to let loose its ordnance

He set his course back for Jeraddo, aiming at a sharp, upward angle, getting plenty of distance between his ship and the base before checking his transponder to see who was still with him. Three shuttles limped behind him, the fourth having straggled somewhere out of atmospheric range. Legan Duravit, Ornathia Nerissa, and Ornathia Sten. Jau's signal was gone.

Numb, Lenaris started to turn back, but his transponder indicated another ship in the vicinity—a skimmer. In fact, two skimmers. No, he checked again, and now there were four, and they were headed straight for him. He increased his speed to sub-impulse and straightened out his trajectory. He would not be leaving the atmosphere just yet, not until after he'd worn these spoonheads out. He checked his transponder one more time for Jau, but his brother's raider was still nowhere within range, and Holem didn't have time to consider it.

"Follow the leader," Lenaris breathed, and dove suddenly back down toward the trees.

## 17

Laren walked at a rapid pace, her legs working to keep up with the longer strides of the men. Keeve was escorting Darrah Mace to his ship, and Bram was close behind. Darrah was giving out the particulars as they walked.

"You're going to need environmental suits," Darrah said.

"Suits!" Bram said, looking flustered. "I thought this was a simple job!"

Laren was thinking much the same thing.

Mace nodded. "It is simple," he said tersely. "Once we get her into the facility, it'll be a simple in-and-out. But Valo VI has no breathable atmosphere—"

"Valo VI?" Bram interrupted. "I always thought there were only five planets in this system."

"Valo VI is barely a planet," Mace replied. "It's somewhere between a dwarf planet and an asteroid."

"The facility is on an asteroid?" Bram looked flabbergasted.

"It will be fine," Laren said quickly, looking to Mace for confirmation.

Darrah nodded. "The facility is underneath a beamshield. You can't be transported directly inside. That's why you'll need the suits."

"What are the Cardassians doing there?" Laren inquired.

"Well, we don't know, of course," Darrah replied. "But

we're hoping to catch them at something that will bring in the Federation."

"Why don't you just kill them?" Laren said. "Who cares what they're doing?"

"Laren!" Bram said sharply.

"It's all right," Keeve said to Bram. He addressed Laren, his tone shifting toward condescension. "I understand why you might feel that way. But you have to remember that everything is interconnected. It's like Torasia's sixteenth prophecy: 'You can cut down the tree, but the roots still hold fast to the rain.'"

Laren made a face. "What does that have to do with anything?" she said. "Those prophecies are all a lot of gibberish."

*"Laren!"* Bram grabbed her by the shoulder, his fingers digging painfully into her flesh. "I've had enough of your blasphemy, your disrespect!" He took a swipe at her, caught her earring in his hand, and flung it to the ground. "You aren't fit to wear that," he told her, snarling.

Keeve waved his hands. "She has to make her own peace with the Prophets," he told Bram. "You can't do it for her."

Bram released her, and she rubbed her shoulder where he'd grabbed her, feeling angry, but mostly surprised. Bram had never put his hands on her like that before. She bent down to pick up her earring. The fleshy part of her ear burned where the ornament had been torn away, and she looked at the chained bits of metal in her hand. It was an old and silly tradition, but this was something of her father's. She put the earring back in her pocket, not looking at anyone.

"We need to do this," Darrah said, clearly uncomfortable.

Bram nodded. "Come on, Laren," he said gruffly, as much an apology as Ro could ever expect to get.

It was a short trip in the high-powered ship Mace flew. Bram and Laren spent most of it getting acclimated to the cumbersome suits they would have to wear. They were old and smelled thickly of the dust of Valo II, having been in a storage locker somewhere at the planet's shipyards. Finding one that could be easily adjusted to Laren's small frame was a challenge. Laren had been impatient to get started, but once they were actually in orbit of the tiny, irregularly shaped planet, her confidence began to ebb, not for the job itself, but for the unsettling novelty of the transporter beam. To her, it was the worst part of the mission, and she was eager to get it over and done with.

Darrah explained the properties of the transporter and gave her a little communications device that could be tapped to hail him back on the ship so that he could transport her back to safety again, but once she was beneath the beam-shield, the transporter beam would not reach her, and she would have nothing but her own senses to rely on. Of course, this would normally be nothing new to Laren, but on an unfamiliar asteroid in a musty-smelling environmental suit that inhibited her freedom of movement, the rules seemed to have changed a bit.

Darrah had said he would do his best to transport them within walking distance of the facility, but when Laren found herself crouched in the middle of unfamiliar terrain, her visibility limited behind the mask of her environmental suit, she at first thought Mace must have made a terrible mistake. There was nothing anywhere in her line of sight, just rocks and misty blackness, but after a half-second of disoriented searching, she found Bram somewhere off to her side, and he gestured to something behind them.

*Behind me.* The facility was only a few paces away, in the opposite direction of where she had been facing. She followed Bram as he scouted around the perimeter of the glinting shield. The shield was dome-shaped, translucent in the misty atmosphere. The buildings beneath it appeared as sprawling, squat boxes. She could not see any feasible way to get inside, until Bram pointed out to her an innocuous passageway with a simple keypad device to admit travelers.

A voice crackled in Laren's head and she started at the odd effect of the radio inside her environmental helmet; it was Darrah, back on the ship. *"Laren? Bram?"*

"We're here," Laren said, almost in unison with Bram.

*"Good,"* Darrah replied. *"Do you see the facility?"*

"Yes," Laren said. "There's just the one passageway, like you said."

*"Can you bypass it?"*

"Yup," Laren said without hesitation.

*"Good. Now, remember. There are usually only two or three Cardassians in there at a time, according to our scans. They have minimum security detail, and only one soldier patrols while the others sleep. There is one soldier awake in there right now, according to the schedule we've logged. He should be in the back part of the building, where we think the center of operations must be. You will have to find a console to hack the system. If you can reconnect the security loop quickly enough, you can just slip out, we'll take off, and they'll never even know we were here."*

*"You think you can handle it, Laren?"* Bram was sounding much friendlier now than he had back on Valo II, probably out of guilt for being so mean, or maybe because he was about to let her go straight into a nest of grass vipers.

"Of course I can," she said stoutly.

*"Well, you've never lacked confidence,"* Bram said, his voice hollow in her earpiece, and the figure in the suit next to her drew its phaser. *"I'll cover you. The minute anything goes wrong—"*

"Nothing's going to go wrong," she assured him, her

own voice echoing oddly inside the curved plastic of her visor. "This is the easiest job I've ever seen. I could do this with my eyes closed."

*"Well, then . . ."*

Laren knew about thirty Cardassian override codes by heart, but she didn't want to take the chance that this system would shut down once two or more incorrect codes were entered consecutively. She'd do better to just hack her way straight inside, and that would also probably disable any security systems that alerted the inhabitants of the facility that anyone was here. Her hands clumsy in the imprecise gloves of her environmental suit, she used the edge of a spanner to pry open the security panel. With the same spanner, she separated a thick wire from the bundle that revealed itself behind the panel. From a pocket in her suit, she retrieved a pair of spring-loaded snips and clipped a few specific wires. The door opened obediently, and she stepped inside. As soon as she crossed the threshold, it closed behind her, and she headed down the short, glassy corridor, sealing her in from the strange terrain outside. Her breathing inside the helmet sounded noisy and labored.

As she approached a second door, she found another panel imprinted with a Cardassian insignia—the same sort of inverted-teardrop sigil she had seen on many pieces of Cardassian equipment. It mimicked the shape of some of their ships, a fan tapering down into a two-pronged blunt spade at the bottom. This one, however, was a bit different. The bottom looked not so much like a spade as a tail, the whole thing appearing as some kind of ugly, poisonous sea creature. Usually she had seen only the outline of this sigil, but this one was filled in with a pale green, drifting to purple at the top. It looked ominous, and her thoughts wandered to things supernatural—the Fire Caves, Pah-wraiths, and angry *borhyas*. She pushed that foolishness away and went about her business.

With the spanner, she punched in a universal encryption sequence at the keypad, and then punched in another, and another. Cardassian passcodes never had more than seven characters, at least none that she had seen. But this one—it was different. She began to feel the finest sliver of worry as she tried another sequence. What was different about this facility? She looked again at the colorful insignia near the door and began to wonder if she wasn't dealing with something a little different from the Cardassian soldiers who tromped around Bajor like automatons.

It was then that she noticed it—faint through the sounds of her own echoed breathing in the spacesuit, but it was there—a discernible clicking noise in her earpiece, as though she were being timed. Shaken, she began to move faster. She had encountered this type of alarm before. If she failed to enter the correct code before the countdown concluded, the system would shut down. She didn't know how much time she had, but she should probably assume that it wasn't much.

After a few feverish moments, she thought she had it. She separated another wire and used her snips to clip a few strands. An arc of electricity spit menacingly before fizzling out, and she released a breath. The door slid noiselessly open, and she stepped inside.

She removed her helmet and gloves and took a deep breath, but the heat in the facility quickly made her feel sluggish. She stuffed the gloves into the helmet and tucked it under her arm, looking around for a computer console and fingering the datarod in the pocket of her heavy suit. She found a console not far inside the building, and, trying to be as stealthy as she could in her clunky attire, she quickly began to hack into the system. She had to hunt and peck at the Cardassian characters on the keyboard. She could read Cardassian letters somewhat, but only piecemeal, one at a time, and she struggled to hurry as she murmured the phonetic sounds under her breath.

She jammed the datarod into a port and waited while the download ran. She entered a code to shield the activity from anyone else who might be in the compound, but stopped tapping as she became aware of a sound. *Voices.*

She plucked the datarod from its port and crouched down below the console, peering just over the edge to see what was going on. She was shocked to see a Cardassian emerge from a doorway built into the floor, and he was talking to someone below him. How could that be? Mace had said that there was only one soldier awake right now, and he was in the other wing of the building. How had he overlooked these two? Could there be a shield that protected them from scans, maybe an underground bunker where they could not be detected? Laren hunkered down further below the console, wondering if she should contact Bram or just try to slip out on her own. The Cardassians had not been wearing armor, he should be easy enough to shoot, if she had to . . .

She peered over the edge of the console again, and what she saw next stopped her heart in her throat. The second man who had come from below looked . . . different from most of the Cardassians she had seen in her life. It was his hair. It was not the same tarry black that the vast majority of spoonheads had been endowed with; no, by some quirk of natural selection, this man's slick hair was a dusty, golden color. A color that Laren had seen on a Cardassian only one other time in all her life. She checked again to ensure that it was true. Of course, it was possible that there was more than one blond Cardassian in the galaxy . . . but no, this was the one. This was the man who had killed her father.

"Varc," the dark-haired one said to him, to the murderer.

"Come here and look at this. The backup security loop is doing something odd."

"What do you mean, odd?" The light-haired soldier peered at his companion's console.

"It looks like there's a breach out there."

Laren clutched at her phaser. Four soldiers she had killed since joining the resistance. She was about to make it six. She squeezed her eyes shut, took a breath—and then she sprang up from her hiding place, phaser at the ready. The resultant flash was blinding, and the first man caught it full in the chest. He flew back, crashing into the light-haired one and pinning him to the console behind him. Ro rushed forward without quite realizing what she was doing, to jam the weapon directly in the face of the man who had taken so much from her.

"You!" she shouted, her voice shaking.

The blond Cardassian was shaking off the blast. "What?" he said blearily, but he could say no more, for Laren squeezed the trigger, and then she turned and ran for her life.

Dukat was in ops, looking over the security logs, when Basso approached him. He gave the Bajoran a look that conveyed it was a bad time, but Basso was impatient to speak, and he did so despite the prefect's unspoken command.

"Sir, it's about the Kira family . . ."

Dukat quickly gestured Basso up the short platform to his office, herding him inside. When the door was closed, he turned to him.

"What can possibly be so important that you would bring up such a topic in the center of operations?"

"My sincere apologies, sir, but you see, this is the time when I normally bring the extra allotment of supplies to the Kira family, and I thought that perhaps—" He stopped, expecting Dukat to quickly catch on to where he was going with this, but the prefect said nothing, only looked even more annoyed than before.

"Do you still need me to make that delivery?" Basso finally asked.

Dukat's eyes narrowed. "How dare you," he said, his voice eerily low.

"Sir, I apologize, again—please, understand—I only want to know what's expected of me, considering the . . . new circumstances."

Dukat looked at a spot on the wall, and then raised his head, his deeply pensive gaze traveling up to the ceiling. "Let me explain something to you, Basso. I loved Meru with all my heart, and promised her—I gave my *word*—that I would look after them for the rest of their lives. Is that clear?"

"Yes, sir, of course." Basso inclined his head, in part to keep the prefect from seeing how florid his complexion had suddenly become. He was deeply frustrated, but there was nothing he could do; if Dukat wanted to alleviate his guilt for having Meru put to death, then Basso was going to have to comply. It was that, or work in the mines with the herd animals, and he'd long ago decided that he was not a man who could live without comforts. Food and a warm bed went a long way toward clearing his conscience. If the rest of them didn't want to cooperate, they could stay in the mines, where they belonged.

He went to see to his duty, cursing the dead Meru.

Lenaris's mother could not be consoled, not by the reminders of her impending status as a new grandmother, not by her surviving son's constant reassurances that he was working practically around the clock to find out what had become of Jau. It was a hollow promise, that he would find Jau alive, and he knew it. He had exhausted every means of locating his brother; none had panned out to anything at all.

It was the week after he'd given up, the week that he was distracted by the baby's quickly approaching due date, when he received word from the Kintaura resistance cell over in Rakantha province that wreckage had been found, not far from the Meiku forest.

"An old raider?" Lenaris asked the woman on the other end of the comm.

*"Not exactly,"* she told him, her voice tinny. *"The ship seemed to have been . . . modified. It was like a raider, but the wings were—"*

"Longer?" Lenaris asked, his heart seeming to stop.

*"Yes, that's right."*

Lenaris let out the breath he had been holding. So it was true. Jau's raider had gone down. "Was there . . . Did you find . . . any remains?" he asked quietly.

*"No, there weren't. In fact, it wasn't so much wreckage as . . . the ship came down hard, but a person could have walked away from it."*

"Really?" Lenaris felt his heart start to beat again. "You think . . . the pilot survived, then?"

*"I do, yes. We've hauled in the raider, we'll be refurbishing it—it hardly sustained any damage at all. We've been keeping an eye out for the pilot, but—I'm sorry to have to tell you this, but there was a recent sweep between Rakantha and Dahkur—anyone found wandering outside Cardassian-imposed boundaries was picked up and taken to . . . a particular work camp."*

Lenaris let out another hard breath. "A camp on the surface?" he asked. Maybe he could stage a rescue effort.

*"Yes, but . . . it's Gallitep."*

"Gallitep!" He didn't have a prayer of getting Jau out. Lenaris clenched his fists, thinking of the stories he'd heard. Severe rationing, death by starvation and exhaustion . . .

medical experiments. Jau was just a boy, he wouldn't last a week in a place like that.

*"I'm very sorry. Maybe I shouldn't have said anything. It's possible he's still hiding in the woods somewhere, if he has survival skills . . ."*

Lenaris wiped his eyes. In fact, Jau was new to the resistance movement, had lived his entire childhood in the relative safety of the refugee camp. Lenaris had been planning on teaching him a few things, after he really started to get the hang of flying . . .

"Thank you for the information, Kintaura Two. This is Ornathia Two, shutting down."

Lenaris turned off the system and rested his face in his hands, allowing himself a moment to catch his breath. He quickly decided to tell his mother that Jau had been killed. If she learned that her son was at Gallitep—

Lenaris was not willing to be the one to deliver a piece of news like that, not to anyone's mother, but least of all his own.

Laren had not yet caught her breath as Darrah's ship shot away from Valo VI. She continued to gasp as she tried to answer Bram, whose questions came so quickly, she didn't have time to answer. "Why didn't you call for me? Laren, you compromised us! Mace and Keeve made it plain that stealth was the prime objective here. Now they'll know an intruder has been there, and they're going to suspect it's the Valo II settlers!"

"What happened back there?" Darrah said.

"I'm sorry . . ." Laren panted. "There were more of them than you said . . . and I didn't have time to think! I was just about to call Bram, or . . . sneak away, but one of them noticed the security loop had been disabled. . . . I had to make a judgment call!"

Bram continued to shake his head. "But you at least got the data," he said.

"I . . ." It hit her then. She'd had to pull the datarod before the download had really gotten going. She had never failed before, not when it mattered—and this mattered.

Bram looked horrified. "You . . . you didn't even get the data?"

Laren started to argue as she caught her breath, but she let it drop, tired and confused. She had expected to feel overwhelmingly triumphant after killing that man, the man who haunted her dreams. But she didn't feel anything except exhausted. Maybe it would come later—though she was beginning to doubt it. Her father was still dead, after all.

*I had to kill him, though,* she thought. *Even if it hadn't been him . . . I had no other choice. They were about to find me, I wouldn't have been able to get away.*

Darrah's ship set down on the old airfield that was dotted with an assemblage of disabled-looking air and ground vehicles, including the freighter, which was off near an outcropping of rock.

Darrah addressed her before they disembarked. "So, what happened back there? You said there were more Cardassians in the place. Tell me exactly what you remember."

"There were two soldiers who came up from someplace underground," Laren told Mace. "They didn't see me at first and I thought I could sneak away, but—"

"I'm sorry," Mace said, and he looked it. "I would never have put you in that situation if we'd known there were more Cardassians in that facility." He turned to Bram. "I'm sorry to have put her in harm's way like that."

Bram nodded. "It's all right, you couldn't have known."

The three climbed out of Darrah's ship. Laren didn't bother to point out that Bram had let her go into much more dangerous situations than that one, and he'd never had any qualms about her being in "harm's way," but she only continued with her report as they left the ship behind and began to head back toward the center of the main town. "I had to think fast, I guess. I might have had time to call for Bram, but then I heard one of them tell the other one that the security feed had been compromised. I thought for sure they'd start looking around for me, and so I took them out."

Bram spoke up before Darrah could. "You mean, they hadn't seen you yet?"

"I don't know!" she snapped. "I told you, I had to think fast."

"It's all right, Bram," Darrah assured him. "She did the right thing. Look, I'll tell you the truth—I don't think we'll experience much fallout from this."

Bram shook his head. "They're going to know it was you!" he argued. "Don't sweeten it for the girl, Mace—she messed up, and she needs to know it!"

"No, no, she did the right thing. I'm telling you—the Cardassian military isn't going to be bothering us over that facility. They probably don't even know about it."

Bram looked taken aback. "How do you mean?"

"The Cardassians at that facility, they aren't military. We don't really know what they do, but we think they're an autonomous body trying to keep their heads as low as possible."

Laren didn't know what Mace could be talking about. Cardassians were Cardassians were Cardassians. Weren't they? Indiscriminate killers. They were *all* the military, as far as she knew . . . Although there had been that unusual sigil on the panel near the door . . .

Darrah went on, though Bram looked dubious. "Of course, it would have been better to have kept this mission a little quieter . . . but let's face it: despite their loss of personnel, by now they'll have figured out that no data was compromised. I don't think we have to fear military repercussions."

Laren stopped listening as they walked through the depressing outskirts of the town, where clumps of refugee camps had gone up, tents blowing in the high morning winds. She became aware of some people approaching from where the older part of the "city" was, and recognized Akhere Bis and his father.

"Mace!" Juk called. "Back in one piece?"

Laren looked at her toes as they approached; she did not want to have to be confronted by Bis when she'd just failed so miserably. Juk had questions for her, and she answered them tersely, without looking at anyone, Bram filling in the rest of the blanks where she could not provide an articulate answer.

"You . . . you killed one of them?" Bis asked her incredulously.

"I killed two of them," she said, trying to sound boastful, trying to feel proud of herself at least for that aspect of the mission—she had finally killed him, the murderer who had robbed her of her father. But she felt nothing. Ashamed, that she'd failed to retrieve the data they wanted.

Bis had nothing else to say. He merely gaped at her while she continued to avoid looking at anyone. She was only half-listening when Juk told Darrah that he could safely take Bram and Laren to a rendezvous with a Kressari freighter captain he knew, who was willing and able to smuggle them back to Bajor.

Laren should have been happy to get away from this desolate rock, but she felt an almost unbearable disappointment, and she wasn't sure where it came from. Was it the failure of the mission? Could it be because she was going to leave Bis behind? Or was it because the face of that blond Cardassian soldier, his eyes blank with confusion before she took his life, had not immediately provided the relief she craved? Again, she hoped it would sink in later, would suddenly be transformed into a euphoric sense of a mission accomplished. But she only felt a chaotic jumble of nervous emotion, none of it very pleasant at all. Keeve had joined them now, and he began asking her questions straightaway. She tried to focus on what she was being asked, but all she could think of was failure and loss, an interminable black spot of grief, as if she would never be happy again.

# OCCUPATION YEAR THIRTY

✦ ✦ ✦

## 2357 (Terran Calendar)

## 18

The loose rocks beneath her feet rocked and cracked against one another as Kira Nerys scrambled up the side of the hill. The wind was bitter up near the ridge, and she pulled her heavy woolen overjacket close around her, her pack shifting on her shoulders. It was a cold day in Dahkur. It would be winter before long, but until then, Kira had to get used to the constant soaring dips and spikes in the temperature. Throughout the fall, the days would be hot, the nights plummeting nearly to freezing after sunset. It wasn't anything new, for Kira had lived in Dahkur her entire life. But now that she had left her father's home, had taken to sleeping outside with the rest of the fighters in the Shakaar cell, she had to get accustomed to waking up with frost over the top of her blankets, the various members of her group huddling together to keep warm while they slept.

The Shakaar cell lived together somewhat communally, though there were a few smaller units within it that took care of their own business. For the most part, the resistance fighters ate together, bathed together, slept together, and divided their chores up among themselves. It had taken some getting used to, but Kira mostly liked it. It made her feel part of something bigger than herself—something important.

"Nerys!" called a woman's voice, echoing faintly from

somewhere down below. Must have been Lupaza, for most of the other women in the cell still referred to her as "you" or "kid" or "little girl." Most of the men did, too, actually, though they were somewhat kinder than the women. Kira resented it a bit, but she knew they were only toughening her up for what lay ahead. As it was, she'd been on scant few combat missions. Mostly she ran errands, bringing food and power cells to those fighters who were in the field, or relaying information back and forth from one cell to another. It wasn't the worst thing in the world, but she was eager to prove her mettle, for she knew she had it in her to be as good a fighter as anyone.

In fact it was Lupaza, calling her name from the base of the hillside, her hands cupped around her mouth.

"What is it?" Kira called down to her friend. "Shakaar sent me up to check the comm relay!" She edged lower to better hear the older woman's reply.

"Oh, come down, Nerys, he only sent you up there to get you out of the camp. You were asking too many questions, he said."

Kira was incensed. "I wasn't either!" she shouted, and began to scoot down the rocky slope, steadying herself against the bigger rocks as she inched lower, trying to avoid causing a slide. "Are you sure?" she asked. "He really just had me go up here to get me out of the way?"

Lupaza nodded. "Yes, he did. He's—"

"He's a lugfish!" Kira yelled, sliding the rest of the way down the hill on a bed of moving gravel. "I could have been killed up here! And for what?"

"Never mind, Nerys. Now come on, let's talk about something fun for a change. Like what you want to do for your birthday! It's your fourteenth, you ought to do something special, with your family, maybe."

Kira shrugged. Her fourteenth birthday was supposed to be an event. Since it signified the passage of her *ih'tanu*, it meant that she was an adult—officially. Of course, Kira felt as though she had already been an adult for some time. A lot of people her age felt that way these days, probably a big part of the reason many girls' *ih'tanu* birthdays came and went without comment.

"Did you have an *ih'tanu* ceremony?" Kira asked her friend.

"Of course I did," Lupaza said. "Everyone in my village had them. Elaborate celebrations . . . lots of dancing, food . . ."

"Did your parents announce your betrothal?" It was an old custom, falling out of practice even before the Cardassians came, but Lupaza had grown up in a very rural region, where some of the old ways had still been observed—possibly were still being observed even now.

"Yes, they did," Lupaza said softly.

"To Furel?"

Lupaza laughed, though it didn't sound happy. "No," she said. "I met Furel much later. The boy I was matched with . . . he went away, before we would have married. He and his entire family—his father went to work for the Cardassians. I never saw him again."

"Oh," Kira said, wishing she hadn't asked. "I—I didn't know that . . ."

Lupaza smiled, artificially bright. "Now, how could you have known? No matter, it was a long time ago, before I got so old."

Kira laughed. "You're not so old, Lupaza. How old are you? Thirty?"

Lupaza snorted. "I *wish* I was thirty," she said. "Now, what shall we do? I'll walk you into Dahkur, if you want to speak to your father about it."

Kira shrugged. "Maybe," she said. "But probably I'll tell him not to make a fuss."

"Whatever you want," Lupaza said softly. "We have to

do our best to stick to our traditions, though. We don't want to forget who we are."

"*I'll* never forget," Kira said firmly. "No matter what the Cardassians do to me, I'll never forget who I am, and where I come from . . . and that they don't belong here." It emboldened her to say these words, especially knowing that she was finally doing something about it.

It was on that note that Shakaar came around a shallow bend in the canyon from the side where the caves were. "Nerys! I thought I told you to adjust the comm signal," he said sternly.

"Oh, drop it, Edon, I told her you were just trying to get rid of her."

"That isn't true!" Shakaar protested, his handsome features pulled into an amusingly rehearsed approximation of indignity.

"I can tell you're lying," Kira taunted, and he didn't get angry, or even argue. She was beginning to feel more a part of the cell every day now, even enough to poke fun at its leader. He wasn't that much older than she, after all, only just in his twenties.

"Come on, Nerys," Lupaza beckoned. "You can help me with the washing."

Washing the clothes was a chore that she would have grumbled about back home, with her father and brothers, but here, doing the washing was different. Here, it was part of the struggle to survive, and to win back Bajor from those who had wrongly claimed it. Kira would happily do washing every single day if she thought it could play a part, no matter how small, in driving off the Cardassians.

"Scratch that," Shakaar said. "I just got a call." He took something ungainly from his pocket, a piece of equipment that Mobara had built from some scrap. The thing squawked twice in Shakaar's hand. "Come back to camp. Dakhana must have found something down in the valley, she's calling for backup. Grab your phasers, let's get down there."

"Me, too?" Kira asked.

Shakaar didn't hesitate. "Of course," he said.

Kira beamed, fishing her phaser from out of her pack and holstering it in the pocket of her tunic.

"You ready?" Lupaza asked her as they scrambled down the canyon.

"Always," Kira said, trying to mean it. For although sometimes there was fear that preceded these missions, Kira had never in her life felt the kind of exhilaration and triumph that came with their conclusion. She had waited her entire life to feel that she was making a difference, to do something that might lead her closer to some facsimile of happiness; and, though she certainly wouldn't consider herself a happy person—not in the sense of being carefree—she was closer to it now than she had ever been before. Fighting the Cardassians, she had decided, was what the Prophets had meant for her to do.

Her head high, she marched forth with her comrades, sure she was ready for anything.

Dukat had always loathed these quarterly debriefing sessions with Legate Kell, but they had become even more unbearable in the past year, during which there had been a noticeable spike in Bajoran terrorist activity. Dukat knew that Kell had been telling anyone who would listen that it was mostly the fault of the prefect's policies, but he was usually more subtle when speaking directly to Dukat about it.

They went through the polite formalities, both men ensconced in their own private offices, separated by much more than time and space. Kell looked old these days, Dukat thought, and wondered what the aging legate thought of the face on his screen. It had been a long and trying year.

"*Gul,*" the legate addressed him, signaling the end of the pleasantries, such as they were. "*May I ask what, if anything, you have been doing to put a cap on the insurgency?*"

Dukat was prepared. "We've had some notable successes. Our latest worry is that in many provinces, the terrorists have taken to moving so far into the forests that we can't locate them, short of burning the forests down—a tack, by the way, which has been performed with some success in a few areas. But it's a tremendous waste of precious resources, especially in the forests that feature nyawood—a rare and valuable commodity on some worlds, as you know. We've barely begun to tap that market."

"*You can't send automated tanks in after them?*"

"The tanks are ill-suited to traversing the wooded areas. I've been thinking on the matter, however, and have an idea that you might find interesting."

Kell narrowed his eyes. "*Go on.*"

"The Federation—our intelligence indicates that they have access to better technologies than our own," Dukat said smoothly. "Here we are, squabbling with them over the pitiful little colonies out on the frontier. But if we had a *treaty* with the Federation, think of the resources we could conserve. Aside from freeing up our troops to be sent to Bajor, we could gain access to Federation military systems—better sensors, better ground travel . . ."

"*A treaty!*" Kell sputtered.

"It would be on our own terms, of course. And we wouldn't necessarily have to hold up our end of the bargain—at least, not in every case. Let me just tell you my proposal—"

"*Your job is not to be contemplating imaginary Federation treaties, Dukat. You are to be concerned with Bajor, and Bajor only.*"

"Certainly, Legate, but you must agree that these matters are all interconnected. The actions of military leaders on the border colonies affect Bajor, decisions made on far-flung Cardassian outposts affect Bajor, and your jurisdiction affects Bajor as well . . ."

*"Since when did you become so philosophical? You sound like one of those damned Oralian fools."*

"Oralians!" Dukat said between his teeth. Perhaps he was a little more philosophical than he had once been, if only as an effect of his age, but he didn't see where that was necessarily a bad thing. For Kell to compare him to the Oralians, though, was perhaps the cruelest implication he could have made, especially considering the fate of Dukat's own firstborn . . . He nearly choked on the reply he would have liked to make, but the legate went on before he could even begin.

*"Yes, and speaking of the Oralians, there are rumors beginning to circulate that there is a resurgence of them here, though I've not been able to confirm it. I would like you to keep your ears open for any news you may hear among our people on Bajor."*

"Indeed," Dukat agreed, remembering himself. The Oralians had been nothing but troublemakers for Cardassia, backward-looking, naïve fools who did little more than damage his people's collective morale—not to mention nearly cause civil war, on more than one occasion. Dukat felt certain that anything Kell had heard was no more than rumor, for the Oralians had all been taken care of many years ago. Dukat would not stand for any alternative.

*"At any rate,"* Kell said, changing back the subject, *"I want to see some quantifiable differences where the Bajoran resistance is concerned. And I want to see them soon."*

"Of course, Legate."

*"Perhaps this truth is lost on you, Dukat, but the citizens of the Union have come to speak your name synonymously with the Bajoran annexation. Whatever way the annexation falls, success or*

*failure, the responsibility rests on you. Not to your predecessors, and likely not to your successors, either, for you are considered to be the true architect of the Bajoran-Cardassian construct. I would advise you to keep that in mind."*

Dukat could find no answer. It seemed that the legate felt resentment about the words he had just spoken, but Dukat was not sure it was something to be envious of, the caliber of responsibility that had just been attributed to him.

The legate started to reach for his console, then paused. *"One last thing. I'm sending a new scientist to Bajor—Doctor Kalisi Reyar. She has been doing interesting things with weapons research, and she has a specific interest in Bajor. I think you will find her to be useful."*

"I thank you, Legate. I will let the director of the Bajoran Institute of Science know that she is to have a new player on her team."

*"Very well,"* Kell acknowledged, and hit his disconnect button, severing their tenuous connection.

The small group of seven Bajorans slipped through the woods, using nothing but the light of the moons to guide their way. It was cold, for Jo'kala, and Ro felt confident that they would not meet many Cardassian patrols tonight—at least, not until they came upon the military compound itself.

The target was not far from the edge of the forest, and they arrived there in very little time, the remaining three from the cell silently bringing up the rear. "We're all clear," Tokiah murmured. "Let's do this."

Ro immediately set about rigging a tricorder to project a Bajoran life sign. She pitched the tricorder within striking range, and a thin, red beam shot out from under the eaves of the squat structure. Ro aimed her phaser at the source of the laser, and took it out neatly with a single shot. She crept closer, beckoning the others, who scrambled behind her, staggering their crouched positions.

It was only a moment before a stiff-legged sentry came out, an exaggerated frown frozen across his features. He was clearly uncomfortable, having been made to stand in the Bajoran elements, and Ro wasted no time giving him a full dose of her phaser. He landed backwards with a nearly comical thud. She leapt forward, stripping him of several pieces of useful equipment, including his comcuff, phaser, tricorder, and padd.

"Hurry, Ro!" Kanore snapped in a loud whisper. "There's no time to pick off paltry bits of equipment when there's a full armory in there waiting to be raided!"

"I'm coming," she muttered, stashing the items away in her clothing. Old habits died hard. She leapt over the sentry's prone form to the entrance of the compound, where she expertly removed the security panel and worked her particular brand of magic on the bypass loop. The door opened obediently, and the seven Bajorans slipped inside.

Ro's thoughts condensed as she entered the compound, her vision focused on each pasty, angry-featured Cardassian face, those lumbering bodies clad in shiny gray. She aimed for the neck ridges, the dimple in the center of the forehead, anywhere they weren't armored, but if she misfired and hit one in the chest, the resultant blast was usually enough to at least disable him for a moment. One soldier caught it just below the shoulder, forcing him a step backward. He shook it off, a tight fist from his uninjured side swinging out to knock Ro's arms sideways. Keeping her pistol clenched tightly between her fingers, she had only enough time to swing her elbows and slam them up under his chin. His knees buckled and he fell, giving her the opportunity to deliver a pulse directly into his face, leaving a gaping, smoking hole where his lizardlike features had once been. Ro coughed and moved on. At least there wasn't so much blood where phasers were concerned. Ro had never cared for the sight of blood.

The Cardassians were outnumbered, a mere skeleton crew on duty in what they thought was a secure facility, and it took very little time for the Bram cell to finish them off. The cell was still named after Bram, though he was gone; injured by a Cardassian phaser last year, he had finally died several months later, though he put up a good fight. Tokiah had stepped in to fill his shoes as an ad hoc leader for the past year or so, since he was the oldest remaining member. Kanore begrudged him the leadership, but it didn't much matter to Ro who led them—she still did pretty much whatever she wanted to do, whether it coincided with her orders or not. Most of the time, she garnered successful enough results to avoid major conflict, but there were those—Kanore, especially—who frequently let her know that she was out of line. Since Bram had left, Ro found that she had fewer advocates for her position all the time, and it had begun to occur to her more and more that Bram might have been the only member of the cell who had really wanted her around for any reason other than her skills.

"In here!" Tokiah yelled. He and two others had found the compound's armory, in a room with flickering lights— a stray phaser shot seemed to have hit the environmental controls, for the lights were winking out all over, and the tinny humming of the building's heat monitoring system had gone silent. Entering the room, Ro immediately saw the force field that protected a long wall of weapons— stacked three and four deep, the aisle as long as three tall men lying end-to-end. There were more weapons than they could carry in one trip, but they couldn't risk coming back for more. Laren quickly found a console, and tapped her way into the mainframe, searching for the correct Cardassian words and phrases among the jumble of foreign text.

"Hurry!" Kanore said.

"When you learn to do this, you can hurry," Ro shot back.

She finally found the right command, and the translucent force field skittered out. Kanore took a step forward before Ro shouted at him to stop. "There may be a secondary security measure," she reminded him, and he obediently froze in place. Ro entered another command, and the lights went out completely, Sadakita and Faon quickly switching on their palmlights to compensate for the close darkness.

"Everyone grab four weapons," Tokiah instructed, as the rest of the cell found their way to the armory. From the farthest end of the line of weapons, Ro promptly selected six rifles and two pistols, to which Kanore wasted no time in rebuking her.

"You can't carry all that, it will slow you down!"

"Maybe it would slow you down," Ro countered.

"Tokiah said—"

Ro bumped his shoulder as she walked past him, heavily weighted down with the massive weapons slung over both shoulders.

"Laren," Tokiah said, and Ro shot him a look. Just because he was older, because he'd been close to Bram, he thought he could get away with using her given name; as though they were friends. They weren't friends. None of these people were her friends, and the look she gave Tokiah said as much. He didn't bother to finish his thought as she left the compound, and she set off into the forest ahead of the others.

It was not long before she was beginning to think that maybe Kanore had been right. To keep the cumbersome weapons from clanking together, she had to carry them close to her body, across the front of her chest, which was putting a tremendous burden on her neck and shoulders. The obvious solution occurred to her, and she set down her weapons some distance into the forest. With another thought, she turned back for more.

"Where are you going?" Sadakita asked her as she passed, heading back toward camp.

"I cached my weapons in the brush back there," Ro explained. "I'm going back for more."

"That's a bad idea, Ro," the older woman admonished her. "I don't have to tell you the facility will be swarming with spoonheads in a matter of minutes. We need to get as deep into the forest as we can."

"What's going on?" Tokiah demanded, coming up with the rest of the cell.

Sadakita looked to Ro, apparently unwilling to directly implicate her. "I'm getting more weapons," Ro said stubbornly.

"Don't be stupid, Laren," Tokiah said sternly. "Let's get going. There's no time to lose."

"I'm going back," Ro said firmly, and continued in the same direction she was headed.

Kanore started to call after her, but she could hear Tokiah telling him to let her go. She drew her phaser—the one she'd taken from the sentry—and jogged back to the facility. How sorry they'd all be when they saw how many weapons she'd lifted from the armory! It would be satisfying to hear Kanore say he'd been wrong.

She was still a considerable distance from the building when she realized that, in fact, the others hadn't been wrong. She could hear the sound of flyers coming in over the tops of the trees, shining lights down into the forest. She clung to the trunk of a blackwood tree for a moment, looking up at the sky until she was satisfied that the patrol's spotlights weren't really very effective at penetrating the tree cover. She felt foolish, realizing that if she wasn't careful, she could lead the Cardassians straight back to her cell's encampment. Defeated, she turned back around and picked her way through the dark forest, eventually stopping to find the place where she'd left the pinched rifles.

Convinced she was safely out of range of where the flyers were searching, she slung all six of the rifles back up across her chest and stuffed the pistols into her waist satchel. She sourly noted to herself that if she'd been smart, she would have just distributed a few of them among the others in her cell, when they were still here to assist her. She could have just admitted she was wrong and asked for help. She sighed as she clanked along laboriously, wondering exactly what it was about her that made her so stubborn.

It was daylight by the time she made it back to camp, and Ro was tired, but there was no time for sleep. After a fairly unpleasant morning during which her actions were soundly denounced by nearly every member of her cell, she went to eat her breakfast by herself on a severed tree stump away from the others, grumbling to herself about the poor quality of food this autumn. The cell had been forced to make do with a soup made from a lichen that grew on the bark of the older nyawoods, and though it prevented starvation, it did little to satisfy the belly—or the palate. Ro knew that the food situation would only get worse this winter. Though Jo'kala's winters were notoriously mild, this had been a lean year around the entire planet. The Cardassians' constant overfarming—not to mention the industrial pollutants from their mining operations toxifying once-fertile soil—were beginning to have noticeable consequences in the quality and quantity of the already minimal harvest.

Tokiah emerged from a shelter made from a piece of canvas stretched around a circle of poles and topped with a conical roof of brush. It was semipermanent, like most of the buildings that dotted the camp—easy to take down, carry, and reconstruct anywhere else in the forest, if push came to shove. It always did, eventually.

"Ro," he said, and she did not look up or answer him, expecting to be scolded again.

"Hey! Ro, I'm talking to you!"

"I hear you," she said in a low voice.

"There's a subspace transmission on the comm!"

Ro finally looked at him. "And?" she said, annoyed. She had no business with the comm system. That wasn't her place in the cell—she bypassed security loops and killed spoonheads. The comm was Tokiah's responsibility.

"They're making reference to you. Someone is looking for you—someone on Valo II."

Ro hesitated only a second before she leapt to her feet and scrambled past Tokiah into the common building.

"It's Ro Laren!" she said breathlessly. "Who am I speaking to?"

The transmission was heavy with interference, and she could barely make it out. Between clicks and squawks she was sure she discerned the words *Jeraddo, meeting,* and *Bis.*

"Akhere Bis! Is it you? Is that who I'm speaking to?"

"*. . . ear me? . . . aren . . . This is . . . khere Bis. I'm . . . ping . . . t . . . Jeraddo.*"

After a few more back-and-forth relays with Ro shouting and the comm spitting back more broken transmissions, Ro felt some measure of certainty that Bis was requesting that she meet him on Jeraddo, Bajor's fifth moon, in two days. She couldn't get more than that out of him, for the comm started to fail in earnest before he could get further, but her mind was made up before his last crackling word. Anything to get her out of here for a while was reason enough to agree to the trip.

"Tokiah," she announced to the cell leader, waiting outside the common building, "I'm taking a raider to Jeraddo in two days."

"You'll do no such thing," Tokiah informed her. "Those ships belong to the cell, Laren. If you want to take a shuttle, it had better be part of an approved mission—for *the cell*."

"This is a mission," Ro said. "I'll be working with another outfit from Valo II, that's all." In truth she had no idea why Bis wanted to meet with her, but that didn't matter.

"You're not taking the raider."

"Really?" Ro said. "So, you wouldn't be willing to part with a ship for a day or so just to have me out of camp during that time? I mean, it's possible I'll never come back, Tokiah. Just think about that."

The cell leader frowned. "You'll dance on all our graves," he said. "You've got more lives than a *hara*, Laren."

"I'm taking a raider, Tokiah, whether you agree to it, or I have to steal one. I'd rather you made it easy for me."

Tokiah said nothing for a moment. "Maybe you shouldn't come back," he finally said, his voice soft.

Ro shouldn't have been surprised, but she was. She'd been a part of this cell for long enough that her memory of her life before it was hazy, existing only in pictures that might not have even had any basis in fact. This cell was the only life she really knew. She swallowed. "Fine," she said, her voice quavering before she cleared her throat. "Maybe I won't."

"Just don't take the *Trakor*," Tokiah said. "That one's my favorite."

"The *Trakor* pulls to the port side," Ro said, her voice low. "I wouldn't want it anyway." She turned and left Tokiah, intending to take a walk by herself. Whatever Bis wanted her for, it had to be better than this. He'd deliberately sought her out; for some reason, he needed her, enough to risk a subspace transmission for it. And that was more than she'd ever gotten from any member of her cell, even Bram—and Bram was dead.

Dukat was on the Bajoran side of the station when he was called to ops to answer a transmission from Gul Darhe'el. He turned from the Bajoran shopkeeper who had been spewing out empty flattery in an attempt to distract Dukat from the fact that he was most likely selling black-market items to some of the wretches in ore processing. Dukat didn't care enough about it to pursue it further—at least, not immediately. He walked away from the shop without further acknowledging the merchant, the swarm of dirty Bajorans parting to allow their prefect to pass.

He accepted the call a few minutes later, apologizing to Darhe'el for making him wait, both of them aware that he did not mean it. Gallitep's overseer didn't bother with any pleasantries, announcing the reason for his call without ceremony.

"It's over," Darhe'el said. "The main vein is played out, and the secondaries aren't worth the cost of running the AI. Besides which, I've had to continue treating the workers for Kalla-Nohra, at considerable expense. I'll need that Bajoran scientist to come to the camp, to shut down the AI. . . . And I'll need your approval for the rest of it."

Dukat felt his body tense. The news wasn't unexpected, but he hadn't thought it would come quite so soon. Gallitep had finally outlived its usefulness to Cardassia.

"The rest of it," he murmured, thinking of what Kell would say. Dukat had long believed that it would be a worthy venture to drill deeper below the surface, but Kell had consistently refused to supplement Dukat's resources with the personnel and equipment that would be necessary to delve that far. Dukat could only hope that the retirement of such a productive facility as Gallitep might persuade Kell to rethink his decision.

"*The workers,*" Darhe'el sneered. "*Unless you want them on your station. I'm sure they'd appreciate dying in the very lap of luxury.*"

Dukat sighed. "I see no great wrong in treating them with basic civility, Gul."

"*Which is why the filthy creatures continue to run over our ground troops, doing as they please,*" Darhe'el said. "*If I were prefect—*"

"Oh, but you're not, are you," Dukat said, enjoying the darkness that swept across Darhe'el's heavy face. "You've done an excellent job at Gallitep overall, I'll give you that. And I'm sure that Central Command will find further use for you, perhaps heading a prison facility, or leading a squadron at the front lines, for one of the colonies. But *I* am prefect of Bajor, and that means that for the time being, you still answer to *me.*"

If looks could kill. Dukat smiled, easing back. "I'll see to it that the necessary technician is sent promptly to deal with the AI. As to the management of the facility's closure, I'll leave that to your discretion. Send me your reports, I'll sign off on whatever choice you make, assuming it's not unreasonable."

Dukat nodded and ended the transmission, wondering if Kell would rethink his position, now that Bajor's most productive uridium mine had played out. Wondering, indeed, what he could do to rework the numbers, to keep Bajor's output level within the Union's very high expectations.

Still, he reflected, he should not overlook the bright side to this turn of events: the end of Gallitep also meant the end of Darhe'el, at least as far as Dukat was concerned. Without the option to elevate him to a higher post on Bajor, Kell would have no choice but to recall Darhe'el to Prime.

"Doctor Mora," Odo said, from where he was sitting in the corner of the lab. Mora waved him off.

"Not now, Odo," he told him, clicking away at his key-pad. "Can't you regenerate for a while?"

"My composition only requires me to regenerate every seventeen hours," Odo replied. His pronunciation was flaw-less, and he'd even begun to learn to put inflection into his voice, though he exaggerated it sometimes.

"Well, maybe you could practice being an insect or something."

"Doctor Mora, are you nervous?" Odo asked.

Mora looked up at the shape-shifter, whose "face" was appropriately inquisitive. "Yes, Odo, I am nervous. A very important man is coming to the laboratory soon, and I've got to be sure that everything is . . ." He trailed off. He didn't know what to do for Dukat, exactly, other than have Odo perform for him. He had to figure out a way to make the prefect understand that his research with Odo was important, but he wasn't sure how to do it without making it seem like a sideshow of some kind.

Yopal had insisted that Dukat would have no inter-est in what Mora was doing, that he only wanted to speak to Daul about something, and that he wanted to discuss something about weapons with a few of the others. But Mora remained unconvinced. He feared that as soon as Dukat was introduced to him, the prefect would begin ask-ing a thousand questions that Mora wouldn't know how to answer, and he would find himself in a labor camp before he knew it. And then what would happen to Odo? Mora looked sideways at the shape-shifter, who watched him with his unique non-expression. It always managed to con-vey sadness, even if Mora couldn't be sure that the shape-shifter was capable of actually feeling it.

Mora's computer chirped, indicating that Doctor Yopal was requesting his presence in her office. He headed down the hallway, absentmindedly smoothing his hair back with his hand. Yopal was not alone in her office.

"Yes, what is it, Doctor?"

"We have a new colleague here at the institute. This is Doctor Kalisi Reyar."

Given leave to do so, Mora turned to regard the other Cardassian woman in the office, a little shorter in stature than Yopal, possibly a little younger, a little more vain; the spoon-shaped concavity in the center of her forehead was filled in with a bit of decorative blue pigment. Other than that, she was nearly indistinguishable from the other women who worked at the institute. They all wore their hair in those peculiarly arranged plaits and bundles, they all had the same wide-open alertness in their eyes. Mora expected to forget her name almost immediately, for he rarely conversed with anyone but Yopal anymore. He extended his hand, and Doctor Reyar looked at it.

"Some Bajorans greet one another by clasping their forearms together," Yopal told the other woman.

"Yes, I know," Reyar said, but she still did not extend her hand, and Mora slowly let his drop.

"I wanted you to meet, because I will be putting the two of you together very soon," Yopal said.

Mora felt his heart skip a beat.

"Not right away, but probably sometime in the coming months. That will give you time to wrap up your current projects."

"Even Odo?" Mora spoke without meaning to, unable to help it. "He needs constant observation, he needs guidance, supervision. Nobody knows him as well as I do, nobody else can—"

"You will still be permitted to work with Odo in your spare time," Yopal told Mora crisply. "Just not as often. I suggest you let him know right away, so that he can become acclimated to the change."

Mora breathed a small sigh of relief. It wasn't ideal, but at least Odo was not being assigned to someone else. Of

course, there was still the matter of this Doctor Reyar . . .
Mora turned to her again. "I look forward to working with
you," he said, trying to sound genuine. He hoped she was
at least as tolerable as Yopal.

"Doctor Mora is one of the good Bajorans," Yopal told
Reyar. "He is cooperative, obedient . . ."

Reyar smiled. "That reminds me of a little joke I heard
on the transport here," she said. "Someone said that the
only good Bajoran is one who is about to be executed."
She laughed out loud, and Yopal chuckled politely. Mora
began to cough, and for a moment he could not stop.

Yopal patted Mora's shoulder. "It's only a joke, of
course."

"Of course," Mora replied, still coughing.

"Perhaps you'd like to see Doctor Mora's pet project,"
Yopal suggested to the new scientist.

Reyar did not appear to have an opinion one way or
the other, but Yopal nodded briskly and the three began to
walk down the hall to Mora's lab. Yopal stood back while
Mora opened the door, and the three entered, revealing
that Odo had been sitting in the same place since Mora
had left him. Reyar gasped.

"What is it?" she asked, and took a step in Odo's direction.

"He is a shape-shifter," Mora answered, walking pro-
tectively toward Odo. "We don't know where he came
from, and we've never seen anything like him. He seems
to be unrelated to any of the known shape-shifting species, with a morphogenic matrix that is utterly unlike the
Antosians, the Chameloids, the Wraith, or the Vendorians.
However, I've begun to make certain breakthroughs. Odo,
this is Doctor Reyar. Why don't you show Doctor Reyar . . .
something that you can do?"

Without a word, Odo morphed into a cadge lupus, a
shaggy, vicious-looking Bajoran animal he'd learned about

from the institute's database. Reyar took a step back and made a frightened noise.

"Something Cardassian," Mora said quickly, and the *lupus* changed into a massive, square-headed Cardassian riding hound, similar to the *lupus* but with longer legs and short, wiry fur.

Reyar seemed no less horrified. "How dreadful!" she exclaimed. Odo changed back into his humanoid form.

"I have upset you," Odo said. Reyar ignored him, turning back to Mora.

"So, what kind of progress have you made with it?" she inquired.

Mora was taken aback, for he'd thought Odo's demonstration illustrated his progress well enough. "Well, I've learned quite a lot about him in the time since I was assigned to him. His optimal temperature, his mass, which, by the way, can be changed at will. I've also taught him the basics of humanoid speech, as you can hear, and he's beginning to learn many things that will hopefully help him to someday assimilate—"

"Yes, but I mean, what have you learned about him that will contribute to the betterment of Cardassian society? For isn't that the ultimate goal here at the institute—and in the sciences in general?"

"Yes, of course," Mora replied. "But I'm learning about a new species, Doctor Reyar. Surely you see the value in that type of research. It is inherently important to learn all we can about—"

"I don't really see the value," Reyar said. "I suppose I'm just a traditionalist that way. But I guess you are to be congratulated for teaching it to do . . . tricks and the like." Her tone was dry, or maybe Mora just imagined it was. Cardassian mannerisms still eluded him at times.

The two women left him alone with Odo, who wasted no time getting to the inevitable questions.

"Doctor Reyar. This is a man?"

"No, Odo, she is a woman."

The shape-shifter nodded. "I thought she looked like a woman. But . . . I thought it was men who did not make good scientists."

Mora laughed, a little puzzled. "Doctor Reyar is probably a perfectly good scientist, Odo."

"But, Doctor Mora, I thought that science, the study of science . . . the study of . . . *me* . . . I thought this was the quest for knowledge, for information and truth about the environment that surrounds us."

He was probably quoting something from one of the informational padds he'd been given, Mora thought, and felt a surge of pride that his project seemed to have internalized what he was reading. "Yes, well, Odo, not all scientists have the same priorities, I suppose. Doctor Reyar believes science is valuable only if it makes people's lives quantifiably better in some way."

"People's lives," Odo repeated. "Whose lives? My life? Your life?"

Mora cleared his throat. He wanted to say *the Cardassians' lives,* but he said nothing. Odo was so naïve, Mora was well aware that anything he said in the shape-shifter's presence was likely to be repeated.

"You are learning so quickly, Odo," Mora finally said. "But it's time for me to check your liquid mass. If you wouldn't mind stepping into the tank, please. I need you to revert to your natural form."

Odo, obedient as always, did as he was told, and Mora shifted his focus to his notes, remembering that he would not be able to devote so much attention to this in the near future. He hoped Odo would understand.

## 19

It seemed a very long time since Daul had used a transporter. The Bajoran Institute of Science was outfitted with one that was used primarily for equipment and supplies, though occasionally the Cardassian scientists employed it to transport themselves from place to place, but the Bajorans were not allowed access to it. This rule was unspoken, but it was very well understood.

Today, however, an exception was being made. The prefect had strongly implied that Gallitep's overseer was a notoriously impatient man, and that Daul needed to begin his new task as soon as possible. Daul was quickly authorized for transport and beamed directly into a long, cool corridor with chrome doors on either end. He was met there by a lean Cardassian who introduced himself simply as "Marritza."

"Gul Dukat recommends you highly for your expertise," Marritza said as he escorted Daul down the corridor.

Daul had the distinct impression that the other man was nervous. He wondered if he was afraid of Bajorans; there was so much propaganda among Cardassians regarding the resistance that civilians probably expected every Bajoran to be ready to spring up and murder their Cardassian neighbors without a second thought.

"I'm flattered by his confidence," Daul said. In truth, he

was anything but flattered. He was disgusted, and he was terrified to consider what he was about to be confronted with at Gallitep. At least last time, he hadn't been made to travel to the actual camp; his software had been electronically implemented into the mine's online system from the institute's database.

"It has been explained to you what you are expected to do?" Marritza inquired.

Daul nodded. "Yes, I'm to reprogram the system to begin a gradual shutdown. It will have to be done in two sessions, however. I trust Gul Darhe'el is aware of this necessity?"

"I will be sure he is informed," Marritza said. "My job is to keep the camp's records and the details of its operation up to date, but I daresay Gul Darhe'el will not wish to be troubled with such minor matters. He has so much else to concern himself with . . ." The clerk smiled then, with a strange trace of what seemed like bitterness.

Daul found the Cardassian to be very unlike any other he had encountered, his expression difficult to read. Of course, Daul couldn't purport to have a very broad understanding of the Cardassian psyche in general, but at least most of them seemed to be motivated by the same things. Marritza seemed somewhat more . . . complicated.

As the two men traveled up the corridor, Daul was made very aware of the intense droning of the mining equipment outside: drills, ore-processing conveyors, smelters, and the rushing water from the great concentrator that delivered slurry to a tailings pond many *kellipates* away from the site.

But beneath the tremendous grinding, echoing din, there was another sound, one that Marritza seemed to be taking great pains to ignore. To Daul at first it sounded like the faint cries of a tyrfox, or perhaps a pack of faraway cadge lupus; but Daul immediately knew what he was hearing—

the cries of the prisoners here, the moans of the dying workers, suffering as they were from Kalla-Nohra. Daul cleared
his throat. "Doesn't Darhe'el see to it that the workers who
are ill are properly treated for their condition?"

Marritza gave a quick nod, almost frantic. "Oh yes,"
he said. "Productivity is of the utmost importance here.
Darhe'el is adamant about the treatment of all victims
of the disease—Bajoran . . . and Cardassian . . . alike." In
the inflection of his voice, which sounded very much as
though Marritza repeated a long-rehearsed falsehood,
Daul thought he detected a single truth—that Marritza
himself was infected with the disease. Without meaning
to, he gave the other man a look of sympathy. Marritza
looked away, and Daul decided to avoid further mention
of the subject.

They reached the end of the passage and Marritza
keyed open a door. Suddenly the narrow, neat corridor was
enveloped in a roar of sound; the floor beneath their feet
gave way to a trembling catwalk, which opened up over
a yawning chasm. The wind whipped fiercely overhead,
the narrow footbridge swinging gently, though it was protected from the relentless gale by the walls of the open-pit
mine, which shot up at a *kellipate* from where they stood.
This bridge had been constructed at what was once near
the very bottom of the mine, but the hole had plunged far
beneath this point in more recent years, and the spindly
catwalk was suspended hundreds of *linnipates* above firm
ground.

Daul glanced up, where the burning sun hung motionless in the cloudless sky, beating down heavily on the workers in the massive pit beneath them. Marritza handed him a
headset, which would drown out the noise and allow them
to talk to each other. Daul stepped gingerly onto the footbridge that spanned the mine.

The vast pit had been gradually but efficiently excavated

over the course of many years, crisscrossed with scaffolds and enormous systems of conveyors to remove the chunks of rock and minerals from the ground. This had once been a massive hillside, likely covered over with trees and foliage and wildlife; now it was a bare, steaming crater, surrounded by many *tessipate*s of complete desolation; it was the closest thing Daul could imagine to the myths about the Fire Caves. Before Terok Nor had been constructed, Gallitep was the center of ore processing in the B'hava'el system. Daul thought that Bajorans could never have conceived of a thing so unsightly and terrible as this place.

The steep, spiraling gravel roads that were cut into the sides of the pit were dotted here and there with workers, some of them disappearing into tunnels that had been dug randomly all around the perimeter of the mine. Though Daul could not see clearly most of the workers from where he stood, those nearest to him staggered on thin, bandy legs, their bare chests and backs covered in open sores and blistering sunburns. They wielded traditional shovels and spades and truncheons, hacking away at the exposed rock, slowly but persistently widening and deepening the abyss beneath them to get at the valuable minerals embedded in the ground. Also visible were a number of Cardassian guards, swaggering between the hapless miners and occasionally stopping to shout criticisms or reprimands. Most of the guards did not venture far into the pit, apparently preferring to remain close to their respective stations, well-built corridors like the one from which Daul and Marritza had just come.

Daul followed Marritza a quarter of the way across the diameter of the pit, until he came to a little building which abutted the swaying catwalk. Here was the center of the system, the brain of this entire operation—the primary server. The artificial intelligence program, which drove the core mining drills, was located here; those drills sought out the richest veins and pointed the scavenging miners in that direction, to pick out and process the precious metals by hand.

Daul began the reprogramming sequence that would eventually shut down the entire system. It was a complicated process, but the clerk waited patiently as he tapped in code. Beneath them, workers groaned and labored, guards shouted, and the machinery ground relentlessly on. As Daul neared the end of the first-stage closure, he found himself compelled to ask his unusual escort a question.

"What will happen to all of them when this camp is closed?" Daul finally asked, looking down into the enormous cavern below him.

Marritza did not immediately answer. "Darhe'el will take care of them," he said in a low voice.

Daul was not sure if he should inquire further, though he did not know what the other man meant. "Oh—I see," he stammered, and went back to his task.

"Do you?" Marritza asked him. He gestured out to the open space that surrounded them. "For Gul Darhe'el—for Cardassia—these workers are valued only for their productivity. You yourself, Doctor Daul, are valued only for your particular expertise here. Is that how it was on your world, in your culture, before we came here?"

Daul considered. Bajor valued its people as more than what they were capable of producing—they were valued as individuals, as relatives, as friends—as *Bajorans*. Daul slowly shook his head.

"When the camp shuts down," Marritza went on, not looking at Daul, "these workers will lose their value. That value has already begun to decline, because of their illness. Do you understand?"

Daul thought perhaps he understood what Marritza was trying to tell him, but he didn't understand the logic—nor did he understand why the Cardassian was telling him, either. "Yes," he croaked, and finished his work.

"Good," Marritza said. "Are you finished?"

"For now," Daul replied. "I'll have to come back to finish the job."

Marritza attempted to smile as he guided Daul back toward the footbridge outside the little building, and again Daul thought he detected bitterness. "I'm sure Gul Darhe'el will be very pleased with your work." He removed his headset as he ushered Daul back inside the cool, stainless chrome corridor, the echoing voices of crying men and women somehow louder now, and Daul was transported quickly and efficiently back to the institute.

Ro was to meet with Bis near the Lunar V base on Jeraddo, a place where another cell had begun stashing ships years ago. Since that time, other cells had begun bringing their own ships here, or using the base as an offworld meeting point to coordinate large-scale attacks that required the cooperation of more than one group.

In addition to her anxious curiosity about why Bis wanted to see her, she could not deny that she was nervous to see him again. In the years since she had been to Valo II, she had never met another boy who had turned her head the way he had, and she had built up a bit of mythology about him in that time. She wasn't sure whether he would be able to live up to it.

Ro docked her little raider, the *Lahnest,* near where she knew the underground base was. What had once been jungle had been partially cleared away to create a suitable landing field, but much of the canopy and brush had to be left behind so as to obscure the Bajoran presence here. In fact, the landing area was smaller than even the poorest farmer's field, and it apparently hadn't been used in a few weeks; the fast-growing vegetation of this moon was already starting to fill in again.

Ro waited for what seemed like a very long time before

she saw another vessel coming, starting out as a dot in the sky, gradually but quickly expanding into a light-capacity ship that she knew was the same one Darrah Mace had used for the rendezvous with the Kressari, three years ago. The ship cracked through the atmosphere of Jeraddo, singing in a telltale high-pitched greeting that took Ro's breath away. He was here.

When he finally arrived, she somehow forgot to be nervous. Here approached a tall man, handsome as he had promised to be as a teenager, his eyes piercing and his smile apparently genuine—he was happy to see her. Ro couldn't remember the last time that had happened.

"Ro Laren!" he exclaimed. "I can't tell you how glad I am you decided to meet me!"

She cleared her throat. "So," she said, trying to sound casual, "what did I come all this way for? I hope it's good."

"Oh, it is good, it is," he said, and she saw him swallow as he came closer to her, scrutinizing her face. She realized that he was very nervous about this meeting, and it occurred to her that he probably had a mythology about her, too. It was entirely possible that she would fail to live up to his estimation of her, just as easily as the reverse could be true.

"Well," he said, "you might remember that we didn't have much in the way of organized resistance on Valo II. But I want to change that. I've been working on an idea for a long time."

Ro frowned. Still no organized resistance? Had she come all this way, pinned all her opportunities on just one idea, still in the planning stages? "What kind of an idea?"

Bis grinned. "Terok Nor," he said.

Ro was a bit taken aback. "Terok Nor?" she repeated. "What about it?"

Bis's smile grew even wider. "Think about it. It's the perfect target, really. It's the seat of the occupation, it's where the prefect lives, and where half the Cardassian ships in this system are docked at any given time—"

"I still don't follow," Ro said. "What do you mean, a target? You just said you don't even really have a cell—you'd need an entire army to attack Terok Nor, and an army is exactly what the whole of Bajor doesn't have. Even with every single resistance cell on the planet, we'd never—"

"That's the brilliant part," Bis said. "We won't be the ones to attack it. We'll get someone else to do it for us."

Ro made a face. "Who?"

Bis's smile finally faded. "Do you remember that Ferengi freighter? The one you—"

"The one Bram and I tried to claim, before Darrah Mace suddenly took us on an unexpected vacation?"

"Right. That freighter is going to be the key to taking out Terok Nor once and for all."

Ro folded her arms, intrigued.

Bis went on. "We never really got much use out of that ship, except to transport refugees, but it was just too cumbersome to be used as a ferry. Something went wrong with one of the engines, and my father—he's one of the best engineers on Valo II—he couldn't figure out what to do with such an alien system. So we started stripping it for useful parts, but other than that—"

Ro nodded, shooting him a "get to the point" look as politely as she could manage.

"Anyway, my father got the comm online a long time ago, and we started picking up a lot of Ferengi back-and-forth chatter. Without even meaning to, we started to learn a lot about some of the Ferengi supply runs—and about the Ferengi in general. Like, for example, they'll do anything for profit."

"So . . . you can spy on the Ferengi," Ro said. She knew next to nothing about the Ferengi, except that they were avaricious and commerce-driven. Some were even pirates. Short pirates.

"Right. They do a lot of trade in and around the Bajoran sector. There's even a regularly scheduled run that goes between Lissepia and New Sydney every two weeks, and they go right through the B'hava'el system."

Ro still couldn't see any significance in the information and she shrugged, waiting to hear more.

"That run is usually carrying a very unstable cargo—unprocessed uridium. They're not supposed to carry more than a certain amount, according to regulation, but they're a profit-minded bunch, and they routinely ignore the rules. They have begun taking on bigger and bigger loads lately, from what we've been hearing. I'm sure they're making an absolute fortune on it."

Ro frowned, beginning to see where this was going. "Those ships . . . if their cargo were exposed to a big enough electrical discharge . . ."

"They're bombs waiting to happen," Bis told her. "Very powerful bombs. And there's one particular Ferengi ship in the fleet that does a routine stopover in this system—"

"—at Terok Nor," Ro finished.

Bis nodded, pleased she had caught on. "That's right," he said. "And that's where you come in, Laren. I don't know anyone on Valo II who has even the faintest idea how to override a security system, but you, you could sneak onto that Ferengi vessel and spike one of the containers with an electrical bomb. It could be set to go off just as soon as the ship docks, and if we get to it just before it heads for Terok Nor—"

Ro was shaking her head. She was vaguely aware of at least one truth about Terok Nor: there were more Bajorans on that station than there were Cardassians. Innocent Bajorans—people who had been brought there against their will and forced to labor in what were supposed to be the most abysmal conditions one could imagine, second only to the horror stories she'd heard about Gallitep.

Bis misread her hesitation, and he smiled reassuringly. "I've thought of all the details, Laren," he told her. "I've been putting this plan together for over a year. Contacting you was the next step, and now that you're here, nothing can go wrong. If you come back with me to Valo II, I can tell you everything. What do you say, are you in?"

Ro looked around Jeraddo, looked at her raider where she had left it, and paused. This plan was madness, for more reasons than she could even begin to address. But she could only think of Tokiah, his saying, *"Maybe you shouldn't come back."*

"I'm in," she said softly, and Bis surprised her by throwing his arms around her and letting out a whoop of triumph. Startled, she hung in his arms like a limp fish, having managed to avoid being embraced by anyone since she was a child. He released her, probably sensing her discomfort, and the two began the walk back to his ship, Bis rattling off more details about his reckless plan, Ro pushing away the uncomfortable thoughts that were beginning to stir her conscience.

For all the worrying Mora had been doing about Dukat's visit to the institute, the prefect paid him approximately no attention whatsoever. Yopal had not been wrong when she'd advised him that Dukat would only be interested in weapons systems, for he spent almost the entire visit talking to Daul and the new scientist, Kalisi Reyar. The prefect left without so much as a hello to Mora—not that Mora would have wanted it any other way.

With Gul Dukat gone, Mora could finally let down his guard a bit. He eased his nerves with a uniformly dull task, performing a routine calibration on some of his tools. Daul entered his laboratory quietly.

"Hello, Pol," the other Bajoran greeted him. Mora hadn't spoken to his colleague since well before Dukat's visit. They hadn't spent much time together at all, in recent weeks.

"Hello, Mirosha. Did you survive your encounter with the prefect?"

"I did, though I won't pretend that I enjoyed it."

Mora chuckled. "I'd bet not. I'm thankful he left me alone."

"Yes, well. He wanted to talk with me about the system at Gallitep. He was pleased with the work I did before, and apparently he found me trustworthy enough to send me to the actual camp, this time."

Mora stiffened. He wasn't sure what to say to his old friend, and he merely followed up with an "Ah," and a clearing of his throat.

There was a moment of silence before Daul softly spoke again. "Are you curious to know what I saw there? Why he wanted me to go?"

Mora cleared his throat again. "Not really," he said.

"No, I'm sure it's easier for you not to think about it, as it would be for me, if I wasn't forced to. It seems that our benevolent Cardassian benefactors have elected to shut down the mining camp. They've finally managed to strip it clean of anything they deem useful. That means the workers there will have to be properly disposed of, since so many of them are suffering from Kalla-Nohra syndrome and aren't worth the effort of transporting elsewhere. As for the others, those who are still healthy—well, my understanding is that it would be inefficient to try and weed out who is sick and who isn't, so . . ." Daul shrugged. "I'm to disable the artificial intelligence program before the . . . genocide begins in earnest."

Mora felt sick. "I—I'm sorry, Mirosha. It's not pleasant, I know, but . . . it's what we must do, to stay alive."

"That's right," Daul said. "And I've heard you're to be paired up with Doctor Reyar. I wonder if you know what she's working on. It's an anti-aircraft system, to shoot down Bajoran raiders as they attempt to leave the atmosphere. I'm told it's a brilliant concept."

"Is that right?" Mora kept inflection from his voice.

"Doesn't this bother you, Mora? Doesn't your conscience trouble you? For you have to know that we are collaborators here. Nothing less than traitors to our own people."

Mora shook his head. "I don't know if I see it that way," he said, his voice still low and careful. "We're following orders, Mirosha. If we tried to do anything differently, we'd be killed, and replaced by someone else."

Daul stared at him a long moment before answering. "That's one way to look at it," he said finally.

Mora continued on with his equipment as Daul left the room, and wondered if it was true, about the anti-aircraft system. *Well,* he reasoned, *everyone knows the rebels are all as good as dead. It's inevitable that they will eventually be killed, or caught and executed. Perhaps I'd be doing them a kindness, helping to speed up the process of putting a stop to the rebellion. They're fools, doing what they do, and for what?*

"For what?" he repeated out loud. *For freedom?* It seemed preposterous. The Bajorans would never be free, not with the hold the Cardassians had on this world. Compliance was the best alternative. At least it was a better alternative than death.

Valo II looked exactly as Ro had remembered it, only somehow even more depressing. Clearly there had been a bit of a population explosion since she had seen it last, for the clusters of shanty structures and tents near the landing field had trickled back farther into the scrubby brush, and the shabby town where Bis's father lived was even more crowded than she remembered it. There were people everywhere, and they all looked unhealthy. Rheumy eyes; hacking, persistent coughs; open sores; drawn, emaciated faces. People were walking through the worn corridors between the tightly packed houses, carrying baskets of soiled rags, dried alien-looking fruits, or headless *porli* fowl. Lean and rawboned women walked surrounded by their dirty children. Old men sat on the ground in scattered hopeless groups, talking reservedly and smoking *hiuna* leaf—a cheap, unhealthy crop that helped to stave off hunger but shortened the life span significantly with its resulting ailments.

In fact, Ro thought, everyone here was slowly dying in one way or another: respiratory afflictions, starvation, communicable disease, or exposure. It sickened Ro to acknowledge to herself that at least the Bajorans back on their homeworld had the Cardassians to feed them—in exchange for slavery. She wondered if, despite its terrible appearance, Valo II might be preferable to Bajor for that reason.

Bis spoke to her as they walked. "In three days," he told her, "the Ferengi captain—DaiMon Gart, he's called—will be docking at the moon of a gas giant not far from this system. That will be his last stop before Terok Nor, and that's where you'll take the device to his ship."

"That simple, is it?" Ro replied, trying not to stare at a woman with an especially prominent neck goiter.

"For you it will be," Bis said confidently.

"But what if I can't do it?" Ro said softly. "I don't know the first thing about Ferengi security systems."

"We can have a look at the freighter," Bis said. "That should give you some ideas, shouldn't it?"

Ro sighed. "It might," she said, but she still felt doubtful.

"Look, if all else fails, you can just bribe him to get on the ship."

"Why would he agree to that?"

"The same reason he agreed to take on such an incredibly dangerous cargo in the first place."

"What am I supposed to bribe him with?"

Bis frowned. "That's one part of the plan that might not work quite so well," he confessed. "You see, we have a stolen Cardassian padd, and we might be able to convince him that he can access Cardassian passcodes with the device . . . but we're not sure if he'd believe it—"

"I thought you had this all figured out."

"Well," Bis said, "there is one other solution."

"What's that?" Ro said sourly.

"Seduce him."

Ro stared at him in disbelief before she broke out in rueful laughter.

"What's so funny about that?" Bis protested. They had come to his father's house, and Ro followed him inside.

"Right. Me, seduce an alien. Me, seduce . . . anyone," she snorted.

The house was dark, and Bis lit a candle on the mantelpiece of a crumbling fireplace. It was likely this house had been built here long before the Cardassians came to Bajor, when the world was still considered an exciting new frontier land, a promising place to settle. Ro looked around the room and saw how those auspicious hopes had eroded. The room, with stone walls and a cracked and deteriorating wood floor, was blackened with the smoke from cooking fires and smelled strongly of ash and dirt. There was almost no furniture, aside from three sleeping pallets that were arranged around the fireplace.

"This is where you sleep?" She gestured to the pallets.

"No," he said. "My cousin's children sleep there. He had no room for them in his own house—he lives with his sister-in-law. His wife is dead, and we took in the children when his sister-in-law's house got too crowded." Bis took the candle and gestured to a corridor that led them to the back of the square house, and Ro followed him before he stopped.

"Why would you say that?" he asked softly.

"Say what?"

"About you . . . seducing anyone?" He looked embarrassed.

"Because it's absurd," she told him sharply.

"Haven't you ever—" He stopped, and she was forced to look away. She considered what he was asking before she replied.

"No," she finally said. "I haven't."

The candle flickering between them, Ro was aware of the sudden awkwardness there, too, standing in the corridor between the tiny rooms of this desolate house.

Bis stepped into one of the small rooms, revealing a bare pallet, a heap of worn clothing. He set the candle on a small, rough chest, the light casting long shadows across their faces, and turned to face her. He put his arms around her then, the feeling strange and terrifying and electric. As she had been on Jeraddo, she was clumsy in his embrace, not sure how to respond. But her body knew, and after a long, warm moment, she felt herself soften to his touch. Nobody had ever approached her this way, and as he drew back to kiss her, his face moving toward hers, she realized, for the first time, how much she had wished that someone would.

Kira pulled a knot of something unpleasant out of her mouth. A bone, perhaps? She hoped it was a bone, for something about the shape of it suggested a tiny little beak. She examined it, decided it was just a bone splinter, and laid it down on the long wooden table where the members of the cell took their meals together. "Ugh," she exclaimed. "Who made this food? Furel?"

"It was Shakaar," Dakhana Vaas told her, nodding toward the back of the cave.

"Oh," Kira said, a little embarrassed. She wouldn't want Shakaar to hear her complaining.

"It's all right, little girl, he knows he can't cook."

Kira resented Dakhana calling her "little girl," since they were only a couple of years apart, and anyway, Kira had been with the cell for more than a year. She silently wished she was taller, or at least as tall as Dakhana.

Shakaar came into the main body of the cave from where he'd been sitting with his precious and notoriously troublesome comm system since just before mealtime. He leaned his hands against the end of the table, his expression suggesting news.

"Listen up," he said, the unusual tension in his voice imploring everyone to look up. The older members of the cell occasionally heckled Shakaar for his tendency to mumble, but he was not mumbling now. "We've got a chance to get into Gallitep."

"Gallitep!" Dakhana exclaimed. "Who's your informant? Is he reliable?"

"I believe so," Shakaar said. "But even if it's just a rumor, this is an opportunity that I don't think we should pass up. It's too important. The Cardassians have decided to shut down the place for good. It's too much trouble to relocate the Bajoran workers, so . . ." he trailed off, passing a hand over his grim face.

"So they're going to kill them instead," Furel said, the disgust in his voice plain.

"Yes," Shakaar said. "Right now, I just need a couple of volunteers to go down and meet with this contact in order to get more information about the plan. It's a little risky—"

"Risky," Dakhana warned. "Shakaar, we're talking about Gallitep! There's no way to even approach that camp; there's nothing around for *kellipates* except booby-traps and Cardassian patrols, the air security has to be the tightest anywhere on the planet, and Gul Darhe'el is—"

"I'm talking about a meeting at a safe location not far from here," Shakaar said. "I wouldn't usually ask anyone to meet with a contact when I can't vouch for his reliability. But like you said, Vaas, this is Gallitep. This person is supposed to have inside knowledge of the camp, and it could be the only way anyone could even—"

Kira spoke up before anyone else could. "I can go."

Shakaar turned to her, hesitating. Kira was sure he was going to say no, but he surprised her. "Okay, I have one volunteer. Who else?"

"Well, I'll go with her, of course," Lupaza said. "So that means Furel is coming."

Furel folded his arms and nodded without a word, his eyes reflecting hard determination. Kira wondered if he might have known someone who had been taken to the camp; almost everyone had relatives who had died or gone to work camps, but Gallitep was different.

"That should be fine," Shakaar told them. "You're to go and meet this person at the Artist's Palette at six-bells tomorrow. Whoever he is, he's asked that we perform some sort of favor in exchange for the information. I don't know what the favor is, but—"

"But I'm sure we can handle it," Furel finished. "We *will* handle it."

Shakaar nodded. "If this information is legitimate, we can't afford to be skeptical. Those people in that camp can't afford it, either. This is their last chance, and it sounds like we don't have much time." His gaze panned around the room. "This is one that we have to get right, no matter the cost."

He had no doubt that Gul Dukat was going to be furious when he delivered this piece of news, but Basso Tromac could scarcely conceal his persistent smile when he approached the prefect's office. Of course, he would not have the satisfaction of saying "I told you so," not to Dukat. Such a move would certainly mean a death sentence for anyone, especially for a Bajoran. But at least Basso would get to see the look on his face; that alone would be worth the outburst that was sure to follow.

"Gul," Basso addressed the prefect as he entered the office, seating himself behind the enormous desk without being asked; his relationship with the prefect had at least become secure enough that he no longer had to wait for permission just to sit down in his presence. Dukat looked up from his filing computer, gave him a nod, and pressed his fingertips together, an expression of impatient expectation on his face.

"I must warn you that what I'm about to tell you is going to be very . . . disappointing," Basso began.

Dukat looked weary. "Yes, you said as much this morning, when you asked to meet with me. Now suppose you get to the point, Basso."

"Of course, sir. You know that I've tried to keep very careful tabs on the Kira family, though in recent years Taban has refused to accept any more of your generosity. He has become quite . . . bitter since his wife—ah, that is, since Meru passed on. I have done my best to keep track of the children, but they are older now, and they tend to—"

"Yes, I'm aware of the Bajoran child's propensity to wander. I wonder if this story has an ending, Basso."

Basso cleared his throat. "Of course, Gul. You see, the daughter, she—"

"Yes, Nerys. Beautiful girl." He sighed. "What's she, about fourteen now?"

"That's correct, sir. She has been increasingly difficult to locate in the past few years, roaming and coming home only on very rare occasions."

"But of course, you have ensured her safety," Dukat said carefully.

Basso began to feel worried. "I have done my best, sir. It's true that Bajoran children are allowed a certain amount of freedom, but certainly not to this extent. I wondered if she might have taken to running away, but when my people in the village spoke to Taban, he seemed entirely unconcerned for her safety. It seems that he . . . knew where she was. She—"

"So, she is safe," Dukat said, appearing to relax somewhat.

"Well, yes, she seems to be safe, but—you see, sir, what I'm trying to tell you is that I have information to suggest that Nerys has joined the resistance movement."

He risked a direct look at the prefect's face. Surprisingly, Dukat did not look angry, exactly. He looked surprised, but not angry. Basso could not quite place his expression, but if he hadn't known better, he'd have said the prefect looked . . . concerned.

"Only fourteen years old," Dukat finally said. "After all I did for her as a child. I saw to it that she was sent to school—art school, as her mother wished, though apparently she didn't take to it. I never would have predicted an outcome like this." Dukat pushed himself up from his chair, folded his arms, wandered toward the back of the room. "Do you know where she is, Basso?"

"Sir, I don't know yet, but I am doing my best to locate her. My contacts have suggested that she must be hiding in the Dahkur hills, with one of the cells in that general vicinity, but we can't nail down which one. It seems possible that even her father doesn't have that information."

Dukat sighed again, pressing his fingers to the bridge of his nose.

Basso could not quite puzzle out the meaning behind the prefect's reaction. Sad, fearful, strangely introspective—nothing like what he'd been expecting. He couldn't help but feel cheated. Dukat spoke again after a moment, and Basso wondered if the Dukat he'd expected to see was about to make an appearance.

"After all I did for her," he repeated, but his voice was colder this time, as if he'd had time to contemplate the meaning of it all. "You must find her, Basso, and you must bring her to me."

"Of course," Basso said reluctantly, realizing that he should have expected this order. Dukat went on.

"And she must be completely unharmed, do you understand me? No excuses."

"Un . . . harmed? Yes, yes . . . certainly," Basso stammered, and left the room without being told to. He knew the prefect well enough to know when it was time to leave him, and anyway, he needed to get away so he could think. What had gone wrong? He'd been expecting an expression of horrified shock, followed by a lengthy tantrum and an order to kill the ungrateful girl, a standing order that would probably never be carried out. Instead, he'd gotten himself a great deal more work, he realized. Locating Kira Nerys, hiding somewhere in the Dahkur hills with one of any number of resistance cells, and bringing her to the prefect—*alive*—that was a tall order. A nearly impossible order. And Basso had no one but himself to blame for it.

Daul had traveled a considerable distance on foot; at least twenty *kellipates*. Such a long walk was rare, a feat he hadn't undertaken since he was a child. Average Bajorans rarely went anywhere anymore, except perhaps to the nearest food ration lines, and Daul didn't have to worry much about that, being one of the few who was still gainfully employed underneath the Cardassians. He had more to worry about from another Bajoran than he did from a Cardassian, for he had all the necessary credentials that could get him out of a sticky situation, if he happened to be stopped by a soldier. It was a mostly comfortable position to be in, though a fragile one. But this journey he had taken today was so far out of his comfort zone, he could scarcely fathom why he had chosen it—for he had come here voluntarily. This whole thing, this was his idea.

He was nearly to the place that was once called the Artist's Palette. It was still called that by the locals, though there was nothing around to suggest its former moniker. At one time, the leaves and flowers on the trees here had been brightly varied in hue; purple and green and pink and orange, from the springtime throughout the fall. Now, the few trees that still produced leaves were uniformly clad in a dull, sickly yellow. The Cardassians had long ago leached the minerals from the surrounding soil, using a process that required an acidic chemical to retrieve the elements used in making certain types of polymers. Those polymers were essential in the construction of Cardassian dwellings. The elements were shipped to a facility on Pullock III where the support structure for the dwellings was manufactured, which were then shipped back to Bajor and combined with other parts, things made on many other worlds, using Bajoran raw materials to power the transport ships—ships built from Bajoran metals and fueled with Bajoran fuel. None of it made a bit of sense, really, when one started to consider it, but Daul supposed there wasn't much he could do about it.

*Yes, there is.* This thing he was doing right now.

Three people were approaching. Three Bajorans. A teenaged girl and a pair of adults, a man and a woman. Were these the people he was waiting for? The palms of his hands felt slick and cool. Perhaps these people were about to kill him for being a collaborator. *Perhaps I deserve it.*

"Are you here to speak to me about . . . Gallitep?" Daul said, hoping his voice didn't betray his anxiousness.

The young girl turned to her companions. "Aren't we

supposed to have a code word?" she murmured, just loud enough for Daul to hear.

Daul remembered quickly—the man he had spoken to had suggested a code word. "I almost forgot," he apologized. "Ah, *rah-vu sum-ta.*" It was Old Bajoran, a word that meant something almost like "child of night"—the classic poetical name for a cadge lupus.

"That's right," the older woman replied. "Okay, then. Tell us what we need to know."

Daul cleared his throat and began to speak, his words tumbling out. "I suppose you are familiar with the setup of Gallitep, the physical characteristics of the camp—"

"Yes," the man said. "It's impossible to approach."

"Except from inside, yes."

"From inside?" This was the woman.

"Via transporter. I am to be taken to Gallitep in a few days, and I think there may be a way to transport a few more people in after me. There is a transporter code that will allow for it, and I think I may have gotten access to the correct code."

"But . . ." The teenage girl looked at her companions. "How would we get access to a transporter?"

"You *think* you may have gotten access?" the man said, speaking over the teenager.

Daul held up his hands. "I believe I have," he corrected himself. "It is risky, but I believe it can be done. There is an industrial transporter at the Bajoran Institute of Science, not far from here. This transporter could not only get people into Gallitep, it could get them out, as well. If someone who can operate a transporter was able to lock on to a large group of people, that person could perhaps transport them out of the camp, and possibly to a place of safety—"

"I don't like all this *perhaps* and *possibly* that I'm hearing," the man said.

"I only want to emphasize that there are risks," Daul

said. "But please believe me when I tell you that the goal is worth the risks. I have been inside the camp, and although I only saw a fraction of what I suspect goes on there, I didn't have to see much to understand that Gallitep is the worst place Bajor has ever seen."

"We can do it," the woman said confidently. "I'm sure we can."

"Why . . . how did you get inside Gallitep—and then back out again?" the teenager asked.

"Shh," the older woman shushed her. "It's not important."

"No," Daul said, inexplicably wishing to be honest with these people. "It's all right. I work at the science institute. I was conscripted to develop the computer system that runs the camp."

The girl's mouth hung open for a moment and then snapped shut. "Oh," she replied, and then looked away.

"Yes, I helped to design it," Daul went on, "and now, I will help put a stop to what it is intended to do. But I don't suppose that will redeem me. Still, maybe I can at least look at myself in the mirror again."

"Maybe," the woman said, and though she tried to remain neutral, she could not mask the tightness in her voice. She despised him, he could see it on her, hear it in that single word.

"I have brought you an isolinear rod with more details. More importantly, this rod will allow you access to the Bajoran Institute of Science. You must wait until nightfall, when everyone has gone home, and you will be required to enter a code to deactivate the security system."

The woman and her companions nodded, listening closely now. At least they could set aside their hate for something so important. At least there was that.

"I will be at the camp when it happens, working on the system. I will purposely delay the work so that I am still there when you arrive. At a given time, I will program the system to simulate a mining accident, which will force the Cardassian guards to corral the workers in a common place. That is where you will come in—someone will have to transport into the camp in order to create a lock-on target for the transporters. The transporters can be programmed to lock on to Bajoran targets only—the procedure is outlined on the datarod. When it is done, when the Bajorans are safe, I will initiate the computer system to destroy the camp. The self-destruct system should kill any remaining Cardassians. At that point, you will have to transport me out as well." He said the last part hopefully.

The man nodded. "I think we can handle that," he said.

Daul started to remark on the second part of the task, but then he remembered something. "I almost forgot," he said. "You'll need these."

The three Bajorans looked curiously at the four little comm devices he produced, relics he'd stolen from a vault at the institute, where examples of Bajoran technology were stored for later study. "These are old, but they still work. They'll be necessary for you to project a signal that can be locked on to by the transporter. You can also use them to communicate with each other, even over great distances. And they operate on frequencies the Cardassians haven't monitored since the Militia was disbanded."

"I know what a combadge is," the man said, a little curtly. He took the devices and pocketed them.

Daul went on. "I suppose your leader told you that I am asking for a favor, in return for this information?"

The woman cleared her throat. "What is this favor, exactly?"

"I would do this myself," Daul explained, "but I won't have the opportunity before I leave, and I have no plans to return to the institute after I'm transported to Gallitep." He hesitated, sensing impatience from the three nameless rebels, and he went on, "Do you have the ability to hack into a computer system, including high-security files?"

"I can hack into any system," the woman assured him.

"Good. The rod will give you more detail. There are specific data files on the institute's computer, and the data in question must be irreparably corrupted. No one can access it ever again. I assume that will not be a problem?"

The woman almost looked amused, which Daul took to be an affirmative reply.

The man raised his eyebrows. "That bad, is it?" he remarked.

Daul thought of the system Mora Pol would soon be implementing, thought of the cold, hard smile of Kalisi Reyar. "You've no idea," he said.

## 20

Ro was not immediately as adept at handling Bis's warp shuttle as she had hoped. She wasn't certain if she could successfully land the vessel, but the other alternative was to transport herself down to the surface of the gas giant's lonely moon, with the expectation that she would have to transport herself back up when her task was completed. The prospect was a bit frightening, as she had never handled a transporter on her own, but she decided it was necessary. She could not afford to damage her vessel; warp ships were few and far between for Bajorans, after all.

With a brief recollection of the encouragement Bis had whispered before kissing her good-bye, Ro beamed herself directly to the moon's surface near a cluster of life signs that she knew to be the tavern where she was to meet her mark. Her molecules having satisfactorily reassembled themselves, she squared her shoulders and entered the little building, advising herself not to come off like an inexperienced, gawking young girl; she had long heard tales of the Orion Syndicate, whose henchmen would kidnap women to be sold as slaves. They sounded no worse than the Cardassians to Ro, but she still wasn't about to take any chances.

Still, she found it difficult not to stare at some of the

people she encountered inside the dimly lit bar—people with brightly colored clothing, not to mention their skin and hair; people with appendages that seemed too long or too short; people with extra sensory equipment, or in some cases, not quite enough; people whose faces looked too smooth, or too lumpy. Ro had never dreamed there were so many different types of people in the galaxy. She knew there were more than just Bajorans and Cardassians, of course, but to be confronted with the reality of it was dizzying. While Bajor struggled, day after day, year after year, the rest of the universe continued to move, everyone carrying on with his or her own business, unaffected by what happened in the B'hava'el system.

Ro had taken a seat behind the bar, a long, black slab with rows and rows of tall colored bottles behind it. A man—Ro supposed it was a man—with bright blue skin and a ridge bisecting his hairless face approached her. "What'll it be, girlie?"

Ro cleared her throat, looking around for Cardassians. She saw none, but she still wanted to keep as low a profile as she could. She wasn't sure what to order. *"Copal?"* she said uncertainly.

"What's that?" He turned an ear in her direction.

"I said *copal—copal* cider? Do you have it?"

The man wrinkled his nose. "Where you from, Miss?"

Ro looked around again, before she answered, quietly. "Bajor," she muttered.

"Speak up!" the bartender told her.

Ro's gaze froze when she saw someone in the back corner of the room, bald as the bartender, but with a swollen, misshapen head. His skin was an unfortunate shade of orange, his mouth full of teeth so sharp and crooked he could not close it all the way. He wore a strange headband with a couple of flaps that concealed the back part of his head, along with a dark-colored uniform trimmed with fur.

He was picking at a plate of ghastly-looking food, and frequently using some kind of tool to remove bits of it from between the varied nooks and crannies of his teeth. But it was his ears that caught Ro's attention; they were round, and cavernous, and gigantic. Bis had expressly instructed her to look for the person with the most prominent ears. This man's ears were nothing if not prominent. She felt certain she'd just found DaiMon Gart.

"Excuse me," Ro told the blue bartender.

"Oh, no you don't," the man said. "You'd better order something if you want to sit in here. Only paying customers cool their heels on my chairs, you got it?"

"Tell you what," Ro whispered. "I have thirty *leks* that're all yours, and you don't even need to pour me a drink."

The bartender glared at her with suspicion. "What's the catch?"

Ro leaned in closer. "I want a look at the Ferengi's tab." The bartender hesitated, perhaps trying to convince himself that the request was harmless. "I just want to see it," Ro assured him. "Nothing else."

"Let's see the money," the bartender said.

Ro held up the brown metal hexagon she'd been clutching since she entered the bar, something she'd taken off the body of a dead Cardassian soldier months ago. Union currency was ugly, but it had considerable value in this part of space. Ro was glad she had decided to save it. "Do we have a deal?"

The bartender glanced past her, as if to make sure the Ferengi wasn't listening. Then he reached toward the counter behind him and produced a padd, which he held facedown on the bar. Ro gave him the coin, and the blue hand flipped the padd over.

Ro found what she was looking for immediately. Gart's

food and drink order didn't interest her, but the two strings of numbers in the upper right corner of the screen gave her an immediate surge of adrenaline: the transponder code for the daimon's ship, and the number of its docking bay—both of which would be essential to pay for anything in a place like this, in lieu of hard currency. Ro had just enough time to commit the numbers to memory before the bartender said, "That's enough," and took back his padd.

Ro thanked the bartender and made for the exit, past the table where Gart was sitting. She hesitated to listen to what he was saying to the person seated opposite him, an alien woman with her scarlet hair in a complicated topknot.

"What a lot of clothing you're wearing!" he exclaimed. "You know, I like that in a girl. Clothing. Especially the part where the clothing all comes off." He laughed, and bits of what appeared to be *worm* violently dislodged themselves from his mouth as he did so. Ro shuddered.

"If my cook weren't trying to poison me," she overheard him say as she left the bar, "I'd never pay this much for a plate of *gree* worms. I tell you, he's had it in for me since he left Ferenginar, but it's his own fault for getting into the mess with the sub-nagus's sister—"

Ro could no longer hear him as she found her way outside in the thin, cold atmosphere of the moon. It was dark here; apparently this part of the moon never entirely faced the sun, and the only light right now was from artificial sources posted between the shabby and sparse buildings that spread out from the spaceport. This moon's sole purpose was as a stopover for travelers . . . especially those interested in conducting illicit business.

Ro made her way toward the spaceport's secure hangar facility, constructed of enormous steel girders and smartplastic dividers backed with force fields to separate the ships. Her first objective would be to break in and find the correct hangar where the Ferengi vessel was docked.

Minutes later, she found it, the massive, awkward vessel looking very much like the one she'd tried to steal years ago, the one that currently lay in pieces at the hangar on Valo II. Ro wasted no time in disabling the force field that would allow her access to the bay. Her next problem would be getting past the Ferengi ship's security features, and while she knew the DaiMon was preoccupied, she knew nothing of the rest of the ship's crew—he'd mentioned a cook, and Ro was nervous at the thought that there could be more than one or two other Ferengi aboard. It hadn't even occurred to her that she'd have to deal with anyone other than Gart. Well, she only needed to get as far as the cargo bay.

She hitched up the satchel around her waist; it held her phaser, comm unit, and the small electrical device that she would soon be leaving inside the vessel. *This is it,* she told herself, and began working at overriding the controls to the drop ramp.

The minutes ticked by. Ro's forehead was slippery with perspiration, but she could not spare a moment to wipe her eyes. How much longer would Gart be preoccupied? If he was successful in his pursuit of the alien woman at the bar, would he bring her back to the ship? It seemed to take forever before the drop ramp began to slowly descend, and Ro scampered inside, finding a shuttlebay much like the one where she had once docked her own raider. She'd walked the remnants of that long-ago ship several times with Bis only yesterday, memorizing its layout. In seconds, she was in the cargo bay, surrounded by massive nonmetallic containers filled with unprocessed uridium. She shivered as she removed the electrical discharge device from her satchel and programmed it to react directly with the impact of the locking clamps at Terok Nor. Then she aimed the bomb's makeshift conducting spike at one of the containers, raised it over her head, and stabbed it through the casing.

She thought she heard voices coming from somewhere to the rear left of the cargo bay, and she quickly scuttled out the way she had come, not stopping to put the drop ramp back up as she ran, removing the comm device from her satchel and placing it in the pocket of her tunic. Once clear of the shipyards, she squeezed the device once, and, like magic, found herself once again on the transporter platform of the little warp ship.

*I did it,* she thought, and knew that Bis would be happy.

Odo usually had very little control of his senses while he regenerated, though certain external stimuli could rouse him from his state of near slumber. And as it was, something had forced him out of stasis on this particular night. Something was not right in the laboratory, though Odo had no concept of what it might be; he only knew that there was a sound coming from somewhere outside the door of Doctor Mora's laboratory, and at this time of night, there should be no sounds at all. He remained a liquid, but he poised himself to be ready to morph into something else if he needed to, though he wasn't sure what that thing might be.

Someone had entered the laboratory. Though the lights were still off, Odo could make out the shape of a humanoid—a Bajoran, he thought. This person looked more like Doctor Mora than like Doctor Yopal and the others, but there was something different about him. Odo wasn't sure what it was right away, but then it somehow dawned on him. This person was a female. This was a Bajoran female, something he'd not seen before. The female was touching Mora's computer. Odo wanted very much to get out of the tank and have a closer look, but he had the distinct sense that she was not supposed to be in here. He wondered what to do, and wished Mora would come, but it was nighttime; Mora would not return until the morning.

"Gantt!" the person said, and Odo wondered who she was talking to. The sound of her voice was like nothing he'd ever heard before. She did not sound like the Cardassian women, and she certainly didn't sound like Doctor Mora.

"Mobara found it, down the hall," said another voice, coming from somewhere outside. "It's done. We need to get to the transporter—it's in the lower level."

"Come in here and look at this," the female in Doctor Mora's laboratory called. "I think this is a Bajoran's laboratory."

"Never mind that," the other person said. "We need to get out of here."

"Yes, but—"

"Kira, we have to go, now!"

"I'm coming," she said, and left the room.

Odo felt relieved that the intruders were going, but he also felt something else, too. He felt an oddly placed regret, for the female had made him terrifically curious—curious in a way he wasn't entirely familiar with. He wanted to know why they had been here, what they were doing. He was too restless to go back into his resting state now, and he contemplated his feelings. He considered that some part of him wished the female hadn't gone quite so soon. He regretted not emerging from the tank to speak to her, though he knew he shouldn't have done that, and it was certainly best that he hadn't. But there was something about her, the novelty of her appearance, her voice—if he couldn't have spoken to her, he wished he could at least have looked at her just a little while longer.

✦    ✦    ✦

Daul had been seated inside the cramped little outbuilding, situated along the vast, stretching footbridge strung across the center of the open-pit duranium mine, for well over three hours now. That was almost twice as long as it should have taken him to complete his task, but the Cardassians didn't know that—at least, Daul hoped they didn't.

The odd file clerk had accompanied him for most of the day, but just under an hour ago, Marritza had explained that he had to get back to his office, and had placed a much less agreeable Cardassian guard in charge of looking after him. The guard had made it abundantly clear that he resented the assignment, glaring at Daul from the only other seat in the little room where the massive computer was housed. But Daul was relieved at the changing of his guard, for he felt confident that this sentry would give him far less trouble than the more observant file clerk would have.

From time to time, the guard shifted impatiently in his seat and inquired as to how much longer Daul was going to take, and Daul's reply was always the same: "I'm not sure, but I don't think much longer."

Finally, the surly Cardassian made an attempt at conversation. "Just what is it that you're doing here, anyway?"

"I'm reassessing the mine's reserve, and reprogramming the system's algorithm to ignore any veins of duridium with inferior percentage extraction. Eventually, the AI will cease drilling when viable duridium reaches 10 percent or less."

"Oh," the guard said, his expression confirming that he didn't know what Daul was talking about. This guard apparently had little understanding of how the mine operated; he was only here to force the Bajorans to work. To Daul's great relief, the guard removed the headset he was wearing—the set which enabled him to hear what Daul was saying. He rubbed his head, and held the set idly in his lap.

Daul glanced at the time displayed on his padd. The resistance outfit had been instructed to transport several of their operatives into a specific mine location in approximately five minutes. Daul had no idea if the terrorists really had the capacity to do all that would be required of them for this undertaking; he had left the most explicit instructions he could conceive of, but even so, his own knowledge of transporter operation was anemic—especially considering the transporter in question was Cardassian technology, and not Bajoran. Still, Daul was an intelligent man, a resourceful man—and he believed the plan was feasible. He had to believe in it.

Sneaking a glance at the bored Cardassian sentry, Daul began to tap into the networked security program. It was lucky the file clerk was not here, for he was obviously a man who knew his way around the facility's computer system and would probably have caught Daul in the act of what he was about to do. Struggling to maintain an aura of calm, he shut down the beam-shield that would prevent unauthorized travelers from transporting in or out of the facility. His task done, he switched back to the AI, thinking it had gone much easier than he would have expected.

He tapped away at the interface, when suddenly, the console began to blink, rattling a line of ominous characters.

WARNING. UNAUTHORIZED SECURITY SHUTDOWN. ENTER
AUTHORIZATION CODE FOR THIS ACTION OR SHUTDOWN
WILL BE CANCLED IN SIXTY SECONDS.

It took the Cardassian a moment to notice the blinking screen. He shouted something, but Daul couldn't hear him without his headset. Daul scrambled to his feet, but the guard caught him by the arm, still screaming.

Daul tried to writhe out of the Cardassian's grip, but

it was impossible. Instead, he lunged forward suddenly, bringing the big man with him as the two crashed into the computer console. The sturdy computer survived the impact, but Daul's ears were ringing from a sharp blow to his chin. His headset fell off somewhere, and Daul could only hear the tremendous, grinding noise from the mine below him.

The screen still flashed: FORTY SECONDS

The Cardassian stood up and pointed his phaser straight at Daul. He spoke into his comcuff, but without his headset, his report would not be heard over the cacophony of the mining facility. Daul threw open the door and scrambled out onto the catwalk. He headed in the direction of the spiraling gravel road that would take him straight down into the belly of the pit, clinging to his feeble hope that he would somehow manage to get past the guards and find his way to where the workers would be convened, and with luck, transported out.

The guard behind him hesitated long enough to fire his phaser, and missed. He gave chase once more, easily gaining on the narrow, swaying bridge, and just as he was about to close in on Daul, the Bajoran doubled back and headed straight for the guard, ramming his head directly into the other man's armored chest. Unhurt but startled, the Cardassian almost lost his footing, and clung to the sides of the unwieldy structure that held him. The bridge swayed more dangerously than ever. Daul grabbed for his phaser pistol, and almost had it, but the Cardassian's grip was too strong for him.

Daul made a quick decision. The computer behind him was the primary server for all systems in the facility. It would have to be destroyed before the security shutdown request could be canceled. With a single burst of adrenaline, he slammed the Cardassian's arm backward and pulled the trigger, aiming straight for the metal cube that housed the AI.

The Cardassian flung his arm back the other way, but not before a shower of sparks lit up the AI station behind them. The little structure shuddered and the catwalk with it, the station pulling away from the narrow footbridge on its legs of crisscrossed scaffolding, tottering backward. In the moments it took to fall across the width of the chasm, before it crashed into the side of the mine, rolling down the steep walls of the pit and exploding somewhere near the bottom, Daul realized that he had not been able to program the system to self-destruct, as he had originally planned. The Cardassian guards would live; Gul Darhe'el would live. It was his last thought, as the guard with whom he still wrestled on the dangerously swaying walkway finally got his phaser pointed in the intended direction, and Daul received a quick, indiscernible blast, full in the chest. He didn't feel a thing.

Kira compulsively looked back at the door of the basement transporter room. Though she knew they were alone here, that Furel was outside waiting to give a signal if anything went wrong, it was terrifying to be inside an actual Cardassian facility. The only missions she'd been part of until now had been attacks from outside facilities or ships; this was the first time she could remember actually entering Cardassian domain, and it made her feel uncomfortably claustrophobic. She couldn't imagine how she was going to feel when she was inside Gallitep. She would never have admitted it, but she was having second thoughts.

"I think I've got it," Mobara said from behind the transporter console. "The scientist said you would be beamed directly into the facility if I use these coordinates; you'll close your eyes, open them, and find yourself standing somewhere in the Gallitep mine."

"I think we all understand the basic concept," Shakaar said wryly.

Kira held her breath. What if Mobara had the coordinates wrong, and she were somehow transported into the solid rock that surrounded the open mine? The thought was beyond horrifying. Kira trusted Mobara's expertise, and she knew that transporter technology had been used safely by the Cardassians for decades, at least. But still . . . it was impossible not to be afraid.

"Are you sure you're up to this?" Gantt said to Nerys.

"Of course I am," she said fiercely, terrified.

Lupaza, who stood close to Kira, reached out to grab her hand. "You'll do fine, Nerys," the older woman assured her, but Kira met Shakaar's eyes for a moment and saw that he wasn't so sure he should have agreed to let her come along.

Shakaar stepped onto the transporter platform. "I stand here?" he asked. Like the rest of them, he'd never used a transporter in his life.

"That's right," Mobara told him.

Lupaza stepped up after him, along with Kira and Gantt. The rest of their strike team would be transported immediately after them, slightly higher in the mine so that they could deal with the guards. There were ten from Shakaar's cell in all—not as many as Daul had requested in his detailed instructions, but several of their group were already on assignment in Ilivia with another cell when Daul had contacted Shakaar, and they were out of reach. Ten would have to be enough.

"Now, just remember," Shakaar told them all. "We get inside, make sure the Bajorans are all in a central location, kill any hostiles we find, and then we contact Mobara with these." He held up one of the comm devices the scientist had given to Furel. Kira fingered hers nervously; it was pinned to her tunic, and she feared she was going to lose it.

She unpinned the small oval of metal and slipped it in her pocket.

"Is everyone ready?" Mobara called out, and Shakaar gave a nod.

"See you on the other side," Gantt said, and Kira shut her eyes tightly.

Lenaris Jau was monitoring one of the dozens of subterranean smelters at Gallitep, so weary that he could scarcely keep his head above his shoulders. So many of the sick workers had died lately, and those who were not affected by disease had to pick up the slack, working nearly round the clock. Jau had no idea how long it had been since he'd slept. Exhaustion and the darkness of the underground tunnels in the mine tended to distort his sense of time. It could have been three hours, it could have been three days. It didn't really matter.

Jau wondered why the number of workers had been dwindling lately. The dead were usually replaced, but lately they had not been. He wondered why the sick workers were no longer being treated. Those who died were unceremoniously dragged from the mines, to be taken to some undisclosed location for disposal, though it was not unusual for their corpses to remain where they had fallen for up to three days, swelling and stinking in the baking sun. The numbers of dead seemed to have escalated quite dramatically lately. Was it only yesterday that over three dozen people had died, in a single day? There were rumors that Darhe'el was planning to shut down the camp, which would not bode well for the workers here. Jau thought he would walk with the Prophets soon, and mostly, he was too weary to care—if anything, death would be a welcome release from the horrors of this place.

Jau had seen the most unspeakable things of his life happen in this place. He had seen plenty of tunnels cave in, had listened to the screams of those left to suffocate inside. He had seen scarcely recognizable corpses retrieved from the vats of chemicals used to separate the rock from the valuable minerals, and even worse, he'd seen the gruesome-looking survivors from similar accidents, forced to go back to work with no hair, no skin—even no eyelids. He'd heard the groans and wails of people who were "treated" in the camp infirmary, more like a torture chamber or the laboratory of a mad scientist, bent on using live subjects. He'd seen dozens of people crippled from injuries sustained after stumbling down the steeper precipices at the very top of the mine. He'd seen people beaten within an inch of their lives for what Gul Darhe'el perceived as insubordination. But Jau was numb to it, mostly. At least, as much as he could have hoped for.

Jau adjusted the smelter's temperature, ignoring the echoing groans and wails all around him. He drew his forearm over his brow, wiping the sweat away, when he noticed that the system of conveyor belts that delivered the ore to the smelter had stopped, and the overwhelming noise that usually accompanied it had ceased as well. It took his sluggish mind a moment to register what was going on, and he looked around, his heart fluttering. Something must have gone wrong with the artificial intelligence system, though in all his time at Gallitep, Jau could not remember that happening, even once. No, it had not happened since the accident, which had occurred before Jau had been brought here. An alarm began to tear through the hollow caverns of the mines, indicating a systems failure—the mine was to be evacuated at once. Jau's breath froze in his lungs; was this going to be Darhe'el's method of disposing of him, and everyone else here?

Before he could think further on it, he was instantly swept up in a crush of panicking Bajorans. Jau began to run, drawing on reserves he didn't know he had, pushing and stumbling until he found himself stepping out onto a wide dirt road that curled down from the very top of the pit all the way down here, just a few *linnipates* from the bottom. He was immediately aware of the heat—more than just the heat from the hot, midday sun that he was accustomed to; it was from a fire, somewhere not far below him. Something burned and scorched with chemical brightness at the base of the pit, sending up great plumes of toxic smoke. Jau began to scramble up the gravel road, trying to get away from the flames below him, but he encountered so many confused Bajorans, he could not get far. The road was packed with people, crying out in panic. Finally, Jau came to the road's widest point, and realized he could go no farther. He would have to wait for the crowd to thin out, which he suspected would not happen before they were all murdered here, en masse—for it seemed logical to Jau that this was really it—Darhe'el's final solution had come.

He looked up once, panned the miserable and frightened faces of the crowd that surrounded him, and did a double take. There was a girl standing there, a Bajoran, and he could have sworn that she wasn't there before. This girl did not look like she belonged here. She looked like one of the younger ones that might have been brought in many months ago, but Jau wasn't aware of any new workers coming in for some time. And there was something else about her too . . . There was a bulge at her hip, underneath her tunic, and Jau felt certain he knew what it was—this girl carried a phaser. She caught his eye and moved closer to him, shoving her way through the tight press of gangly limbs and exposed rib cages, bruised beneath too-tight skin.

"Don't worry," she said to him, and suddenly, he did worry—he found he still had the capacity to worry, even after feeling mostly nothing for such a very long time.

✦   ✦   ✦

Ro had not expected to feel so conflicted as she warped back to Valo II. She had been on and off the Ferengi freighter in less than ten minutes; the entire operation really had been as easy as Bis had said it would be. She kept reminding herself of the wonderful, risky, and brave thing she had just done, but the thoughts were not quite resonating within her, and she was eager to find Bis and hear his reassurances.

Still wary of landing the valuable warp ship on her own, she left it in orbit of Valo II, hoping that Bis would be able to retrieve it later. But she could not immediately find him once she materialized on the planet's surface. He had implied that he would meet her near the landing field when she returned, but she was back much faster than expected, and she did not know where he could be. She went to his house, but he wasn't there, so she wandered the dusty, tightly packed village, asking those people who bothered to look up as she walked by. It was in the center of the crowded town that she encountered Keeve Falor, the old politician she'd met those years ago with Bram. She did a double take as he passed, and he stopped to regard her.

"You look familiar to me," the man said, stepping back as he tried to place her.

"I'm Ro Laren," she said, feeling suddenly as sulky as her younger self.

"The little girl from Jo'kala?" Keeve mused. "Is that right. What are you doing here?"

"I'm helping Bis with something," Ro said. "Akhere Bis."

Keeve immediately looked alarmed. "Helping Bis!" he exclaimed. "Tell me he hasn't recruited you for that foolishness with the alien ship?"

Ro wasn't sure if Keeve was talking about the plan she had just undertaken, but since he seemed not to approve, she supposed she'd better not confirm her involvement. "I haven't decided if I'm going to help him," she lied.

"Prophets help us," Keeve said. "Bis is young and reckless—he doesn't understand the great cost that would be suffered by destroying Terok Nor. Thousands of Bajoran lives . . . It simply doesn't make sense, to sacrifice what we are trying to preserve."

"If those lives buy millions more, maybe the sacrifice is worth it."

"Is that how your resistance is going to save Bajor?" Keeve asked in disgust. "Using arithmetic to decide who lives, and who dies? That isn't what the Prophets teach us."

Ro felt a flash of anger at the sanctimonious mention of the Prophets. "At least . . . at least it would be doing something to fight the Cardassians, instead of hunkering down on this world like a coward, hiding here where they won't trouble you, and letting them do as they please with Bajor!"

Keeve studied her a moment. If he was angry, she didn't see it; he only looked tired and sad. "Perhaps to you, I seem a coward," he said, after a moment. "But I know that when the people on this world still listened to my advice, we were learning things that could have brought the Federation in to aid us in our struggle. We had warp vessels, we had trade relations with other worlds. But that is changing, and the people here have begun to grow impatient. We've lost most of our warp ships, and we have to rely on charity from others within this system for our very survival. We've fallen out of favor with the Federation, especially since the unfortunate incident that occurred on Valo VI. The Federation once had a lot of questions about what that little group might have been doing there, and I suppose now they have much less of a chance of ever finding out." He looked at her very pointedly when he said it, and Ro felt a strange thing, a thing she thought might be guilt.

Troubled, Ro looked past Keeve to see that Bis was

approaching her, his face unable to contain its excitement. Sensing that Ro was done with him, or wishing to avoid confrontation with Bis, Keeve moved on down the road, toward his own residence.

"Is it done?" Bis asked her eagerly, and Ro gave him a single nod, her head feeling heavy. This time, she did not respond when he grabbed her tightly, lifting her nearly off her feet.

"We have to celebrate," Bis said. "Come with me, we'll have spring wine at my friend Lino's house." He gestured toward a dwelling not far from where they stood.

"We did a good thing, didn't we?" Ro said.

"We did a brilliant thing," he said. He laughed out loud, a picture of jubilation.

"And . . . the people on the station . . ."

"What people?" Bis said, beginning to walk.

"The Bajorans," she said. "They'll . . . walk with the Prophets? Is that what you believe?"

Bis looked puzzled. "That's right," he said, but his voice sounded a little less excited now. He stopped walking. "Come on, Laren. Just think. We're going to be responsible for killing Gul Dukat! Gul Dukat and Kubus Oak, all their henchmen. We're going to destroy Terok Nor! Do you have any idea of the significance of it?"

"Yes, I know," Ro said. "But Keeve Falor just told me—"

"Forget Keeve Falor!" Bis said, and he sounded angry now. "Just wait—once Terok Nor is really gone, once the prefect is dead—Keeve and the others will see that I was right."

"Of course," Ro said. She thought of the botched mission on Jo'kala, her last. She'd been so sure the others would see that she was right—but she hadn't been.

"I left the ship in orbit," she told him.

"That's for the best," Bis told him. "We'll pick it up tomorrow, when I take you back to Jeraddo."

Ro swallowed. Back to Jeraddo? "Right," she said, feeling her chest tighten.

Bis's friends Lino and Hintasi were both inside a little house with a dirt floor, one nearly identical to Bis's, but older and smaller. It was mostly dark inside, with dirty and mildewed fabric covering the open windows. A pile of blankets was heaped in a corner, making do for a bed. There were several bottles of spring wine on the floor where Lino and Hintasi were sitting, and they saluted with a bottle as Ro entered, shouting their congratulations and pushing a bottle into her hands. She was only too happy to drink it, thinking her nerves deserved it.

She took a sip, wanting to make it last, but she found herself drinking deeply, thirsty for the effect. "I hope it was worth it," she said, coming up for air. She sat on the floor, took another drink.

"It's worth it," Bis assured her. "I can't think of a better reason to finish off the last of my father's spring wine. The last time we drank a bottle was—"

"No, I mean—all of it. I mean—what if the Cardassians just send another prefect? What if they just build another station? What if it's all just—"

"Don't be ridiculous," Lino interrupted.

"Why is it ridiculous?" Ro asked, and as she said it, she began to think, to really think, about what she'd done. To the Cardassians, Bajor was just one little planet. Killing the prefect might not matter much to them at all. Certainly, the destruction of Terok Nor would mean a setback, but perhaps their resources were truly infinite. Perhaps there were exponentially more of them than there were Bajorans. Ro suddenly recognized that maybe Keeve Falor had been right, all those years ago when he'd sent her on the cautious reconnaissance mission; maybe gathering information about the Cardassians before fighting them was the better approach, after all.

"Come on, Laren," Bis said, starting to sound a little upset. "Don't you remember what you said all those years ago? About just killing the Cardassians on Valo VI? And then you did it! You shot them, all by yourself. Even though I would have been scared to death, I never would have been able to—"

"It was a stupid thing to do," Ro interrupted. "I didn't have to kill them. I could have gotten out of there before they would have seen me, I could have called for Bram, but I compromised the mission, and I killed them anyway." She took another deep drink from the bottle. "I thought . . . I thought if I killed him . . . I'd never have another nightmare, I'd stop feeling so terrible about what happened to my father, but it made no difference. None!" She dropped the empty bottle on the dirt floor, fighting tears.

No one spoke for a moment. "Laren," Lino finally said. "I think I understand how you feel. But those Bajorans on the station, they'll walk with the Prophets soon, can't you see that? And—"

"How comforting it must be for you!" Ro interrupted. "To have something to believe in, to have something to justify what we just did. What I just did!" She tried to reach for another bottle, but thought better of it. The wine had hit her fast.

"I want to be alone for a while," she announced, and pushed herself up off the floor. She stormed out of the little house, a strange, buried part of her almost wishing that Bis would follow her, but he let her go.

## 21

Kira fought down the panic that threatened to overtake her—for it appeared that something had gone very wrong. The Bajoran scientist who had briefed the Shakaar about this operation had neglected to mention anything about the burning wreckage that was currently at the base of the pit. He had indicated that the Bajorans would be corralled by the Cardassian guards, but instead, Kira was confronted with a brace of panicking people, pushing at the slowly moving queue that spread out across the entire perimeter of the pit, the line of Bajorans undulating in an upward direction. But Kira needed to bring them all in together, and she did not know how four people could possibly round up all these hysterical wretches in one central location. Hysterical and terrible in their weakness, their sickness, their injuries and too-thin bodies. There were no Cardassians to be seen, but she heard phaser fire and screams coming from some of the upper tunnels. Gallitep was a nightmare, worse than she'd imagined.

She caught the eye of a man who seemed to have a recognizable degree of lucidity, and she moved closer to him. "Don't worry," she told him. "Help is here. I need someone to help me gather everyone together in a central location. Can you do that?"

The man, who Nerys quickly realized could not be

more than a few years older than she was, cleared his throat with difficulty. "I can try," he croaked. "Someone needs to tell them to calm down, or people are going to start shoving each other off the paths and we'll all wind up down there." He nodded toward the pit, where the flames from the crashed building were finally dying down, its three broken and twisted legs crookedly awry, but the smoke was thick, and many people were beginning to hack and cough.

Nerys began to shout, her eyes streaming from the chemical smoke below. "People, people! Please, try to calm down!" Her voice was lost over the crying and shouting, and the man did his best to shout along with her, until the people nearest them began at last to still.

"We've come to help!" Kira shouted, though she didn't know if her voice could be heard. Above her, she could see Gantt, attempting to calm down another small group that surrounded him on an even narrower road than the one where she stood. She hoped Shakaar was with him. She couldn't see Lupaza anywhere.

"We need to get these people together in one place," Kira told the man urgently. "Is there any way—"

"One of the larger tunnels," the man replied. "The one I just came from goes back far enough to get everyone inside."

"Let's do it," Kira said. The smoke was getting even thicker now.

"They may be reluctant," he warned her, beginning to cough. "It was in one of the tunnels that the accident happened a few years ago—the one that caused so many to become sick."

"We'll have to convince them," Kira said, and began to beckon to those closest to her, while the young man led them back in the direction of the tunnel. Kira saw the signs of protest, but she was firm. "Please!" she insisted. "You have to listen to me! We're going to get you out of here, but you have to trust me, just follow him—" She pointed to her nameless assistant, and wormed her way through the people to get to Gantt, to tell him what was happening.

"Gantt!" she screamed, and after a few more shouts he finally saw her through the smoke, and looked down in her direction. She could not get to him without walking the full rotation of the circular road, at least a *kellipate*. "Get them down here! This way! If you see any of the others, tell them—there's a big tunnel down here where we can herd them all together and transport them out!"

"Transport us out?" someone cried, and many more people began to talk at once, shouting back and forth in an excited, squabbling rumble, through the coughing and choking from the smoke. "Are we being transported out?" "Where are we going?" "Who is taking us there?" "Where are the Cardassians?"

"We're taking you someplace safe!" Kira shouted, and repeated the words again and again until they began to spread throughout the crowd, hopefully to those on the other side of the pit. Kira could no longer see them through the haze, though it seemed to be clearing—either that, or she was getting used to it.

The process of herding everyone into the tunnel was slow and painstaking, and many people continued to resist, trying to move in the opposite direction and holding up progress, but Kira had help from others who apparently felt that the chance to get out, no matter how slim, trumped their fear of some kind of trick. By the time Kira entered the black, sweltering tunnel behind the enormous crowd of people, she began to have second thoughts. Not only was it hot and dark in here, but the smoke had made it almost impossible to breathe. By the time everyone could get to the tunnel, many of them might suffocate.

But there was no time to reformulate the plan; there

were a hundred things or more that could go wrong. Kira still had no idea what had happened to Shakaar and Lupaza, nor any of the others who had been transported after her, although she thought she could hear phaser fire above her. She saw no guards, and feared they might have all been transported into the offices above, only to come back at any moment—or worse, bring in reinforcements to put a stop to the escape. Worse yet, there was the possibility that Mobara and Furel, who were back at the Institute of Science, had been caught at the industrial transporter. Then they would all be trapped here with no other means of getting out.

People in the back of the tunnel were coughing and crying. "I can't breathe!" shouted a woman. "Get us out of here, please!"

Standing at the mouth of the tunnel, Kira recognized Lupaza coming closer with more people. "Lupaza!" Kira cried out. "We have to get these people out of here, quickly! It's going to take too much time to get everyone together, we'll have to begin transporting them now!"

Lupaza turned to regard the long rope of people still advancing toward the tunnel through the thinning smoke, listened to those at the back of the cavern who cried out in the claustrophobic darkness, and gave a quick nod. She pressed her comm device.

"Mobara, it's Lupaza! I'm here with Nerys—we have to start transporting people out right away."

*"How many would you estimate are with you?"*

"I have no idea," she said. "Can't you just lock on to our signals and get as many out as you can?"

*"I think so,"* he said. *"I hope so,"* he added. *"I don't know the first thing about what this transporter beam is capable of, but I'll widen it to its full distance capacity and see where that gets us."*

Kira shut her eyes tightly and felt a distinctive pins-

and-needles sensation in her limbs and torso. When she opened her eyes, she was somewhere else; somewhere in the Dahkur woods—and she was surrounded by dozens of bewildered-looking people, malnourished, injured, coughing, and crying—and then muttering and exclaiming their amazement over what had just happened.

"Wait!" someone standing near Kira cried out. "Where's Tynara?"

"Tynara will be here!" Kira shouted. "Please, remain calm, everyone. Just stay here with me, the rest will be here soon." She hoped it was true.

Many people had now fallen to their knees, shouting with joy, others were crying, though Kira couldn't tell if it was from fear or jubilation. Some still appeared to be in a daze, rubbing their faces in confusion or simply staring up at the trees as if they'd forgotten what trees looked like. Many were calling out for missing family and friends, searching for people who were not here yet—and who might not ever come, Kira thought, for even if Shakaar and the others made it with the rest of the survivors, plenty of Bajorans must have died today, either as a result of the accident that had caused the fire, or from having been too close to fleeing Cardassian guards who haunted the upper reaches of the mine.

After what seemed like a very long time, Gantt and Shakaar arrived with a smaller group of people.

"Did we get everyone out?" Kira pressed Shakaar.

"As many as we could see," he told her, his tone hasty and dismissive, looking among the faces for the rest of his cell. Kira recognized others from the Shakaar cell in the growing, noisy crowd, Dakahna and Ornak and the young couple from outside Tamulna who had just joined the cell, but two were still missing, and Shakaar was trying to get clear word from Mobara regarding what had happened to them.

"Edon," Lupaza prompted him, "we need to get these people to safety."

Kira interrupted. "The scientist," she said. "What about him? Mobara is supposed to . . ."

"Nerys," Lupaza said gently, "the scientist is gone. He was in the structure when it fell from the suspension bridge above us."

Kira shook her head. "But . . ." she said, "you can't be sure . . ."

Gantt put his hand on her shoulder. "He's gone," he told her. "Now, we've got to get these people out of here. We'd better let Mobara know to get him and Furel back to the camp, and we've got to get these people somewhere safe."

Swallowing hard, Kira nodded.

Valo II had grown dark, the people in the tents and rotted wood huts and eroding brick houses all gone to sleep. Ro knew that somewhere, Bis was probably looking for her by now.

Ro made her way to the landing field on Valo II, where the Ferengi freighter lay scattered in pieces. But she knew the comm was still functional, the comm that Bis and his friends had used to formulate their careful plan—the plan that she was now about to sabotage.

She managed to contact DaiMon Gart quite easily; Ro still recalled the comm code she'd seen on his bar tab. His face appeared on the tiny screen alongside the aural device. "DaiMon Gart," she shouted, hoping the universal translator was still working.

*"Who are you?"* the Ferengi DaiMon said gruffly.

"I'm a . . . terrorist, DaiMon Gart. I wanted to let you know that . . . I put a bomb on your ship."

The Ferengi's eyes suddenly went wide with fear, and he began to shriek. *"What?"* he cried. *"Why would you have done such a thing? I'm an honest man! Is this about the ion coil assemblies? Because they were in perfectly good shape when I sold them, I assure you!"*

"No . . . it's not . . . it's . . . look, DaiMon Gart, you have to eject your cargo, now, or it's going to react with the bomb and you'll never see another . . . ion coil assembly . . . or anything else . . . ever again!"

The man stopped screaming, and looked suspicious. *"Eject my cargo? Are you mad? Do you have any idea how much latinum I'm going to be making with this run?"*

"Which is more important to you, DaiMon—latinum, or your life?"

The Ferengi considered for what Ro thought was an absurdly long time before finally making his decision. *"My life,"* he said grudgingly.

"Then you're going to have to eject your cargo, DaiMon. I'm sorry. If you don't believe me, you can send someone back there to confirm that there's a device in the bay, but I'm not sure I'd advise tampering with it. The men who built it were a bit on the amateur side."

The DaiMon appeared to consider this for a moment. *"I believe you,"* he said. *"You've got an . . . honest face."* He said the last part with clear revulsion. He muttered to himself for a moment, looking over his control panel. *"Yes,"* he said, *"you're telling the truth, aren't you? My scans show an object of unidentified origin and composition in the cargo bay . . ."* He looked positively miserable. *"Why would you do this to me?"* he cried.

"Hey, I'm saving your life right now!" Ro pointed out, but it seemed of little consolation to the Ferengi.

*"Fine,"* he practically sobbed, and began to mutter to himself again, though it sounded quite distinctly mournful this time. With an exaggerated and deliberate gesture, he stabbed at a control panel on his sensor array. Ro sighed with relief, and left the comm without so much as a goodbye to the Ferengi.

She wandered away from the landing field and walked aimlessly around the perimeter of the village, finding the copse of trees where she had once taken a little walk with Bis, to hide from Bram. She remembered hoping that he would kiss her. It was so foolish, she recognized now, not just the thoughts she'd had as a younger girl, but that she'd been so easily convinced to take part in such a dangerous and costly plan by the promise of . . . what? Love? She almost laughed out loud at it now. Even after all she'd shared with him, all of herself that she'd given him, Bis had just been expecting her to go back to Jeraddo, go back to Jo'kala, without a second thought of him.

Where would she go now? She could not very well wait for Bis to take her to Jeraddo; he'd be so angry with her when he learned what she had done that he would be sure to . . . She didn't know what he would do, but she had no intention of finding out. She didn't want to go back to Bajor, anyway. The way she saw it, she had only one choice.

Before she'd gone to the moon of that gas giant, she'd known that there was much more to the universe, that it was crammed with people who took no notice of the simple dichotomy between Cardassian and Bajoran. But it had never occurred to her that she might somehow be part of that other universe, a universe where she might be regarded as something beyond the identity she'd somehow stumbled into. Orphan, pickpocket, resistance fighter—she didn't want to be any of those things anymore. She just wanted to be Ro Laren. The trouble was, she didn't know who Ro Laren could be.

She took one last look at the copse of pathetic little trees, thought that she would miss the majestic forests of Jo'kala, and then she squeezed the comm device that was still in her pocket, the device she'd neglected to give back to Bis. She felt a strange whirring deep in the very essense of her body's composition as she was transported into the pilot seat of the shuttle, one of the last warp vessels on Valo II. It was a shame that she had to take it from them, but she could think of no other way. The defeat she saw on her world, the petty squabbles and the justification of such heinous acts in the name of liberation—maybe now she could go to a place where she could really make a difference. Maybe now she could find out who she really was, and what she really wanted.

"How can this be?" Kalisi Reyar was shouting, and Mora could hear every word as he poked his head out of his laboratory.

"It's a very good question," Yopal answered her. "I don't understand how you could let a thing like this happen, Doctor Reyar."

"It was a security measure!" Reyar answered, her voice high and angry. "I assumed the system here was safe! Why would I risk copying my research, leaving it where anyone could get hold of it, could steal it from me—"

"Protecting your work from terrorists should have taken precedence over your concerns regarding provenance for your achievements." Yopal's voice had gone cold.

"How was I to know that a terrorist was working right alongside us?"

Mora turned to Odo's tank, where the shape-shifter was apparently regenerating. "Odo," he said, keeping his voice authoritative, though the conversation down the hall had him very frightened.

After a moment, the shape-shifter writhed and twisted into partially humanoid form, his features glassy and liquid. "What is it, Doctor Mora?"

"Odo, did you . . . happen to . . . notice anything unusual happening in the laboratory last night?" His voice had dropped, the worry showing through.

Odo's features solidified. His eyes were devoid of expression, but his hesitation suggested he was afraid to answer.

"Never mind," Mora told him. "Odo, if you saw anything, you must not repeat it to anyone, do you understand? If anyone asks, you didn't see anything happen here last night."

"I . . . saw nothing," Odo said, and Mora didn't know if he was telling the truth, or only following Mora's instructions. Either way, it would have to do. Mora left Odo in his tank and headed for where Yopal and Reyar were still arguing.

"Good morning, Doctors," Mora said with convincing neutrality.

"Doctor Mora!" Yopal exclaimed when she saw him. "A terrible thing has happened! Doctor Reyar's research has been stolen!"

Mora took a step back. "You don't say!"

"It was your friend Daul!" Reyar shouted. "I suppose you heard what he did—he sabotaged the work camp he'd been assigned to! And then he stole my research!"

"You don't say," Mora said again, his voice growing faint now. "I . . . I hadn't heard." Daul? So he was behind this?

"It's all over the comnet, Mora!"

"I . . . don't have access to the Cardassian comnet," Mora said. His personal laboratory computer was programmed to block him from the Cardassian channel.

"Yes," Yopal sighed. "Unfortunately, it does seem that our Doctor Daul is responsible for wreaking quite a bit of havoc. Last night, the main computer server at Gallitep was sabotaged—destroyed. Nearly all the Bajoran prisoners escaped, several guards were killed in the accident—and Doctor Daul was killed, as well."

Mora heard himself gasp, and then quickly shut his mouth. "How . . . terrible," he said.

"On top of all of that unpleasantness, Doctor Reyar's research has been destroyed, the permanent files on her computer corrupted," Yopal went on. "Apparently, Daul was working in conjunction with a group of terrorists. Our transporter was accessed last night, and Daul's passcode was the last one used. The security cams have all been wiped, as have all the last transporter coordinates. Only Daul could have orchestrated something like this. I knew it was foolish to allow him to use the transporters."

"What did you know of this?" Reyar asked Mora accusingly. "What did Daul say to you?"

"Nothing!" Mora insisted, feeling like a terrible coward. He couldn't believe Daul had the wherewithal—the courage—to pull off a thing so spectacularly dangerous. "I . . . haven't spoken to Daul in almost a week. I assure you, if he'd said anything regarding sabotage—or theft—I would have reported him!"

Yopal turned to Reyar. "I'm sure our Doctor Mora knew absolutely nothing of this."

Mora did his best to conceal a sigh of relief.

Reyar went on. "I'll have to start practically from the beginning!" she complained.

"That's enough, Doctor Reyar. We should think of the forty-seven brave Cardassians who lost their lives trying to protect Gallitep."

Reyar was undaunted. "It was my life's work, and now it's all gone!"

"Well, at any rate, you'll be able to recall most of it, of course," Yopal said calmly.

Mora distinctly read uncertainty in Reyar's eyes before she answered. "Yes, of course."

Yopal went on. "You'll just need someone to act as a scribe. And Doctor Mora is going to help you do that."

Mora thought about what Reyar had been working on—the anti-aircraft device, something to shoot down terrorist raiders. He felt oddly triumphant on Daul's behalf, through his fear and guilt—and it quickly occurred to him that maybe he could do something as well—nothing so grand, but something nonetheless.

*So,* he thought, *I'm going to be helping Doctor Reyar salvage her research, am I?* Well, he intended to make it very difficult for her; he decided it right then and there.

"Meanwhile, Mora, there is something else I'd like to discuss with you," Yopal said, and her artificial smile looked more forced than ever. "I've decided that it might be more . . . comfortable for you if I make a little . . . place for you to stay, here at the institute. That way, you won't have to be bothered with traveling such a long distance back to the village. You see, we Cardassians all live at the nearby settlement, but you've got such a lengthy commute from the village . . ."

"I'm to live here?" Mora said, surprised. It immediately dawned on him what was happening—he was no longer permitted to leave.

"Yes, I think that would be best, don't you?"

Mora nodded, for there was nothing else left to do. He supposed he should be grateful, after what had happened with Daul, that they weren't simply sending him straight to a work camp. He was the last Bajoran here, and he'd better not forget it. The Cardassians obviously weren't going to.

"Gul Dukat, I have something to show you!" Basso burst into the conference room with the isolinear recording in hand, and the prefect looked up from the long table where he was seated with his visitors, a damage assessment team from sciences.

"Basso! I believe I've asked you numerous times not to—"

"It's about Gallitep, sir."

Dukat immediately stopped what he was doing and excused himself from his visitors. The sabotage of the camp took precedence over all else; Dukat was eager to amplify the blame laid on Darhe'el for the disaster, no small task. Gul Darhe'el had been away from Gallitep when the mass escape and near total destruction of the camp had taken place; at worst, he was guilty of poor timing, although he *had* specifically asked for that Bajoran scientist, the one who'd acted on behalf of the terrorists. Dukat had gone out of his way to say as much in every report heading back to Cardassia Prime. If there was anything Basso could tell him that might be useful in his quest to see Darhe'el disgraced, Dukat was eager to hear it.

Leaving the conference room, he walked briskly back to his office, the Bajoran at his heels. When the door had closed behind them, he nodded for Basso to continue.

The Bajoran was breathless—from excitement or exertion, Dukat didn't know. "I reviewed all the security rods from the day of the disaster, as you asked me, and I found one that has something you need to see."

"Very good," Dukat said, and sat down at his office desk.

Basso quickly plugged the recording into a nearby monitor and found the sequence he was looking for. Dukat squinted to view the footage. "Enhance," Basso told the computer, and the focus pulled in on a group of people edging along one of the narrow roads that lined the openpit mine.

"There," Basso told him, pointing to the screen. "That's Shakaar Edon, the leader of a cell just out of Dahkur."

Dukat nodded. "So, we know who is responsible for Gallitep. But this doesn't get us any closer to—"

"No, no, sir, there's more." Basso progressed the recording a few steps further, to show another crowd shot on a road further below the first point. "Enhance," he said again, and pointed to the slender red-haired figure that appeared onscreen. He didn't need to say more.

"Nerys," Dukat breathed.

◆   ◆   ◆

Kira mostly felt triumphant, for she'd just taken part in one of the biggest missions in the history of the Shakaar cell. She'd personally had a hand in liberating the worst camp on all of Bajor. She felt dizzied from all the praise that was being heaped on her, from not only Lupaza, but Dakhana, Mobara—even Shakaar himself had commended her courage and clear thinking.

The Shakaar cell had taken proper time and measure to grieve as well as celebrate, for two members of the group had not made it back. Mobara had been unable to get a lock on two of the communicators, and made the assumption that they had been destroyed. Ornak later confirmed that Matram Tryst had blown himself up, taking at least twenty Cardassian guards with him—along with Par Lusa. Par had been only eighteen years old, and Matram not much older than that. But they'd known the risks . . . just as Kira did.

She couldn't stop thinking about one small thing, certainly small against the overwhelming sense of victory that had accompanied the sight of all those Bajorans suddenly appearing in the forest of Dahkur, many of them so near to death that Kira knew they would not have made it for one more day inside that camp. They could go home now, and those who were sick could at least live out their last moments in freedom, hopefully with their families or loved ones. But there was one Bajoran who wouldn't ever see his loved ones again—the scientist who had made it all possible. And that small thing kept at her, throughout the celebration, throughout the glowing aftermath of Gallitep's liberation.

She had gone to sit outside the cave, watching Bajor's moons as they very slowly crept from behind the mountains in the west, one after the other. The closest moon was a deep orange, tinted by the haze in the atmosphere. She wondered what it had looked like in the days before the Cardassians' various mining and manufacturing interests had tainted the air with billowing clouds of pollution. People said the moons were once the color of fusionstone, nearly white sometimes on summer nights. Kira absently drew circles in the dust with a stick, briefly calling to mind thoughts of her mother, the artist, and wondering why she'd never had any talent of her own.

"Nerys," called a gentle voice—Lupaza, of course, emerging from the cave.

"I'm here," Kira answered her, setting down the stick.

"What are you thinking about?"

Kira shrugged. "Nothing," she said unconvincingly.

Lupaza pursed her lips. "You're not still thinking about that scientist, are you?"

"No," Kira said. "Yes. A little bit."

Lupaza squatted on her heels. "Nerys," she said. "You need to understand something right now. That man—he was a collaborator. It's true that in the end, he did what he could to compensate for the evil he'd been responsible for, but . . . it's only right that he ultimately gave his life for the struggle. Do you understand?"

"Yes," Kira said listlessly, picking up the stick again.

"Nerys," Lupaza said, her voice not quite so gentle now. "If you want to fight in the resistance—if you really want to be in this cell, or any cell—you'd better get used to the idea that Bajorans have to die sometimes. Not just the people in your cell, which is bad enough, but sometimes . . . Bajorans have to die, and we have to kill them. It doesn't matter how brave you are, how strong—if you can't come to terms with killing collaborators, then you'd better go home to your father right now."

Lupaza stood up, and made to go back into the cave. "Really, it's a good thing that scientist was killed. Because if I were him, I don't think I'd be able to live with myself, after seeing what those people in that camp looked like."

"You're right," Kira said quickly, before Lupaza could go inside. "I know you're right." She managed a weak smile at Lupaza, genuinely feeling a little better. Lupaza smiled back, and held her hand out to pull Kira to her feet.

Lupaza went on. "It's difficult to understand, maybe, but this war we're fighting . . . it's not just a matter of Bajorans versus Cardassians. This is a fight between what's right, and what's evil. And the face of evil sometimes looks unsettlingly like your own. It could be someone that you know. It could be a member of your own family. It could be the boy that . . . the boy you were supposed to marry, the boy you thought was the love of your life. But it's still evil, nonetheless."

Kira nodded, remembering what Lupaza had mentioned of her *ih'tanu*.

"Let's go inside," Lupaza told the younger girl, changing her tone. "There's a glass of *copal* in there with your name on it."

"*Copal!*" Kira exclaimed.

"Sure," Lupaza said. "You're old enough to handle something like Gallitep, I think you're beyond old enough to have a little old glass of *copal*."

Kira nodded, eager to taste her first cider with the rest of the cell. For if Gallitep had been her formal initiation into the cell, the event that would finally persuade the others to stop calling her "little girl" would probably be a round or two of *copal* with Shakaar. It would do the job better than an *ih'tanu* could have.

A cheer went up as Kira and Lupaza entered the cave, one of many cheers that had been erupting throughout the evening, and Lupaza poured Kira a stoneware tumbler full of strong cider. Kira took a hesitant sip and willed her face not to crumple with the potent sour flavor that stung the back of her tongue. Another cheer went up as she opened her eyes and raised her cup with a smile.

As the evening blurred into a haze of warm triumph, a cacophony of friendly cheers and songs of victory, Kira recognized that the old ways were really gone for good now. Bajor was a different place than it had once been, a new place. It would never be the same as it was before Kira was born, but her world *would* be free again. Kira would have a hand in ensuring her people's freedom, she decided—no matter how many Bajoran collaborators she had to kill to do it. This would be the last time that she would ever mourn the loss of someone who had caused the kind of suffering that she had witnessed at Gallitep. Tonight, she was truly a resistance fighter.

# Epilogue

In his office, housed in the business sector of Cardassia Prime, Dost Abor was putting his papers in order as he did every day before he went home. He was a ritualistic person, and though the task was almost entirely meaningless, to neglect it without just cause would have been unthinkable.

When the chime on his comm sounded, he answered it with eagerness, for he was a man whose particular line of work dictated that he had to be ready for anything, at all times. He was anticipating a call, but then there were always those calls that he wasn't anticipating, and it was important to be just as prepared for the unexpected as for the expected. Abor was nothing if not flexible.

*"Mister Abor,"* said the woman whose face appeared before him. It was the turnkey in charge of the storeroom at the Ministry of Science, the very person Abor had been expecting to contact him this evening. *"We received your request for the item, and it appears that your credentials are all in order. But . . . we have unfortunate news."*

"And what might that be?" Dost asked, annoyed but unsurprised. The ministry was an inefficient body, even compared to the idiots in Central Command. He already knew the object was lost, he only needed to gather a little more information regarding its disappearance.

*"I'm . . . sorry to have to inform you of this, but the object in question seems to be . . . missing."*

"Missing!" Abor repeated, with mock surprise. "Tell me, Madam, with an organization as tightly run as yours, how could that possibly be the case?" He did not bother to conceal the sarcasm in his tone.

*"Mister Abor, I do apologize, and I can tell you that I don't know how a thing like this could have happened—nobody has looked at that artifact in years."*

"Who was the last person to see it?" Abor asked her. "Surely there must be an information trail."

*"Well, going by memory alone, I do seem to recall that a former student looked at it, a very long time ago . . . There was some kind of a to-do about the security system, and the object was classified, but since then—"*

"I don't want you to go by your memory," Abor told her coolly. "I want you to go by the records. Find out who accessed that object last, and then contact me."

*"Without the container in hand, that may be difficult to ascertain."*

Abor smiled coolly. "Well then," he told the woman, "I imagine you'll want to begin looking for the container right away."

*"May I ask why this is so important?"* the woman asked him, plainly annoyed at the manner in which she was being spoken to.

"No, you may not," Abor told her. "It does not concern you."

A knowing expression came across the woman's eyes, and Abor punched the disconnect button. If she thought she knew what was going on, she probably couldn't guess the half of it. But she almost certainly suspected the Order was involved. No matter, Abor decided. If she became a problem, the Order could get rid of her. Tain might be reluctant to arrange it himself, but Abor supposed he had enough influence to make that call on his own.

Of course, it would be ideal to do it before he was sent back to the Valo system. Abor had no intention of allowing another agent to take credit for a breakthrough that was deservedly his to claim. It had been Abor who had uncovered the long-overlooked transmission that he believed might lead the Order to the heart of the risen Oralian Way.

Enabran Tain may have been far less interested in the Bajoran artifacts than his predecessor, but that didn't mean that Dost Abor had lost interest in them. Abor had recently learned that the artifact from the Ministry of Science was the only one that had ever gone on record as causing anyone to have any kind of so-called "mystical" experience since it had been removed from Bajor.

Abor was not certain, but he believed that the artifact in question had been removed from Bajor under the authority of Rhan Ico, one of many agents who had disappeared during the upheaval that followed Tain's assumption of office. There was a short interim during which the vast and untraceable contents of the Order's storage facility had been ransacked by several agents who protested Tain's impending status; those agents had all disappeared shortly following the incident—and so had at least one of the Orbs of Bajor.

Tain was unconcerned about the breach; the old man was convinced that there was no weight to the stories surrounding the artifacts, the suggestion that whoever possessed them might be privy to a kind of second sight, an indefinable source of knowledge and power. But Abor, who had been in the Order at the time of the first artifact's retrieval from Bajor, remembered a few details about that original group of Oralians, those the Order and Central Command had conspired to exterminate. The Oralians had developed a particular fascination with Bajoran religion, and the artifacts that came with it. Now that the Oralians were said to be growing in numbers once again, Tain was sure that it was only a matter of time before Central Command began to tolerate them, and possibly even to condone their foolish, imaginary ideologies. Enabran Tain made no secret of his disdain for many of Central Command's "softer" policies, believing that the military was weakening due at least in part to the sudden influx of wealth from Bajor, turning soldiers who had once been hard and ruthless into soft, complacent politicians—most notably, Gul Dukat.

Reviewing old transmissions when he was last stationed on Valo VI, Abor had discovered an archived communiqué between Yannik Reyar, the military's liaison with the Order, and his daughter, who apparently worked at the Ministry of Science several years before. Their conversation referenced a Bajoran artifact, one that Dost Abor was certain had been taken from the Obsidian Order, somehow finding its way to the ministry. Tain had shown little interest when Abor sent word that he might have located an item that had been missing from the Order's catalogued inventory. But, Abor hoped, when he assembled his case, Tain would take notice—for Abor had done a bit of digging since he first came across the transmission, and he intended to find not only the Orb, but the woman who had handled it last— the woman who had apparently attempted to hide it—the woman he believed to be the Guide for the Oralian Way.

THE TEROK NOR SAGA
CONTINUES IN
*DAWN OF THE EAGLES*

# Appendices

The following is a guide to many of the specific characters, places, and related material in *Night of the Wolves*. Where such an item was mentioned or appeared previously in a movie, episode, or other work of *Star Trek* fiction, its first appearance is cited.

## APPENDIX I: BAJOR

### Characters

**Akhere Bis** (male) resident of Valo II

**Akhere Juk** (male) resident of Valo II, father of Akhere Bis

**Arin** (male) kai of the Bajoran faith (*Terok Nor: Day of the Vipers*)

**Aro Seefa** (male) resistance fighter, member of the Ornathia cell

**Basso Tromac** (male) personal aide to Gul Dukat. (DS9/"Wrongs Darker Than Death or Night")

**Bram Adir** (male) resistance fighter, leader of the Bram cell

**Crea** (female) resistance fighter, member of the Ornathia cell

**Dakahna Vass** (female) resistance fighter, member of the Shakaar cell

**Darrah Mace** (male) resident of Valo II, former member of the Bajoran Militia (*Terok Nor: Day of the Vipers*)

**Daul Mirosha** (male) researcher at the Bajoran Institute of Science

**Dava** (male) a kai who lived several hundred years prior to the Cardassian occupation

**Faon** (male) resistance fighter, member of the Bram cell

**Furel** (male) resistance fighter, member of the Shakaar cell (DS9/"Shakaar")

**Gantt** (male) resistance fighter and medic, member of the Shakaar cell (DS9/"Ties of Blood and Water")

**Halpas Palin** (male) resistance fighter, leader of the Halpas cell

**Hintasi** (male) resident of Valo II

**Istani Reyla** (female) monk, friend of the Kira family (*DS9/Avatar*)

**Kanore** (male) resistance fighter, member of the Bram cell (TNG/"Preemptive Strike")

**Keeve Falor** (male) resident of Valo II, former member of the Bajoran Chamber of Ministers (TNG/"Ensign Ro")

**Ketauna** (male) artist, follower of Opaka Sulan

**Kira Meru** (female) mistress of Gul Dukat, mother of Kira Nerys (DS9/"Wrongs Darker Than Death or Night")

**Kira Nerys** (female) resistance fighter, member of the Shakaar cell (DS9/"Emissary")

**Kira Pohl** (male) brother of Kira Nerys (DS9/"Wrongs Darker Than Death or Night")

**Kira Reon** (male) brother of Kira Nerys (DS9/"Wrongs Darker Than Death or Night")

**Kira Taban** (male) father of Kira Nerys (DS9/"Ties of Blood and Water")

**Kubus Oak** (male) special liaison between Gul Dukat and the Caradassian-sanctioned Bajoran government (DS9/"The Collaborator")

**Lafe Darin** (male) resistance fighter, member of the Halpas cell, lifelong friend of Lenaris Holem

**Legan Duravit** (male) resistance fighter, member of the Ornathia cell

**Legan Fin** (male) resistance fighter, member of the Ornathia cell

**Lenaris Holem** (male) resistance fighter, former member of the Halpas cell and later the Ornathia cell (DS9/"Shakaar")

**Lenaris Jau** (male) resistance fighter, member of the Ornathia cell, brother of Lenaris Holem

**Lenaris Pendan** (male) father of Lenaris Holem and Lenaris Jau

**Lino** (male) resident of Valo II

**Luma Rahl** (female) friend of Kira Meru (DS9/"Wrongs Darker Than Death or Night")

**Lupaza** (female) resistance fighter, member of the Shakaar cell (DS9/"Shakaar")

**Matram Tryst** (male) resistance fighter, member of the Shakaar cell

**Mesto Drade** (male) resident of Rakantha Province

**Mobara** (male) resistance fighter and engineer, member of the Shakaar cell (DS9/"Shakaar")

**Mora Pol** (male) researcher at the Bajoran Institute of Science (DS9/"The Alternate")

**Opaka Bekar** (male) husband of Opaka Sulan

**Opaka Fasil** (male) son of Opaka Sulan (Opaka's son is first mentioned, but not named, in DS9/"The Collaborator")

**Opaka Sulan** (female) priest at the Kendra shrine, later kai of the Bajoran faith (DS9/"Emissary"; Opaka's given name was established in DS9/Rising Son)

**Ornak** (male) resistance fighter, member of the Shakaar cell (DS9/"Shakaar")

**Ornathia Delle** (female) resistance fighter, member of Ornathia cell, cousin of Ornathia Lac

**Ornathia Harta** (female) resistance fighter, member of the Ornathia cell, cousin of Ornathia Lac

**Ornathia Lac** (male) resistance fighter, leader of the Ornathia cell

**Ornathia Nerissa** (female) resistance fighter with the Ornathia cell

**Ornathia Sten** (male) resistance fighter, member of the Ornathia cell, cousin of Ornathia Lac

**Ornathia Taryl** (female) resistance fighter, member of the Ornathia cell, sister of Ornathia Lac

**Par Lusa** (male) resistance fighter with the Shakaar cell

**Petra Chan** (female) childhood friend of Kira Nerys

**Porta** (male) priest, friend of the Kira family (DS9/"Accession")

**Res** (male) resistance fighter with the Ornathia cell

**Ro Gale** (male) father of Ro Laren (Gale's name comes from a computer screen graphic in TNG/"The Next Phase")

**Ro Laren** (female) resistance fighter, member of the Bram cell (TNG/"Ensign Ro")

**Sadakita Rass** (female) resistance fighter, member of the Bram cell

**Shakaar Edon** (male) resistance fighter, leader of the Shakaar resistance cell (DS9/"Shakaar")

**Shev** (male) resident of Yarlin, follower of Opaka Sulan

**Sorash Mabey** (female) resident of Dahkur Province

**Tancha** (female) resistance fighter with Ornathia cell

**Thera Tibb** (female) resident of Relliketh

**Thill Revi** (male) resident of Rakantha Province

**Tiven Cohr** (male) resistance fighter and engineer, member of the Halpas cell

**Tokiah** (male) resistance fighter, member of the Bram cell

**Tora Naprem** (female) mistress of Gul Dukat, mother of Tora Ziyal (DS9/"Indiscretion")

**Trakor** (male) ancient religious figure, writer of prophecies (DS9/"Destiny")

**Tynara** (female) Gallitep laborer

**Vusan** (male) resistance fighter, member of the Ornathia cell

**Winn Adami** (female) monk, friend of the Ornathia family (DS9/"In the Hands of the Prophets")

## Places

**Artist's Palette**: area of Dahkur Province

**Berain Valley**: near Relliketh, its main port is Berain city

**Denorios Belt**: ring of charged plasma in the Bajoran star system; where the *odo'ital* was found (DS9/"Emissary")

**Derna**: Fourth moon of Bajor, former site of a Cardassian base (DS9/"Image in the Sand"; the base was established in *Terok Nor: Day of the Vipers*)

**Gallitep**: Cardassian-run labor camp and mining facility (DS9/"Duet")

**Genmyr**: ruined city in Kendra Province

**Jalanda**: population center in Hedrikspool Province (The Jalanda Forum was first mentioned in DS9/"Sanctuary")

**Jeraddo**: fifth moon of Bajor; site of the Lunar V base (DS9/"Progress")

**Jo'kala**: population center in Musilla Province (DS9/"Starship Down")

**Karnoth Mountains**: range near the city of Relliketh

**Kendra Shrine**: religious temple in Kendra Valley; the second to be built on the site after the first was destroyed in *Terok Nor: Day of the Vipers* (Kendra Valley first mentioned in DS9/"The Collaborator"; Kendra Province first mentioned in DS9/"Penumbra")

**Meiku Forest**: wooded area just outside Rakantha Province

**Mylea**: population center in Kendra province (*Worlds of Star Trek: Deep Space Nine, Volume Two—Fragments and Omens*)

**Naghai Keep**: ruined ancient castle in Kendra Valley, former ancestral home of the Jas clan (*Terok Nor: Day of the Vipers*)

**Sahving Valley**: region of Kendra Province (DS9/"The Homecoming")

**Tamulna**: city in Dahkur Province (DS9/"The Reckoning")

**Tilar**: a Bajoran peninsula, famous for its temperate climate and beautiful landscape (*DS9/Unity*)

**Tozhat**: Cardassian settlement on Bajor, governed by Exarch Kotan Pa'Dar (DS9/"Cardassians")

**Valo II**: habitable planet in the Valo system, home to many refugee Bajorans (TNG/"Ensign Ro")

**Valo VI**: barren planetoid in the Valo system, site of a Cardassian listening post

**Yarlin**: settlement in Kendra Province

## Food and Drink

*alva*: grapelike fruit (DS9/"Resurrection")

*copal*: ciderlike alcoholic beverage (*Terok Nor: Day of the Vipers*)

*deka* **tea**: hot brewed beverage (DS9/"Wrongs Darker Than Death or Night")

*jumja*: tree with a sticky, sweet sap from which a popular confection is made (DS9/"A Man Alone")

*kava* **root**: edible tuber, part of the extremely versatile kava plant (DS9/"Starship Down")

*makara*: herb known for its medicinal value, particularly to pregnant women (DS9/"The Darkness and the Light")

*moba*: sweet, tree-grown fruit (DS9/"Rejoined")

*ratamba* **stew**: good eats (DS9/"For the Cause")

## Other

**balon**: fuel source abandoned before the occupation because of its notorious instability, later revived by the resistance

**batos**: big, smelly, domesticated herd animal (*DS9/Section 31: Abyss*)

**borhya**: ghost (TNG/"The Next Phase")

**bell**: benchmark of time, similar to "o'clock" (*Terok Nor: Day of the Vipers*)

**B'hava'el**: the star of Bajor (*Star Trek: Deep Space Nine Technical Manual*)

**cadge lupus**: large canine predator, similar to a wolf

**dolamide**: versatile material that can be used, in very pure form, to manufacture explosives (DS9/"Dramatis Personae")

**Fostossa virus**: source of an epidemic that swept across Bajor during the occupation (VGR: "Nothing Human")

**fusionstone**: ancient building material (*Worlds of Star Trek: Deep Space Nine, Volume Two—Fragments and Omens*)

**grass vipers**: gray-skinned snakes (*Terok Nor: Day of the Vipers*)

**hara cat**: large feline predator (DS9/"Second Skin")

**hiuna leaf**: Bajoran tobacco (*Terok Nor: Day of the Vipers*)

**Ih'tanu**: traditional celebration of a Bajoran girl's fourteenth birthday (DS9/"Accession")

**Kalla-Nohra**: unique medical condition suffered by Bajorans and Cardassians who were exposed to the effects of a mining accident at Gallitep in 2353 (DS9/"Duet")

**kellipate**: unit of distance (DS9/"Progress")

**kelbonite**: material known to interfere with various types of scanning equipment (TNG/"Silicon Avatar")

*kosst*: swearword or curse, derived from Kosst Amojan (DS9/"The Reckoning"; however, the word's original meaning was simply "to be" (DS9/"The Assignment")

*linnipate*: unit of distance, roughly two or three meters (*Terok Nor: Day of the Vipers*)

**lugfish**: large, slow, and ugly fish (*Terok Nor: Day of the Vipers*)

**nyawood**: type of wood similar to mahogany (*Terok Nor: Day of the Vipers*)

**Orb**: also known as a "Tear of the Prophets"; one of several religious artifacts that sometimes impart visions or insights upon those who gaze into them (DS9/"Emissary")

**Orkett's disease**: affliction being studied at the Bajoran Institute of Science (VGR/"State of Flux")

*porli* **fowl**: chickenlike food animal

**raider**: generic name for a small attack craft used by the resistance

*ra-vu rum'ta*: Old Bajoran expression meaning "child of night"; the classic poetical name for a cadge lupus

*salam*: type of grass (DS9/"Shakaar")

**sinoraptor**: animal known for its fierceness and eyes that face opposite directions (DS9/"Shakaar")

**spoonhead**: slur used by some Bajorans when referring to a Cardassian (DS9/"Things Past")

*tessipate*: unit of area (DS9/"Progress")

**tyrfox**: wily canine predator (*Terok Nor: Day of the Vipers*)

**uridium**: mineral that, in its unprocessed state, is highly unstable; uridium ore is processed on Terok Nor (DS9/"Civil Defense")

## *Religious Ranks*

The following is a breakdown of known ranks in the Bajoran religion, in ascending order.

**prylar**: a monk

**ranjen**: a monk specializing in theological study

**vedek**: a high-ranking priest, typically a regional spiritual leader

**kai**: the world leader of the Bajoran religion

## D'jarra *Caste System*

Until recent times the Bajorans had a series of castes called *D'jarra*s. This is a rough order of ranking for the ones that have been established so far.

**Ih'valla**: artists (above Te'nari) (DS9/"Accession")

**Te'nari**: unknown, but below Ih'valla (DS9/"Accession")

**Mi'tino**: low-ranked merchants and landowners (*Terok Nor: Day of the Vipers*)

**Va'telo**: pilot, sailor, driver, and similar professions (*Terok Nor: Day of the Vipers*)

**Ke'lora**: laborers and lawmen (*Terok Nor: Day of the Vipers*)

**Sern'apa**: unknown (*Terok Nor: Day of the Vipers*)

**Imutta**: those who deal with the dead, the "unclean," and lowest ranking *d'jarra* (DS9/"Accession")


## *Resistance Cells*

The following is a list of the established Bajoran resistance cells and their areas of operation.

**Bram**: active in Jo'kala (Musilla Province)

**Halpas**: active in Relliketh (Hedrikspool Province)

**Kintaura**: active in Rakantha Province

**Kohn-ma**: active in Dahkur Province (DS9/"Past Prologue")

**Ornathia**: active in Tilar Peninsula (Hedrikspool Province)

**Shakaar**: active in Dahkur Province (DS9/"Duet")

# APPENDIX II: CARDASSIA

## Characters

**Abor, Dost** (male) operative of the Obsidian Order, assigned to Valo VI listening post

**Astraea** (female) traditional name of the ceremonial "guide" or religious leader for the Oralian Way (*DS9/A Stitch in Time*)

**Dalak** (male) official of the Cardassian Information Service, superior of Natima Lang and Veja Ketan

**Damar, Corat** (male) military officer serving on Terok Nor (DS9/"Return to Grace")

**Darhe'el** (male) military officer, overseer of the Gallitep mining facility on Bajor, political rival of Gul Dukat (DS9/"Duet")

**Dukat, Athra** (female) wife of Skrain Dukat (*Terok Nor: Day of the Vipers*)

**Dukat, Skrain** (male) military officer who served under Danig Kell during the formal first contact with Bajor, later prefect of Bajor and commander of Terok Nor (DS9/"Emissary"; Dukat's given name was established in the DS9 novel *A Stitch in Time*)

**Ico, Rhan** (female) Letin Pasir's handler in the Obsidian Order (*Terok Nor: Day of the Vipers*)

**Kell, Danig** (male) military officer and member of Central Command, direct superior of Skrain Dukat (DS9/"Civil Defense"; Kell's first name was established in *Terok Nor: Day of the Vipers*)

**Ketan, Veja** (female) correspondent for the Cardassian Information Service

**Kieng** (male) code name for Joer Varc, an operative of the Obsidian Order

**Kretech** (male) military officer serving on the scoutship *Kevalu*

**Kruva** (male) commander of the patrol ship *Drakamair*, assigned to the Pullock system

**Lang, Natima** (female) correspondent for the Cardassian Information Service (DS9/"Profit and Loss")

**Marritza, Aamin** (male) military officer and file clerk serving at the Gallitep mining facility on Bajor (DS9/"Duet")

**Mendar** (female) professor at the Ministry of Science on Cardassia Prime

**Moset, Crell** (male) civilian physician and exobiologist who worked on Bajor during the annexation (VOY/"Nothing Human")

**Ocett, Malyn** (female) military officer in command of the scoutship *Kevalu*, assigned to patrol the Bajoran system (TNG/"The Chase"; Ocett's given name was established in *A Stitch in Time*)

**Pa'Dar, Kotan** (male) former scientist, later exarch at the Tozhat settlement on Bajor (DS9/"Cardassians")

**Pasir, Letin** (male) operative of the Obsidian Order, assigned to Bajor posing as a vedek (*Terok Nor: Day of the Vipers*)

**Prang, Limor** (male) operative of the Obsidian Order (*A Stitch in Time*)

**Ratav** (male) military officer commanding a base in Hedrikspool Province on Bajor

**Regnar** (male) code name for an operative of the Obsidian Order (*A Stitch in Time*)

**Reyar, Kalisi** (female) civilian scientist

**Reyar, Yannik** (male) civilian liaison between Central Command and the Obsidian Order, father of Kalisi Reyar

**Sa'kat** (male) military officer assigned to patrol the perimeter of Cardassia City

**Tain, Enabran** (male) head of the Obsidian Order (DS9/"The Wire")

**Tedar** (male) military officer stationed in Dahkur Province on Bajor

**Thrax** (male) chief of security on Terok Nor (DS9/"Things Past")

**Trach** (male) noncommisioned officer serving on Terok Nor

**Vara, Miras** (female) civilian scientist

**Varc, Joer** (male) operative of the Obsidian Order, code name "Kieng"

**Veda** (male) military officer serving on the scoutship *Kevalu*

**Yopal** (female) director of the Bajoran Institute of Science

## Places

**Lakarian City**: population center on Cardassia Prime, site where ancient Hebetian culture was said to have flourished long ago (DS9/"Defiant")

**Cardassia City**: capital city of Cardassia Prime (*A Stitch in Time*)

**Letau**: the innermost moon of Cardassia Prime and the site of a maximum-security prison facility

**Ministry of Science**: center of learning and scientific research in Cardassia City (DS9/"Destiny")

**Paldar Sector**: residential district of Cardassia City (*DS9/A Stitch in Time*)

**Pullock V**: habitable planet in the Pullock system; site of a Cardassian manufacturing complex (DS9/"Shakaar")

**Terok Nor**: space station orbiting Bajor; the main ore processing facility as of 2346 and the command post for the Bajoran annexation

# Other

**Drakamair**: *Hideki*-class patrol ship under the command of Dalin Kruva, operating in the Pullock system

**kanar**: alcoholic beverage (TNG/"The Wounded")

**Kevalu**: scoutship under the command of Dalin Malyn Ocett, operating in the B'hava'el system

**Koeder**: *Keldon*-class warship

**marga**: fish with a smooth, pink belly

**metric**: unit of time, roughly equivalent to a minute (*Terok Nor: Day of the Vipers*)

**Obsidian Order**: intelligence bureau of the Cardassian Union (DS9/"The Wire")

**Oralian Way**: religion dating back to the First Hebitian civilization on Cardassia Prime, forced to go underground during the era of the Bajoran annexation (the Hebitian civilization was first mentioned in TNG/"Chain of Command, Part II; the Oralian Way was established in the DS9 novel, *A Stitch in Time*)

**riding hound**: large canine animal (DS9/"In Purgatory's Shadow")

**rokassa juice**: nonalcoholic beverage with a very distinctive odor (DS9/"Cardassians")

## Military Ranks

The following is a list of Cardassian ranks and their Starfleet analogs. This system borrows from the work of Steven Kenson's unpublished *Iron & Ash* supplement for the *Star-Trek* Roleplaying Game from Last Unicorn Games.

**garresh**: noncommissioned officer
**gil**: ensign
**glinn**: lieutenant
**dalin**: lieutenant commander
**dal**: commander
**gul**: captain
**jagul**: commodore/rear admiral
**legate**: admiral

# APPENDIX III: MISCELLANEOUS

**Antosians**: species capable of cellular metamorphosis (TOS/ "Whom Gods Destroy")

**Chameloids**: shape-shifting species (*Star Trek VI: The Undiscovered Country*)

**Ferengi**: spacefaring species known mainly for their pursuit of profit (TNG/"The Last Outpost")

**flyer**: generic term for a small aircraft

**Gart** (male): Ferengi DaiMon (captain) whose ship routinely stops at Terok Nor

*gree* **worms**: edible soft-bodied invertebrates favored by the Ferengi (DS9/"Little Green Men")

**Kressari**: spacefaring species known mainly for being traders in botanical DNA (DS9/"The Circle")

**Lissepia**: inhabited planet on DaiMon Gart's trade route (DS9/ "The Maquis, Part II")

**New Sydney**: inhabited planet on DaiMon Gart's trade route (DS9/"Prodigal Daughter")

*odo'ital*: Cardassian designation for the mysterious shape-shifting life-form that was discovered in the Denorios Belt in 2345; translates as "unknown sample" (DS9/"Heart of Stone")

**skimmer**: generic term for a near-ground hovercraft

**Valerians**: spacefaring species known mainly for trading with the Cardassians (DS9/"Dramatis Personae")

**Vendorians**: shape-shifting species (TAS/"The Survivor")

**Wraith**: shape-shifting species (ENT/"Rogue Planet")

# ABOUT THE AUTHORS

**S. D. (Stephani Danelle) Perry** writes multimedia novelizations in the fantasy/science fiction/horror realms, for love and money. S. D. lives in Portland, Oregon, with her excellent family, and is working on an original thriller in her spare time, of which she has very little.

**Britta Burdett Dennison** once had pipe dreams of becoming a comic book artist, before fully realizing just how many little panels she would have been required to draw, and so turned to writing instead. She is an enthusiastic newcomer to the *Star Trek* universe. She currently lives in Portland, Oregon, with her husband and daughters. This is her first published book.